DIXON'S EDGE

DENNIS O'KEEFE

ISBN: 0-9702160-0-9
Library of Congress Card Number: 00-192747

Printed in the United States of America.

Parintel Books are published by the Parintel Publishing
Company, 4195 Valley Fair Street, #104
Simi Valley, CA 93063

I dedicate this book to my darling wife
Sadako.
May she rest in peace.

ONE

*P*atrick 'Pappy' Patterson sat on the wooden stoop of the clapboard two-bedroom house. The lump in his throat was so large it was like he had swallowed one of his five hundred head of cattle that were being slaughtered. The gunshots had been going on continuously since mid-afternoon. He could hear the pitiful moaning and bellowing of the panicked cattle. Even with their dim brains, they sounded as if they knew what was going on.

Pappy was trying hard to hold back the tears as he watched his oldest son, Colt, who stood with both fists shoved deep into the pockets of his bib coveralls.

Colt stared out across the fields looking through the dust stirred up by the milling and running cattle.

The evening sky looked red through the dust. The sun had almost disappeared below the low-lying dunes of sage and mesquite when the shooting finally stopped.

The county sheriff, followed by the stranger from Austin, walked up. Pappy could see the grim look on both their faces. Sheriff Grimes looked like he had just completed the worst duty of his life. As he walked up to where Pappy was sitting, the sheriff took off his white Stetson and wiped his face with his neckerchief for a moment before speaking.

"Mr. Patterson, I can't tell you and your family how sorry I am about all this. I know how many years you worked building up this ranch and to have to destroy your herd this way, well dammit, it just doesn't seem right. Hell, I never even heard of anthrax before last week. Not until all those cows out at Miller's place started dying."

He motioned to his grim companion and continued, "Mr. Stallings here says that we have to burn the carcasses and the fields where you had those cows. Mr. Stallings says that it's possible that the anthrax could infect you, your family, and all your other critters. I hate to pile worse news on bad news but I guess we have to get rid of your other livestock too." Pappy just nodded his head.

The sheriff couldn't bring himself to look at Pappy. He stood making a senseless circle in the dust with the toe of his boot and kneading his hat with both his hands.

Finally the sheriff looked up at Pappy and said with a slight catch to his voice, "Ah shit, Mr. Patterson, I'm sorry."

He turned and yelled to one of his deputies, "Okay Carl, round up all the other stock, including the horses, and drive them into the corral. Keep your own horses out of that field. Saddle up Mr. Patterson's horses, and let's drag those carcasses into a pile. When you're done, shoot the horses and burn them too."

Colt couldn't watch anymore. He rubbed the tears from both eyes using his dust-covered forearm and walked back into the house. He saw his father sitting on the stoop, staring straight ahead. Pappy and Colt were the only ones staying in the small house.

Pappy had sent Colt's mother, Edina, and his twelve-year-old brother over to the Hunt's to stay. Pappy didn't want them to be there to watch the destruction of twenty years of their life and all their dreams. Colt had never heard of anthrax; according to the sheriff it must have come in with some Mexican cattle that his daddy and Mr. Miller both had bought. The sheriff said the disease could actually get into the ground and could infect any livestock that even walked on it.

The man that the government had sent down, Mr. Stallings, said their only hope of avoiding an epidemic was to slaughter all the livestock and burn them. They'd also have to burn the grass where any of the stock had been.

Colt thought, "Hell, that was damn near the whole thousand acres." There was so little grass that the cows had to be rotated, using all the fields. Colt sat just inside the dark interior of the house look-ing out the front door. He couldn't see Pappy anymore. He must have gone to talk to the sheriff.

*

Pappy watched Colt walk by. The boy was obviously trying to hold back his emotions. This was just too much for Pappy to bear. He and Colt had worked so hard. Every posthole, every stump cleared, and every strand of fence was dug and strung by his and Colt's hands. Even the house and barn had been built by them. He was so proud of his son. He was proud of the rest of his family, too, but there was something special about a man and his son, especially his first born, building something together. Now, in just a few days since they got the news, it was all over. Pappy stood and walked the hundred feet to the barn.

*

Colt sat staring at the shadows. The shooting had stopped for a couple of hours while the sheriff and his people apparently dragged the cattle into a pile. A few more shots rang out. Colt knew that would be the horses. He could hear men talking but they were too far away to make out what they were saying.

It was dark now and Colt sat still looking out the door. He could smell the evening dust and for some reason it smelled good. He could smell the house that had the fine scents of cooking, lye, and leather. He could pick out the other smells that were typical, yet unique in their own way, of every well-maintained house. It seemed to Colt that the personality of each member could be picked out just by the smell.

The night air soon carried the sharp acrid odor of kerosene. The smell soon became overwhelming.

It wasn't long before the fires of the burning carcasses lighted up the night. Revulsion swept over Colt.

He was drawn to the door where he looked out at the carnage.

A huge fire was engulfing the cattle. A second fire was in the cor-ral, burning their now dead horses. He could see smaller fires springing up all over the ranch. They were burning the fields. Colt went back into the house.

He walked into the bedroom and flung himself across his bed. He pulled the blanket over his head to keep out the kerosene smell and to stifle his sobs.

Colt had no idea how long that he lay there. It could have been minutes or hours because he began to doze.

*

Colt awoke with a start. The smoke had increased to the point where he could barely breathe and the heat was intolerable.

The wind had picked up and was blowing toward the house stronger than it had been. He removed the covers from his head. The light from the window was a bright red from the fire and was lighting up the darkened room. The smoke was like a bright, heavy fog. He got up and went to the door.

The flames were leaping twenty to thirty feet in the air. It was preheating the grass in front of the main fire until it reached its combustion point. The fire would leap forward as the grass before it exploded. The ranch house was being threatened by the southeastern winds.

He ran outside looking for Pappy. Sparks and embers were flying everywhere. The thermal wind created by the fire was almost at hurricane force.

"Pap! Pap! Where are you?" He couldn't see his father. "Pap, I think the house is gonna go!"

The roar of the fire was so loud that he doubted if Pap could hear him. He found a blanket and wrapped it around his nose and face. He again looked around for Pappy, but he was nowhere in sight. Colt ran through the smoke to the barn.

He went inside and froze. Through the smoke and light of the fire he saw Pap gently swinging. A sawhorse was turned over nearby and the rope around Pap's neck was drawn tight by his weight. His neck had stretched to twice its normal length and was bent at an angle.

Colt screamed. "Pap, oh no! Oh no!"

He ran to his father and cut him down. Pap was already stiffening up and Colt knew that he was dead. Colt knelt by his father, cradling his head in his arms. This time he didn't try to hide his anguish. He held his father and rocked back and forth, crying as he had never cried before.

Slowly he came back to himself and lay his father's head down. He noticed a folded sheet of paper protruding from his father's pocket. He opened it and by the light of the raging inferno, he read:

Edina, Colt and Douglas
Please forgive me
Pap

Colt crumpled the paper and shoved it in his pocket. He leaned over and again cradled his father. "Why now, Pap? Why now?"

The crackling of the flames grew louder. The haystack outside the barn was burning and it would be only seconds before the barn was engulfed.

Colt picked up his father and carried him back to the house, oblivious to the heat and smoke created by the hell surrounding him.

He sat all night watching his father. There was no doubt that the house would go next but somehow he just didn't care.

Colt dozed and when he awoke, it was daylight.

The stench of burned grass, lumber, and cattle was heavy in the air but the fire was out.

He stood and walked to the door. He saw that the barn, chicken house and corrals were only ashes. The fields were black as far as he could see.

The charred remains of their cattle and horses could be seen scattered throughout the fields of blackened ashes. Smoke was still wafting into the still morning air.

Colt looked at his father. "Pap, what am I gonna tell Ma and Douglas? That you hung yourself? You know you've killed her, too, by doing this. Pap, if we ever needed you before, we really need you now. What the hell am I gonna tell Ma?"

Colt left the house and walked to what was left of the barn and tool shed. He rummaged through the ashes until he found the remains of a shovel, a hammer and saw. He found that the ashes from the crack of the whip as it cut into the back of his foster father, Alchisay.

He knew that each blow should have been his, for it was he that had stolen the chickens and was so careless as to pluck them outside their wickiup.

He watched Alchisay's body jerk with each lash. That was six but so far his father hadn't uttered a sound.

A steely-eyed sergeant, mounted on a horse, counted each blow aloud.

Charley wanted to scream out that it was he who had stolen the chickens but he was too afraid. Each time the whip cracked it was as though it was cutting into his flesh.

The sergeant finally reached ten. He said, "Okay, that's it. Cut him down and drag his ass to the infirmary." He turned his horse away and looked down at Charley. He smiled and nodded. He said, "It was you that stole that chicken, wasn't it, you little bastard. You could've saved your papa a lot of pain if you'd been man enough to own up to it."

As the sergeant prodded his horse through the crowd, Charley felt the eyes of the eyes of everyone looking at him. He was filled with shame and a white-hot anger at both himself and the soldiers.

*

Colt walked with a heavy heart, his boots making a soft whistling noise in the sandy South Texas soil. The moon was high and the white sand made it almost as bright as day. He walked briskly, head down, listening to the slight breeze as it dusted the light powdery sand across the desert.

He walked until midnight, then rested and ate the cornbread and beans.

Colt started no fire. He would only be there for a few minutes, and he knew that a fire could be seen for miles.

The Lipan Apache hadn't caused much trouble lately, but one could never tell. He heard the high-pitched barking of a coyote and felt even more alone.

He dreaded the task of telling his mother and little brother about Pap. He'd been thinking about the problem for hours. He decided that he would tell her only that Pap's heart stopped. That was true. The fact that his heart stopped is what killed him. The hanging was only the way he made it stop.

Ma could always tell when he was avoiding the truth. Colt tried really hard not to ever tell a hard lie, but he'd tried to reshape the truth a few times and Ma always seemed to know. Maybe he ought to just tell her what happened. Well, he'd decide when he saw her.

Colt could tell by the stars that it was after midnight, and he calculated that he still had four or five more miles to go.

He shouldered his pack, picked up his rifle and left.

*

Colt reached the Hunt's ranch about two o'clock in the morning.

Hunt's two mongrel dogs came running out barking up a storm. The dogs didn't know him and he was afraid they would bite him.

A voice called out. "Who's there?"

"It's Colt Patterson, Mr. Hunt. Call off your dogs!"

"Skeeter, Blue, get back here!"

The dogs reluctantly turned back and Colt walked up to the house. He saw a lantern light and Orville Hunt on the front porch with his shotgun.

Hunt raised the lantern to get a good look at Colt's face. "What the hell are you doing here this time of night?"

Another voice asked, "Who is it, Pa?"

"It's Colt Patterson. What's wrong, Colt?"

"Pap's dead, Mr. Hunt. I have to talk to Ma."

Mr. Hunt's eyes widened. "Oh my Lord, how'd that happen? Myrtle! Better wake up Edina! Come in, Colt. Come in. What the hell happened? Lordy, when it rains, it pours. Myrtle, I said wake up Edina and put on some coffee!"

Edina shouted, "I'm awake, what's wrong?"

"Colt's here. You'd better come into the kitchen."

Colt and Hunt walked into the kitchen where Hunt put the lantern on the table.

Edina stood in the bedroom doorway looking at Colt, absent-mindedly fumbling with the tight-fitting collar of her nightgown.

Douglas could go there for a while. Maybe I could find a job in San Antonio for myself."

Colt looked at the man and said, "Mr. Hunt, are you sure you want to do this?"

Hunt lit his pipe and took a deep puff. "Well, after I heard about the problem with you folks and Mr. Miller, I talked to that man Stallings. He said that the fire ought to kill it and somebody could put a few cows on it in the spring. I figure I could do that."

"Just what is anthrax, Mr. Hunt?"

Hunt puffed his pipe thoughtfully. "It's some kind of thing like the plague. Hits livestock real bad and sometimes, according to Mr. Stallings, it hits humans too. He said some people call it black leg. I'm not sure myself, but it's some real bad stuff."

THREE

Frank Stallings had ridden all day following the events at the Patterson and Miller ranch. It was way past dark when he quietly rode into the light of the campfire near where the Cotulla and Annarose Road crossed the Nueces River.

The lone man sitting at the campfire said, "Get down and sit. I have some coffee."

Stallings remained mounted. "No thanks, I won't be visiting. Do you have something for me?"

"If you're Stallings, I do." The man at the fire got up and withdrew a small leather bag from his bedroll and walked over to Stallings.

Stallings took the bag and opened it. He counted twenty-five Double Eagles. He put the money back in the bag, drew the drawstrings tight, and placed it in his pocket.

He asked the man, "Why'd you want to burn the grass? You people knew those cows didn't have anthrax."

The man said, "The boss said to burn it because even if those boys figured out a way to pay off their loans and bought more cows, they'd not be able to afford to buy enough hay to feed them. He said he didn't want them having any grass of their own. Besides, the boss said that the ashes give them nutrients or something like that. Are you sure that you don't want any coffee?"

"No, thanks. I have to go." Stallings quickly rode off into the night. He didn't like what he had done. When he'd been approached, it had seemed a simple matter, and he needed the money. He had no idea that he would be involved in something that would destroy so many people. It was too late now. What was done was done. He would have to stick with the anthrax story.

*

The next day Mr. Hunt and Colt drove Hunt's buggy to Cotulla. Colt told the sheriff about Pappy and showed him the note.

The sheriff's face tightened. "I just don't know what to say, son. I feel like somehow I caused all this, but I had no choice in the matter. According to Mr. Stallings, an anthrax outbreak here not only threatened every rancher in the area but also could kill half the people within a hundred square miles. Hell, it was all I could do to talk him out of putting you folks and the Miller family in quarantine. I sure am sorry, boy."

Colt only nodded. He took a deep breath and walked outside. Hunt had stepped out the door and was waiting on the boardwalk.

"Well, Mr. Hunt, we might as well go to the bank and straighten out this mess. "

*

Elroy Peoples, a.k.a. Doctor Sam Pritchett, had just climbed upon his green and red medicine wagon when he saw Colt and Mr. Hunt crossing the street. He noticed that both glanced in his direction and he purposely turned his head away. He snapped his whip at his team and headed out of town.

Colt saw the tall man on the wagon and asked Mr. Hunt, "Who's that? I've never seen that wagon before."

Hunt glanced at the wagon and said, "I don't know. Probably just some drummer passing through."

*

At the bank, Mr. Goodhew drew up the papers and gave them to Colt. Goodhew suggested that since they were heading for San

Antonio, Colt should have his mother sign the papers before a notary.

Hunt gave Colt five hundred dollars right then, even though Edina had yet to sign the bill of sale.

Colt stated that he had to go and pay off the account at the feed store.

Hunt said, "You go ahead, Colt. I'll meet you back here when you're through."

*

Two hours later they were headed back to the Patterson ranch. Colt had tried to pay off their account at the feed store, but Mr. Hatfield, the owner, said that he couldn't find an account.

Colt told him that he was sure they owed him at least fifty dollars.

Mr. Hatfield refused the money, saying, "If I can't find an account, there is no account. Now, your daddy was a friend of mine, and even if there were an account, which there isn't, I still wouldn't be able to find an account. No, you just go along and take care of your mother. She's a mighty fine lady, and with all your problems you sure don't need to be worrying about any feed bill."

Colt rode in silence. With all his heartache he couldn't help but be touched by all these fine people who offered their support.

Colt turned to Mr. Hunt. "What about the Millers?"

"They rolled out yesterday, heading someplace back east. It's just too damn bad. Really fine folks, they are. It's just too damn bad."

When they got to the Patterson ranch, Colt had a hard time controlling his emotions. He'd been there and had lived through the fire, but just couldn't believe the devastation. Everything was ash. Bloated and burned carcasses were everywhere.

Hunt turned to Colt. "Are you sure you're up to this, son? I can come back later and get your things."

"Thanks, Mr. Hunt, but let's get on with it. I don't want to ever see this place again."

They loaded up what few personal items they could, and left the furniture.

They walked over to Pappy's grave and stood in silence.

Hunt, holding his hat in hand, said, "Son, I'm gonna build a nice picket fence around your daddy's grave and make sure it's tended to proper. He was a fine man. I'm sure gonna miss all you folks."

Colt, holding back his tears and swallowing the lump in his throat, said, "Thanks, Mr. Hunt. I sure appreciate all you've done. Can we leave now?"

Hunt fixed his hat back on his head. "Sure, son, sure. Let's get you back to your family."

*

Outside, the night shone brightly, but inside their hut it was dark except for the yellow light of the fire. Charley heard a dog's bark somewhere in the distance and smelled the wood smoke from the fire. For some reason the smell of smoke always made him hungry, and since they had been forced to come to this place he was always hungry.

He lay in his blanket on the dirt floor and watched silently as his aunt's face glistened from the heat in the yellow light of the fire as she bathed Alchisay.

The wounded man was racked by fever from his festering wounds. There were no medicinal herbs to be found in this hell that the whites called Bosque Redondo. The drunken doctor at the camp hospital had given his aunt some stinking yellow salve and told them to take Alchisay home. Charley knew that it was just as well, for the hospital's dirt floors were not a place for healing—only a place for dying.

He thought of his fourteen-year-old sister who had been taken there after a breeched birth. She, like most of the others there, had died.

He thought of her stillborn baby with the blue eyes, fathered by one of the many white soldiers who had paid her the white man's money to lay with them.

Charley was ashamed that he had cowardly stood silent as this good man had taken his punishment. Tears blurred his vision as he remembered how Alchisay had silently accepted the pain as the whip cut into his flesh time and time again, and he was ashamed of his tears.

He realized that Alchisay had defeated the whites by denying them the pleasure of hearing him cry out.

As he watched the dying man, he vowed to kill a white for each and every rasping breath that he heard from Alchisay.

Yes, he thought, *I will escape this place of bitter water and scorched ground and I will leave the bones of the white race scattered over it.*

Charley had no idea how to live off the desert. The only knowledge he'd ever obtained was what he'd learned from listening to Alchisay and others as they sat around telling stories of the days before Basque Redondo.

He had no memory of his real parents and sometimes fantasized that his real father might have been a chief. But he knew that a chief would never abandon his son and leave him under a tree where Alchisay had found him and given him the name Tree. The whites at the school had given him the name Charles.

He understood and liked the name Tree. He hated the name Charley. It had no meaning. What made it worse was that the white teachers at the school had assigned it to him.

*

Charley hadn't realized that he had slept but it was morning when he awoke to the wailing of his aunt.

He stood and went to Alchisay. He knelt and tried to lift his head but noted that the body was rigid. Even in his young years, Charley had seen enough death in this place to realize that the man he had known as his father had been dead for several hours.

He wanted to weep but now the tears wouldn't come. Suddenly he had to get out of this place. He stood and quickly went outside where several people had gathered.

Charley looked into the faces and saw only misery and hopelessness. Even the young men and women looked old. He saw the children with skin pulled tightly over their bones, with their joints and stomachs swollen. He saw old people in the same condition. His hatred for the white race was like hot coals in his belly.

He would leave this place. He would make the white man pay many times for this. He would find Goyathlay and help rid the earth of the festering sore that called itself the white race. Before he killed them he would teach them about pain.

*

Two days after the fire, Mr. Hunt took Colt, Edina and Douglas to San Antonio. It took six days to travel the twenty miles to Cotulla and the additional seventy-five miles to San Antonio. They got to San Antonio late and Mr. Hunt insisted on paying for all their rooms at a boarding house.

The next morning they went to a nearby bank and had Edina's signature on the bill of sale notarized. They then went to the stage station. Again Mr. Hunt insisted on paying for Edina and Douglas's tickets to Fort Worth. They bid their farewells and thanks to Mr. Hunt, who started back to his ranch.

Colt kept fifty dollars for himself and gave the balance of the money to his mother. Two hours later Colt watched the stage roll out of sight and Edina and Douglas were on their way to Fort Worth.

During the two hours that he'd waited at the stage station, he heard that a big cattle buyer by the name of Jim Lassiter might be hiring drovers. He was coming through with a large herd of cattle bound for St. Louis, and was expected to arrive in San Antonio within the next few days.

Colt found the livery stable and made arrangements to sleep there for a couple of days in exchange for helping out.

As Colt secured his bedroll and equipment in the hayloft, he was thinking either the livery owner didn't know or didn't care, but storing hay over the horse stalls could give the horses a lung condition from all the dust and pollen that continuously dropped down on them. Oh well, it wasn't his place to say anything. He tossed a few flakes of hay to the floor, climbed down the ladder and fed it to the horses.

There were only four horses, but there were ten more empty stalls; most of them hadn't been cleaned since the last occupant left. He made sure each horse had water and while they were eating their hay, he began cleaning the stalls.

Colt was just finishing when Mr. Foster, the livery owner, came into the barn.

After looking around he said, "It looks pretty damn good, boy. I didn't expect that much from you."

Colt shrugged. "I had nothing better to do while I'm waiting."

"Who are you waiting for, if you don't mind me asking?"

"Well, sir, I was told that a Jim Lassiter was coming through here in a couple days with a big herd of cows and I thought I might could get a job."

"Do you know anything about cows, son?"

"Yes, sir. My pap owned a small place down south. I learned a little back there."

"I know Mr. Lassiter. He's a hard man, but he's mostly honest. I'll introduce you to him if you like."

"That'd sure be nice, Mr. Foster. I'd really appreciate that. I'm about through here so I thought I'd walk to that restaurant down the street for some dinner. I'll be back later."

"Hell, boy, why don't you come on to the house for supper? My wife always fixes more than enough. It isn't fancy but it's always plenty. It's closer anyway."

Colt was embarrassed. He needed a bath. His hair and what few whiskers he had on his chin were too long. "I appreciate that, Mr. Foster, but, well, I don't want to put you out. Besides, I'm not too presentable, as you can see."

Mr. Foster stared at him with a twinkle in his eye. "Why don't you just clean up in the water trough. There's some lye soap in the tack room and a mirror. If you don't have a razor, I'll loan you one. You get cleaned up best you can and don't worry about what you can't. I'll warn my women not to be too shocked at your wild an' woolly ways."

Colt knew he was being kidded and finally grinned. "Thanks, Mr. Foster, I'd really enjoy some home cooking and your family's company."

"You just get cleaned up and come on over. You go out this door here, turn left and it's not fifty feet to my house. It's the first one on the left." Foster turned and walked out.

Thirty minutes later, Colt had combed his hair and tried to shave with Pap's straight razor. All he was successful in doing was knocking off a few of the longer hairs and nicking his face in several places.

He changed into some spare clothes that Ma had made.

The pants were what Pap had called 'tin pants' because they were so stiff and tough. They'd been made from a heavy brown canvas and were so tough that mesquite thorns had a hard time going through them. He put on a brown cotton shirt that was a much lighter and softer material.

He wrapped his weapons in a blanket and stashed them in the hay. He climbed down from the loft and went to the Fosters'.

Mr. Foster opened the door immediately. The combination living room and kitchen was small but cozy and clean.

Mrs. Foster turned and smiled, then sat a granite pot on the table.

She wiped her hands on her apron, and with a bright smile, shook Colt's hand. "Please come in. My husband has told me a lot about you. Sit down. Dinner is ready."

Mr. Foster took Colt's hat and hung it on a peg. He motioned Colt to sit at the head of the table and took the chair on the opposite end.

Mrs. Foster finished delivering the food. There was fried ham, potatoes, and greens, corn on the cob, cornbread and gravy. She also placed a large pitcher of milk on the table.

Colt sat on the proffered chair, feeling awkward and as if he were intruding.

Shortly, Mr. Foster looked up and said, "Colt, this is my step-daughter, Miriam."

Colt looked up and saw a beautiful girl about sixteen years old. Her mischievous smile showed in her eyes. She had a heart-shaped face with dimples, full red lips, white even teeth and the bluest eyes Colt had ever seen. She had light blond hair done in braids around her ears. All of this, Colt took in for the brief moment that it took him to look upon the prettiest, largest breasts he had ever seen. Her dress was buttoned to her throat but there was nothing she could do to hide those beautiful treasures.

He stood up so suddenly that he almost knocked his chair over.

Colt forced his eyes away from such a sensitive area, but not so quickly that Miriam didn't see his interest.

Thank God he had his back to Mr. and Mrs. Foster. He knew that Miriam had caught his look and he blushed all the way from his ears to his boots.

Miriam, seeing his discomfort, put a special little curl in her smile that made Colt feel as if he were standing nude in front of her.

He stammered, "Glad to meet you, ma'am."

Still smiling, she said, "I'm not ma'am. I'm Miriam and I'm glad to meet you too. What on earth happened to your face?"

Colt stammered, "I must have cut it shaving."

"My word, it doesn't look like you shaved. You must have a very heavy beard, Mr. Colt."

"It's not Mr. Colt, Miss Miriam, it's just Colt. Colt Patterson."

She offered her hand and Colt didn't know what to do. Was he supposed to kiss it or shake it? He numbly grabbed her hand and pumped it like a well pump. As he withdrew his hand he noticed that just for a fraction of a second she held on seductively, sliding her hand from his. He quickly grabbed her chair and slid it out for her.

She stood in front of the chair, waiting.

Colt didn't know what to do. Should he just shove the chair towards the table and hope he timed it to be in the right position before she sat? Or should he wait for her to sit and try to catch her before she fell on the floor?

Miriam solved his dilemma by grasping the chair and saying, "Why, thank you, Mr. Patterson." She sat and scooted it to the table.

Colt was sure glad that was over. He sat down in his own chair and tried not to look at Miriam. He tried to be very polite, making sure he took small portions and passing everything to his left.

Miriam, seated immediately to his left, was very proper each time he passed plates of food to her, but each time she had that mischievous look in her eyes and that damnable, sexy, half-smile.

Colt had just taken the gravy dish from Mrs. Foster, placed some on his plate and was about to pass it over to Miriam when he felt her foot brushing against his leg. He realized that she had discreetly removed her shoe. He almost dropped the gravy.

Colt had a hard time keeping his mind on things like passing the food and carrying on some intelligent conversation with Mrs. and Mr. Foster. He tried to concentrate on eating and ignore the foot that was rubbing against his leg.

Miriam always looked very proper and never missed a beat in the conversation as she massaged her bare foot against Colt's thigh.

Colt had just stuffed his mouth with cornbread and had taken a big swallow of milk, when Miriam's toes found their way between his legs.

He coughed, spraying milk and cornbread. He jumped back from the table and stood, this time knocking his chair completely over. Cornbread and milk went down his windpipe and he coughed as hard as he ever had.

Miriam could see Colt's filled-out pants, the front of which Colt was able to turn away from Mrs. Foster. Miriam jumped up and used her napkin to brush the cornbread and spilled milk from Colt's shirt. She was quick enough to get a couple of swipes at the front of Colt's pants while looking him right in the eye.

Colt coughed even harder and struggled outside, all bent over and still coughing. It wasn't the fresh air he wanted. He wanted darkness before Mr. and Mrs. Foster saw what little Miriam had done to him.

The Fosters, trailed by Miriam, followed Colt to the front porch.

Finally Colt was able to get his breath. He kept his back to the Fosters as much as he could and was grateful that it was dark.

Mrs. Foster said, "Are you Okay, Colt? Would you like some water?"

"No, ma'am, I'm okay. Gosh, I'm sorry. I guess I have something down my windpipe."

Miriam walked around in front of him and again started brushing at his shirt. "That's all right. These things happen."

To Colt's excitement and embarrassment, she brushed his pants again.

He said, "Mrs. Foster, thank you for a great dinner, but I think I really ought to go now."

"Hang on, Colt," Mr. Foster said. "I have a jug of some real prime whiskey. Made it myself. Why don't you and I have a sip of it? Maybe it'll clear your throat."

Miriam looked at Colt with a coquettish smile and went back inside. "No, thanks, Mr. Foster, I really think I ought to go." Colt quickly said goodbye and went back to the stables.

*

Colt lay awake until late. This had never happened to him. Ever since he was about twelve he had been getting these feelings, but nothing like this. He was almost ready to go after that girl in front of her momma and daddy. It would have gotten him shot probably, but it had almost been beyond his control.

Miriam had left no doubt that she wanted it too.

He briefly considered sneaking into her house. If he had known which window was hers, he sure would have.

He lay there in the hay, hoping that he could go to sleep and his problem would go away. He couldn't sleep, however, and his problem didn't go away.

Colt lay there with the biggest erection that he'd ever had. He felt as if he was ready to explode. He checked Pap's watch. It was ten after one.

He still couldn't sleep. The moonlight was so bright through the open loading door that he could have read a book.

Colt heard a slight rustling down in the barn. It sounded as though it was someone that didn't want to be heard.

He forgot about his erection and quietly pulled his Savage. He cocked the hammer and pointed the gun at the trap door to the loft.

Someone was quietly climbing the ladder.

He saw Miriam's smiling face appear through the hole to the loft.

Colt thought, " Oh Lord, my dream's come true." He quickly de-cocked the Savage and lay it aside.

"Colt, are you there? It's me, Miriam."

"Yeah, I'm here. Every bit of me."

Miriam giggled. "I thought you might like some company."

"Lord'ee, I sure would. Especially your company. But what about your parents?"

"They're asleep," she said. "I could hear them snoring. I knew you wanted me to come. I could just tell."

Miriam climbed onto the loft.

Colt stood with his pants about to bust wide open. The moonlight allowed them to see each other completely.

She deftly pushed the shoulder straps off her nightgown, let it drop and stood naked in the moonlight. Her perfectly shaped breasts stood out with the nipples erect.

She moved close to Colt, and as they kissed, her hands hungrily groped for his belt, loosened his fly and reached inside.

*

Colt exploded inside her almost instantly. It took awhile, but soon she had him excited again. This time she set off and made so much noise, Colt was afraid someone would hear them. Miriam seemed oblivious to the outside world as she exploded again and again until Colt fired for the second time.

They lay there in the moonlight, exploring each other's body with their fingertips.

Miriam looked at Colt. "Was this your first time?"

"No," he lied. "Was it yours?"

"Yes," she lied.

𝕵𝕺𝖀𝕽

It was morning when Colt awoke and found Miriam gone. He checked his watch and was shocked to see it was almost seven. He could hear someone down below moving around. He stuck his head over the loft and saw it was Mr. Foster pitching hay to the horses. *Oh Lord*, he thought, *how am I gonna face him?* If he remained quiet long enough maybe Mr. Foster would go away.

"Colt, are you up there?"

There was no choice but to answer. "Yes sir, I sure am."

"Come on down. The wife's got breakfast almost ready."

Oh Lordy, Colt thought, *how can I get through another meal like last night? How can I sit and face Mr. and Mrs. Foster after what happened? How will I be able to look at Miriam without getting a hard-on?*

Colt leaned over from the loft and said, "Uh, Mr. Foster, I don't feel so good, I really don't feel like breakfast this morning."

"Nonsense, boy, come on down. The missus will be real put out if you don't show. She already has it cooked."

Not seeing any way out, Colt dressed and followed Mr. Foster to his house.

Over breakfast Miriam hardly looked at him. She conducted herself properly, much to his relief. He made sure to refer to her as Miss Miriam; dreading, yet hoping, for the touch of her foot that never came.

Mr. Foster spoke up around a mouth full of food and said, "I hear

Mr. Lassiter is gonna be a few days late. It seems like there's been an outbreak of black leg down south and he is detouring around. I figure it will be Saturday before he gets here. That black leg is sure enough bad news when it hits. What cows it don't kill, you have to shoot the rest and burn them."

Colt looked at his plate of half-finished ham, toast and eggs and didn't say anything. Suddenly he wasn't hungry anymore.

He stood and said, "Begging your pardon, Mrs. Foster. It was a delicious breakfast, but I don't feel so good. Would you excuse me?"

As he walked out the door, he could hear Mr. Foster saying, "He said he didn't feel good earlier. Maybe he's caught something."

*

Miriam came the next two nights. The last night, a Friday, Miriam asked Colt if he loved her.

Colt didn't know what to say. He sure as hell liked her, and it was hard to think about her and anything else at the same time. But he wasn't sure about that word love.

"I don't know. Maybe."

"Will you take me with you when you go?"

"I don't see how I can," Colt said. "I'm not even sure Mr. Lassiter is gonna hire me, and if he does, it will be for only a couple of months. Maybe someday I can come back this way, but right now I don't know where I'm going or what I'm gonna do."

"You have to take me with you."

Colt felt the intensity of her statement. "Why? Why can't I come back later for you?"

"Because I'm going to have your baby, that's why!"

Colt was shocked. After three nights, they'd made a baby! "How do you know?"

"A woman knows these things."

What she didn't say was that she had known for several weeks before she'd met Colt.

"Oh, Lordy, I never expected anything like this! Are you really sure?"

Miriam said, "Of course. I told you, a woman knows." *So did her mama,* she thought. *And so did her stepfather. Especially her stepfather—and Mama had suspected for a long time what Mr. Foster was doing with her daughter.*

Colt hesitated. Everything was happening too fast. "I guess...I don't know. Are you sure? I mean, how can you tell that soon?"

No one had bothered to explain to Colt all of the facts of a woman's cycle. He knew what made babies; he just didn't know all the details.

Miriam could see Colt's confusion, which suited her fine. She now knew that he was so dumb about women that he would never know it wasn't his.

She put her hand against his face and said, "Colt, no matter what you do, I'm going to name the baby after you. I guess if you don't love me, why I'll just have to run off someplace and have the baby alone. I thought you loved me, otherwise I wouldn't have given myself to you."

Colt, stunned, just looked at her. "I don't know. I guess that if it's my baby I don't have any choice but to marry you. Are you sure?"

Miriam didn't answer. Instead she shed some very large tears. *The best I've ever done*, she thought, and just nodded her head.

Colt sighed. He sure wished he'd kept his britches on. Now what was he gonna do?

He didn't know much about women, but somehow he just didn't believe her. He looked at Miriam and said, "Don't worry, I'll do the right thing."

Miriam brightened and hugged him. She kissed him right on the mouth. "I knew you would, I just knew you would. The moment I laid eyes on you, I just knew you would." She scrambled down the ladder and was gone.

Colt just sat there. *What did she just say? "I knew you would when I first laid eyes on you?" Hell, they hadn't done anything when she first laid eyes on him. Maybe she didn't mean it that way. Maybe I ought to get some advice.*

He dressed, climbed down the ladder and walked to the business district of town.

*

Colt eventually saw a sign that said 'Doctor Payne, DDS.' He did-n't know what 'DDS' stood for, but a doctor was a doctor. He went inside and talked to a young lady sitting behind a desk. "I'd like to see the doctor." Colt sat down and waited with his hat in his lap.

He heard a man's yell and cursing. "Goddamn, Doc, that hurts."

"Shut up, Homer, it's supposed to hurt! Why the hell you think my name is Payne, anyhow?"

A few minutes later an elderly man in run-down boots and faded denims came out of the examination room holding his jaw.

This must be Homer, Colt thought.

Homer's face was pasty gray as he asked, "How much?"

The secretary smiled and said, "That will be two dollars and four bits."

Homer threw the money down and stomped out holding his jaw and cursing to himself.

The secretary smiled at Colt. "The doctor will see you now."

Colt got up and went into the doctor's office.

Payne pointed to a large funny-looking chair and motioned Colt to sit and then said, "Open your mouth."

Colt, puzzled, did as he was told.

The doctor looked into his mouth. "Which one's bothering you?"

"Which one is what?"

Payne asked, "Which one's bothering you?"

Colt, again, asked, "Which one what's bothering me?"

Payne said, "Well, hell, you don't see a dentist if your teeth ain't bothering you, so which one is it?"

"There isn't anything bothering my teeth, Doc. I just need some advice."

"I'm a dentist, I ain't no counselor. What kind of advice you need, boy? Legal advice? The only advice I can give you is teeth advice."

"I thought since you were a doctor, you'd know about women having babies."

"Son, my woman's had nine young-uns, and naturally I learned a little about the human body in dental school, but I'm not the kind of doctor that can deliver a baby, nor give you any advice on how to do it."

"Just answer me this," Colt said. "How does a woman know when she's gonna have a baby?"

*

A little while later, Colt came out of the doctor's office. The secretary said, "That'll be two dollars and fifty cents."

Colt paid and left. He'd made up his mind about Miriam. Either she wasn't gonna have no baby, or she was gonna have somebody else's. If she was, she was gonna have it without him.

He immediately went back to the livery. While checking closely for Miriam or Mr. Foster, he quickly gathered his belongings and got out of there as fast as he could.

*

As soon as Miriam left Colt, she ran home and gushed out to her parents that Colt had asked her to marry him.

Mrs. Foster, knowing the condition of her daughter, thought that it was just wonderful.

Mr. Foster hurried off to find Preacher Holcomb.

Miriam and her mother spent the next several hours making wedding plans.

In the meantime, Colt was disappearing into the mesquite of the desert.

*

Colt ran the first mile or so, then settled into a walk for several hours until he came to Sandy Creek.

Looking at the creek, he knew why they called it Sandy Creek. It was solid sand. There wasn't a drop of water.

He checked his canteen and figured that he had enough for about one more day. If Lassiter didn't show up tomorrow, he would have a long walk back into San Antonio. Worse than the walk, Miriam was back there.

He wondered how long he could stay at Sandy Creek without water. Maybe he could last more than a couple days after all. Colt found some firewood and lit a fire. He was only a little concerned about Apaches, but he was very concerned about Miriam and her daddy.

He spread one of his blankets on the ground, rolled up in the second one and went to sleep.

*

At daybreak, Colt woke feeling something crawling across his face. He swatted his face and sat bolt upright. Cold chills rippled over him. A large scorpion, its back broken, was trying to sting itself to death. One had never stung him, but he'd heard they hurt like hell, and some people got so sick they died.

He jumped up and stomped it in the ground. He stood there looking at where the scorpion had been. He shook out his boots and blankets until he was convinced there weren't any more.

Stoking the coals and adding some mesquite, he soon had a small fire going. In his rush to leave the Fosters', he'd overlooked taking food, so he got a fist full of mesquite beans and chewed on them. It only made him hungrier. He spotted a cluster of cactus filled with prickly pear nearby.

Butcher knife in hand, he chopped off a few and took them to his fire. He roasted the thorns off them and ate the purple fruit. It wasn't much, but he was hungry.

Colt waited until noon. He was nearly out of water and the cactus didn't do much to sate his hunger.

If Lassiter didn't show soon, Colt knew he would have to head back to San Antonio. He scanned the horizon to the south and saw no sign of anyone approaching Sandy Creek.

He climbed the mesquite tree for a better view.

There was still no sign of the herd. If they were within five miles, he ought to see a dust cloud from the cattle at least.

As Colt turned to climb down, something caught his eye. He glanced to the north, and sure enough, there was something heading toward him. Whoever it was, they were at least a mile away. It looked like a wagon.

Oh Lordy, Colt prayed, *don't let it be Miriam or Mr. Foster*. What was he gonna do if it was? He sure wasn't gonna marry that girl, no matter what. Hell, if old man Foster believed he'd gotten her pregnant, there might even be a shooting.

Please don't let it be Miriam. I'd rather it be outlaws or Apache. Colt thought, *Outlaws! Outlaws will try to rob me!* He shinnied down the tree, walked about fifty feet and scooped out a shallow hole. He set five dollars aside and buried the rest. He used a piece of brush to spread out the dry sand and placed a dead cactus over it. He brushed out his tracks as he returned to the fire.

He checked the Spencer and made sure it was loaded with all seven rounds. He checked the Savage to insure all the caps were seated on the nipples.

"Hell," he thought, "*maybe I'm over-reacting. It might be some traveler just like me. If it is, maybe I can beg or buy some food and water off them.*"

Deciding he needed some kind of barricade and something at his back if it was Apaches or outlaws, Colt dragged a dry log near the embankment of the creek bed. The creek was only about three feet deep, so he would have to lay mighty low if it came to shooting. He placed his powder flask and pouch of .36 caliber balls for the Savage nearby, and then filled his pockets with as many of the 56-50 rim fire cartridges for the Spencer as he had. He sat on the log and waited.

The sun was almost directly overhead and Colt began to feel the heat. Gnats swarmed around his face and his sweat-stained white felt hat was too damn hot for this weather.

He mopped his face and waited. He sure hoped that it wasn't Miriam.

FIVE

Colt watched the wagon approach. Eventually he could make out the figure of the driver as that of a tall man, wearing a dark suit and a black stovepipe hat. A portly woman sat next to him. When they got closer, Colt could see the man wore a full black beard with some white showing around his chin.

Thank the Lord! It wasn't Miriam and it wasn't Indians either. It looked like just a man and his missus; still, he kept his hand near the Savage and remained seated on the log.

"Howdy," the man said. "We weren't expecting to see anyone way out here. My name's Moses Crawford, and this lady is Flossy. She works for me."

Flossy smiled and waved. "Hi, I'm Flossy."

"Dammit, Flossy, I just told him that."

Moses put his foot on the wooden brake bar and brought the wagon to a creaking halt. "So what's a fellow doing out here just sitting on a log in the hot sun? What happened? Did you lose your horse?"

Colt stood and said, "Nope, I'm just waiting for somebody."

"What's your name, young fellow?"

"Colt Patterson, and I didn't lose my horse. I don't have one."

Moses asked, "Mind if we all get down and stretch? It's about time for a nooner, anyway. Any water in that creek?"

Colt shook his head. "Nope. Not a drop. I reckon you can get down if you want. It's a free country."

Moses hopped down. Although Colt stood at nearly six feet, Moses seemed a good two inches taller. He looked about fifty, muscular and without any spare fat.

Colt thought they seemed friendly enough and he began to relax.

Moses extended his hand. "Glad to meet you, Colt. My ladies and me are heading out to meet a herd. Most of those cowboys are gonna want to go into town to kick up their heels, but some are gonna have to stay with the herd. I figured those that are going to stay will want some refreshment and entertainment."

Flossy climbed down from the wagon and yelled, "Pearl, get your ass out here. You've been complaining about needing to pee for the last hour. Now's your chance. Besides, there's a mighty pretty man out here and he looks a might lonesome."

She looked at Colt and smiled. "You got any money, handsome?"

Colt said, "Not much, ma'am."

"Do you have two dollars for a poke?"

Colt looked at her puzzled. "A poke of what, ma'am?"

Flossy laughed. "A poke at me, darling, or if you like them skinny, a poke at Pearl."

Moses had walked behind the wagon and was relieving himself when Pearl climbed down.

Flossy ambled around the mules and walked up to Colt.

Although they both appeared under thirty, they were each missing some teeth.

Colt figured Flossy weighed around three hundred pounds and Pearl was so skinny that if she turned sideways she wouldn't cast a shadow. He sure didn't want to poke either one, not even for free. Besides, he remembered Miriam and had decided he was gonna be mighty careful about dropping his pants in front of a woman. At least for a while. Of course, if one came along that didn't look like a cow or a fence post, he might reconsider.

"No, ma'am, I don't have any money for that, but I do have a little that I could spare for some water and maybe something to eat. I'm kind-a hungry and almost out of water."

Moses came back around buttoning his fly and asked, "Well, how much do you have, boy?"

Colt hesitated, and then said, "I have close to five dollars."

"That's it? That's all you have?"

"Yes, sir, that's what I have."

"Hell, boy, that ain't more than a toot in a whirlwind. I don't reck-on I could sell you much for five dollars."

"How much to fill my canteen, some beans and coffee? Maybe even some salt pork or bacon?"

Moses spotted the watch bob hanging from Colt's pocket and asked, "You got the time, boy?"

Colt pulled out the watch and snapped the cover. "Yes, sir. It's almost two o'clock."

He put a friendly hand on Colt's shoulder as they walked towards the log by the mesquite tree.

"Let me see, that's a mighty fine-looking gold watch you have there, so I tell you what I'm gonna do. I'll give you a pound of beans, a sack of cornmeal, hog drippings, a pound of coffee and a whole rack of bacon for five dollars and that watch." He winked at Colt and added, "Plus you can have as many pokes with my ladies as you can stand. Now, that there is as fair a deal as a man could ask."

Colt looked at him. "No, sir. There's no way that I'm gonna sell this watch. This was my pap's watch. Since he died this is about all I have left of him. That, and this old pistol."

"Well, that's understandable, boy, and I admire your reasons; but you know, a man's gotta do what a man's gotta do. Out here is a hard land, and without something to eat and something to drink, a watch isn't gonna help you much, is it? I tell you what. I'm a real gener-ous man. I can see that's a mighty fine watch and that it means a lot to you. I have real, honest-to-God canned tomatoes and canned peaches. I'll throw them in, too. Plus," Moses hesitated, "I'll throw in a jug of some of the finest whiskey you ever wrapped your lips around."

Colt said, "No, sir, I couldn't hardly do that. I'll buy what I can for the five dollars and just make do."

"Suit yourself, boy. I really admire a man that's loyal to his loved ones; I surely do, so you keep your watch. I'm going to let you fill your canteen from my water barrel. I'll give you some beans and enough coffee to make a pot or two, but for only five dollars, that's about the best I can do."

Colt knew that in town he could buy ten times that for his five dollars but he was in no position to turn down the offer.

Moses could see that, too, and he still wanted that gold watch. He said, "Hell, son, I know that's no bargain. It's just hard times and I'm not used to dealing too much with decent folk like you. I tell you what; you just go ahead and give me the five dollars. Take all the water you want and whatever supplies you think is fair. I apologize. It's just that I'm so used to dealing with hard people.

"Flossy, come on over here. I want you to put together a big pot of your famous stew for this man. He hasn't eaten for a couple days."

Moses looked at Colt and continued, "If this man doesn't mind, I'll just stir up that fire and build us a pot of coffee. I might even find something to splash in it."

He winked at Colt. "You ever put a little corn whiskey in your coffee? It's mighty good. Couple cups, you might even feel like a poke. If you do, boy, it's on the house."

Colt didn't want to take advantage of Moses' generosity but he did fill his canteen and asked for a pound of coffee beans, a like measure of pinto beans and corn meal, salt pork and a can of tomatoes.

Moses put it all in a gunnysack. "Boy, I saw you eyeing those peaches, so I'm throwing in a couple cans. No charge."

*

Later, they were all sitting around a campfire that was much too large for Colt's liking, but he had good company, a full stomach, and Moses was passing around the bottle. They sang religious songs, bawdy songs, and Colt felt better than he had in a week.

Flossy and Pearl were looking better and better to him every time Moses passed the jug.

After a while, Colt had to head for the bushes. He staggered away from the firelight. He felt real good and yet everything kind of swirled around him. He had a hard time unbuttoning his pants and he wasn't sure that he was going to make it.

Somehow he finished his business and stumbled back to the fire. *Boy!* he thought. *These are some really nice and fun folks.*

The ground seemed to be swaying and Colt was having trouble buttoning himself up, which struck him funny. He giggled as he made his way back to his log. When he tried to sit, he completely missed it. He, along with everybody else, thought this was hysterical and they all laughed. *People can say what they want about whores and pimps,* Colt decided, *but these are mighty good folks.*

*

Colt awoke lying face down in the sand with his head pounding. His stomach didn't feel good and every time he inhaled, he breathed dust from the ground.

He wondered if it would be better to stay where he was and smother, or move and suffer what he suspected his head was going to do to him. He managed to roll over onto his back. His stomach and head told him that he should have stayed where he was.

He smelled the wood smoke that last night's fire was still giving off in thin wisps.

"Oh Lordy, Moses, that was some night. Wow, my head hurts!" When he didn't hear any response, he rolled his head toward the wagon and risked opening his eyes. The wagon wasn't there.

It took a moment to register but when it did, he sat straight up. Gone! The wagon was gone. He jumped up and noticed he was barefoot. Hell, he didn't remember taking his boots off. He looked around. His blankets were gone. His Savage was gone and his money was gone.

The coffeepot was gone from the fire ring along with his skillet and all the goods that he'd bought the night before.

With relief, he saw his boots standing neatly by the fire. He hopped over to them; sand burrs and goat heads stabbed his feet as he went.

A note was stuck in his boot. It read:

They don't fit, 'sides I wouldn't leave anyone afoot out here with no boots. Enjoyed the visit.

Moses

P.S. I hated to do it, but I couldn't afford to have you sneaking up on us some night, so I took your guns.

Colt looked around. He couldn't believe it. They were such nice folks!

He remembered his watch, but knew even before he felt his pocket that it was gone.

Feeling sicker than ever, he just sat down on the log. It seemed like he'd lost everything possible. He'd even lost Pap's watch.

He was looking for a branch to stir the fire when he saw his butcher knife partially buried under the sand.

Colt thought, *At least they didn't get that.*

He remembered the money he'd buried. He quickly put on his boots and ran over to the spot and kicked away the cactus.

To his profound relief, the money was still there. That was the only smart thing he'd done in a long time. It would be a long, hot, dry walk back into San Antonio but he could make it if he started right away.

*

Charley lay in the sand not more than a hundred feet from the crazy white man. Even though he'd been forced to attend white man's school for three summers, he didn't think he would ever understand them.

*

Two days after the death of Alchisay, Charley had sought out his two cousins, Yanahosa and Ka-e-tennay, and told them what had happened.

They decided to leave Bosque Redondo and join forces with warrior Indians. They'd heard that Victorio and Goyathlay, the man who yawns, were raiding along the border between New Mexico and Texas. Goyathlay, or Geronimo, as the white man called him, was especially active in Texas.

They'd left New Mexico, headed due east and had managed to

travel half way across Texas without being caught. Along the way they'd been able to snitch a few chickens and eggs from farmers and had even managed to steal horses complete with white man's saddles. They had actually stolen five horses, but had eaten two to get to where they were.

Although they bragged among themselves what they were going to do to white men, there had been little chance until now. For weapons, they only had a knife each and some poorly made clubs. Ka-e-tennay had a bow he had stolen from his father, along with a quiver of eight arrows. Since he was better armed, physically bigger and one summer older, Ka-e-tennay was the self-appointed chief of their three-man war party.

They'd seen the bearded man with the foolish hat and his fat and skinny women leave hours before. Foolish Hat was very well-armed so they had decided not to confront him. It was too dangerous, even for his wagon full of supplies. And, though young and full of the flames in their loins, none of them thought Buffalo Woman or Skinny Woman was worth fighting someone as well-armed as Foolish Hat. So they waited until the one crazy white man, who sits on a log, was alone.

*

Colt sensed that something was wrong. His shoulders stiffened and his hair stood up on his neck.

He slowly scanned the mesquite, cactus, and sand dunes around him. He didn't see anything, but he felt something watching him. He touched the butcher knife in his waistband.

*

Charley thought, here was their chance. A white man, whom at the most, had a knife, against three fierce Apache warriors. Admittedly, none had ever been in combat before, but they had the blood of the warrior, handed down from the Athapascan to their fore-fathers.

Charley and his cousins had left their horses back in the mesquite. Like their fathers and uncles had taught them, they had decided to attack on foot.

They quietly surrounded the lone white man on three sides. Killing him would be good sport. If Charley Tree could kill him, maybe he could get enough prestige to take away Ka-e-tennay's leadership.

*

Colt heard a whisper of a sound and instinctively ducked behind the mesquite tree. An arrow glanced off the mesquite and embedded itself into his buttock.

*

Charley was furious. Ka-e-tennay was using his bow, trying to get the white man before any of the others had a chance.

He let out a yell and charged the white man before Ka-e-tennay could loose another arrow.

Yanahosa, not to be outdone, charged also.

Ka-e-tennay dropped his bow, pulled his crude war club and joined the fray.

Charley chased the white man around and around the mesquite until Yanahosa finally hit the white man across the back of the head, knocking him cold.

Yanahosa let out a victory yell and grabbed the white man's hair, intending to take the scalp.

Charley and Ka-e-tennay stared at him angrily.

Ka-e-tennay grabbed Yanahosa's arm and said the scalp was his, since his arrow was the first to strike the white man.

Yanahosa argued that the scalp was his since he was the one who knocked the white man down.

Charley, being the first one to engage the white man, felt the scalp was his. Ka-e-tennay's arrow almost missed the white man, and, in fact, the wound was a joke. On the other hand, wasn't he, Charley Tree, the only one to face this knife wielded by the white man? Wasn't he the first one to engage him in combat?

Charley wanted the scalp bad enough to kill Ka-e-tennay and Yanahosa. If they ever met up with Goyathlay—or, if really lucky, the great Victorio—it would be important to have a scalp tied to his lance. Of course, he'd have to find a lance to tie it to.

After a heated argument, they finally calmed down and began to discuss a method to settle the argument.

It was decided that they would first kill the white man in such a manner that each would guess the exact moment when he would die. The one who guessed right would get the scalp.

This, of course, created a new problem. How could they devise a way for him to die that would be precise enough?

They discussed the problem for quite some time, but it was all too complicated. Finally, they decided to just burn the white man and be done with it.

They lifted the unconscious man and tied him to the tree. They piled brush around him and waited for him to regain consciousness. After all, it would be no fun unless the white man was alive to know what was happening.

The Indians squatted down to wait for the Man Who Sits on Log to wake up.

*

Billy rode with his chin almost touching his chest. The thought of giving up the ranger business was back on his mind. It had all started when his horse had kicked down the widow Tucker's corral fence.

He'd ridden onto her farm to ask directions and water his horses. The widow had not only allowed him to water his horses but also offered him some peach cobbler.

The only water trough had been in the corral and he'd unsaddled and locked his horses in the corral while he'd sat on the porch swing with Ms. Tucker eating the cobbler.

They'd heard a ruckus and Ms. Tucker had said, "Oh my Lord, I forgot about my mare. She's in heat!"

By the time they'd run out to the corral, his grulla had kicked down the plank fence and had mounted the mare.

Billy had stayed over for three days repairing the damage done by his horse. Those three days had done something to his mind.

The widow Tucker had pitched in like a man and worked right

along with him.

Each evening they sat in the porch swing watching the sun gently settle. For some reason he felt at peace for the first time in his life. He noticed that beyond the widow's tired look, there was a quiet beauty in her face. He was stricken with the gentle way that she cared for her teenage son, Calvin. Billy had noticed from the beginning that something wasn't right with the boy. Apparently his mind hadn't grown with his body.

Billy had never been shy with the ladies, but there was something about the widow that made him feel like a kid on his first date. There were a couple of moments when he wanted to hold her but wasn't able to bring himself into making the move.

He'd visited her several times since; each time he found himself looking for something to fix. He'd repaired the windmill, mended fences, and repaired the roof. On his last visit he'd helped the mare foal a healthy filly.

He didn't know whether to blame the horse or the peach cobbler. He only knew that his mind had been acting funny ever since he showed up that first day.

The widow was on his mind as he nodded off, sleeping as he rode.

He awoke to the heat of the sun on his back.

Dixon halted his horse, pulled off his brown canvas duster, rolled it up and tied it behind his saddle. He took his canteen and stepped down.

He poured some water into his hat and let the grulla drink. He did the same for the roan. Only then did he take a drink for himself.

He wiped his mouth, smearing the alkali dust that coated his face. He figured that he had a long way to go, but if he were right, it would be worth it. The warrants in his pocket covered five fugitives and totaled twenty-one hundred dollars. One was wanted dead or alive.

He knew from past experience that most fugitives wanted four things. They all seemed to want food, drink, sex and safety. When the heat was on they usually headed to Mexico. There were hundreds of small settlements just across the border but only a few that offered any semblance of entertainment and civilized conditions. Matamoros, which was good, but too far east. Reynosa was a little closer. Ciudad Camango and Nueva Laredo were closer still.

He was gambling that it would be the latter. According to his information, all of the fugitives had been seen in San Antonio within the past few months. Nuevo Laredo had everything. The town could provide accommodations, entertainment and security. He guessed that most, if not all, of his fugitives were there.

He took another drink from his canteen and climbed back into the saddle. It was then he heard a yell.

In his twenty-plus years as a Texas Ranger, he'd fought Indians many times. There was no doubt about that yell.

He quickly dismounted, leaving his horses on low ground. He took his Henry .44 rim-fire and crawled to a low sand dune. There were at least three Indians chasing what looked like a white man around a tree. The Indians soon swept over the white man and he was down.

There wasn't a damn thing he could do if he didn't get closer. He followed the low ground, moving as fast as he could without making too much noise.

SIX

Colt's head really hurt. It took a moment to realize that he couldn't move. He saw the three leering Indians squatting around him.

He saw the brush lying around the tree and his blood ran cold as he realized what they were going to do.

Colt thought, *Not that! Dear Lord, please don't let 'em burn me*!

The tallest of the three Indians stood and walked toward Colt with a burning branch in his hand.

He was about five feet from Colt when suddenly his chest exploded in gore.

With a surprised look, he was knocked to his knees as the sound of a rifle shot echoed across the desert. The Indian tried to stand up, stumbled, and then fell again.

Charley and Yanahosa saw Ka-e-tennay fall and knew what had happened even before the sound of the rifle shot died. They were off and running in different directions as fast as their moccasins could carry them.

Yanahosa suddenly dropped like a sack of potatoes, followed by a second shot.

Charley ran even faster, fully aware that he was running in the opposite direction from where they had left their horses. He kept running until he disappeared into the chaparral and cactus of the desert.

*

Colt was in shock. One minute he was sick with the thought that he was going to be burned, and the next his tormentors were gone. Two shot down with the other beating feet into the desert.

*

Dixon was disappointed that he hadn't hit all three but that one little bastard was really fast.

As he approached the man tied to the tree, he saw that he was just a kid, not over eighteen.

He looked at the Indian lying nearby. He was lung shot and wouldn't last more than a few more minutes.

Dixon kicked out the burning branch and glanced at the boy. "You okay, boy?"

"Yes, sir, I guess so. Mister, I'm sure glad to see you. They had me good. They were gonna burn me."

"Yep. It sure looked that way." Dixon took out a clasp knife and cut Colt loose. "Boy, you watch this son of a bitch here. I have to check on the other one."

He went to Yanahosa and saw that he had been shot just above the right kidney. He was moaning and rolling back and forth.

Dixon placed the muzzle of his Henry behind the Indian's left ear and said, "Indian, I'm doing you a favor," then pulled the trigger. Yanahosa convulsed for a moment then lay still.

Dixon studied the dry desert, but saw no sign of the one that got away.

He rolled the Indian over and noted that he couldn't have been over sixteen years old.

He removed the Indian's knife and beaded sheath and stuck it in his belt. The Indian's club was crudely made and consisted only of elongated rock strapped to a wooden handle. He left it and walked back to Colt, examining the knife as he went. The knife was the exact opposite in quality from the club. Most Indian knives were crude modifications of butcher knives or made from scrap metal. An Indian obviously hadn't made this one.

The blade was about ten inches long with a slight curve toward the tip. The top of the blade, from the tip back toward the handle, was as finely honed and sharp as the bottom. The knife was Damascus steel with a blood groove milled on both sides. The handle was horn, with a nickel or similar metal guard and end cap. The only thing Indian about it was the sheath.

Colt was standing by the wounded Indian when Dixon walked up, still examining the knife.

Dixon could see that Colt's left buttock was bleeding from the arrow. He also had a nasty bump behind his left ear.

"You sure you're OK, boy?"

Colt said, "Yes, sir. My head hurts a little, but this here arrow didn't go too deep."

"Well, sometimes these heathens dip their arrow points in shit to cause infection. If they'd dipped it in snake poison, you'd be dead now. I have some rubbing alcohol back at my horse. I'll look at it then."

Colt nudged the Indian with his boot and said, "What about him?"

"Shoot 'em and let's get out of here."

"Can't we do anything for him?"

Dixon looked at him in surprise. "Hell, boy, they were gonna roast you. Besides, can't anybody do anything for him now. He's lung shot. You'd be doing him a favor if you just shot him or cut his throat. He's in a lot of misery."

Colt said, "I don't have a gun."

"What in tarnation would anybody be doing out here without a gun?"

Colt, a little sheepish, said, "Well, I had some guns but a drummer and some whores stole 'em. They took everything else including my blankets and canteen."

"I won't even ask how you let that happen. They take your horse, too?"

"No, sir, I didn't have no horse. I was walking."

Dixon just shook his head. He moved over to the Indian. Bloody froth emitted from his lips and nose as he struggled to speak.

He knelt down close to the Indian so he could hear what the Indian was saying.

The Indian whispered, "Tell Man Who Sits on Log he fight like a woman. I don't think he would have died so good."

"Where'd you learn English, boy?"

"White man's school. They cut my hair; made me wear white man's clothes. Made me speak white man's tongue and eat white man's pig. Now white man kills me."

Dixon nodded his head. He took a deep breath and shot the Indian in the head.

When the shot sounded, Colt jerked almost as much as the Indian.

"We'd best be getting out of here. I have my horses tied back over there. These heathens have theirs tied about half way to where I have mine."

Colt stumbled after Dixon, looking back at the Indian and the campsite. He would have a long memory of that mesquite tree where they were going to burn him. He didn't really feel sorry for the Indians, it was just that he had never seen anyone killed before and this stranger did it like somebody killing a hog.

"My name's Billy Dixon. What's yours?"

"Colt Patterson."

Dixon turned and looked at him. "I had a gun once that was a Colt Patterson. Is that your real name or just one that you made up?"

"That's my real name. Why would I make up something like my name?"

Dixon grunted. "Maybe you have something to hide. Most everybody does, and when it gets real serious, oftentimes people change their name or go somewhere else. Now, here you go traipsing off out in the desert, no gun, no horse, no supplies and you give me a name like Colt Patterson. It sounds like to me you left someplace in a mighty hurry. Now, don't fun me, boy, what's your name? For sure, now, don't fool with me or I'll leave you with those Indians over there."

"Colt is my real name. I guess I did leave San Antonio in a little hurry but I didn't do anything wrong. I just came out to meet a man called Lassiter who's running some cows through. I thought I might could get me a job."

Dixon eyed Colt suspiciously. "Usually when someone says they didn't do anything wrong, that's exactly what they did. I can't afford to have anyone back shoot or stab me when I'm asleep, so you'd better tell me before I get to my horse or I'm leaving you right here."

Colt told him about Miriam.

Dixon stood for a minute then started laughing. "Boy, if what you said is true, you did real good by getting out when you did. Looks like Mr. Foster won't be bothering you any because old lady Foster blew his head off yesterday. I was in talking to the sheriff and he told me that Mr. Foster had been poking that daughter of hers and done got her pregnant. According to the sheriff, it seems like just about every male in San Antonio had been poking her. That is, except the sheriff. At least according to him. It was right smart of you to leave when you did.

"According to the sheriff," Dixon continued, "Mr. Lassiter isn't coming this way. He said the herd had to detour and was heading through Southerlen Springs. He said something about a cow plague down south and Lassiter didn't want to risk his cows. You'd a been here for quite a spell waiting for him, I reckon."

They reached a small ravine and found the Indian horses tied to some chaparral. They were all saddled and two had bridles. The third had a hackamore instead of a bit.

Dixon said, "It looks like you done got lucky, boy. There's your ride back to San Antonio. Two of those horses have brands on 'em, and you can bet the owner's going to be real upset if they find anybody riding 'em. The third one seems like he has no brand, unless he's been tattooed on the lips or ears. He's so damned ugly, though, I doubt if anybody but an Indian would want him. Seems like he's got some belly on him but his feet are easty-westy. Looks like if one foot went one way, the other one would have to go another."

Colt looked at the horse and laughed. He had to agree.

"It looks like somebody took a whole bunch of left over horse parts and tied them all together."

The horse's withers were lower than his rump, which ought to make a rider feel like he was riding down hill. His neck was too long for his stubby body and he had a hammerhead that looked completely out of place. His throatlatch was so thick, the halter strap barely reached. He was an odd steel gray with light brown, almost pink, freckles. Some people would call him a strawberry, but he was uglier than any strawberry Colt had ever seen. The most remarkable thing was, one of his eyes was blue and one was brown.

Dixon went to the horse. "Whoa, boy, easy boy. Let me check and see if you're marked."

The horse let Dixon grab his head and waited until he tried to lift his lips, then the horse bit him hard, right where his thumb joined his wrist.

"You son of a bitch!" Dixon jumped back, holding his hand. "Shit, he's as mean as he is ugly."

Colt looked at the other horses. Both of them were obviously well bred, maybe a cross between a Quarter horse and Morgan. "You know, I think I'll pass on the ugly one; I'll take one of those. But I'm not going back to San Antonio."

Dixon said, "I'd think twice about riding around on another fellow's horse, especially one that's branded. You're liable to get yourself hung. As ugly and mean as that one is, he doesn't have a brand that I can see. You might get bit to death but he's the one to take. Do what you want, but if your gonna ride a branded one, don't ride close to me. I sure wouldn't want to get hung along with you."

Colt had a feeling Dixon meant it.

Dixon continued, "If it was me, I'd keep the ugly one and turn the others loose. Maybe they'll find their way home, maybe they won't. At least you won't get your neck stretched. I'd pull those saddles off 'em first. It wouldn't be right to leave 'em on. You might as well pick the best one for yourself."

Colt really wanted to keep one of the better horses but what Dixon said made a lot of sense. He'd managed to get himself into one problem after another here lately and he sure didn't need any more trouble.

He removed the bridles and saddles from the other two horses and they took off heading back toward San Antonio. Colt took the best saddle and blanket over to the remaining horse. The ugly thing was staring at him suspiciously, its brown and blue eyes rolling. As he approached, Colt noticed that both of the horse's ears laid back.

"Easy, boy, steady…whoa, boy."

The horse allowed Colt to untie the cinch strap and Colt was lifting the saddle off when the horse bit him on the left buttock. Colt yelped and jumped in the wrong direction. The horse kicked him with his rear hoof, catching him in almost the same place he'd bitten him. The force knocked Colt to his hands and knees. The horse continued kicking and bucking as Colt scrambled away.

Dixon stood laughing and shaking his head. "Boy, that old horse has done got you buffaloed. Horses are a whole lot like women. Most of 'em only need a little love and understanding. Once in a while you run across a salty one, and with those you gotta get their attention."

He picked up a rawhide thong from one of the saddles and said, "Here, now you pay attention."

Dixon made a loop and caught it around the left rear foot of the stubborn horse and ran the other end through where the bridle connected to the hackamore. He pulled it tight, forcing the hoof off the ground. He walked to the rear of the horse and slapped him on the rump. The horse tried to kick out with both rear feet and instantly went down.

The horse managed to get back up standing on three legs. Then Dixon yanked on his tail. The horse tried to kick and again went down. Dixon then twisted his tail until the horse kicked and he went down for the third time. The horse struggled back up and was looking at Dixon with hate in his eyes, his ears pinned back against his head.

Dixon reached down and pinched the tendon near the hock on the horse's rear leg and again the horse kicked. Again he went down. The horse's eyes were rolling as he stared at Dixon, but suddenly he quit kicking.

He walked all around the horse, touching him as he went. The horse didn't kick. He pulled his mane and then bent his left forearm toward the horse's mouth.

The horse bared his teeth and tried to nip.

Dixon jerked his arm away and hit him full force in the side.

The horse, surprised, jerked his head away.

Dixon offered his arm up again to be bitten and the ugly horse tried to bite again.

Dixon pulled his arm away just in time and smacked the horse again.

He repeated that process five or six times until, no matter what Dixon did, the horse didn't try to bite.

He patted the horse and said, "I think you can saddle him now."

Colt thought he knew about horses, but he'd never seen this.

Dixon watched as Colt switched saddles and replaced the hackamore with a regular bridle. "You think I'm a mean man, don't you?"

Colt didn't want to say anything, but that was exactly how he felt. Billy had shot those two Indians after they were already dying; and although this was, without doubt, the meanest horse he'd ever seen, he didn't like to see it abused.

"Mr. Dixon, you sure saved my bacon, and I'll do whatever to repay you. I truly owe you my life, but you are a puzzlement, I'll admit that. You just don't seem to have any feeling for man nor beast."

"That might be what it seems, boy. But you ought to think about something. There really are only two kinds of people, and two kinds of beast. There are those that's gonna hurt you, and those that ain't. Those that ain't gonna hurt you, you can afford to be nice and gentle. Those that's gonna hurt you, you gentle mighty quick or you kill 'em. There's nothing in between."

Dixon went on, "Now, those Indians were gonna burn you. One, at least, went to our school and he was still gonna burn you. He could never be tamed. Now he's dead. There was never any choice in the matter. It isn't about what's right, because when I really think about it, maybe he was right in wanting to burn you. I think, though, if I asked you about getting burned, I'm pretty sure your viewpoint would be a little different. So it really comes down to living or killing. Not necessarily who's right or wrong. I shot those Indians the first time to help you. The second time was to help them. There was no way they were gonna survive that first bullet. They were in agony. The second bullet stopped their misery."

Colt had to admit that what Dixon said made sense.

"As for this ugly old horse, you ought to see what a mare does to a colt that's acting up. Why, hell, she'll kick his ass to kingdom come. Somehow they always survive it. What I did is nothing his own momma wouldn't have done. Now, as you can see, that horse is saddled and he isn't biting any more."

After they had gathered Dixon's horses, Dixon removed a bottle of alcohol from his pack and said, "I gotta look at that arrow wound in your ass. Sometimes those heathens dip their arrows in shit and it causes blood poisoning real quick. Drop your pants and bend over."

Colt did as he was told.

Dixon grinned as he pulled out his huge knife and quickly lanced the wound.

Colt's trusting expression turned to surprised agony as he screamed and jumped, tripping over his pants. He got up and turned an accusing glare toward the laughing Dixon.

"Hold on, boy, I'm not through."

"That was evil, Mr. Dixon. You should'a warned me!"

"If I had, your ass muscles would've tightened up an' it would've hurt a lot worse. Now bend over. I gotta clean that cut."

Colt grudgingly bent over again and the grinning ranger poured a liberal amount of alcohol over the cut.

He clenched his eyes as the fiery liquid scalded his rump and said, "I don't know about this, Mr. Dixon. Maybe I'd have been better off if you hadn't rescued me."

Dixon bandaged the cut and slapped Colt on the rump, making him wince in pain again.

"Okay. I'm all done. You can pull your britches up and then I'll check that cut on your head."

Colt pulled up his pants and Dixon cleaned and bandaged the head wound.

Colt put on his hat and said, "I reckon I'm ready. Where are we going?"

"Well, I don't know where we're going, I only know where I'm going. I'm going to Laredo and maybe even further. As far as you're concerned, you ought to go back to town. You're gonna stay in trouble out here and sooner or later you're gonna get killed."

Colt said, "I'm not going back to San Antonio. If you don't mind,

I'll ride along with you for a ways. Maybe we'll run across that snake that stole my watch and guns."

Dixon swung into his saddle. "Boy, I'm not sure you want to go where I'm going. Where I'm going there's gonna be a fight and a good chance of a shooting. I have warrants on five separate people. One of them is dead or alive. I get five hundred each for three and a hundred dollars for the other two. I figure the whole passel of 'em has headed to Nueva Laredo."

Colt stared. "Are you some kind of lawman?"

"Yep. I've been a ranger for nigh on to twenty-five years. The State hasn't paid us in over four years, but they do allow us to keep our bounty. Now, that's what I do and I don't have time to fool with any baby who's gonna be second-guessing every move I make. Whether it's shooting Indians, getting a horse's attention or maybe having to pickle up some outlaw's head to take back."

"What do you mean, pickle up somebody's head?"

Dixon looked at him and said, "Never mind. I don't think you'd understand."

Colt climbed on his ugly horse and they rode side by side, heading south.

Colt said, "I've never had to kill anybody, and never really wanted to. I sure would've killed those Indians, though. I just didn't have anything but a knife."

"Boy, did you hear what that Indian said about you?"

"Yes, sir, he said I fought like a woman. I don't think I fought like a woman. I tried to cut one, but hell, one of 'em snuck up on me and whacked me across the head."

Dixon said, "Yep, and you found yourself about to be roasted. Now, ain't that right?"

"Yes, sir, there's no doubt about that. If you hadn't showed up when you did, I figure I would've done some real hard dying."

Dixon studied him, and then asked, "Do you know why that Indian said that you fought like a woman?"

"No, sir, I sure don't."

"Because a woman fights backing up, and you were backing up the whole time. A warrior always attacks the enemy. If you'd been that Indian, and there was three white men, they might have still killed you, except there would've been at least one or two of them dead. You see, son, you're so worried about staying alive that you can't fight to win, so you lose. When you lose, in most cases, you die. If you quit worrying about dying and start thinking about killing, sometimes you win. Those times you win is when you don't wind up tied to a tree waiting for somebody to burn you.

"Even if they shoot you or cut you, it's better than being tied to a tree to burn. No offense intended, but that Indian was right. If you're gonna survive out here, you ought to be thinking about that. Avoid a fight if you can, but if you have to fight, God dammit, fight. Don't worry about fair, worry about winning."

Colt said, "But you just can't back shoot somebody. Everybody deserves a chance."

Dixon looked at Colt in surprise and said, "Now, just what kind of fool would want to give some asshole a chance to kill 'em? Hell, boy, you're not playing checkers out here. When you're in a fight, there's but one rule. Win. Your enemy's gonna make up their own rules as they go. You better do the same. Give 'em no chance to win. Sometimes a fight's won by only the smallest margin. Take every margin you can. If you have to kill a man, back shoot 'em or sneak up and shoot them while they're asleep if you can. If you get the drop on them and they're dumb enough to pull on the drop, everybody'll know they committed suicide."

Colt stared straight ahead, wondering at this hard man who had saved his life.

"I'm telling you the truth, boy. I've been doing this a long time, and I'm still alive. I know those dime novels talk about face-to-face shootouts where one guy lets the other guy draw first. That's bullshit. Never did happen. Don't ever draw down on somebody unless you're serious. If you have no choice, get the drop on him before he knows you're there. If he so much as sneezes after you told him to freeze, kill him. Don't try to wing him. Kill him. Don't try any fancy head shots either. Shoot for the center of his body and keep on shooting until you run outta lead or he quits wiggling. If you try any other way, boy, you're dead and that's a fact!"

They rode in silence. Colt had a lot of thinking to do. He didn't like what he was hearing, but it did make some sense—and look at what had happened to him in only the last two days. Yep, this would take some thinking.

Colt began lagging a little behind Dixon and he noticed for the first time that Dixon was not only carrying a gun on each hip, but he had a small ivory-handled pistol in his waistband near his back. He had a long-barreled pistol, butt forward, on his left hip and a shorter-barreled pistol on his right hip. There were two other pistols every bit as big as Colt's Savage in a holster on either side of Dixon's pommel. Dixon's Henry was shoved in a saddle scabbard beneath his right stirrup, butt forward.

"Mr. Dixon, I must say, you're well-armed."

"Son, I've been in horse races where I was shooting at people and they were shooting back. If you ever tried to reload a pistol or rifle riding a horse at a dead run, well, it just don't work real good. Generally, whoever runs out of bullets first loses. I always have as many guns as I can carry. If you need a weapon, you most likely are gonna need it sudden and if it's ten feet away, it might as well be in the next county. Anytime you find a weapon, be it a knife, gun or whatever—or if you can get a special good deal on one—get it and keep it for a spare. I have several with me an' I have a whole bunch more at home."

Colt pulled alongside of Dixon. "If you have any extra guns, I'd sure appreciate buying one or two. I'd especially like to buy a rifle."

Dixon said, "Well, I don't have any rifles to spare. I do have a couple pistols on the packhorse. I took 'em from an old boy that decided that he didn't have any more use for 'em. They're Allen and Wheelocks .44's. The only thing wrong with them is they're nickel plated with ivory handles."

Dixon studied Colt for a few moments. "Do you have any money, boy? I thought you said that you'd been robbed. I don't think real favorable of credit, 'specially someone that I hardly know."

Colt thought for a moment. If he told him about the forty dollars, all Dixon had to do was take it. He was unarmed and Dixon had a lot of guns and had proven that he would use them almost without thinking.

Now it was too late. He'd already offered to buy the guns, which implied that he had money. All Dixon would have to do was pull out one of those pistols, make him strip, take his money and leave him in the desert again. Or shoot him. He'd probably just shoot him, judging by what he'd been saying.

Colt bit his lip and thought that he'd just made another blunder. When would he start using his head? Oh hell, he might as well go for broke. He pulled up real close to Dixon, figuring if Dixon tried anything, he would try for the gun on Dixon's left hip or one of those on the pommel.

"Mr. Dixon, I have a little money. That drummer didn't get it because I buried it before they got to my camp. I dug it up when they left."

Dixon smiled. "That was probably the only smart thing you did. How do you know I won't just stop this horse right now, shoot you and take your money?"

Colt said, "I guess you could. But if you try, I'll do my best to wrestle you off your horse. If I'm lucky, I might even grab one of them fancy guns. I'm real close right now and I think I'd have a chance. I sure hope you don't do that, Mr. Dixon. I figure that I owe you my life. I'd feel awful bad if I had to kill you. I'd hate it, but I'd do it."

Dixon laughed. "It seems like Man Who Sits on Log has some fire in him after all. How much do you have, boy?"

"Mr. Dixon, I might have enough if you're willing to sell."

"Well, those pistols that I have would run about ten dollars apiece in a store. The belt and holsters about five dollars. I have a bullet mold and a powder flask. If everything was brand new, I figure it would be worth about forty dollars."

Just when Colt was thinking he couldn't make a deal, Dixon continued. "Of course, they aren't brand new, and I'm not a store. Besides, they didn't cost me anything. So how about twenty dollars for everything and I'll throw in a pound of powder and this Indian knife? It's a damn good one. Better than the one I carry."

"Maybe I have enough for that, and maybe a little extra for some food and a canteen of water."

"Nope. I can't sell any food or water. As long as you're with me, you're welcome to share. Save your money until we get to the next town and buy it there. Maybe I'll have to share yours before it's over."

Dixon hauled back on the reins, stepped down from his grulla and walked off a short distance to relieve himself.

Colt slid off Blue Eye, as he called his horse. Just as he turned away, the horse bit him under his right shoulder blade. Without thinking, Colt swung his fist and hit Blue Eye right in the muzzle. Blue Eye jerked his head back and gave Colt an accusing but surprised look.

Dixon said, "I'm glad you got his attention, but don't ever hit a horse in the head. It makes 'em head shy and then it's hard to put a bridle on 'em. Hit 'em in the chest. It gets their attention and don't sour 'em."

Colt wondered if he'd ever do anything to impress Dixon. He held the reins as he relieved himself. When he was through, he turned back and saw Dixon walking toward him with the pistols and the rig. The double-rigged holsters were set up so that both butts pointed forward. He showed Colt how the pistols were loaded and carried.

Colt had fired Pappy's old Savage a few times but he'd never learned to hit anything with it.

He said, "Mr. Dixon, I'm a fair shot with a rifle, but I don't know much about pistols."

Dixon looked at Colt and said, "It's getting late and we've made about fifteen miles, so as soon as we get someplace where there's a decent field of fire, we'll call it a day. I doubt if we'll find any water before tomorrow but I think we got enough to make some coffee and give the horses a little sip."

"Mr. Dixon, what's a field of fire?"

Dixon looked at Colt and shook his head. "Boy, you sure don't know a whole lot about staying alive, do you?"

Colt's ears burned. "I guess not. It'd sure be nice if you'd show me a few things before I up and got killed."

※

SEVEN

*A*fter they set up camp, Dixon showed Colt the basic art of the shootist. He had Colt load, unload and reload each weapon for a solid hour. When he decided Colt could do it without shooting himself, he had him unload them again.

He showed Colt how to carry the weapons in their holster.

"Boy, it doesn't matter a whole lot where you carry your guns as long as they're somewhat comfortable and you can get to 'em when you need 'em. No matter where you decide, though, always carry 'em exactly that way. You don't want 'em off so much as an inch. You sure don't want to be fumbling around if you're in a real hurry and the target's real close. Now, check and make sure that gun's unloaded."

Colt said, "I just checked it."

"Well, dammit, check it again. I sure don't want you shooting me or yourself." Colt made sure the pistols were empty.

Dixon said," Now put those weapons in your holster and watch me."

Colt did as he was told.

Dixon slowly reached his right hand down to his own gun and gripped the butt. His trigger finger was pointed straight down outside the holster while his remaining three fingers curled around the walnut grips. His thumb was placed against the leather thong that was slipped over the hammer spur.

He held that position and said, "Now, watch my hand. The most important thing is to always get a good solid grip on the butt of your weapon. Don't just grab at it. Get a good solid hold on it the first time. You're not gonna have time to be adjusting your grip after you pull leather. Now, see how my shooting finger is outside the holster and not around the trigger?"

Dixon looked at Colt and continued. "That's on purpose, son. I don't want to shoot my foot off—and if you get in the habit of curling your finger on the trigger before you're ready to shoot, I guarantee you that you're gonna shoot yourself one day. Some damn fools cut away their holster just so they can get their finger on the trigger real quick. Now, there's no sense in doing that while the gun's in the holster. You don't want that finger on that trigger until just before you're ready to shoot. Now, watch this."

Dixon removed his hand from his gun and let it hang to his side. He moved his hand in slow motion in a smooth movement to his holster, his thumb pushing the thong off the trigger spur. The thumb came back and slowly cocked the hammer while his index finger was pointed straight down outside the holster. His remaining three fingers curled around the grip. He pulled the gun slowly and deliberately straight up until the barrel cleared the holster. He stopped the movement, freezing his hand in place.

"While I'm looking at my target, I bring the barrel up." Dixon started slowly bringing up the barrel. When he got about forty-five degrees from level, he stopped. "Now, this is about where I put my finger on the trigger." He then pulled the gun up until it was level and pointed it in front of him.

"Now, notice how I have my elbow against my body and it's locked close in. I could probably get a good hit on somebody about waist high if they were real close. It isn't much good over about ten feet. Now, if they were more than that, why, I'd just shove the gun straight out, moving my elbow out from my body. Then I'd bring the gun up to eye level, line up my sights to my target 'til I have a good sight picture, place a little backpressure on the trigger and ka-boom; I'd shoot the son of a bitch. Now, I want you to practice what I showed you with that gun empty."

Surprised showed on Colt's face. "Empty?"

"It's okay to dry fire if you put caps on the nipples. Now you're gonna have to practice this a whole lot before it comes natural."

Colt took a deep breath and dropped his hand along his side, concentrating to duplicate Dixon's movements.

*

Dixon and Colt spent several hours going over the basics of the art of the use of the handgun.

Colt had no idea there was so much to learn about the simple act of pulling a gun out of its holster, pointing and shooting it.

They had made camp during the late afternoon near some good water with enough grass for the horses to graze. Colt practiced until it got too dark to see.

After Dixon dug a hole and started a fire, they prepared a quick meal, and then Colt practiced even more.

*

Charley lay patiently watching the huge rattlesnake. He was hungry and thirsty and he hoped the snake would move just a few feet closer. He might be able to hit it with his club even at this distance. He was tempted to try but he knew if he missed, the snake might make it back to the heavy patch of cactus and be lost to him, so he lay very still watching.

He'd run several miles into the desert after the shooting the day before. Their water skins had been left with the horses, as had the little food they had. His medicine had not been good yesterday, but he had gotten away. He'd heard two shots and seen both Ka-e-tennay and Yanahosa go down. He was sure that if he and Yanahosa had not run in opposite directions, whoever had shot might have gotten him too. That was something to remember. If you have to retreat before a superior force, disperse.

The old rattler nudged a little closer, its black tongue flicking in and out, tasting the smells before it, moving its head from side to side, aiming its thermal sensors in all directions before it moved again.

Charley threw his club, striking the snake just behind his head.

Its back broken, the snake twisted and turned, trying to strike at its unseen tormentor.

He ran to the snake and stepped on its head. He grasped the snake behind its head and held its twisting body to the sky. He felt like yelling in triumph but he was afraid the whites might hear so he merely smiled.

Charley lay the snake on the ground and quickly cut off its head. He held the severed end toward his mouth and let the blood drain into his throat. There wasn't much blood in the snake, but it was enough to quench his thirst and put moisture back into his dehydrated body.

He opened the snake's belly and removed the spleen, pricked it with his knife and squeezed the greenish peppery liquid into his mouth. He stripped the snake's skin and bit into the succulent white meat.

Feeling refreshed and having a full stomach, he removed his red bandanna and tied the snake's head into a bundle. Later, he would dry it for his medicine bag. The poison would be good in which to dip his arrows, when he could make or find some.

After finishing, he stood and looked over the desert from which he came. He had few choices. He was unfamiliar with this part of the country. He knew that if he watched the direction that the birds flew, he might find water. He also knew that it could be twenty miles away.

He could strike out and hope to find a farm where he could steal food and water. Perhaps he could even steal a horse.

He'd seen no evidence of any kind of settlement or farm. Other than the road where they tried to burn Man Who Sits on Log, there were no signs of roads, tracks or anything else to indicate people were anywhere within walking distance.

Going to San Antonio was out of the question. If he lay in wait for a traveler, he could wait days.

There was yet another choice, and this one appealed to him. He could follow Man Who Sits on Log and whoever had saved him. They had killed his cousins and made him run like a rabbit. He knew that a man on foot could out walk a horse. Even if there were too many to kill, maybe he could steal a little food, water, and a horse.

He headed back to where his cousins had been shot. He had no idea that he had run so far. It took him much longer to get back than he had anticipated. He found Ka-e-tennay.

His body was already bloated and the flies almost covered the corpse. It was hard to believe this rotting piece of meat had been his cousin. He didn't want to touch the stinking, bloated body and he ignored it.

He searched the ground, looking for Yanahosa's tracks. Perhaps he was still alive. As he searched, something partially buried in the sand caught his eye.

It was his cousin's bow and quiver lying near the log that they had sat upon waiting for the white man to awaken. He couldn't believe his luck.

Charley easily found the tracks of Yanahosa and followed them. It wasn't long before he found his rotting corpse. There was nothing useful there.

He had no means to dispose of the bodies properly so he left them to the elements.

He walked bent and low, pointing his finger in front of him like a divining rod. He circled in an ever-widening spiral. He saw only two sets of tracks. This was good. Two white mans was not too many.

Charley followed their footprints to where he and his cousins had left their horses the day before. The horses were gone and he saw only the two saddles lying in the sand.

He saw one set of horse prints co-mingled with the two men's footprints, and he followed them another hundred yards.

He laughed to himself as he recognized the splayed front hooves of the horse's tracks. These crazy white mans left the good mounts for this crazy worthless horse. The only thing this horse was good for was eating. These must not be smart white mans. If he could catch them, they should be easy to kill.

Charley continued and saw where they had picked up two other horses. One had deeper tracks. Either there was an additional rider who was very heavy or the third horse was a packhorse. This was good. A heavily laden packhorse would slow them down.

He began a slow jog, running beside the road rather than on it.

Every mile or so he would go back to the road to confirm the tracks were still there. He noticed fairly fresh wagon ruts co-mingled with the horses of Man Who Sits on Log. The horses' tracks overlaid the wagon tracks so he knew the wagon had preceded the riders.

He ran until the beating sun became too hot.

Charley finally stopped at mid-day and scooped out a depression in the sand. He lay down and scooped the sand over his body. He covered his face with dried brush for shade and slept.

*

Colt and Dixon left their camp at daybreak. For the first half-hour the horses were full of energy and wanted to trot. Finally, Colt told Dixon, "If you don't mind, let's either walk or run these horses. This damn horse trots like a donkey. It feels like I'm sliding up and down on Ma's rub board."

Dixon slowed his horse, as did Colt.

"Damn horse is about to beat me to death. I've never seen anything like it. The last few minutes there I think I'd rather be afoot."

"Yep, that sure isn't much excuse for a horse. I'm sure glad he's yours and not mine!" Dixon mused, "I wonder who belongs to those wagon tracks?"

Colt said, "Most likely that drummer and them whores that robbed me. Do you think that we can maybe catch up with them? I'd sure like to get that watch back."

"Not much doubt if they keep heading south. There're only so many places that has water."

"That's a fact, for sure," Colt said.

"If you can know all the places where there's water, boy, that's where you look. Now, I've been man hunting, one way or another, for over twenty years in this part of the country. I've made me a map of every waterhole, farm, creek and town I ever heard of. Now, this wagon is probably heading to Laredo or someplace else like Pearsall. If they stay on this road, though, they better have a few barrels of water, because there isn't any water before the Frio, and that's another thirty miles. Their horses are gonna need a lot of water, pulling that wagon in this heat."

Dixon was quiet a minute, then continued, "Thinking on that, our water's gonna play out before we reach the Frio as well. Now, we can do something they can't. According to the way those wheels are cutting into that dirt, that wagon's pretty heavy and wouldn't get far in this sand, so they're committed. I think what we ought to do is cut west. The Hondo can't be more than four or five miles. We do that, we'll have water to spare. We can follow it all the way down to the Frio and then cut back to the road. It's about ten-mile further, but our horses will be fresh all the way. We'll probably catch up to your gold watch by tomorrow."

Colt instinctively wanted to continue straight ahead until he caught up with the wagon, but so far, every decision he'd made just got him in trouble.

"So far, you've been right all the way, Mr. Dixon. If you don't mind, I'll just follow your lead."

They turned west toward the Hondo, leaving the road behind.

*

Moses was worried. The wagon's front axle was squeaking like crazy. It sounded as though the hub was dry of grease.

He didn't have a jack and if he lost a wheel they'd be in real trouble. He had a keg and a half of water and if he had been told right, they shouldn't be more than a day from the Frio. As a matter of fact, they might make it this evening. There they could make camp with plenty of water and he might find enough timber to rig up a means of lifting the wagon enough to re-grease the wheel.

"Hey, Flossy," he yelled, "get out that map and hand it up here."

Flossy stepped through the front curtain and sat down on the driver's bench next to Moses. "How much further you reckon it is to the Frio, Flossy?"

Flossy scrunched up her face while she looked at the crudely drawn map. "I don't know, Moses. How far since we left Sandy Creek?"

"Hell, counting yesterday and today, I'd say," he pulled out the gold watch and said, "we've been rolling about ten hours. Figure two or three miles an hour, average. I reckon we have come about twenty-five to thirty miles, maybe a little more."

Flossy said, "Well, if that's true, it ought not be more than ten or twelve miles."

Moses did some quick figuring. "Hell, if that's all it is, we ought to be there in four or five hours."

*

A badger cautiously sniffed his way to a dried bush lying on a mound of sand.

Badgers are fairly small, rarely over thirty pounds, but, pound for pound, are one of the meanest, toughest animals in the world.

Suddenly a hand holding a club sprung from the sand, striking the animal in the head.

The badger leaped backward as Charley jumped up.

The badger prepared to charge when Charley hit him again and yet a third time.

Nothing seemed to faze the snarling and drooling animal. It leaped, snapping its jaws at Charley's foot.

Charley leaped away just in time and hit the badger again.

This time the badger went down.

Charley struck it another solid blow to be sure.

He was pleased. He had his evening meal and more blood to quench his thirst.

Charley soon found where the white man had left the road and cut west. The wagon tracks continued straight.

He could follow the horses or he could follow the wagon. The road had the best chance of leading him to a settlement or ranch, he thought. Plus, he might catch up to the wagon. A wagon meant horses, more chance of water and food. Besides, the friend of the Man Who Sits on Log was well-armed and no doubt skilled at killing Indians. The wagon was probably Foolish Hat and the whores. It could also be just a farmer and his family.

He could tell by the horse droppings that the wagon was moving slow. The droppings of the wagon teams were closer together, whereas the riders' horses were further apart. The wagon wheels also cut deeply in the dirt.

Charley picked up the droppings from the horses from the wagon.

They were only a little drier than those from the horses ridden by Man Who Sits on Log and his companion.

He decided to go for the wagon. He knew he was only a few hours behind it. He began trotting, heading south.

EIGHT

Charley knew he was close to the wagon. It would be dark in about three hours. He stopped and unwrapped his bandanna with the snake's head and sat it on a rock. He ate the remaining parts of the badger except for the liver, which he set aside.

When he had eaten, he removed the arrows from the leather quiver and set them nearby. He took the liver and, using the stick, he worked it into a paste.

Charley took the snake's head and forced the mouth open with the stick. He placed the stick back against the snake's jaws, locking them open. Using his thumb and forefinger he pressed on the sides of the snake's head and watched as the yellow venom dripped into the liver paste.

Using the stick, Charley stirred the poison into the paste. When it was thoroughly blended, he took each of the eight arrows and coated the entire arrowhead with the mixture.

He knew he was good with the bow, but a person couldn't always count on a killing shot. Now, if the arrow didn't kill, the poison and rancid liver would—or at least it would make the target very sick.

He was becoming thirsty again. If he didn't catch the wagon soon, he'd be too weak to continue. He replaced the arrows in the quiver, picked up the bow and began his mile-eating jog again.

Charley ran parallel to the road and several hundred feet to one side. He didn't want to clear a rise or round a bend and stumble on to the wagon accidentally.

Pearl sat on a pallet near the rear of the wagon. The canvas top provided shade but did nothing to keep the heat and dust out. The main problem was the dust that wafted up from the floorboards. The front wheels of the wagon acted like paddles, churning the dirt and dust so that it was a continuous cloud, making it difficult to breathe.

The tuberculosis that had ravaged her body for the last two years was finally taking its toll, and the dust aggravated her lung condition, causing her to cough almost continuously. The damp cloth she held to her mouth did little to keep the dust out. She'd tried covering her nose with it, but the water and dust clogging the material made it almost impossible to breath.

She called out, "Flossy, how about changing places with me. This damn dust is gonna kill me."

Flossy yelled back, "Hell, no, Pearl. I've told you a hundred times that I don't sit back there. Now, if you don't quit your whining and that damn coughing, I'm takin' one of Moses' guns and put you out of your misery."

Flossy looked at Moses and said, "Why don't we just throw that whore's skinny ass off and leave her? She isn't worth anything. She's too damn skinny and a boy has bigger tits. When was the last time anybody poked her? Even that last time, she got to coughing so bad that old boy just pulled his britches on and left. Why're you still keeping her, anyway? Sometimes you don't make any sense, Moses."

Moses lowered his voice and said, "Flossy, you're right. She isn't much account anymore and I've been doing some thinking on it. We'll leave her at the next town. It wouldn't be hardly Christian just to leave her out here."

Flossy said, "Hell, Moses, I don't think I can wait much longer. All her bitching and coughing is driving me crazy. You just pull over here an' I'll go back there and just shoot her and be done with it."

Moses shook his head. "No, Flossy, you aren't gonna do any such thing. You aren't gonna touch a hair on her head. If you do, you're gonna answer to me before you answer to God, and there won't be much time in between. You hear what I'm saying, Flossy? Now, I mean that."

Although Moses was trying to keep his voice down, Pearl heard every word. She knew Moses was a no-account, but he was a good old boy anyway. That fat bitch Flossy was something else, though. Hell, she wanted to de-nut that boy they robbed, just for the fun of it. If it hadn't been for Moses, she would have, too. Maybe she ought to shoot Flossy, or maybe stab her when she was sleeping. Flossy was so damn big and she was so weak, she couldn't do anything if Flossy was awake.

Pearl smiled to herself as she remembered all the times that she'd intentionally coughed in Flossy's face, hoping to give her consumption. Maybe that bitch would catch it yet.

While these hopeful and pleasant thoughts were going through her mind, she sat in the rocking and creaky wagon, watching the small streams of dust stirred up by the wheels.

Did she see something moving? It looked like something was loping along a few hundred feet behind and to the west of the road. It was gone now, but she was sure she saw something.

Pearl thought, *Maybe it was a coyote. But why would a coyote be tracking our wagon? Maybe it was an Indian. Hell, the Indians hadn't been causing any trouble for years.*

"Moses, honey," she yelled. "I think I saw something following us."

"What do you mean, you saw something? What kind of something?"

Pearl looked again but saw nothing. "I don't know, maybe it was just my imagination, but I saw what might-a been a coyote or maybe somebody running behind us and off the road to the west, kinda. I don't see it now."

Flossy turned and leaned out of the right side of the bench seat so she could see around the wagon. "I can't see anything, Moses. You don't reckon it could be that pretty boy from Sandy Creek, do you? I told you we should have killed that son of a bitch. At least if you'd let me de-nut him, he wouldn't be in any shape to be following us."

"Dammit, woman, there's no one following us. We've been making good time and nobody is gonna be running on foot in this heat. If they were on a horse, we would've known. It's probably just a coyote or some other critter, but I doubt that. So just hush up. All of y'all are beginning to get on my nerves. All this bickering and complaining is just getting to be too damn much for me. If you don't shut your traps, you're both gonna be walking."

*

Colt and Dixon arrived at the Hondo about an hour before sundown. They found some cottonwood trees about a hundred feet from the river. There they unsaddled their horses and led them to the river to drink.

Colt knelt and wet his face. He was about to take a drink when Dixon said, "Hold on, son. I'd be careful about drinking that water if you don't have to. There're all sorts of critters in there that you don't want in your innards. We still have a little water in our canteens. Let's use that for now."

Colt looked at Billy and asked, "If we can't drink from the river, what good is it?"

Dixon said, "I didn't say we couldn't drink it directly. Now, it's a slow moving river so it wouldn't be too bad in a pinch. Sometimes you have no choice. But like I said, always give yourself an edge. Come on back and I'll show you something."

They walked back to the cottonwoods where Dixon drove two stakes in a grassy area and tied the horses. He left about fifty feet of slack in each rope to give the horses room to graze. He took a short-handled shovel from his pack and motioned to Colt. "Come on, boy, now it's our turn."

They walked until they were about a hundred feet from the river's edge, where Dixon started digging. It wasn't long before he had a hole about three-foot square and as deep.

When water started seeping into the hole, Dixon quit digging and said, "Son, you can't always do this, depending on the ground. But if you can dig a hole about a hundred feet from a river or creek, or even a stagnant mud hole deep enough to get seepage, you can get pretty safe water. That is, if there isn't arsenic or some such thing in the ground. The ground works pretty good to clean up the water. Now, if the ground is clay or hard bedrock you couldn't do this. In that case, you'd best boil the water. If you can't do either one, well, you just take your chances and go ahead and do what you have to do.

Now, I'm gonna take a bath and wash the dust out of my clothes. You stand watch. When I get through, I'll watch while you take a dip."

A half-hour later, Colt and Dixon had finished their bath. They walked back to the cottonwoods, wearing only their boots, hats and guns. Colt felt as ridiculous as Dixon looked.

Colt asked, "Why don't we camp near the river?"

"Well, there's lots a reasons. First reason is that somebody could swim across the river at night and come up real sudden. The second reason is, all kinds of critters go to the river to drink. Skunks, badgers, coyotes, cougars and everything. I sure don't want to wake up with any skunk in my blankets or no snake in my boots. Skunks and snakes killed more people out here than outlaws and Indians combined."

Colt asked, "Skunks?"

"Damn right, boy! Skunks. It seems like those critters are born trying to figure out how to catch that hydrophobia. I've known some—and heard about a whole bunch of other cowboys—died from being bit by a hydrophobied skunk that crawled in their blankets. I sure don't want any of that."

Colt shuddered at the thought and said, "Me either."

"Now, if we were to get into a standing fight, we're close enough to keep 'em off the river. If they come from this side, we have a clear field of fire all the way to the river, plus the width of the river. In the meantime, we have those cottonwoods to hide in. We also have our own secret waterhole that we just dug, so we don't have to expose ourselves trying to get any river water. If we can keep them off the river, we can thirst them out."

Colt thought that he'd learned a very important lesson.

After they strung their wet clothes to dry, Dixon unfastened his gun belt from around his waist and dug a hole for the fire.

He said, "Boy, while I'm digging, you gather up some real dry wood."

Colt did as he was told and when he was finished he went back to the river and picked up several rocks. He took them back to camp where he dropped them near the fire hole. He'd turned to go back for more when Dixon said, "What are those rocks for?"

Colt said, "For the fire. We can put our pans on them for cooking."

"That's a good idea, boy, but find some other kind of rocks. Those are river rocks. They may look dry on the outside but on the inside sometimes one will still be wet. If you put it in your fire, it's liable to explode. It could sure mess up your day."

After they'd eaten, they dressed in their almost dry clothes and Dixon said, "It'll be dark soon. I dug that fire hole pretty deep, so we can keep a real small fire going all night. No one will be able to see it from more than a few feet away. These cottonwood trees will spread what little smoke there is. Unless someone is right on top of us, they ought not to know that we're here. Now, boy, why don't you get those two pistols of yours? Don't load them, just bring them to me."

Colt did as he was told. Dixon took the revolvers and handed Colt the tomato can they had emptied during their supper. "Go set that can up about twelve paces toward the river. That ought to be about thirty feet."

While Colt was gone, Dixon loaded three rounds and spun the cylinder.

When Colt came back Dixon stood up, brushing the sand from his damp pants and said, "Now son, most gun battles with pistols are between zero and about twenty-five to thirty feet. Some are further. A handgun will shoot accurately up to about a hundred feet; but anything beyond about fifty feet, you ought to be thinking about using a rifle.

Of course, you can kill a man a lot further away; it's just hitting 'em that's the problem. Now, boy, here's what I want you to do. This gun holds six bullets. Now, I put in some bullets. Maybe I put in all six, maybe only one or two."

Colt started to look at the chamber.

"No!" Dixon snapped. "Don't look, dammit. I'm trying to teach you something."

Colt froze, waiting to hear what Dixon had to say.

"Just listen, now. I've been telling you about sight picture and trigger control. You've been dry firing and it looks like you understand the theory. Now, we don't have a lot of powder or ball to waste so we're only going to do a little shooting.

Now, the problem with most people is, they are anticipating the sound of the gun and the recoil. So what happens most times is, even if they got a good sight picture, just as they pull the trigger and the hammer drops, they tend to dip the gun down. They don't know they're even doing it, and if you told them, they'd call you a liar. Also, this same anticipation makes some people squeeze their hand tighter and their thumb pressure causes the gun to move to the outside of the shooting hand. Now, go ahead and line up on that can. Let's see you hit it in the brisket."

Colt lined up the revolver, aimed very carefully, inhaled, exhaled part of his air and pulled the trigger, trying to keep his sights lined up as he did. The gun fired and kicked in his hand. The can flew about a foot before it landed. He was surprised and pleased that he'd hit the can with his first shot. He turned to Dixon smiling.

Dixon said, "Missed it clean."

"Missed it, hell! It flew a couple of feet."

"Nope. You missed it. Go look at it and sit it back up."

Colt did as he was told. He would bring the damn thing back and show it to Dixon. He reached the can expecting to find a large hole in it. He couldn't believe it. The can was only slightly dented. He sat the can up and walked back.

Dixon said, "I told you that you missed it!"

"No, I creased it."

Dixon said, "Nope, you missed it clean. If there's any dents it was caused by dirt or rocks kicked up by the bullet. Even if you'd nicked it, the can would've been torn. You shot low and a little to your right."

Colt didn't believe he'd dipped the gun.

"Okay," Dixon said, "let's do it again. This time don't try to control your breath. Get used to shooting and doing normal things like breathing at the same time. In a real gun fight, you're not gonna have time to go through all those exercises that target shooters go through."

Colt was careful to hold the sights on the can as he aimed again.

When the hammer dropped there was only a surprising click. Colt could easily see the barrel dip down.

Dixon looked at Colt and said, "See, you would have missed again. Don't feel bad. Most people have that problem. Try again. Now, this time let the gun surprise you. Try not to anticipate it firing."

Colt cocked the hammer and slowly squeezed the trigger. The gun bucked in his hand and the can went sailing off about twenty feet.

"Well, you sure got it that time. That there can is almost fifty feet away. I don't know if I could hit it from here. You want to set it up again, or try from here?"

Colt didn't think he could hit it, but it would be easier to shoot at it and miss rather than walk over to it, so he said, "I think I'll try it from here."

He slowly aimed and pulled the trigger. Again it clicked. This time neither he nor Dixon noticed the barrel dipping.

"That's good, boy. I'm more proud of that than I am of that shot. Now I know that you weren't just lucky. Try it again."

Colt cocked the revolver, aimed and pulled the trigger. There was another click. Again he held the gun steady. Dixon just nodded, but Colt could see a slight smile of approval.

Dixon said, "Try it again."

Colt pulled the trigger and he was surprised when the gun fired. He was even more surprised when the can sailed in the air and landed in the river.

"You did real good. It looks like we've lost our target, though. That's enough shooting for now, anyway."

They walked back to the fire. It was getting too dark to see much, anyway.

Dixon said, "Go ahead and load 'em up. Only put five in each and let it ride on an empty cylinder. That way if you drop it, you won't shoot yourself. Now, if you know you're going into a fight, load 'em plumb full. You may really need that extra bullet."

Colt spread his blanket near the fire.

Dixon said, "Unless it's really cold, I don't recommend you sleeping by that fire."

"Why not?"

"Lots of reasons. One is that if you get to rolling around in your sleep, you might wake up with your foot in it. Another reason is that snakes are cold-blooded animals, but they like the heat. They like to curl right up, cozy like, next to a good fire like everybody else. The third reason is, if somebody snuck up on us, you'd be a real good target. I recommend moving off into the shadows. You should arrange a log, rock, or even dig a little hole to give you some cover, in case somebody decides to take a shot at us.

Also, don't get in the habit of staring into the fire. Sit with your back to it. It'll warm you up the same and your night vision isn't ruined. Like I keep telling you, son, always give yourself a little edge. Even like now when we aren't expecting any trouble. When you feel the safest is when you're in the most danger. That's because you don't take any precaution."

Colt moved his blankets about twenty feet away. Dixon agreed to take the first watch and moved into the trees, telling Colt he'd wake him about midnight.

He lay there smelling the wood smoke and watching the stars. He'd learned a lot this day. No wonder Dixon was still alive. He had all these edges working for him. He wondered what time it was. He sure wanted that watch back.

*

Charley was trotting along, barely out of sight of the wagon. He'd caught up with it before he realized it. He then dropped back immediately. He thought he heard a shot.

He stopped to listen. He heard nothing but his own heart beating and his heavy breathing. It must have been his imagination. He started running again.

Charley heard the sound again. This time he was sure. He stopped again to listen. He heard yet a third shot. There was no doubt about it. Someone was shooting. Whoever it was, was too far away to be a threat. Probably Man Who Sits on Log and his friend. He started running again.

NINE

Moses heard the squeaking of the wheel just before it fell off. The left front of the wagon dropped and dug into the dirt, almost throwing him from the seat. Damn! They'd almost made the Frio. He could see the trees of the river less than a half-mile away. Flossy had managed to hang on and was cussing up a blue streak.

Pearl yelled from the back, "What happened?"

"We lost a wheel." Moses climbed down and, mumbling, stared at the axle. "Son of a bitch!"

He walked around to the back of the wagon and told Pearl, "You might as well get out and stretch your legs. It looks like we're gonna be here for a while."

While Pearl and Flossy climbed down, Moses went to the water keg on the side of the wagon and took a dipper of water. He poured it into his hat and took it to the horses.

He made several trips until the horses had enough to keep them satisfied for a while. They were down to about a gallon. Thank goodness they were almost to the river.

Moses told Flossy and Pearl, "I'm gonna take the two lead horses and go on to the river. I have to find some poles or something to rig a jack to pick up this wagon. I want y'all to stay with the wagon while I'm gone. I'll leave the shotgun and the pistol with you. Flossy, do you still have that pepper box that you shot me with a couple years ago?"

Flossy said, "I still have it, and if you try to beat up on me again, I'll shoot you with it one more time."

"You and Pearl stay here. I ought to be back before dark."

"Like hell. I'm not staying here to listen to Pearl bitch and cough. I want to go with you. Pearl can stay here."

"No! I don't like leaving a woman alone, 'specially no sick woman at that."

Pearl spoke up. "Hell, let her go. If she stays here, I'm like as not to take that scattergun and blow her damn head off. I'll stay with the wagon; I don't feel like walking anywhere."

Moses shook his head in frustration. "Hell, y'all suit yourself. I don't really care anymore," Moses said. "I'm getting mighty tired of all your complaining. Next town we come to, I'll just leave you two to go on about your business."

Flossy laughed. "Moses, you old bastard, you threatened that a hundred times. You aren't gonna leave us. How are you gonna make a living? I don't think you're gonna make a whole lot of money renting yourself out for pokin'."

Pearl had to laugh with Flossy. She had a vivid imagination and could picture Moses trying to do that.

Moses said, "Come on, then, we're losing daylight."

He handed Pearl the Savage and unhitched the horses from the wagon.

There wasn't anything for the horses to graze on, so he just tied a long rope to the halter of the horse he was leaving behind and the other end to the wagon.

He saddled two of the remaining horses and put a lead rope on the last one.

"Pearl," he said, "give this horse a little grain. Save some water for yourself and if we aren't back in a couple hours, give the rest to the horse."

He and Flossy mounted and, leading one horse, they headed toward the river.

Pearl waited for them to get out of sight then went into the bushes to relieve herself. She could have done it right by the wagon, but somehow that didn't seem right.

She spread her shawl on the ground and lay the pistol on it. Just as she squatted down, something struck her in the back. It didn't really hurt, but when she looked down, she saw an arrowhead sticking from her chest.

She screamed and grabbed the pistol. She fired wildly as she ran staggering toward the wagon.

Suddenly the pain hit her and she screamed again, both from fear and pain.

She could hardly breathe and her chest felt like there were hot coals inside of her.

Pearl made it to the wagon and managed to crawl in.

She grabbed the shotgun and turned just as she saw the flash of someone's face by the tailgate.

She pulled the trigger just as the head ducked. She was still screaming. She could feel her heart beating so fast she thought it would explode. She lay on her back and waited. The pain was even more severe but she couldn't get enough air to scream. She thought she was screaming but only whispered rattles escaped her lips.

She was light-headed and fell back against the bags of grain and supplies.

Pearl didn't feel the arrow as it pushed through her chest.

She didn't see the face as it appeared through the weather flap at the front of the wagon. She didn't feel the knife as it sliced through her throat.

She was unconscious when the knife made a circular cut from her hairline to each ear and then across the top of her head. She didn't feel the pressure of the foot as it pressed against her neck, or hear the wet pop as her scalp was pulled from her skull.

*

Moses and Flossy heard the screaming and several popping sounds. He yelled, "Oh Lord, Pearl's in trouble!"

Flossy asked, "What the hell?"

"Pearl's in bad trouble!" Moses spun his horse around and headed back toward the wagon.

Flossy said, "You gonna get yourself killed. It's too late, whatever it is."

"Too late, hell, that's my wagon back there, woman."

He kicked his horse into a dead run. The horse that he'd been leading followed.

Flossy didn't know what to do. She sure didn't want to be left alone with only a four shot pepperbox pistol.

"Moses, damn you," she yelled. "Come on back here, you're gonna get us both killed."

*

Charley grabbed a sack and quickly started filling it. First went some cans of food, salt, dried beans, flour, a box of percussion caps and a powder flask. He threw a saddle and blanket out on the ground along with a bridle.

He found a box of matches, a slab of salt pork and a pot. He grabbed various other supplies and placed them in the sack.

He found a large canteen and ran to the water barrel. He quickly filled it and ran back to the horse, threw the canteen over the pommel of the saddle and mounted. He could hear hoof-beats and he knew he had only seconds.

Charley kicked the horse in the flanks and headed into the desert.

*

Moses came around the bend in the road in time to see the back of someone riding away on one of his horses.

He raised the Spencer and fired, just as the man and horse dipped down behind some dunes out of sight. He galloped to the wagon and jumped off his horse.

Not knowing what to expect, he cautiously looked under the wagon and, seeing nothing, he eased his head around the rear of the wagon and looked inside. He saw Pearl covered with blood. She had an arrow sticking out of her chest and her throat was cut. He almost threw up. Her scalp had been removed, taking part of her face.

About this time, Flossy came riding up. She grabbed the reins of Moses' horse that was dancing around.

Flossy yelled, "Damn you, Moses! Where's Pearl?"

Moses yelled back, "Inside the wagon! She's hurt real bad!"

Moses helped Flossy climb into the wagon. He said, "Watch yourself. Indians did this. There may be more about."

Flossy knelt by Pearl, lifting her head into her lap and sobbed, "Oh, Pearl Baby! Pearl, honey, just look at you! It's okay, sweetie. It's okay. Flossy's here, baby."

Moses looked away with tears in his eyes.

Flossy said, "Moses, Goddamn you. Don't just sit there, do something!"

Moses just shook his head sadly and said, "There's nothing to be done. She's gone, Flossy."

Flossy said, "No, she ain't, she's still alive! You gotta do something!"

Pearl let out a sigh and went limp.

Flossy, crying, said, "Oh, no, Pearl! Don't leave me, baby. Don't leave me!"

She looked up at Moses and said, "She's gone, Moses. I think she's dead. What am I gonna do, Moses? She was all I had."

Moses let out a deep breath and nodded. "She never had a chance, Flossy. There was nothing anybody could've done."

Flossy held Pearl and gently rocked her and cried.

*

They buried Pearl beside the road. By this time it was full dark. Moses said, "We'd better stay right here with the wagon tonight. If there isn't any more trouble, maybe we can go on to the river and get something to fix the wagon with. We might as well build a fire. If there're any hostiles about, they already know we're here and that we aren't going anywhere."

Flossy said, "Why not? We still have three horses. We could leave this old wagon and be in Cotulla by morning."

Moses said, "I told you once and I'll tell you again. I'm not leaving the wagon. Everything we own is in it."

Flossy said, "Everything you own, you mean. Everything in it belongs to you, including the wagon."

He said, "That's how it used to be. Now it's different. Now it's everything that we own."

Flossy moved closer to Moses, twisting her handkerchief in her hands. She whispered, "What do you mean, Moses? How is it different?"

Moses turned away from her and leaned against the wagon. He said, "I don't know. It's just different, that's all."

Flossy touched his shoulder. She said, "Tell me how it's different, Moses."

Moses looked at Flossy and said, "I thought you hated Pearl. You two were always fighting and carrying on. Hell, one time she took a knife to you and another time you beat the shit out of her. I thought that you'd be glad to see her dead."

Moses turned away to hide his tears. He said, "The way you acted back there about tore my heart out. If you loved her so much why were you always fighting?"

Flossy looked down at her feet and lowered her voice. "I don't know. Maybe it was because of you. Before she got sick, she was kind of pretty. She was a lot prettier than me. I was always fat. I've always been fat. I guess that by being mean, it was my way of telling people that I didn't need anyone to love me. Before you came along and took us in, we was all each other had. I don't think I knew that until I saw her all butchered up that way."

Flossy turned away and exclaimed, "Oh, what am I saying? I'm just a fat old whore with most of my teeth knocked out. Pearl was the same except that she wasn't fat. Maybe that's why I hated her. She wasn't fat. But Moses, she was all I had."

She looked up at Moses and whispered, "Moses?"

Moses looked at Flossy and asked, "Yeah?"

"Please don't beat on me, but I don't want to be no whore anymore. I don't want to rob any more pretty boys, either. Just leave me here with Pearl. I'll be all right."

Moses reached out and hugged Flossy. He said, "I ain't gonna hit on you, Flossy. Not ever again. I don't want you to whore for me, either. I ain't ever said this to a woman before but I need you. We ain't much but we're all we got."

Flossy put her head on Moses' shoulder and cried. Through her tears, she said, "I'm sorry, Moses. I didn't mean that about whoring—but I did mean the part about not robbing any more folks. I'm just not gonna do it."

Moses stroked her hair as he held her close. "Flossy, from now on the only person that I want pokin' you is me. Don't you worry none about robbing nobody, either. We ain't gonna do that anymore."

Flossy pushed Moses back and looked him in the eyes. She said, "Moses, honey, you don't want to be pokin' me."

"Why not?"

"Because I got the clap. There's a whole bunch of cowboys riding sidesaddle right now."

Moses laughed and said, "That don't matter. Your whoring days are over."

Flossy asked, "If I don't whore for you, how are we gonna make any money?"

"I don't know, Flossy. I really don't. I grew up on a pig farm back in Missouri. Maybe we could sell the wagon. With that and what little we got stashed away, maybe we could buy us a few pigs. I know how to cure bacon. I bet the folks in this country never had good country ham before."

Moses turned and swept his arms around in a grand gesture and said, "Just look at this country, Flossy! It ain't worth nothing. I'll bet they'd give it to us and pay us to take it. It ain't no good for either farming or cattle but it'd be fine for pigs. Pigs ain't like cattle. Hell, we'd only need about ten or twelve acres."

"Do you really mean it, Moses? No more whoring and robbing? It'd be just you and me with a bunch of pigs? I like that, Moses. I like that a lot."

*

Colt had stood the night watch from midnight on. To keep himself occupied, he unloaded one of his guns and spent three hours slowly drawing his weapon and dry firing. It was too dark to see his sights so he practiced the close-in method. It wasn't long before he could find the gun, draw, fire and replace it in his holster without looking.

He spent an equal amount of time using the cross draw with his right hand and the reverse draw with both hands.

When Dixon rolled out of his blankets, he saw Colt in the early dawn, practicing. It looked like he was doing it correctly, at least.

Dixon stood and walked over to the latrine he had dug the evening before and relieved himself.

Colt was back at the fire when Dixon returned.

Dixon said, "If you have to take a dump, go ahead. If you'll cover up the shit hole, I'll cover the waterhole. When you cover it, plant a dead cactus or brush over it and dust up your tracks. That coffee ought to be ready by the time we're through, then I'll fry up some bacon and make a little hoecake. I even have some preserves I've been saving."

While Dixon was cooking, he said over his shoulder to Colt, "If you don't mind me asking, boy, where're you from?"

"We used to have a little ranch a few miles east of Cotulla but we lost it. My pap died and so I went to San Antonio looking for work. I didn't find nothing but trouble, though."

Dixon said, "Well, I was born and raised in Texas. I've been to Arizona and as far east as Mississippi. I didn't much like that part of the country. Too damn many ticks and skeeters. Also snakes. They have every kind of snake there is back there. They have 'gators, too. Some of 'em are so big they can take your horse right out from under you. I don't much like those 'gators. No, sir!"

He flipped the bacon over to brown on the other side. "I never had a ranch of my own. I worked on a few, though, and drove lots of cattle. I've been rangering most of my life and I used to do pretty well until after the war. Then that damned reconstruction governor cut our funding. The only way that we've been able to make ends meet and feed our horses is that they let us keep the bounty on those we bring in. I may wind up with a farm, though."

Colt looked up in surprise. "Yeah?"

"Yes, sir, there's a mighty pretty widow woman that has a little spread up around Austin. I've been sparking her a little. Mighty fine woman, too. She isn't like a lot of the women that I've known. She isn't always complaining and trying to change a man. Good cook, too. Not like what I'm fixing."

Billy stirred the food and continued, "She has a boy, almost as old as you, but he doesn't act like he's more than three or four years old. Always grinning though. He was kind of sceery when I first laid eyes on him but I have come to be right attached to him. He follows me around like a little puppy.

I've been saving up my money kind of secret. When I get a little more, I'm gonna ask that woman to marry me. I think that I'll fix up that farm and see what I can do for that boy. I have a pocket plumb full of warrants. One of 'em is worth five hundred dollars all by itself."

"Five hundred dollars!" Colt exclaimed. "What'd he do?"

Dixon checked the hoecakes to see if they were about done. "They say he's a poisoner. He poisoned a couple of his wives and even poisoned a fellow's dog once. He is one real asshole. Then there's the Baker brothers. Tyrell and Eldon. They aren't worth much, but together they are worth almost as much as the poisoner. I have a few others, too, but I don't think they're in this part of the country. I know the poisoner and the Bakers are heading south.

I'll bet you that I'll find at least three down in Nueva Laredo. That poisoner, he's calling himself Doctor Sam Pritchett. That ain't his real name though. His real name is Elroy Peoples. He drives a red and green medicine wagon. You can't mistake that wagon."

Dixon put the hoecakes into two tin plates and handed one to Colt.

"How long ago you leave the ranch, boy?"

Colt sat on a log and stared at his plate. He got a lump in his throat. It sure seemed a lot longer that it actually had been.

He swallowed and said, "Just a few weeks, Mr.Dixon. We had a real good start, but our cows got sick and the sheriff had to shoot 'em. Then they burned the grass."

Dixon looked at him and said, "Are you folks the ones that had the cow plague?"

Colt said, "Yes, sir. They called it anthrax. Pappy and our neighbor bought some cows from a Mexican named La Gordio. They figure there were some sick ones in the bunch."

Dixon said, "How come they think the Mexican cows had it? Hell, I know the La Gordio family. They're real fine folks."

"Well, Mr. Dixon, only the Millers an' us got it. Even the Hunts, whose ranch is right between ours, didn't have it. It had to be those Mexican cows."

"Son, I'm sure sorry to hear that," Dixon said. "I'm surprised that your family didn't catch it. I've heard about anthrax. That's one of the most terrible diseases there is. It kills about everything in sight."

Colt said, "I never heard about it before about three or four weeks ago. I woke up one morning and a couple of our milk cows were acting funny, and pretty soon other cows started getting sick. Mr. Miller started having the same problem at almost the same time. He got somebody down from Austin and they said it was anthrax. They made the sheriff shoot all our cattle and burn our grass. I guess it was too much for Pap. His heart just couldn't take it and he died." Colt didn't tell him that his Daddy had hung himself.

Dixon stirred the coals on the fire and sat silent a few minutes. He said, "Anthrax! Now, something just doesn't seem right. You said your milk cows came down with it first?"

"Yes, sir."

"And was your family drinking that milk?"

Colt said, "Yes, sir. I'd milked them the night before. They seemed okay then. I got damn near a gallon from each cow. The next day, two of 'em were already down and the others were staggering around."

"Whoee, you mean you drank the milk from them diseased cows and nobody got sick?"

"Yes, sir."

"Did the Millers get sick?"

"Not that I heard," Colt said. "Their milk cows got it, too. They have a whole bunch of kids and so they drink a lot of milk."

Dixon asked, "How long did it take that man from Austin to get down?"

"Almost a week. Mr. Miller telegraphed them from Cotulla as soon as his cows started dying."

"How many cows actually died from it, son?"

Colt took a long sip of his coffee and sighed. "Well, we lost about thirty head right off. We didn't know what it was so Pap and me, we separated the herd into different fields. It seemed to help, because only the cows in the one field got sick."

Dixon brought the food off the fire. He fixed a steady gaze on Colt. "Something is wrong, boy. If it took that man a week to get down, all your stock should've been dead. If both you folks and your neighbor had been drinking that milk, you should have been dead, too. At least some of you should've been real sick. I'm no expert, but it just doesn't sound right to me."

"It doesn't?" Colt asked. "What makes you say so?"

"What I just said." Dixon poured himself some coffee and blew into the cup before taking a drink. "Tell you what. The La Gordios don't live far from Nuevo Laredo. I haven't seen 'em for a while. If you folks got anthrax, he sure as hell would have got it too. Why don't you ride on down with me to collect them hombres I'm after? If we have time, maybe we'll ride over and talk to Mr. La Gordio. I could use somebody watching my back, anyway. How about it?"

Colt said, "Mr. Dixon, I owe you an awful lot, including my life. If you asked me to eat those coals in that fire, I reckon I'd be happy to do it. I'm no man killer, and I've never shot anyone, but if some-body was gonna shoot you, I'd do my best to shoot them first."

Dixon smiled. "Good. I guess I have me a partner. And if we find those fellows, I'll give you part of the bounty. Hell, boy, you done found that job you're looking for."

They loaded their packhorse, saddled and rode south, following the Hondo.

TEN

*M*oses and Flossy worked most of the morning hauling cotton-wood poles from the Frio back to their wagon. Moses, using a small crosscut saw, cut some of the poles into several three-foot lengths and one about fifteen feet in length.

He rigged an A-frame from the shorter pieces then he and Flossy placed the longer pole under the wagon and lay it across the A-frame.

Together, they pulled down on the long pole until the wagon lifted.

He had Flossy sit on the end, which held it down firmly.

Moses greased the worn but serviceable shaft and remounted the wheel.

Flossy eased up from the pole and the wagon was sitting back on four wheels and they pulled out.

They arrived at the Frio about mid-afternoon and while Moses unloaded the wagon, Flossy started a fire.

He first washed out the floor then took some of his whiskey and poured it over the bloodstains. They'd lost only a little of the food but all the blankets were soaked with Pearl's blood. Those he let soak in the river.

Flossy, watching from near the fire, said, "Moses, you might as well throw those damn blankets away. There's no way that I'm gonna sleep on blankets with Pearl's blood all over them."

Moses said, "If you get cold enough, you will. Now leave me

alone or you come over here and clean up this mess."

*

Charley had ridden west the evening before. He had no particular reason except that it was away from the white man that had shot at him. He'd cooked a good meal and for the first time in two days he wasn't thirsty.

During the early morning he came upon the river unexpectedly. He let his horse drink and graze. He laid the shotgun and pistol nearby and removed his moccasins and waded into the shallows of the river.

He was ever watchful, for he knew that Man Who Sits on Log was behind him with his friend. The white men could arrive at any time.

Charley knew that he couldn't stay long, but both he and the horse needed rest. He unsaddled the horse and lay the blanket in the tall grass.

He lay for a while watching his back trail and soon fell asleep.

The sun had crossed overhead while he slept and when he awoke it was mid-afternoon.

He couldn't believe that he'd fallen asleep. He was acting like a white man. *You catch his influenza, small pox, his softness and laziness.* He was getting lazy. He also knew it would get him killed. He was soon on his horse and headed out.

*

Colt and Dixon had followed the Hondo down until it spilled into the Frio River. They took the left fork, which would take them east back to the road.

Just before sundown, Dixon held up his hand and said, "Hold on!"

He pulled his Henry from the scabbard and slowly walked his horse forward.

"Stay with the pack horse, son. Something doesn't seem right."

Dixon rode to where he had seen the grass flattened like a horse had rolled. He was watching the tree line and tried to look in all directions. He couldn't see anything, and didn't smell any smoke. If it were Indians, he probably wouldn't see them until it was too late.

When he reached the flattened grass, he saw a moccasin track in the soft mud.

He dismounted, keeping his Henry ready and his eyes sharp. He walked to the edge of the river and squatted down, studying the water. Beneath the surface of the water about a foot from the shore, he saw a bare footprint.

An Indian had sat here, taken off his moccasin and gone for a swim.

Dixon walked to where the grass was flattened. It was an area about four feet by five or six feet. Someone had laid here. He leaned over to the flattened and broken grass and smelled.

He walked a short distance away, broke some more grass and smelled again. The grass that he'd broken smelled stronger. Some time had gone by since whoever was here had left. The track in the slow moving river could still be seen, so he figured that someone had been here two or three hours ahead of them. He stepped out of the trees and motioned for Colt to come on in. He didn't want to whistle or yell because sound would carry a long way on the water of the river.

When Colt arrived, Dixon mounted and said, "Let's keep going, boy, but keep your eyes peeled. We got at least one Indian ahead of us and he's riding a white man's horse."

"How do you know that?"

"It's wearing shoes. If I'm not mistaken, it looks like the same shoe prints off one of them horses that were pulling that wagon on the road. You see that print there?"

Colt looked to where Dixon was pointing.

Dixon said, "That's because that horse is dragging the right rear hoof just a little. No two horses walk the same way. I've seen that same track up on the road. It looks like some Indian has stolen one of those horses. I believe it's a Mescalero Apache."

"Why Mescalero? How do you know it's not Lipan or Comanche?"

"The Mescalero have their own way of sewing their moccasin on the side. That means that Indian isn't from around here. Mostly what we have is Lipan Apache down here. Although they are both Apache, the Lipan and Mescalero don't usually get along too well. I think those marks in the track were caused by the stitches on the moccasin. Also, the foot size is about the same as the one that tried to burn you. I figure that little son of a bitch somehow caught up with those watch-stealers and swiped himself a horse."

Colt asked, "How could he have caught up with them? They had a half day head start and that Indian was on foot."

"Son, any man, especially an Indian, can run a horse down any day. A horse is a lot faster but only for a mile or two. A man, especially an Indian, can run at a good lope all day and half the night. The Apache, especially. They haven't had horses as long as some Indians and even today they'd rather fight on foot. They only like horses for carrying them someplace or for eating. An Apache doesn't care too much for their horses like other tribes do. An Apache will cut a little nick in a vein and drink his blood if water's scarce. They'll bleed him plumb dry if they have to. Then they'll eat him. Yep, I figure our Indian is back amongst us, so keep your eyes peeled."

*

Flossy was sitting on a rock waiting for the coffee to settle while Moses was in the process of loading all of their supplies back into the wagon.

She stood to get the coffee just as an arrow, aimed for her back, stuck her in the right cheek of her ample rump.

Flossy let out a squeal and jumped forward, right into the fire, knocking the coffeepot over and scalding her foot. She squealed even louder as she hopped around.

She thought that she had been snake bit because she hadn't heard anything.

Moses heard Flossy screaming, grabbed the Spencer and started running. "What's wrong, woman? What the hell's wrong with you?"

*

Flossy was still hopping around and yelling. "I think I done been snake bit! Bit me right on my ass! Oh, Moses, you have to get the poison out! Oh, I'm gonna die!"

Moses saw the arrow. "You aren't snake bit, you've been shot with an arrow. Get your ass down!"

He turned back to the wagon for cover when something hit him in the back, knocking him forward. A loud explosion followed instant-ly.

He stumbled and fell, face down, by the wagon wheel. Something was wrong. He could see and hear, but he couldn't feel his body. He heard Flossy screaming. He tried to reach the Spencer but his hands wouldn't move.

He tried his legs and it was as if he had none. He knew that he'd been shot and wondered why he felt no pain.

Moses tried to roll over to see Flossy but nothing worked.

Flossy pulled her pepperbox from her thigh holster and looked around. Her rump was on fire and the burning pain was running up to her right shoulder and into her neck. Her heart was beating much too fast. She thought, *I gotta calm down, I gotta calm down.*

She saw Moses by the wagon. She ran as fast as she could but stumbled just as a second arrow embedded itself into the wagon, snapping the shaft in half.

Had Flossy not stumbled, the arrow would have hit her square between the shoulder blades.

She fell on top of Moses. She grabbed the Spencer, rolled over and sat up. She howled in pain as her movement broke the arrow that was lodged in her rump.

Flossy thought she saw movement and fired the Spencer.

One of the horses stumbled and went down.

I gotta calm down, she thought. *I have to get rid of some of this weight. I've never had a heartbeat like this.* She was feeling light-headed. *Oh, Lord, don't let me pass out.*

Suddenly she saw stars as something struck her head.

She was semi-conscious as she felt herself being dragged. She was vaguely aware of her clothes being removed and someone was doing something to her hands and feet. Then she felt someone was on top of her, poking her. She'd been raped before and she got paid for being poked, so she wasn't too upset. It's just that she hurt so badly. She could feel the sweaty body of the Indian as he humped her and for the first time was glad that she had the clap. This Indian was going to wish he'd raped someone else. If she didn't hurt so much, she would have laughed.

*

When Charley was through, he walked over to the white man.

He was still breathing, his eyes were aware but he wasn't moving. One of the nine pellets from the double ought buckshot had embedded into his spine.

Charley counted seven other bloody and ragged holes in his back. He laughed. It was good the white man was awake. He would know it when Charley took his scalp. He took his knife and made a circular incision, put his left foot against the white man's neck and pulled the scalp off with his right hand. The man's eyes clenched tight and he made a deep animal noise from his throat. Charley said, "See, white man. You take our land. You take our food. You feed us wormy corn and sick cows. Now look what you did. You lost your scalp to Charley Tree. Now watch what I do to Buffalo Woman."

He dragged the man around, facing Flossy. Flossy was almost wide-awake and her heart was beating even faster.

She thought, *I have to calm down. He'll leave me alone now. He's got everything, including a free poke.*

Flossy felt a foot press across the bridge of her nose and someone pulling her hair. A white-hot pain covering the front part of her head was overwhelming. Suddenly, she realized what was happening.

"Oh, my God! Oh, my God! No! Oh, my God!"

The pain exploded into agony as she felt her scalp being pulled away. Her body went into convulsions. She was convulsing so violently that she pulled one of the stakes out.

Charley caught her arm and, by placing all of his weight on it, was able to re-secure it.

He ignored her screaming convulsions as he calmly rummaged through the wagon.

Charley found a few dollars in a tin box. He pocketed the money and tossed the box away.

He took two blankets, a hatchet and some rope. He found a sack of flour and emptied it on the ground. He used the empty sack to load as much contraband as he could carry.

Charley found one dead horse, evidently shot by Buffalo Woman. He saddled one of Moses' two horses. He tied a lead rope to the remaining horse and loaded the supplies on it.

He walked over to the white man and saw that he was still alive. He searched him and found a gold watch, a pipe made of some white, yellowish material and a tobacco pouch.

He loaded the pipe and struck a match. He smiled as he inhaled.

Charley searched the man once more and found a few silver coins and a small gold ring on the man's finger.

He tried to get the ring off, but, try as he may, the ring would not come off, so he cut the finger off at the middle knuckle. He smiled at the man, who was watching the entire time.

Charley walked back to the woman, who had settled down to only a blubbering whimper.

He squatted beside her. "Hey, Buffalo Woman. I speak pretty good English, you think so? How you like the way Charley fuck you? I think pretty good, maybe. Charley got a surprise for you. I think next time I rather fuck real buffalo. Why you not laughing? Charley think tell good white man joke. White man always say Apache fuck buffalo. Now Apache fuck buffalo. Charley don't think it a pretty good fuck." Charley stood up and walked to the wagon for a shovel. He got a shovel full of coals and carried them to the white man and emptied the coals over his face.

The white man's head flopped and animal-like noises came from his mouth, but the rest of the body remained still.

Flossy smelled an awful stench. Through all her pain, she was able to open her eyes just as Charley threw a second shovel full onto Moses' face. Suddenly all of her past pain was forgotten as her horror shoved it aside.

She screamed, "Oh, dear Jesus, not that! Please shoot me! Not that! Oh, dear God, no!"

Charley turned and smiled at her. "Soon Charley gonna cook a buffalo."

He took another shovel full and walked over to Flossy. He smiled as he poured the coals over her huge stomach.

Flossy screamed and rolled, the motion casting most of the coals aside as she writhed and tossed.

Charley went back for another shovel full. He walked back to Flossy and said, "It's pretty hard to cook a buffalo sometimes." He poured the coals between her legs. Flossy was screaming and twisting, scattering the coals everywhere.

Flossy's back arched, her mouth opened and her eyes rolled. Then she lay still as the venom finally made her heart stop.

Shooting her with the poisoned arrow was the nicest thing Charley had ever done. Charley climbed into the saddle, grabbed the lead rope from the spare horse and calmly walked the horses away.

*

Dixon and Colt heard the two shots. It sounded like it came from the road. In a direct line the road couldn't be more than a mile or two, but following the winding river it was about four miles.

Dixon said, "Sounds like somebody's in trouble. Maybe our Indian has done found himself some more horses. We better hurry, boy. Maybe we can lend a hand."

They'd been hearing horrible screaming for the last ten minutes but the screaming had abruptly stopped.

They put their horses into a full gallop until they were within a couple hundred yards of the river.

Dixon pulled up and said, "We'd better get off this road. Let's cut to the right here and head for those trees. I think we'd better come on this pretty easy until we find out what's going on."

They didn't know it, but that was just about the time Charley was riding off.

It took another twenty minutes for the two men to get to the wagon.

Colt was immediately sick.

Dixon checked the woman and found that she was dead. He walked over to the man. He wasn't tied up like the woman but his face was almost black with charred meat and wood ash. Dixon knelt down.

The man's lips were moving, but only guttural sounds came out.

Dixon took his canteen and poured a little down the man's throat.

Colt, wiping his mouth, walked over to Dixon. "That's Moses and Flossy. They're the ones that robbed me. They took Pap's watch, but I sure didn't wish this on them."

Moses said, "Indian. His name is Charley. Indian, Charley."

Colt said, "Mr. Dixon, there's one missing. A skinny gal named Pearl."

Dixon said, "Moses! Moses, now listen. I know it's hard to talk, but where's Pearl? Where's Pearl, Moses?"

"Dead yesterday, same Indian."

"Moses, how many? How many Indians?"

Moses let out a breath and died.

Dixon removed his hat and wiped his brow. "Colt, according to the tracks I think there's only one and I bet my saddle it's the same damn Indian I let get away. He's one murdering son of a bitch. If he ain't stopped he's gonna do this to a lot more people. Let's get these poor folks underground and see if we can't catch up to him."

Colt stared at the carnage. He'd never wanted to hurt anybody in his life, but he could easily kill whoever had done this and the only emotion that he'd feel would be relief.

Then he remembered his watch. As bad as he hated losing that watch, he didn't want to sound disrespectful of the dead and he sure didn't want to have to search Moses' bloodied body. He started to turn away when Dixon began searching the body. He said, "Colt, it doesn't look like he has your watch. Let's search the wagon; maybe it's there."

They searched the wagon and found plenty of canned goods and other staples, but no watch.

Dixon said, "It looks like whoever done this musta took your watch. Let's get these folks underground and then see if we can't catch that son of a bitch."

*

After the burial, Colt and Dixon walked back to the camp.

Dixon saw the broken arrow embedded in the wagon. He worked what was left of the shaft up and down while he pulled on it until it was free. He picked up the broken end from the ground and held the pieces together.

"Something don't make sense," he said. "This is an Apache arrow. They're longer than most Indian arrows."

Colt said, "Well, the Lipan and Mescalero are all over down here. What would you expect?"

Dixon ignored Colt as he studied the arrow. "I've never heard of any Apache, Lipan, Mescalero, Chiricahua or any others take scalp. They have no use for 'em. They're practical people. They raid, steal, kill and run as necessary. This Apache has taken up the habits of other Indians. He acts more like a Comanche.

Another thing, I think this arrow has been poisoned." Dixon held the tip near his nose and sniffed. "It smells like he dipped it in putrid meat. If he found a sand toad and let the skin rot, he'd have some right nice poison. He might've found himself a rattler and mixed the venom in with it. Even if it weren't a killing shot right off, the infection could kill you. I think we have a crazy Indian here. Considering his bad habits, I think he's been hanging around Indians other then Apache."

Dixon tossed the arrow aside and continued, "The most likely place would be off some reservation where they have different tribes gathered. Like Bosque Redondo up near Fort Sumner, maybe. They have Apache, Navajo, Comanche, Ute and a whole passel of others all mixed up together. They force all the young ones to go to white man schools. The whites make them cut their hair and dress up like white folks."

Colt said, "That makes some sense. All three of those that were gonna burn me had short hair. They were wearing Apache loin cloths and high moccasins but two had on white men shirts."

Dixon said, "He's no ordinary Apache. Apache don't act this way. This is just a mean little son of a bitch, whoever he is."

*

They took what supplies they could find from the wagon to supplement what they already had, especially two bottles of whiskey. They also found a bottle of chloroform and one of laudanum. They added that to their kit, climbed in the saddle and took off after the one that they called Indian Charley.

Their quarry was now a good two hours ahead of them. He had two good horses and was traveling light. After an hour, Dixon pulled up.

As Colt came up to him, he said, "Colt, we have to admit we aren't gonna catch up with that Charley son of a bitch this way. We have too many supplies and we need it all.

We have two good horses and that mean crowbait that you're riding between us. That Indian's gaining on us every minute. We're gonna kill our horses and we still aren't gonna catch him. He can swap horses and keep right on going when we have to rest ours. Also, that Indian won't mind killing both of those horses. He'll just drink his fill of their blood, cut off a slab of meat an' keep going on foot."

Colt asked, "What do you think we ought to do?"

"What we ought to do is cut back over to the road, slow down and just keep on heading the way we was. That Indian is heading south as fast as he can an' you can bet your life he's looking to join up with some party raiding back and forth into Mexico. I hear Victorio and Geronimo done split up and Geronimo is working down south of here while Victorio is raising hell up around New Mexico. I figure we'll run across that murdering bastard eventually, but we aren't going to outrun him and that's for sure."

Dixon removed his hat and wiped his brow. "I think if we head on down to Cotulla and warn the sheriff, he can telegraph Austin and let the rangers know what's happening. He can also telegraph the law all the way down south. Eventually, somebody's gonna find that mean little bastard."

Colt was disappointed but had to agree. Dixon was still making sense. They stopped, rested their horses for an hour and then angled southeast to intersect the road.

*

Charley kept the horses in a lope, changing mounts every hour.

He kept the Spencer in his hand with the bow and quiver strapped to his back. The revolver was in his waistband. The shotgun was in a saddle scabbard on the spare horse.

He didn't even stop when he switched horses. He would slow the one he was riding, loop both reins over the head of the one he was on and simply lean over, grab the pommel of the other and swing over.

Both horses were breathing hard and blowing out their mouths. He knew that even with swapping them over, they couldn't take much more.

He'd learned to tell time in the white man's school and he snapped open the gold watch that he'd hung on a thong around his neck. He'd been running these horses for over two hours. He was sure that if anyone had followed him, they were now far behind.

He slowed to a walk. He looked back and could see no signs of pursuit. He walked them another hour to gradually cool them and then stopped.

There was no water in sight so he dry camped. He took one of the two lariats and cut two short lengths and made some hobbles for the horses. He could let them graze on what little grass there was without fear of them running off.

He took one of the two blankets and, using dried mesquite limbs, made a small shelter to keep the sun off. He dug a hole, built a fire and cooked a meal.

He checked his water supply and decided to give them a little. It would help them carry him a little further.

After giving the horses water, he spread the three scalps, flesh side up, and scraped them. They would dry enough by morning so that he could tie his trophies to the barrel of the Spencer. He was now a warrior. He'd fought the white man and won. He had weapons, scalps and horses to prove it. When he met Goyathlay he would ride with his head high.

He next checked his weapons. The shotgun was a single barrel, 12-gauge, breach loader. All he had to do was to turn a catch behind the breach and the shotgun would break open, making loading from the rear easy and fast. Much faster than the old muzzle-loaders.

He looked at the printing engraved on the side and phonetically tried to pronounce the words. It read C.O.L.T. There were some numbers following 'S/N.' He didn't know that word S/N.

Charley set the shotgun aside and picked up the Spencer. He wasn't familiar with this rifle. He read the words and tried to pronounce the word "Spen kur, Spen kur." He didn't know 'Spen kur' either. The number 56-50 he knew was the size of the bullets.

He operated the hand lever and to his surprise, a bullet was ejected. He slowly opened the lever again. A second bullet came out. He repeated it a third time. Another bullet came out. He rapidly operated the lever several more times and noted there were seven bullets. He'd never seen such a gun.

He studied the rifle. There didn't appear to be any place to put the bullets in. Finally he looked at the rear of the stock. He saw a flat piece of metal protruding from a recessed hole. He pulled on the metal and it didn't move. He twisted the metal and it rotated. He pulled the tubular magazine from the rear of the stock.

Charley placed seven bullets in the hole in the stock and pushed the tube back into the rifle. He moved the lever and nothing happened. He moved it a second time and a bullet was ejected. Now he knew how it worked.

He unloaded the rifle again. This time he tried to load eight bullets. He couldn't get the tube to go all the way in. The gun would hold only seven bullets. He looked at the rear sight. There was a flat piece of metal about two inches long lying lengthwise on the barrel. Toward the front was a notch for the sight. It looked unusual in that it also had a hinge right under the notch. He caught his fingernail under the metal and saw that it would lift up. Was this a second sight? He noticed another piece of metal that would slide up and down on the now vertical piece of metal. He noticed numbers engraved on the side of the flat metal. He now understood that for long distance he would raise the sliding metal up and for short distance, down. He wanted to fire the Spencer but was afraid the sound would carry. He didn't have that many bullets anyway. Maybe tomorrow when he was further away he might risk one or two of his precious bullets.

He looked at the Savage. He tried to read it, remembering his English. He pronounced it Sa Bage. "Sabage," he repeated. He'd picked up a powder flask, caps and a leather bag of bullets. He'd not thought about a bullet mold.

Charley hefted the pistol in his hand. It was a huge gun and appeared to have two triggers. The rear trigger was a ring large enough to put his finger through. The front trigger was like all other triggers he had seen. He pulled the front trigger and nothing happened. He pulled the rear trigger and noticed the hammer raised and locked in a back position. He pulled the front trigger and was shocked when the gun discharged.

The black powder smoke was very thick, and his ears were ringing from the report.

He found a lever running lengthwise beneath the barrel. There was a catch at the very front. Grasping the catch and pulling it toward the cylinder, the lever would swing down, pushing a rod into the cylinder. So this was how it worked. He could pour powder in from the side, place the ball in behind the powder and pack it by pulling down on the lever.

Placing the percussion caps on the cylinder was easy. He didn't know how much powder to put in, so he decided that he would put in as much as the cylinder would hold and still accept the ball. He reloaded the spent cylinder. He noticed that this looked different from the other five cylinders. Someone packed what appeared to be grease over the ball. Well, he could do that, too. He would use the drippings from the bacon.

Charley had never felt so good in his life. He had three firearms, his knife, bow and all the food he wanted. He had water and two horses complete with white men saddles. Most of all, he had three white scalps and the memory of watching them squirm. Maybe he would now go back and find the white man that made him run like a rabbit and killed his cousins. Maybe finish burning Man Who Sits on Log, too.

The more he thought about it, the more he liked the idea. If he had five scalps and more horses he would demand much respect from Goyathlay.

ELEVEN

Colt and Dixon were back on the road within the hour and rode until sundown. They made a dry camp and ate some dried beef and a can of tomatoes each.

They took turns standing guard.

The next morning, after they'd eaten and relieved themselves, Dixon said, "Boy, do you know how to use that knife I sold you?"

Colt looked surprised. "Sure, I've been using a knife most of my life."

"Hell, I don't mean using it to cut twine or a bull's nuts. I mean if you had to use it on a man."

Colt sipped his coffee. "No, sir, I've never thought about having to cut anyone."

Dixon said, "Well, if that Indian was gonna do to you what he almost did—and what he *did* do to that poor woman—and all you had was your knife, what would you do?"

Colt said, without hesitation, "Well, I reckon I'd sure cut him."

"Stand up, boy," Dixon said. "Take that knife and sheath. I want to show you something. Now come at me like your gonna cut me. Now, get serious. You can't hurt me too bad with the sheath on it."

Colt spread his legs and faced Dixon. He crouched down and held the knife about waist high. He lunged at Dixon, who had been standing sideways with his left shoulder toward Colt.

Dixon's arms were relaxed but as soon as Colt lunged, Dixon's left arm swept to his front, striking Colt's forearm. His right hand swept up and grabbed Colt's wrist; at the same time, Dixon slid his left wrist down to support his right hand. He then pivoted on his left foot, swinging his right leg around behind him.

Colt was pulled forward off balance and tripped over Dixon's left knee.

The next thing Colt knew, he was down on his knees with his right hand bent back and his arm being twisted.

Just when Colt thought his arm would break Dixon said, "Now, boy, if this was a real fight, I'd just bend a little more and pull your shoulder right out of its socket. If I was really pissed, I'd stomp my knee or boot right on your shoulder as I lifted up, and I'd damn near tear your arm clean off. Now get up an' let me show you what I did."

*

Dixon went through it several times until Colt seemed to understand it. Then Dixon showed him the proper way to hold the knife close to his body while turning sideways to the opponent.

"Boy, you make a smaller target sideways and your vitals aren't facing the knife. Also, if you're sideways, you can lunge in toward your opponent further than if you're facing him. Now, watch this. Face me like before, all crouched down."

Colt did as he was told.

"Yeah, like that. Now, boy, see how your knees are bent? If I'm standing sideways, I can kick your kneecap right off as soon as you lunge with that knife. All I have to do is just go in right under your swing. If you cut me, it's going be my ribs or my arm. It won't be anything that'll kill me. Now, as soon as I kick, you're going down and, well, I just naturally cut your throat right at your juggler. Now you try it." After the lesson, they saddled up and rode out.

Colt had always imagined that he would be as good as any man in a fight. He'd never imagined how many ways people could kill him. He was going to get as much information from Dixon as he was willing to give.

They rode on to Cotulla, arriving after dark. They found the livery, unsaddled their stock and paid the livery man three dollars to rub their horses down, grain them, and give them some water.

Dixon took his saddlebags and weapons. He suggested, "Why don't we get us a store-bought meal, have a couple cold beers and then find us a bath and a real bed for the night?"

Colt looked embarrassed and said, "Mr. Dixon, I ain't got much and what I have, it has to last until I can get some more."

"Hell, I thought we were partners. Come on, I'm buying. It'll be your turn as soon as we fetch up those that we're chasing. Tomorrow we have to get you a good rifle."

*

Charley backtracked for several miles, traveling in a circular direction. If anyone were following him, he would eventually cut their tracks. If he did, he would be behind his pursuers. If not, he could relax and concentrate on finding Goyathlay, or maybe Victorio. If he found any tracks, he would follow and kill whoever it was.

During the mid-afternoon he found three sets of tracks. All were shod horses. He recognized the track of the blue-eyed, crazy horse immediately. They were heading east back toward the road. The tracks were fresh enough that the wind had not yet had time to smooth the crisp edges of the track.

Charley followed the tracks slowly as he studied them. He found what appeared to be fresh horse droppings.

He dismounted and picked up one and crushed it in his hand. It was fresh and moist but not warm. He thought he was one or two hours behind the white men. He'd follow them until they made camp. He was sure he could kill one with his bow before they even knew he was there. The nice new rifle that shot seven times without reloading would guarantee him success against the other one.

He smiled as he imagined himself being given a hero's welcome by Goyathlay. He would have many scalps, weapons, horses and supplies. He could see himself riding side by side with Goyathlay. He imagined how Goyathlay would tell his followers that if he were to fall, they should follow Charley Tree, the great warrior. Charley smiled as he followed the two white men.

*

Dixon and Colt went into the Cattleman's Cafe. The cafe was about to close and the waitress had already left. Mr. Felterman recognized Colt and looked at him with surprise.

Colt said, "Good evening, Mr. Felterman, this is my friend, Billy Dixon. It looks like you're about to close, but if it isn't too much trouble we'd like a couple of steaks. Actually, we'd like anything that we don't have to cook ourselves."

Mr. Felterman came over and said, "Colt, your daddy was one of the best men I ever knew. Your momma was a fine lady, too. Any friend of yours has got a lot of credit with me. I'm sure sorry about everything that's happened. It doesn't seem right that a fine family like yours could be wiped out just like that.

I was just cleaning up, but I have some choice beef, some calves' liver, and I have onions. It won't take long to stoke up the stove and I could even boil some potatoes. I have real butter, honey, and some biscuits left over. I could even make a nice salad."

Mr. Felterman threw out the remnants of the coffee and pumped fresh water into the pot. "You boys just sit down wherever you like and while the coffee's making, you can start off with some fresh milk and biscuits with butter and honey."

Colt and Dixon sat down. Colt felt funny the way Mr. Felterman talked about his family in the past tense. His pappy was gone, but he, his mother, and Douglas weren't past tense.

Dixon ordered calf liver with onions, mashed potatoes, gravy and a salad. Colt ordered the same except he ordered a steak. The steak was good but when he smelled the liver and onions he wished that he had chosen differently.

When they finished their meal, both felt bloated. Dixon stood and put his hat on. Followed by Colt, he went up to Mr. Felterman who was tallying up the day's receipts behind the cash register.

Dixon said, "That was the best damn meal that I have had in a long time. How much do we owe?"

Mr. Felterman looked up and said, "Well, it's after hours an' I don't have to pay anyone but myself. I never did get to pay my proper respects to what happened to this boy. Let's just say that it's on the house, just this once."

Colt reached into his pockets and withdrew some money from his meager funds. "Mr. Felterman, I appreciate that, but I don't feel right about it. How much for those two meals?"

"Colt, I mean it. Tomorrow when you come in here, you pay like everybody else. Tonight if you don't let me buy your supper, don't bother coming for breakfast."

Dixon turned to Colt. "That's pretty clear, Colt. I think the man means it."

He turned back to Felterman. "Mr. Felterman, Colt and I appreciate it, an' you can bet we'll be here for breakfast. By the way, where could we get a bath and a bunk for tonight?"

Felterman said, "Martha Albright lets out a bed from time to time. She nearly always has three of four customers sleeping in her attic. I've never been there, but folks that have said if you can stand the snoring, it's at least clean."

Felterman gave them directions. "You'd better hurry because I hear that she turns off the lights at 10:30 and it's 9:30 now."

Dixon and Colt left and walked the short distance to the boarding house. Dixon had wanted to stop by the Longhorn Saloon for a cold beer but if he wanted a bath they wouldn't have time.

They got a bunk that was located in an attic that was a single room that extended from one end of the house to the other. Several bunks were lined up in two rows, one on either side of the room. Partitions of white canvas separated each bunk, with another curtain that could close off the aisle-way.

Albright, a hefty, smiling, but no-nonsense woman, led them to the back porch where she had arranged other canvas curtains around six tin bathtubs.

She boiled water and filled two of the tubs with a mixture of hot and cold water, so that it was slightly more than lukewarm. She handed both men a strong smelling brown bar of lye soap, two towels and washrags.

She admonished them to hurry their baths because the lights were going out in twenty-five minutes and she was locking the doors at that time.

She said, "Everybody gets woke up at seven in the morning all at the same time. Nobody leaves between 10:30 when the lights go out until everybody leaves at the same time at six in the morning. That way, if anybody steals anything from the other guests, there's a chance of getting it back. Those are the rules. If you don't like the rules, go someplace else."

They accepted the rules. For a while, at least.

*

Colt's bunk was next to Dixon's, which was next to one of the two windows leading out to the roof of the front porch.

Dixon was lying by the open window, feeling the pleasant but warm breeze as it gently moved the sheer curtains. He could hear the tinkling of a piano and people laughing. He'd missed that in the desert.

He whispered to Colt, "Are you awake, boy?"

"Yeah, I'm awake, and if you don't quit talking, I'll probably stay that way."

Dixon quietly laughed. "Listen, boy, why don't you an' me just kind of creepy-crawl out my window here, shinny down the porch and have us a beer? If we carry our boots, and are real quiet, we shouldn't disturb anyone."

Colt was tired and the meal made him even sleepier. The feather bed was much more inviting then a beer and a lot of loud noise.

He didn't want to disappoint his friend but he sure didn't want to leave his bunk. He was silent for a few moments.

"Colt, did you hear me? Let's go get us a cold one. Hell. That old biddy won't know we're gone. Come on, boy."

Colt, trying to think up an excuse, whispered, "Just getting dressed, we'll wake up everybody here. More than likely they'll be pissed off."

A voice said, "God dammit, shut up, there's people trying to sleep!"

Colt lowered his voice even more. "See, we're liable to get our asses whipped before we even get dressed."

Dixon whispered, "Hell, we'll wear our johns and roll up our clothes and take 'em with us. When we get down we can dress.

Nobody can see us. It's pretty dark."

"You go ahead, Mr. Dixon. This bed feels mighty good an' I'm not much on beer, anyway."

"Suit yourself, boy. I'm gonna get me a beer."

Dixon, wearing his long johns, strapped on his gun belt, put on his hat, rolled up his pants and shirt and crawled out the window carrying his boots.

The slope of the porch was steeper and shorter than he'd anticipated. He immediately slipped, dropping his boots and bundle of clothes, and slid off the porch. He landed flat on his back on the ground, ten feet below.

The actual fall didn't make much noise, but Dixon's loud expletive "God-damn-son-of-a-bitch!" didn't go unheard.

Colt, just beginning to ease into the euphoria of sleep, was brought wide-awake by Dixon's loud yell. He heard a crunch and several men's voices saying "God dammit, I've had enough of this."

A voice said, "Knock it off. I have to get some sleep!"

Another very deep and powerful voice said, "If I have to get up out of this here bed, I'm gonna knock some goddamned heads together."

Downstairs, Martha Albright heard the disturbance. One thing she didn't put up with was a bunch of pea-brained men carrying on after she had laid down the rules.

She pounded the ceiling with her broom handle. "If you don't shut up, you can just get out! I told you the rules and all of you agreed, now shut up. The next peep I hear out of anyone, I'm going to just start blasting rock salt from my scattergun right through the ceiling. Do you hear me you uncouth, loud-mouthed, stinking heathens? Just one more peep!"

Colt lay very still. No one made a sound. Not even the big-sounding voice. It was so quiet that he thought he could hear just the whisper of the sound of someone crawling away.

Dixon's back hurt. He couldn't believe that he'd dropped his pants and boots, which were now somewhere on the roof above him. It hurt to move but all the commotion was beginning to attract attention. He crawled into some bushes and waited for the commotion to die down. All of his money was on the roof of the porch along with his boots.

The way his back hurt he wasn't sure he could shinny back up that four-by-four post.

Mrs. Albright sounded real pissed off and if she didn't dust his ass with some birdshot, there was no telling what those fellows up in their bunks would do to him. He'd fought Indians, bad guys and gun-slingers but he'd never been in a fix like this.

He thought, *Hell! Maybe I ought to just go and have a beer like I planned in the first place.*

The Longhorn Saloon was just getting up to speed with its usual evening festivities when the piano player stopped in the middle of his piece.

The overly-painted singer stopped in mid-song and all of the card players and dealers stopped in mid-play as everyone turned to stare at the apparition in front of them.

Dixon felt everybody looking at him as he walked into the Longhorn. *Well, you have to do the best with what you have,* he thought.

He put his shoulders back, pulled his hat over his eyes and walked right up to the bar. He hadn't noticed what just about everyone else had already seen. One button from the trapdoor on his long johns was missing, exposing the left cheek of his rump.

He planted his bare foot on the brass rail and waited for the bar-tender who, with a strange look, came over. The music started again and soon people were talking and laughing.

Billy heard a few remarks that he knew were directed towards his means of attire. He pulled out his pistol and laid it on the bar. Suddenly, everything got quiet again.

Oliver Wimbleton had been a bartender for thirty years of his fifty years of life. He'd never seen what he had just seen. An old man in his mid-fifties or early sixties, white, grizzled beard, barefoot, wear-ing nothing but his underwear, hat and two guns strapped to his waist, walked up to his bar. He was waving one of his very large guns around.

Oliver whispered out of the corner of his mouth to Phillis, one of the bargirls, "Better go get the sheriff. We have a live one."

Phillis, agreeing completely, disappeared out the back door.

Oliver smoothed his walrus mustache and discreetly picked up a small billy club from beneath the counter. He kept the club hidden until he was facing the crazy old man in the underwear.

Dixon laid his pistol on the bar and said, "I done got locked out of my room and all my money is in my pants on the roof. I'd sure like a beer, and I'll leave my pistol for collateral. Give me a couple of beers and I'll pay you in the morning."

Oliver knew opportunity when he saw it. This crazy man, dressed in only his underwear, was willing to give up one of his guns for a beer.

Oliver said, "Yes, sir." He laid his billy on the shelf under the bar. He took a mug, filled it with beer and slid it to the crazy man. He picked up the pistol and placed it on the shelf next to his billy.

The crazy man sucked off the head of the beer, took a long drink, smiled, belched, and then collapsed as Oliver hit him right across the left ear.

Sheriff Grimes walked in the door at just about the time Dixon hit the floor. The sheriff walked to where Dixon was lying.

"Okay, Oliver, what's going on?"

Oliver said, "This here crazy man just walked in wearing nothing except what you see, offering to leave one of his guns here for collateral and wanting a beer. I got his gun and knocked 'im cold."

Grimes asked, "Why'd you do that, Oliver?"

"Hell, Sheriff, see for yourself. He ain't wearing anything but his underwear. He ain't decent."

The sheriff said, "It does seem a little peculiar, but I don't know of any law that says a man can't dress the way he wants as long as he covers his privates. I don't think you should've hit him. Did he threaten anybody?"

A big man standing next to the bar was laughing. He said, "No, Sheriff, other than walking in here dressed like a jaybird, I don't reckon he did anything. I have to admit, he had us a little worried, though."

Grimes asked, "Is that right, Oliver? You cold-cocked this man because you were worried?"

"Well, yes, Sheriff, just look at him. I've never seen the likes. He ain't wearing anything but long johns and those guns."

Grimes shook his head. "If and when he wakes up, he just might prefer charges against you, Oliver. You can't hit a man just because you don't like the way he's dressed. If he goes and dies on you, you're really gonna be in trouble."

The sheriff looked around the room. "How about a couple of you men help me get him to the jail. I'd appreciate it if somebody would fetch Dr. Barstow. I don't want anyone dying in my jail."

"I'm glad you're locking him up, Sheriff," Oliver said. "I think he's dangerous. He sure ain't decent."

"Oliver, I'm not locking him up. I'm just loaning him a bunk for the night. If I have to lock anybody up, it's gonna be you. You're just a little too sudden with that club of yours. Now, first thing in the morning, you come on over to the jail and maybe you can talk this man out of pressing charges. If you aren't there by seven o'clock, I'm gonna be looking for you at about five after. If I have to do that, I'll arrest you for obstructing my investigation. I'll hold you for the circuit judge and he isn't expected for a couple of weeks. Now, I reckon you ought to close up a little early tonight."

Grimes turned to the few customers and said, "Fellows, drink up whatever you have going, this place will be closed in ten minutes."

With the help of Oliver and two patrons, Grimes carried Dixon's limp body out.

Dixon's trapdoor was fully open and now dragging the floor. His exposed, bare rump brought out the humor of the situation, causing quite a few discreet giggles and remarks, especially amongst the bargirls.

*

At about the time Dixon was being drug off to jail, Charley realized that he was approaching a white man's town.

The town wasn't very large but he knew that if the white men stayed overnight, they wouldn't tie their horses where they slept. Living with the whites as he had, he knew the white men would leave their horses at a livery and sleep somewhere else.

They could be just passing through, but due to the time of night he didn't think so.

He sat on his horse in the moonlight, studying the tracks in the white sand that were almost as clear as if it were day.

Charley sat on his horse thinking. Eventually, a thought occurred to him. If he couldn't kill Man Who Sits on Log and his friend, perhaps he could steal or kill their horses. It'd be a small payment for the death of his cousins and making him run like a scared rabbit.

Maybe when the sun showed its face again, he could see where they left their horses.

Charley unsaddled his horses and hid them in some mesquite brush. After covering his tracks, he walked obliquely to as close to the town as possible, being careful to stay away from the road.

There were no hills and certainly no mountains in the generally flat country, but there were areas higher than others. He sought out such a higher elevation, burrowed into the sand and slept.

TWELVE

The next morning when Dixon woke up, he didn't know where he was and his head and back hurt. He forced himself to sit and swung his legs off the bunk. He sat for a moment, holding his head in both hands with his elbows on his knees.

When the room finally quit spinning, he looked around and saw that he was in jail.

That was curious. He didn't know why he was there. The cell door was open, so whatever he'd done to land himself here must not have been too bad. He remembered crawling out of the window from the rooming house. He had no memory of anything else.

Sheriff Grimes was leaning back in his chair with his feet on his desk and looking at his watch. Oliver had five more minutes before he would go looking for him. He heard a noise from behind him and said, "Well, it's about time you woke up. How do you feel?"

Dixon asked, "How'd you know it was me?"

"Because besides me, you're the only one in my jail." He took his feet off his desk, letting his chair rock forward just as his boots hit the floor. "You have to be the silliest sight that I ever saw. Button up your trapdoor before your ass freezes."

Dixon looked over each shoulder and saw that the back door of his johns was indeed open. He fumbled for a few moments until he found both buttons missing. Dixon mumbled, "I must've lost the buttons."

Grimes asked, "Do you always dress up that way when you go out drinking?"

"What difference does it make how a man's dressed as long as he's dressed?"

Grimes laughed. "Well, some folks might be offended. As a matter of fact, one of 'em was so offended, he cold-cocked you last night at the Longhorn."

Dixon asked, "Why am I in jail? Did I hurt somebody?"

"Nope. You didn't hurt anybody. As far as I can figure, you haven't broken any laws. I brought you over here just to give you a bed until you woke up. I was kind of curious why somebody would run around in their drawers to get a drink."

"Well, it's sort of a long story. I'm a Texas Ranger heading south. I stopped in with a friend of mine for the night and we got us a room over at Miss Albright's. She done locked the door at 10:30 and I was thirsting for a beer. I remember crawling out the window and falling. I must have lost my pants somewhere along the way. Hell, I don't even know if I got a beer."

Grimes said, "Well, you had a beer, at least part of one. You got cold-cocked before you had more than a sip."

Grimes looked at Dixon, measuring him. "So you claim to be a ranger, huh? Can you prove it?"

"Yes, sir. If I can find my pants I can. I have me a badge and my commission letter in my pants."

"What's your name, Mr. Ranger?"

"William Dixon. Everybody calls me Billy or Mr. Dixon. Take your choice."

Grimes said, "It seems like I heard that name before. Where would that be?"

"I don't know, Sheriff. I've been pretty much all over."

Grimes stood and put on his hat. "Okay, Mr. Dixon, you go find your pants. It looks like I have to track down the man who hit you."

About that time, the door burst open and Oliver stood in the doorway, puffing. He stared at Dixon with more than a little trepidation.

"Sorry I'm late, Sheriff. I got here as quick as I could, just like you asked."

"I didn't ask, Oliver. I told you. Another thirty seconds I was gonna come looking. Now get your ass in here and talk to this man."

Grimes looked to Dixon and said, "Oliver here has done admitted cold- cocking you. He used some real bad judgment because it doesn't appear that he had good reason. Now, I wanted him to come over to see what you wanted to do about it. You'd be within your rights to prefer charges against him. We have a ten dollar medical bill from the doctor and I don't think the county is gonna be real happy about that."

Oliver, feeling less the hero than the villain, was beginning to realize that he could really go to jail. "Don't you worry, Sheriff. I'll be happy to pay for the doctor and whatever damages this man thinks he has coming. Within reason, of course."

Oliver turned to Dixon and said, "Mister, I'm sure sorry. I was plumb out of line. It's just, nobody ever came into my place wearing nothing but a hat and their underwear. I thought you were plumb crazy. I'm real sorry."

The sheriff said, "Oliver, do you have any idea who you hit? You cold- cocked a famous Texas Ranger. This here is Texas Ranger, Billy Dixon."

Grimes wasn't sure Dixon really was famous, but the fact that the name was vaguely familiar gave him license to put the fear into Oliver. "This man here once gunned a man down just because he didn't take his hat off in front of a lady. He personally out-gunned ten men in a saloon who had the drop on him. He was a hero in the battle of Hornsby Bend and killed over twenty Apache before he ran out of bullets. Then do you know what he did, Oliver? He took his empty rifle and clubbed five more to death before the rest broke and ran."

Grimes wasn't sure about any of the details of Hornsby Bend, but hell, somebody there must have been a hero and it might have been somebody like Dixon.

Dixon sat there in one of the office chairs holding his aching head in his hands. His rump was cold on the oak seat. He really wasn't interested in what Grimes and Oliver were talking about.

Oliver's eyes got large and his heavy walrus mustache quivered. *My God, what had he done?* "Mr. Dixon, like I said, I'm sure sorry, and I want to make things right. What can I do to make it up to you?"

Dixon asked, "What did you say?"

"I want to make it up, Mr. Dixon. Whatever you say."

Dixon, not feeling very well and not much caring one way or another, said, "Well, I'd really appreciate it if you wouldn't go hitting on me again."

"Oh, no, sir," Oliver said. "I sure won't do that no more. What else can I do?"

Dixon rubbed his hand across his head. "Well, I don't think I ever did get my beer. You reckon you could fetch me a bucket of beer? I could take some back to my partner at the rooming house."

The sheriff said, "Are saying you ain't gonna press charges against old Oliver here?"

"No, Sheriff, I reckon not," Dixon said. "I can't afford to stay around for any court hearing. I have things to do that are more important, which reminds me. I'd appreciate it if you could send a couple of telegrams for me."

"That's a possibility."

Grimes turned to Oliver and said, "I suggest that you fetch that man his bucket of beer. The next time I hear about you using that club of yours, you'd better have one hell of a reason. Now get the hell out of my office."

Oliver took two steps out the door and was gone.

Dixon wrote out two telegrams and gave them to the sheriff. One was to the Indian agent in Fort Sumner in New Mexico requesting any information on any Apache between fourteen and twenty that had recently jumped the reservation and went by the name of Charley or Indian Charley.

The second telegram was to the Texas State Department of Health. The telegram was short, and requested the names and addresses of individuals or institutions that had conducted studies of bovine diseases.

The sheriff looked at the telegrams and said, "Is there anything I ought to know about this so-called Charley fellow?"

Dixon told the sheriff the story. "Yes, sir, we have us one unusual Apache. I've never heard of any Apache taking scalps, but I'm pretty sure that's what he is. He's one mean son of a bitch, whoever he is. If he isn't caught real soon, he's gonna kill somebody else and he doesn't kill pretty."

Grimes shook his head. "It looks like we got a whole passel of strange Apache. A group of six or eight took over a stage relay post up near Killeen. They killed the hostler, his wife and his boy. They were wearing regular white men clothes. When the stage arrived, they killed the driver and his guard. They then killed two men and a woman passenger. There was a boy on board, but they don't know what happened to him. The Indians probably took him to sell in Mexico. Funny thing, though, they took the cash box. Never heard of any Indian stealing money. Looks like them reservation Indians are picking up white man's bad habits."

Dixon was silent for a moment. He'd seen what one crazy Apache could do. Six or eight more could be a real problem.

Grimes said, "We have about twenty volunteers out looking, but so far nobody has seen hide nor hair of 'em."

About this time, Oliver came in with a bucket of beer. He handed it to Dixon.

Billy blew off the head and took a long swig. He wiped his mouth with his sleeve and belched. "I think I'll go and fetch my pants. I figure my partner ought to be waking up and he might enjoy a swig of this beer."

The sheriff handed Dixon his guns. He strapped them on, put on his hat, and walked out into the early morning.

The street was beginning to fill with ranchers and their wives, merchants and rawhiders. Dixon hesitated on the boardwalk.

He raised his chin, pulled his shoulders back, coughed and stepped into the street. He walked stiff-legged and purposefully through the mixed crowd.

Dixon looked neither right nor left as some of the ladies giggled and some were heard to utter indignant phrases like, "My word!" and "He ought to be ashamed of himself."

The men weren't so generous with their remarks and Dixon thought he just might have to shoot somebody yet. Of course, he had both his shooting hands full, one carrying the beer while the other held his trapdoor closed as best he could.

He reached the front door of the rooming house just as Miss Albright came out. She froze in her tracks and said, "I declare! Now look at you. That's indecent. Just where do you think you're going?"

"I have to go in and get my pants," Dixon said.

Albright blocked his path. "You're not coming in this establishment dressed, or should I say, undressed like that."

"Begging your pardon, ma'am, but you see, I have to go in and get my pants before I can get proper dressed."

He tried to push by her and she swung her broom handle at his head. He dropped the trapdoor on his drawers and caught the broom with his left hand. He took the broom away from her and said, "Ma'am, with all due respect, I'm going in there to get my pants."

A crowd of about twenty of the good and proper citizens had gathered by this time.

Sheriff Grimes sat across the street, leaning back in his chair on the boardwalk. He had an amused grin as he watched the awkward scene unfold.

Dixon started to brush past Miss Albright when a huge and hairy arm reached out and grabbed him from behind.

The brute's thumb was pressing on his left ear while the giant's fingers pressed against his right jaw.

The man's voice sounded like the rumbling of a volcano. "Mister, if Miss Albright says you ain't going in, you ain't going in."

Dixon stopped and the unseen stranger relaxed his grip. His head started hurting again and he turned, prepared to bust whoever it was right in the mouth.

When he turned, he was looking at somebody's chest that looked as wide as a barn. He had to look up to see the giant's face. The man was about forty and was at least seven feet tall. He had to weigh three hundred and fifty pounds if he weighed an ounce. His long red hair matched his beard.

Dixon swallowed. "You're right, mister, I'm not going in that door. I done changed my mind."

Miss Albright said, "Thanks, Huey, it's okay now. You don't have to hit him. Come on in and I'll find some pie for you."

Huey stared at Dixon for a moment as though he couldn't decide whether to pound him into the boardwalk or not. Finally he said, "Whatever you say, Miss Albright." He walked around Dixon and followed Miss Albright into the house.

Dixon let out an audible sigh of relief. He set his pail of beer on the boardwalk.

As soon as Miss Albright and Huey were safely out of sight, he commenced to climb up the porch that he had fallen from the night before. As he climbed up the porch, he had to use both hands and his trapdoor dropped completely down. It was unintentional, but as he reached the roof and bent his upper body forward to pull himself up, he mooned the good citizens of Cotulla.

*

Grimes was watching all of this with a great deal of amusement. Maybe he'd have to arrest this fellow after all, because what he just saw was indecent. That Dixon fellow was the strangest ranger that he'd ever met.

*

Dixon found his pants and put them on. He gathered up his shirt and boots and went to the window and tried to open it. It was locked.

He brushed the dust away and peered inside.

All he saw was Huey, slowly shaking his head.

Dixon put on his shirt then sat as he put on his boots. When he was fully dressed he stood, went back to the edge of the roof and shimmied down, just in time to see a big yellow dog pissing in his bucket of beer.

Now, that about tore it. It looked like he wasn't going to get any beer in this town. Dixon picked up the pail of beer and knocked on the door. He could hear Huey's lumbering steps as he came down the stairs and approached the front door. The door opened and Huey stood there just behind Miss Albright.

Dixon said, "Ma'am, I'm all dressed and I still have some things upstairs. I'll just be a minute."

Miss Albright stepped aside. "Alright. Get your things but be quick about it. I run a decent establishment and I don't want the likes of you here. You done embarrassed me before half the town."

As Dixon passed Huey, he handed him the bucket of beer and said, "Mister, it looks like this beer has caused me enough trouble. If you want it, you can have it."

Huey, for the first time, smiled.

Dixon went upstairs and saw Colt just getting dressed.

Colt asked, "Where've you been?"

"Out getting a beer. Come on, let's go get some breakfast." As they left Miss Albright's, Dixon saw Huey sitting on the boardwalk drinking the beer.

Huey waved and smiled at Dixon. "Thanks for the beer."

"You're mighty welcome to it."

*

Grimes watched Colt and Dixon leave. He recognized Colt and crossed the street to follow. As Grimes passed Huey, he asked, "Did you and that fellow get everything sorted out?"

Huey looked up with foam covering his mouth and said, "Sure did, Sheriff, he wasn't a bad sort. He even gave me this beer."

Grimes, never breaking his stride, said, "I don't blame 'im. I'd a given it to you, too. A dog pissed in it."

Grimes didn't look back as he heard a bellow and gagging. He was going around the corner when the gagging stopped, followed by the loudest cussing that he'd ever heard.

The sheriff thought, *Maybe I ought to get the doc. Dixon might need him again.*

*

Grimes didn't see Colt or Dixon. He figured they must have gone into the Cattleman's Restaurant. The telegraph office was just down the street so he decided he'd send the wires first. That way, he would know how much to charge Dixon when he saw him. Maybe he should have made Dixon send them himself; but Grimes was right proud of Cotulla, and Dixon, strange as he was, had been sorely mistreated by some of the townsfolk. Besides, Dixon was a lawman, too.

*

Dixon and Colt were just finishing up a chicken-fried steak, eggs, gravy and biscuits. They were on their third cup of coffee with real sugar and cream when Grimes walked in.

He walked over to where Dixon and Colt were sitting and said, "Do you mind if I join you?"

Dixon said, "Hell, no, Sheriff. Sit down and have a cup of coffee."

Grimes took his hat off and laid it on the remaining chair and sat. He ran his fingers through his short brown hair and looked at Colt. He said, "I thought that was you, Colt. How have you been holding up?"

Colt said, "OK, I guess. Mr. Dixon here helped me out. Saved my life actually."

"Son, I'm real sorry about everything." Grimes put a hand on Colt's shoulder. "First your ranch, then your dad, and now your ma and little brother. I don't see how you can stand it."

"What do you mean, my ma and brother? They're in Fort Worth by now."

Grimes looked at Colt in disbelief. "You mean you don't know? Son, I received a wire the other day. Your ma's dead, son. We don't know where your little brother is. A bunch of Indians attacked the coach and it looks like they took your little brother. They killed everybody else. Hell, son, I'm sorry. I thought you knew."

Colt was stunned. This couldn't be. He felt cold inside. He was amazed that he didn't feel like crying. The hurt was too deep for tears. Colt asked in a whisper, "How did it happen, Sheriff?"

Grimes told him what he knew, which wasn't very much. He said when he got the wire he was told to be on the lookout for the renegades.

The wire also asked him to notify the next of kin. Since there were none in Cotulla the sheriff had gone to Mr. Hunt, who told him about the relatives in Fort Worth. The sheriff wired the relatives, who had the body shipped there for burial.

Colt felt rage boiling inside. He would've killed any Indian walking in that cafe at that moment.

He said, "Mr. Dixon, I'm gonna go find me some Indians."

"Well, boy, since it seems like those Indians are heading south and that's where I'm going," Dixon said, "I reckon I'll just go with you. How about we get our supplies and head out in the morning, first light?"

Colt said, "I want to leave right now."

Dixon said, "We got some shopping to do and by then it will be pushing on noon. Not only that, but I had the sheriff send a couple of telegrams for us. One of them was about that Indian called Charley. If we get an answer, it might help."

Colt thought about it. Dixon so far had been right about everything and he had been wrong about everything.

"Okay, Mr. Dixon, whatever you say. But if those bastards have my little brother, I can't sit here too long."

"We'll leave at first light. Now, let's go do some shopping."

Dixon turned to Grimes. "Excuse us, Sheriff, and thanks for all you done."

Grimes looked up and said, "Oh, one more thing. I think Huey may be looking for you."

Dixon asked, "Why?"

"He found out about the dog piss in the beer. Huey isn't a real bad boy and he isn't real smart, but that old boy can lift a wagon. I'd hate to see you get hurt."

"You and me both, Sheriff. See you around."

"And by the way," Grimes added. "Huey isn't armed. Ranger or no ranger, I'd be mighty upset if Huey got shot."

Dixon said, "Sheriff, I promise that I won't shoot anyone that I don't have to."

*

Charley had ridden completely around the small town, staying far enough away so that no one could see him.

On six different occasions, he hid his horses in the mesquite and crawled up close enough to the town to study its layout.

He found the livery sitting alone to the west of town about a hundred yards away from the nearest building. He couldn't see the signs on the stores from this distance, but could figure out by the number of wagons pulling up to various stores which one was probably a feed store and which one was the general store.

The livery would be easy. All he had to do was wait until after midnight when the fewest people would be expected to come or go, sneak across a short, empty field, then steal or kill the white man's horses.

The general store where he might replenish his supplies was more difficult. It was the third building east of the livery and on the same side of the dusty street.

He could hide his horses in the brush behind the livery, go to the general store, steal what he could find; then go to the livery to get the horses and no one would know he was there. Charley returned to his horses and waited.

THIRTEEN

Dixon and Colt walked about three doors down to Jacobson's Mercantile and General Store and went inside.

Colt, somewhat embarrassed, watched Dixon select a duster similar to his own. It was made of coarse, light brown canvas.

Dixon held it out for Colt and told him to try it on.

It generally fit, except the sleeves were about a half-inch too long and just a little large in the shoulders.

Colt was about to suggest a smaller size, but Dixon nodded his head in approval. "That's perfect. Come winter, a coat under that ought to fill it out nice and proper."

They selected a pair of soft tan leather gloves, a heavy brown denim shirt and matching pants.

Colt had his eye on a striking bright red shirt, but Dixon shook his head. "Nope, wrong color. On hot days, light colors keep the heat off you but they're just as bad as bright colors. You can see 'em a mile away. At night, they're worse. Moon reflects off light colors real well. They also show dirt a whole lot worse. Nope. Brown works just fine in our business."

Dixon gave Colt a head-to-toe inventory. "Your boots is OK, but that white hat ain't gonna make it. We'll soak it in some coffee and take care of it. Pick out a pair of good wool socks. They may seem hot, but if you have to do any walking in hot sand, that wool is good insulation. Wool also wicks off the sweat better than cotton. Come winter, if you still got them, they're a whole lot warmer. Even if they get wet they'll provide some warmth."

They took their bundle to the counter and Dixon asked the clerk for a one-pound can of beeswax.

Dixon told Colt, "We'll melt that beeswax and rub it into your duster. It collects dust, but it works pretty good to keep out the rain."

Dixon asked the clerk to show him a Winchester 44-40 and a double-barreled shotgun.

He said, "If we're gonna do any real Indian fighting, we ought to get us something that will reach out and touch somebody further than these saddle rifles."

The proprietor laid out a near-new Winchester and a 12-gauge shotgun.

Dixon said, "Let me see that Whitworth, also." The clerk handed him the weapon.

As Dixon examined the weapon he turned to Colt. "This old Whitworth is only a single shooter but it'll send that .45 ball a long ways and bring down a buffalo. If you hit a man with it, he ain't gonna get up."

Dixon bought two pounds of powder and a pound of lead. "How much for all this?" Dixon asked the clerk.

Colt whispered, "Mr. Dixon, I don't know if I'll ever make enough money to pay you back for all this."

"Hell, it's for sure gonna come outta your half of whatever we collect," Dixon said. "Besides, I'm not doing it just for you. We have a bunch of hell-raisin' Indians out there cutting hair. I need somebody at my back that is well-armed and has staying power. You got staying power, boy?"

"Mr. Dixon, I reckon I'll back you 'til hell freezes over."

"You know, boy, I think you would."

The clerk said, "The whole bill comes to one hundred and sixty-eight dollars. Make it one hundred and sixty dollars even, considering how much you bought. What the hell you boys gonna do, fight a war?"

"Good Lord! A hundred and sixty dollars?" Dixon slapped Colt on the back. "Come on, boy. This man's trying to rob us. Let's go."

The clerk waited until they had reached the door before he shouted, "Hold on there, fellows. Maybe I can make you a deal."

Dixon smiled and winked at Colt and they went back to the counter.

The clerk made a show of licking his pencil and then he worked on the bill. He glanced up and said, "I want to help you boys out and the Whitworth's been sitting for a while."

The clerk risked a glance at Dixon's face and quoted a price that sounded more like a question. "A hundred and fifty sound okay?"

Dixon said, "A flat hundred would sound better, but I'd go a hundred and twenty-five."

After a little more negotiating they walked out with their purchases, having paid a hundred and thirty dollars. Dixon had him throw in a jar of licorice candy.

When they got out on the boardwalk, Colt glanced over his shoulder to make sure they were out of hearing range and said, "That was some negotiating, Mr. Dixon."

"Nah, everybody always asks for more than they'll take. All you have to do is to offer less than you're willing to pay. That way it kind of comes out even. Come on, we have to find a blacksmith shop."

Colt said, "What're we gonna do at a blacksmith?"

Dixon held up the double-barreled shotgun. "We're gonna do a little modification of this here scattergun."

After asking a passerby, they found the blacksmith shop. Dixon told the smithy to cut the barrels off even with the wooden fore-piece. He then had the smith cut off most of the stock except about two inches behind the checkered pistol grip. He had him drill a quarter-inch diameter hole through the two-inch portion behind the pistol grip.

When the smithy was through, what had been a nice fowling piece was now a mean-looking weapon.

Colt watched all of this, not understanding any of it. Dixon paid the two dollars the smithy asked for and they walked back the way they had come.

Dixon said, "I seen a sign pointing off Main Street that said something about a hotel. Let's get us a real room tonight. One where we can come and go as we please without me having to go sneaking out a window in my underwear."

As they approached the front door of the hotel, they heard a deep booming voice.

Dixon froze. His shoulders hunched up and the hair on the back of his neck stood as the deep rumbling voice of Huey said, "You, yes, you! Just hold on! I'm gonna kick your mangy ass all the way out of Texas."

Dixon turned around to face the mountain coming at him. He handed his bundle to Colt, keeping the empty Winchester. "Here. Hold this, Colt."

Huey crossed the twenty feet with fury in his eyes.

Dixon said, "Hold on, Huey, I thought we were friends. Hell, I even gave you my beer."

"Yeah, because a dog pissed in it."

"Who told you that?"

"The sheriff."

"Now hold on, Huey. What would I be doing carrying around a beer with dog piss in it?"

"How the hell do I know? Same reason as you was prancing around in your underwear, because you're crazy. I'm gonna whip the shit out of you. Everybody's laughing at me."

Dixon looked at the brute. "Huey, you're a friend of mine and I don't want to hurt you, so just back off."

Colt dropped his load on the ground. He knew that there was no way that his grizzled old friend wasn't about to get hurt real bad. It was doubtful if ten men could take Huey down, but he had no choice but to back Dixon. He knew that both he and Dixon were in deep trouble.

Huey charged and swung what looked to Colt like a full-sized ham of a fist.

What happened next was almost too fast for him to follow.

Dixon ducked into a deep, almost squatting position just as the freight train of a fist cut the air where Dixon's head had been a fraction of a second before.

He swung the barrel of the rifle like a baseball bat at the outside of Huey's left knee.

Huey let out a bellow and fell just as Dixon sprung to his right, jumping up and back.

Bawling in pain and cursing a blue streak, Huey fell. He rolled around until he was sitting on his butt holding his left knee.

"You old son of a bitch! Damn, this hurts! I'm gonna squish you now."

Dixon held the rifle like a batter and warned, "I said I didn't want to hurt you, Huey. Now, if you get up, I'm gonna have to hurt you worse."

"You asshole! First, you make me drink dog piss, now you damned near broke my leg. Fuck you." He rolled to his good leg and with surprising speed, lunged from a sitting position to tackle Dixon.

Dixon took one step back and brought the Winchester down on Huey's right collarbone.

The bone broke, instantly paralyzing Huey's entire right side.

Huey went down, rolling around and bawling like a wounded buffalo. A group had gathered by this time.

One spectator said, "I'll be damned, I never thought anybody could put ol' Huey down."

Dixon said, "Goddamn it, I said I didn't want to hurt you. Now, next time I say back off, maybe you'll listen."

Huey gasped, "I'm gonna kill you for this."

"Maybe," Dixon said, "but by the time you're able to walk, I won't be around."

They left Huey cursing in the dirt and carried their supplies to the hotel.

They were surprised that they could get a room with two beds for just a dollar more than the rooming house. There was also a covered walkway that led to the outhouse with individual stalls so there would be no waiting. Dixon made sure that they could come and go as they pleased without any silly rules.

The clerk said, "We only have three rules. No spitting, no shooting and no women in your rooms unless it's your wife."

They went up to the room, spread out their supplies and examined the weapons. Dixon showed Colt how to break down the shotgun and the Winchester for cleaning. While Colt was cleaning them, Dixon cleaned the Whitworth.

After the weapons were cleaned, Dixon took the shotgun and ran a leather thong through the stock and made a loop. He had Colt stand up with his arms out to his side. He held the loop up so that the shotgun dangled from Colt's right shoulder. He adjusted the thong until the pistol grip of the shotgun was just even with Colt's hand. He tied the thong and stepped back.

"OK, Colt. Reach down with your right hand and grab the butt piece of that scattergun."

Colt did, and found that he didn't have to move his hand at all. The butt piece was exactly even with his hand when his arm was dropped casually at his side.

Dixon said, "Now, swing it up and bring your left hand up to the fore-piece. Your right thumb should be cocking those hammers as you bring it up."

Colt found it easy and fast, even without practice.

Dixon told him to let the weapon hang and put on his duster. After Colt had the duster on, the shotgun was almost invisible.

"When you expect trouble," Dixon said, "wear that rig just like you have it and leave that duster unbuttoned. Those double barrels sawed off that way will clear out a wall covered with man-killers. Most intelligent people would never pull on you facing that, no matter how many they are. Of course, you can always get that one that thinks he's fast or one that's got a death wish. But, boy, don't you ever pull a gun on anybody unless you're sure that you have the salt to use it. If somebody draws on you and you hesitate, you're probably gonna get dead."

He gave Colt a serious look, as though he was evaluating him. "Now, let's put this shit away and go buy some groceries for our trip. As a matter of fact, I have to check with the sheriff on some telegrams I sent this morning. Why don't you go get the groceries while I do that? I'll make up a list of things to get and here's some money. Take your time. After I check with the sheriff, I'm going over to that Longhorn and have me a beer yet. You bring those supplies here and wait, or you can find me over there."

They left the hotel and split up. It was getting a little later and the sun was just beginning to set. The dust stirred up by the day's traffic of buggies and horses was beginning to settle.

As Dixon walked toward the sheriff's office, he heard groups of men and some women murmur and whisper to each other as he walked by, but no one said anything loud enough for him to make out what it was. As he walked down the boardwalk, two men actually stepped off into the street to let him pass.

When he arrived at the sheriff's office, Grimes looked up from his desk. He was filling out a report and talking to three men sitting around his desk.

Grimes didn't look happy. When he noticed Dixon, he motioned to the men and said, "Okay, I figure I know what happened. Thanks for your help."

The three men cast furtive glances at Dixon and quickly left the office.

The sheriff said, "Dixon, I thought I told you that I didn't want any trouble between you and Huey."

"Sheriff, I remember you telling me not to shoot him and I didn't. I told him I didn't want any trouble, but he was bent on killing me anyway. He thought some dog pissed in his beer."

Grimes leaned back in his chair and let out a long sigh, tossing his pencil at his report with enough force that it bounced off the desk. Grimes rubbed both of his eyes and said, "Goddammit, Dixon, you and I both know that damn dog pissed in that beer. Now, I can't hardly blame old Huey for being upset."

"Nah, I reckon not," Dixon said. "But if you hadn't told him, it would've been our little secret. He tried to rough me up and wouldn't let me get my pants. Hell, it was fair punishment."

Grimes said, "Well, maybe you're right. Maybe I have some responsibility. Now, technically—according to witnesses—Huey did swing at you first, and considering old Huey's about the size of a house, I reckon you didn't have much choice. So I have to put it down as self-defense. But I have to tell you, Ranger Dixon..."

Dixon interrupted. "Billy. Call me Billy."

Grime's voice became very even. "I have to tell you, Ranger Dixon, if I see any more of your antics, any fights, or if I see you parading around in your underwear, I'm gonna personally whip your ass, drag you in here and lock you in a cell. Then I'm gonna go on vacation for about a month. I don't think I like you very much, Ranger Dixon."

"Well, I'm sorry, Sheriff. I didn't mean to get out of line. By the way, did those telegrams ever come back?"

Grimes looked at Dixon with disdain. "I really don't know. I sent them like you asked, as a courtesy. I walked six blocks over to the telegraph office—six blocks that you could've walked—and paid seventy-five cents of the county's money. Now, I expect you to reimburse the county. Then you can walk your ass over to the telegraph office and find out for yourself. I'm not doing you any more favors. What you did to Huey was legal but it wasn't called for. The doctor says that it could take months before he can walk without a limp. Now, if you hurry, you just might make it before they close."

"OK, Sheriff. We'll be gone before daylight. Thanks for all your help." Dixon left the sheriff's office and went directly to the telegraph office.

Sure enough, he had two telegrams. The one from Fort Sumner essentially stated that three Mescalero Apache had disappeared from the reservation almost three weeks prior. They were identified by the agent as being Charley Tree, about sixteen years of age, and his two cousins—Yanahosa, around fifteen to sixteen, and Ka-e-tennay, age seventeen to eighteen. Dixon thought they fit the general description of the two that he shot and Indian Charley.

He read the second telegram, which gave him the name and address of a Professor Keenan at the University of Albany in New York.

Keenan had done extensive research on bovine diseases. Dixon sent a telegram requesting any information regarding anthrax in cattle: specifically, symptoms, incubation period, how it was transmitted and diagnostic procedures. He paid the telegraph operator and left.

He went to the Longhorn Saloon and walked up to the bar.

Oliver nervously brushed at his mustache and hurried over to Dixon. "Good evening, Mr. Dixon, glad to see you again, sir. What's you pleasure?"

"Well, if you promise not to hit me again, I'd like to have a beer. I'd also like some of those boiled eggs and pickled sausage that you have in those jars there."

Oliver said, "Yes, sir, anything you want. It's on the house tonight."

"Like hell it is. I only let my friends buy me a drink, and you sure as hell aren't my friend."

"Yes, sir, Mr. Dixon. Whatever you say."

Dixon looked around the room that had suddenly fallen quiet. Between the exaggerated reputation the sheriff gave Oliver, and Oliver's embellishment of it—plus the exaggerated story as to how Dixon had whipped big Huey—the crowd in the bar viewed him with respect mixed with resentment.

Dixon had no idea that he'd built such a fearsome, if mostly false, reputation. He thought it was because of his running around in his underwear.

He turned his back to the crowd and tried to enjoy his beer.

Dixon was on his third beer, and had consumed six hardboiled eggs with as many pickled sausages, when Colt walked in.

Colt drank two beers while Dixon had two more.

Finally Dixon said, "Feel like a little cards, boy? They got a game over yonder. That card slick has been cleaning out everybody he's been playing. He's cheating, but he isn't very good at it. Watch his right foot. Now, watch the deal. There it goes. Now look real close at the floor under his right foot."

Colt looked and could barely make out what appeared to be a loose board moving under his foot.

Dixon said, "Now, watch that man on his left. If he rubs his chin, he's gonna fold on the second card he gets. Now, watch, the dealer's gonna shift the deck to his left hand and slide the cards sideways. There you go. See it? Now, look over to the wall behind those other two players. There's a room behind that wall, and I guarantee you, there is a peephole in that wall. Somebody is behind there signaling to the dealer what those other boys have. They have a rocker under that loose board with a wire or string tied to it."

Dixon sipped his beer. "That fellow on the left is the shill. The dealer wins only a modest hand once in a while but the shill always wins the big pots while the suckers only win enough small pots to keep them interested. That dealer has the cards shaved so he knows the low cards and the face cards. One is shaved on the long side in a wedge shape and the other is shaved on the short side. That way, depending on which way he deals, he can give the suckers whatever he wants."

Colt and Dixon watched another hand and then Dixon motioned to Colt. "Come on, boy, bring what little you have. We're gonna make us a little money. As soon as two of those suckers gets tapped out, you an' me are gonna sit in."

Colt cleared his throat. "I'm not sure that I know how to play poker, Mr. Dixon."

Dixon chuckled. "That's even better. You let the dealer know that and he'll be real glad to teach you. Don't you worry now, boy, you just watch. They're using red Bicycles. I have some of those up in my saddlebags. While we're waiting for some spots to clear, why don't you run up and get them."

Colt left while Dixon had yet another beer. Colt was back before Dixon finished his beer and discreetly handed the cards to Dixon. "Watch my beer, boy. I have to go to the pisser. This beer is getting to me."

By the time Dixon got back, two of the suckers, having been cleaned out, got up to leave.

He whispered to Colt, "Now, boy, you just bet normally. You aren't gonna win anything but small hands. You're gonna lose all the big ones. Don't worry, because before the night's over we are gonna skin some skunks."

Dixon, followed by Colt, walked over to the table and asked, "You fellows mind if we buy in?"

FOURTEEN

The dealer smiled at Dixon like a wolf looking at fresh meat. He made a grand gesture to the two empty chairs. "Please do, gentlemen. Perhaps you'll be able to change my luck. The gentleman to the left seems to have all of it tonight."

Colt and Dixon took seats. Dixon said, "What's the rules?"

"Dollar ante and pot limit."

"Sounds okay to me." Dixon pulled out five double eagles and said, "I'll need some change."

Colt pulled out his meager twenty-two dollars and laid it on the table. The dealer snapped his fingers and yelled to Oliver. "Ollie, these gentlemen need some change."

Dixon said, "Just change one of those double eagles for now."

By the time the change came, the dealer had already started dealing. Like Dixon expected, they were allowed to win two small hands each. Dixon knew that was to get them hooked.

Of the next three hands, two went to the shill and one went to the dealer.

The remaining sucker folded and left the table, saying, "That cleans me out."

The dealer said, "Well, I prefer five to play poker, but I guess four will do. Shall we continue, gentlemen?"

Dixon said, "Suits me."

Colt said, "Me too."

The dealer dealt the next five hands, allowing Dixon and Colt to win two each and the shill picking up one.

Dixon figured that at any time the shill would start raising the bet.

Sure enough, the shill said, "Hell, I have to get home, so let's make it interesting."

The stakes went up.

Dixon pulled in seventy-five dollars on the next hand.

Colt said, "Well, that cleans me out," and started to get up.

"Hold on, boy. You have property. I'll give you fifty dollars for your saddle and that Winchester."

Colt sat back down.

The dealer, looking somewhat concerned, glanced at his shill. Something had gone wrong.

He dealt another hand.

Dixon intentionally held his hand so that whoever was peeking could get a good look at it, and raised the bet. Colt passed and the dealer raised again.

The shill raised and bumped.

Dixon raised and bumped the shill. He'd been given three tens, an eight and a five.

The dealer knew what Dixon and Colt had and made sure that he dealt the shill what he was positive was his third ace. He kept two pair for himself.

Knowing what everybody had, the dealer saw and raised, giving the shill another chance to bump him.

Colt dropped out, having lost his second fifty. There was now over five hundred dollars in the pot. Dixon asked for two cards, the dealer took one and gave the shill one.

Dixon, who opened, bet fifty dollars. The dealer, knowing that Dixon had him beat but only wanting to sweeten the pot, saw him and raised another fifty dollars. The shill, having two pair, but convinced that the dealer knew he had the sucker beat, saw and raised another fifty.

Dixon saw the bet and said, "I have three tens with an ace kicker."

The dealer smiled, thinking the shill had three aces. "That beats me."

The shill sat looking bug-eyed and said, "That ain't possible."

The dealer, alarmed, said, "What are you talking about? Lay down your cards."

Dixon slid out his pistol and laid it in his lap.

The shill said, "All I have is two pair," and looked accusingly at the dealer.

The dealer, stunned and wide-eyed, said, "That's all you have? How can that be? I mean, with all that betting, something is wrong here."

Dixon stood. "Yep, there's been something wrong here all night." He casually held his pistol, generally pointing it in the direction of the dealer and the shill.

He told Colt, "Boy, pick up the money.

Mr. Dealer, if you don't want me to shoot you right now, you're gonna hand over that shaved deck. You're also gonna get your ass out of that chair and we're gonna look at that board under your foot. Then you and that asshole shill are gonna go with me into the back room and then we're gonna have a chat with your friend who's been peeking at our cards."

Colt had gathered the money by this time.

Dixon said, "Colt, I'll be all right. You go and get the sheriff. Before you do, tell Oliver to get his ass over here. I think he's part of this."

Dixon marched the three men into the peep room and found a homely, heavily-painted woman hanging a picture over the peephole. She looked up, obviously very frightened.

"Woman, get away from that wall," Dixon said. "I wouldn't shoot no lady, but that leaves you out. Get your ass over here and stand by these other assholes."

Dixon backed to the door and stood sideways where he could watch both the captives and the small group of customers who were gathered in the main bar.

He said, "We're waiting for the sheriff, the bar's closed. Drink up whatever you have going and get the hell out of here. Don't worry about your tab. It's on the house!"

About this time Sheriff Grimes walked in, followed by Colt. Grimes was not happy. "Dixon, what the hell are you doing now? Every time I turn my back, you're raising hell. Until you came along, I was almost retired."

"Sheriff, if you'll just remove that picture yonder off that wall, you're gonna find a peephole. If you'll check the floor right below it, you'll find a loose board on a rocker. You'll find another loose board under the table where the dealer sits. I think if you look real close, you'll find two rockers under those boards are gonna be connected by a wire or something. If you check those cards, you're gonna see the deck has been shaved. The low cards are shaved on the sides.

Sheriff, I watched these two sidewinders skin three of your good citizens out of over two hundred dollars. Cleaned them out. When I saw how they were cheating those poor fellows, I decided to get involved."

The sheriff glanced at Oliver, who said, "Sheriff, I don't know anything about this."

The dealer and the shill looked at Oliver and the dealer said, "The hell you don't!"

The sheriff checked and, sure enough, everything was like Dixon described. "Ollie, you're shut down. All four of you are under arrest."

Dixon handed the sheriff some money. "Sheriff, here's two hundred dollars. I figure Ollie can give you the names of them boys that got slicked. I'll be keeping the rest."

"No, you aren't. All that money is evidence. Besides, you're gonna have to stick around and testify."

"Sorry, Sheriff," Dixon said. "I can't do that. I have to leave in the morning."

The sheriff said, "If you don't testify, I don't have a case. I could hold you here as a material witness."

Dixon said, "Yes, you could, but I don't think you want to. We have a little boy out yonder that's been taken by a bunch of savages. I have a poisoner down south that's killed several people, including a few of his wives. I also have the Baker boys to pick up. That's not to mention a crazy Indian that's running around scalping and burning people. Now, if you insist on me staying, you're gonna have to arrest me. If you do, my partner here is gonna send a wire to Austin. I don't think the governor is gonna think your priorities are the same as his."

The sheriff thought for a moment, then said, "Well, then, I'm gonna have to turn them loose."

He turned and looked at the gambler and his shill and said, "I don't ever want to see you in my county again. If I do, I'll make up something to arrest you for."

He focused on Oliver. "Ollie, I'm shutting you down permanent as a public nuisance. I suggest you find somebody to sell this place to and follow your friends. If I see you around here a week from now, I'm gonna arrest you every time you spit. Take your whore with you."

The whore popped up and said, "I ain't no whore!"

The sheriff laughed. "Prissy, everybody in the county knows that you're a whore. If you had as many peckers sticking out of you as you had stuck in, you'd look like a porcupine. Now get out of here." The sheriff turned to the gambler. "Now, I'm gonna ask you one time and one time only. How much did you skin those other fellows out of?"

The gambler stared down at his boots and said, "Maybe a couple hundred."

The gambler suddenly had a flash of what he thought was a brilliant defense. He pointed to Dixon. "Sheriff, this isn't fair. Now, you have us cold on that cheating business, but this man was cheating too. How else could he have won?"

The sheriff looked at Dixon and said, "The skunk's got a point. If they were cheating so much, how'd you win?"

"Sheriff, you ask those boys whose cards they were. You ask them who dealt every hand. You ask them who cut every hand. Then you tell me if you have any evidence that I was cheating."

The gambler said, "He must have switched cards, Sheriff. Have him empty his pockets or take off his boots. He has to have those cards on him someplace."

Grimes motioned to Dixon. "Strip. If I find a single card on you,

I'm confiscating all that money."

Dixon nodded. "Whatever you want, Sheriff." He stripped all the way down. The sheriff checked all of his clothes and didn't find a single card.

"He has to have 'em, Sheriff. Maybe he gave 'em to that kid. They were together and sitting side by side."

Dixon looked uncomfortable.

Grimes looked at Colt. "Strip."

Colt shrugged his shoulders and did as he was told. Again, no cards were found.

The sheriff studied the gambler and Dixon, then Colt. "Well, ain't no doubt you figured a way to out-skin the skinners. Leave two hundred dollars with me and I guess you get to keep the rest. Now, I don't want to see you around here again, Mr. Dixon, unless it's on official business. I want you gone by the time I open my office tomorrow."

He looked at Colt. "Son, your pappy and all were fine folk, but the next time I see you, I don't want to see you in the company of this reprobate."

Grimes turned to the small group of onlookers and said, "This is none of your affair. I have some business with these gentlemen so everybody clear out. This establishment is officially closed."

*

Charley looked at his white man's watch. It was eleven o'clock at night and most of the lights in town had gone out, except for one building.

He could hear a piano playing and loud laughter coming from it. That was probably a white man's saloon and it was several streets away from the livery. It was time. He secured his horses in the brush and ran silently across the open field.

He decided to go to the general store first and steal or kill the horses last.

He reached the alley behind the livery and froze when one of the horses snorted. He crept like a shadow until he reached the second building.

It was obviously a white man's house instead of a store. A privy was next to the alley. Just as he reached the back of it, he froze again. He heard what sounded like a screen door opening. From his position he couldn't see who came out, but he could see the halo of light from a lantern. The light undulated as the person carrying it walked towards the privy, crunching the gravel as he approached.

Charley's heart was in his throat. He removed his club from his sash and waited. He heard the lantern being set on the ground and the door to the privy open. He stepped around the privy and saw a man standing with his back to the open door, urinating into the toilet.

Charley hit him in the back of the head. The man grunted and fell forward, but caught himself by extending both arms and bracing against the back wall of the privy.

Charley hit the man again and yet a third time before the man collapsed.

He grabbed the lantern and moved it inside the privy and closed the door. He took out his knife and quickly had the man's scalp. He picked up the lantern and dropped it into the privy.

He was just about to leave when he heard a woman's voice.

"Henry, are you all right?"

He stepped back inside the privy and gently closed the door. He heard footsteps on the gravel as the woman approached.

"Henry, honey. What's wrong? Are you alright?"

The woman opened the door. She never saw the club as it struck her in the forehead, killing her instantly.

Charley dragged her into the privy and quickly had another scalp.

He closed the door and, like a ghost, disappeared down the alley.

At the back of the general store, he tried the door and found it locked. He moved silently around to the side of the building, being careful to stay in the shadows. He found a window, but it was also locked.

If he broke the window someone might hear. Using his knife, he gently pried out the putty that sealed the glass to the wooden frame. He moved his knife very slowly, catching the dried putty in his left hand lest it rattle as it struck the ground.

Once he stopped as he heard footsteps on the boardwalk and froze.

The footsteps faded and he began working again.

Soon he had the pane loose. He gently pulled it from the window and set it quietly on the ground. Reaching in with his hand, he found the latch and twisted it. He raised the sash slowly, stopping to listen periodically. Soon the window was all the way open.

He listened again. Still hearing no sound, he eased himself into the window. His moccasins made only a whisper of noise as he landed on his toes inside the store. The interior was in shadows, but some light from the gas lamps on the street shone through the front windows.

Charley found two gunnysacks and started filling them with supplies. In the dark, he wasn't sure of everything he took. He bumped into some salted bacon hanging from the ceiling and took two of them. He rummaged around and found a blanket, shirts, pants and a hat. He found some boots in boxes and tried several before he found a pair that fit.

The next time he had to sneak into town he would dress like a white man.

He went to the gun counter, where he picked up two pistols. He couldn't tell the caliber but they looked like a .44 caliber. He took the pistols and a small keg of powder. He took four boxes of 56-50 rounds.

Charley finished filling the bags and eased them out the window. Not seeing or hearing anyone, he lowered them to the ground and silently dropped after them. He closed the window and disappeared down the alley toward the livery.

*

Fifteen-year-old Thomas Gray lay in the hayloft in the livery. He covered his head with his blanket in a futile attempt to shut out the loud piano and other noise coming from the Longhorn.

Sometimes he didn't think the fifty cents a night he earned by sleeping here was worth it. Nobody had ever tried to steal a horse from it in his memory. He wasn't sure what he would do about it even if they did. The old single-barreled shotgun hadn't been fired or cleaned in years. Its rusty barrel was full of dust and it even had cobwebs on it.

Damn, he wished those folks would go to bed. Thomas could hear the horses milling about and stamping their hooves.

He heard a whisper of a noise that could have been one of the many rats that made their home in the barn. Then his head exploded with a bright white light and he heard no more.

*

Charley had his sixth scalp. He left the body of the boy and quietly walked over to the stalls. Only four were occupied, one by that crazy blue-eyed horse. He wasn't worth taking and would be a lot of trouble.

He would take the other three and cut the throat of the crow bait.

He found three halters with lead ropes and soon had all three standing quietly in the center of the barn. He took out his knife and crawled through the wooden rails into the pen.

Charley had one leg inside when he felt an excruciating pain in his neck as the horse bit him.

He stifled a scream and lashed out with his knife.

The horse spun and kicked him just as he got completely inside the pen.

A well-placed hoof caught Charley in the right side, knocking him flat. The horse kicked him about the head and chest with his front hooves.

Charley again lashed out with his knife, striking only air.

Desperate, he managed to get to his knees and dive for the rail of the pen. Just as he went through, he caught a glancing kick to the side of his head. He fell to the sawdust outside the door.

The rails went down after the third or fourth kick and the horse came charging out, crow-hopping and kicking.

Charley managed to crawfish out of his way just in time. He watched as the crazy horse headed for the open rear door of the barn, spooking the other three horses as he went. All four horses galloped off into the dark.

Charley, gasping for breath and holding his side, staggered to where he'd left his supplies. One gunnysack was light enough to carry on his shoulder, but he had to drag the other. The pain in his side was so intense that he had a hard time breathing. In spite of it, he managed to reach his horses, tie on his supplies and head off into the desert.

*

It was after midnight when Dixon and Colt stepped outside.

Colt saw old Blue Eye crow-hopping down the street.

He said, "Hey, that's my horse. What's he doing loose?"

They turned around just in time to see three more horses running out of the livery. It took Colt, Dixon and the sheriff ten minutes to calm and collect Dixon's two horses and the third one belonging to someone else. It took all three of them another half-hour to catch Blue Eye.

Dixon, Colt and the sheriff walked the horses back to the livery. When they got there, the interior was dark.

While Dixon and Colt held the horses, Grimes struck a match and found the lantern. A second match soon had the lantern going.

Grimes said, "That Gray kid ought to be a lot more careful. How the hell did he let them horses get out? Why did three of 'em have lead ropes?"

Grimes held the lantern high and saw three open stalls. The fourth stall's gate was closed but the planks to the pen had been broken. "What the hell!" He stopped mid-sentence when he saw young Thomas Gray lying in a pool of blood.

"Oh, no!" The sheriff hurried over to the boy. His head had a flattened lopsided look to it. Grimes could see it had been bashed in and his throat had been cut from ear to ear.

"Oh, hell! Boys, we got trouble. This boy's dead and he's been scalped. Put them horses up. Colt, you and Dixon go down the street to the rooming house and the hotel. Get everybody down here that you can. Tell them to arm themselves and send some men out to warn everybody they can. We got serious Indian trouble."

Dixon said, "Colt, you go ahead, I'll be along." He went over and peered at the dead boy.

"I thought I told you to go wake people up," Grimes said.

"My partner can handle that. This boy's only been dead a few minutes. If you don't mind, I'll saddle up and see what I can find. I'll bet you my saddle that you don't have an uprising here. What you have is one crazy Indian. It's that Charley Tree fellow, I bet you. If I start now, I might be able to get a lead on where he's heading and I bet it's south. It's pretty dark, so I'll need the lantern."

Grimes said, "If you take that lantern an' whoever did this is still around, like as not, you're gonna get shot."

"Yeah, I know, but there is no other way to follow tracks in the dark. When you get everything organized here, tell Colt where I went and have him follow. I'll be moving slow and I'll leave a clean trail. If you have anybody to spare, send them with the boy."

Grimes reluctantly offered Dixon the lantern. "All right, but you're taking one hell of a chance."

Dixon nodded. "I'll be back for the lantern, Sheriff." He saddled his horses and then walked them over to the hotel and loaded all of their supplies on the packhorse.

He told the night clerk to get everybody up and have them meet the sheriff at the livery, briefly explaining what happened. Just as he was mounting his horse, Colt walked up.

Dixon said, "Colt, I left your guns up in our room. I have every-thing else loaded. Grab 'em and come on down to the livery. I have old Blue Eye all saddled up. I want to pick up a lantern before we leave. That son of a bitch can't be too far."

Dixon turned his horses back toward the livery while Colt ran up to their room.

Colt was able to catch up with Dixon just as he was coming out of the barn with the lantern. A few other men came running up.

Grimes shouted, "Hold it, everybody. Meet me out front. I want somebody to guard this alley until we have a chance to check it out."

*

Dixon had Colt hold the reins to the horses while he took the lantern and studied the tracks in the alley. He held the lantern low as he followed the tracks toward the general store.

He stopped by the outhouse, drew one of his revolvers, set the lantern down, eased around and suddenly pulled upon the door, ready to shoot.

What he saw made his stomach turn. He examined the bodies and saw that they were beyond help. Their brains had been bashed out, their throats cut and their scalps gone.

Dixon left the bodies and continued following the tracks.

He could see them going and coming, so he was pretty sure the Indian wasn't ahead of him.

Dixon found the window to the general store and noted that one of the glass panes was missing.

He returned to the livery and saw that the tracks led into the field.

Grimes came out of the barn.

"Sheriff," Dixon said. "We have two more dead bodies over in that privy yonder. It's a man and a woman. It looks like whoever did this killed them first, broke into the general store and probably stole everything he could get his hands on. Then he came back here to steal the horses. I guess the boy was just unlucky. It looks like who-ever done it got three horses out, haltered them up and was going for old Blue Eye. It looks like old Blue Eye had other ideas."

Grimes shook his head. "Those other victims have to be the Schneiders. That's where they live. God dammit to hell! That black-souled son of a bitch! What you say makes sense, Dixon. There's blood over yonder in Blue Eye's pen. There's also blood on the floor here, running outside. It could be blood from that poor boy's scalp but I figure it's likely old Blue Eye done hurt our killer."

"I think you're right, Sheriff. It looks like whoever done this was dragging something when he left. Probably supplies from the store. He might be hurt, because he didn't drag it from the store. If we get on with it, we just might catch him."

Grimes said, "Well, all of my boys are out looking for them six Indians that killed those folks up at Killeen. I'll get some volunteers and we'll try to catch up tomorrow. I have one part-time deputy that I'll leave in charge. We have to leave enough people here just in case it's more than one Indian. Remember Victoria? They plumb wiped that town out a few years ago."

Dixon said, "Yeah, you may be right. I still think we are talking about one Indian plus that bunch from Killeen. I don't think you have an uprising here."

Dixon lowered his voice so Colt couldn't hear. "By the way, Sheriff, them folks up at Killeen, was they scalped?"

The sheriff scratched his head. "I don't think so. They didn't say so, but I think they would have told me if they were. Crazy thing, though, they took the money. Indians usually don't do that."

"How do you know it was Indians?"

"Oh, it was Indians, all right. The stage driver was still alive and swore to it. The stage crew and passengers was all shot up but the folks that ran the stage stop were killed with clubs and arrows. The arrows were Apache, but they weren't Lipan. Looked like Mescalero. But I didn't hear about any scalps being taken."

Dixon said, "I'm sure this is the work of Charley Tree or Indian Charley. He kills them and after they're dead, he cuts their throat. He always takes a scalp. He's Apache, but not like any Apache I ever saw.

Well, Sheriff, you get however many men you can, then follow as best you can. Colt and me will head on out."

Dixon stopped and turned back to the sheriff. "I hate to impose on you again, but I'm expecting a telegram. I may not be coming back this way for a while. Could you have them forward it to Laredo? I ought to be there in three or four days."

"Yeah, I'll do that for you. As soon as the telegraph opens tomorrow, I'll tell 'em. I expect we'll pull out right after that. You won't make good time 'til daylight, so we shouldn't be too far behind you. We ought to catch up by sundown tomorrow."

"Okay, Sheriff, and if you can, bring a couple kegs of water. Our horses are gonna get mighty thirsty by then."

Grimes said, "If you're going south you'll find water down at Artesian Springs. After that, you have about forty miles to go before you find any for-sure water. There are a few creeks and buffalo wallows, but they tend to dry up when you need 'em most. I'll bring some empty kegs as far as Artesian Springs and fill 'em there."

Dixon and Colt left on foot, with Dixon holding the lantern, studying the tracks, and Colt leading the horses.

The trail of blood had disappeared before they reached the point where Charley had mounted his horse.

JIJTEEN

Charley alternated his horses between a walk and a trot. It was too dangerous to run them at night for fear of one of them stepping into a gopher hole. Trotting was the best choice, but the jostling of the uneven gait of the horses hurt his side so much that he could only take a few minutes of it at a time. He walked them most of the time as he headed west.

He stopped and painfully dismounted.

Using his knife, he cut a blanket into strips and wrapped his ribs as tight as he could. He found he could now breathe deeply without gasping.

He looked around in the moonlight and gathered some dead brush. He tied them into the remnants of the blanket and rolled the blanket into a tube, placing a few rocks into the bundle to give it a small amount of weight. He tied his lariat to the ends of the bundle and looped the rope around the saddle horn of his packhorse.

Charley then changed directions and headed south, dragging the bundle behind. He knew the bundle would leave its own mark but the hoof marks would be obliterated. The marks left by his drag would be spread out and shallow. Any slight breeze would soon erase them.

Once, when he rode up a slight rise, he thought he saw a light several miles behind him. It was seen for only the briefest moment before the pinprick of light disappeared. It might be his imagination, but somehow he didn't think so. He was being followed already. No matter. Soon they would lose his trail.

*

While Colt rode, Billy walked almost the entire way. It was almost daylight when Dixon held up his hand.

He told Colt, "Take a breather. Those tracks have plumb disappeared. Charley's probably made himself some kind of drag. Maybe when the sun comes up we can see better. I'll tell you one thing, though: this here is definitely our crazy Indian. That's the same tracks we followed from the Frio, no doubt about it."

They unsaddled and hobbled their horses, letting them graze on whatever vegetation they could find.

Colt spread a ground sheet and sat their saddles on it.

Dixon dug a hole and built a small fire. Although it was summer, the night air of the desert was chilly.

He said, "Let's make us some coffee and fry up some bacon. Maybe even have us a little sip of that whiskey while we're waiting."

Colt broke out the coffeepot and frying pan while Dixon got the coffee, bacon and his jug of whiskey. They pulled some coals aside from the main fire to set the coffeepot on.

"While that coffee's making, let's pull back away from the fire," Dixon said. "Being down in that hole the flames can't be seen, but if we sit too close the glow on our faces could be seen a million miles away."

They pulled back and sipped their whiskey in silence.

Colt wasn't used to drinking hard whisky and it felt as though he was swallowing barbed wire. It warmed his stomach, though, and after a while it began to go down a little easier.

Colt said, "Mr. Dixon?"

"Yeah."

"How did you do it? I mean with those cards?"

Dixon laughed. "Son, it was pretty simple. When I went to the pisser, I took my razor and shaved a duplicate set. I didn't know if they were shaving the sides or bottoms of the high cards or them low cards, but I knew they'd pick the lowest and highest. That meant all the cards from five on down to the deuce were shaved one way, and all the face cards and aces were shaved the other. So what I did was take my deck and shave all the cards from five through ten. I shaved the five, six and seven on the bottom, and the eight, nine and ten on the side. Every time I got a card from those old boys, I just substituted the same card of mine and kept theirs. We played eleven hands. By the time we got to the last two or three hands, I had most of their cards and they had most of mine. I would've had them all except that I'd get some of my own cards back."

"How could you tell that they were your cards?"

Dixon said, "I took my entire deck and made a hairline cut across one bottom corner. I couldn't see it but I could feel it. I want you to know one thing, boy: it wasn't like the sheriff thought. I never did cheat. I played every card they gave me. I only tossed the substitute back in the pile after each hand was played. Now, if they'd been honest, it wouldn't a made any never mind. But since they were cheating and going by their shaved cards, eventually I switched most of their cards and when they thought they were dealing a face card, they were really dealing a low card and vicey versey. Now, I figured they'd let us win the first few hands to get our interest, but by the time they got serious, I had most of their cards switched. I kept putting their cards in your right pocket. The way you were playing, nobody could accuse you of cheating. When the sheriff searched me I wasn't worried, but when he searched you, I almost shit myself. What did you do with 'em?"

"I felt you sliding those cards into my pocket and I knew you were up to something. When I went after the sheriff, I dumped them in the privy. Are you sure that wasn't cheating?"

Dixon said, "Nope, I played every hand they dealt me. I just let them cheat themselves."

"How much did you get?"

"You mean how much did we get? I don't know. Let's find out."

Dixon reached into his pocket and pulled out a roll of bank notes and double eagles. "Let me see, here's your twenty-two dollars, your fifty, and here's my hundred." He set that money on the groundcloth and continued. "I gave the sheriff two hundred to give back to those poor old boys that got skinned and we got, let me see here…" Dixon counted out the remaining money. "We got four hundred and twenty-five dollars even. That comes to two hundred twelve dollars each, plus one silver dollar that we'll flip for." He handed Colt his share.

"Mr. Dixon, you keep that extra dollar. You earned it."

"Nope," Dixon said. "Fair's fair and even is even. You call it, boy."

Dixon flipped the dollar in the air.

Colt said, "Heads."

They both looked at it. It was tails.

Dixon picked it up. "Well, I guess I do keep it."

The coffee was made and they drank that while Dixon fried the bacon.

When they were finished, Dixon scrubbed out the frying pan with sand, threw out the coffee grounds and replaced everything in the pack.

Colt covered up the fire pit, spread the sand around it, brushed their trail away and dragged some dead cactus over the area. It would take a sharp eye to see that someone camped there.

They saddled up just as dawn was breaking. Colt, counting out one hundred and thirty-five dollars from his pile, walked over to Dixon and handed it to him.

"What's that for?"

Colt said, "That's for you buying those guns and things."

"Oh, I almost forgot. Glad you didn't. Well, I reckon now we're even."

"No, sir, we're not even by a long shot."

They mounted their horses and followed the faint marks of the drag. While Dixon kept his eyes on the ground, Colt watched the horizon in front, both sides and to the rear. It was his job to make sure that no one was sneaking up on them.

To pass the time, Colt would unload one revolver at a time and practice drawing and firing. Although the horses were walking, he would simulate a canter or gallop by exaggerating his body movements to the horse's movement; then sight and fire just as his body reached the apex of his movement.

He would practice replacing his revolver in the holster, without looking, while he moved up and down in the saddle. He'd been doing this in all of his free time since Dixon had showed him and he was pleasantly surprised to notice that he could do it almost without thinking.

He was proud to note that, although he might not be fast, he was smooth. Every part of the movement was correct. His gun came into alignment with his eye with no conscious effort on his part. How many times had he done this, he wondered. A hundred? No, more like a couple thousand. Dixon had said that it would take a hundred thousand times before he would even begin to be pretty good. He kept practicing.

About noon, the wind started picking up and soon Charley's tracks were completely gone.

Dixon shook his head in disgust. "Well, it looks like he shook us. I figure we are about even with those artesian springs that the sheriff was talking about. It ought to be eight or ten mile over to our left."

He motioned with his head. "Why don't we head over there and meet up with the sheriff? Our boy's making a beeline south. If he don't get some water real soon, he's going to have to slow down or kill those horses. I figure we can meet the sheriff, let our horses water good and probably still catch him. Besides, he'll wear out his drag pretty soon and by that time he ought to feel safe enough to quit using it. We'll pick him up again, you can be sure of it." They turned the horses east and headed for Artesian Springs.

*

The sand, picked up by the desert wind, stung Charley's eyes.

Squinting, he saw what appeared to be cottonwood or willow trees in the distance. Either one could indicate much needed water.

His horses were almost played out and normally he wouldn't care, but he had too much to carry and the way his side hurt, he was in no shape for walking.

For some reason, his testicles hurt and it really hurt to urinate. Every time the horse took a step, it felt like someone kicked him in the groin.

He rode on for another half-hour before he reached a small recession. The water was brown and shallow.

It was a buffalo wallow. He could see hundreds of hoofprints and the water stank. He picketed the horses away from the water, removed his knife and started digging a hole about fifty feet from the nearest water. It was slow and painful digging, but after an hour and almost full dark, he could feel the water seeping in.

He groaned as he stood, then walked to the muddy pond and sat in it. The water had a cooling effect on both his groin and his ribs. His head had quit hurting but his right eye was swollen. His eyebrow was painful to the touch and there was crusted blood on his face. He knew better than to use the water from the shallow pond to wash it.

Charley sat in the water for a good hour, then stood and went back to his horses. Only then did he unsaddle them. It was slow and painful work, but he finally got it done.

He led the horses to the hole, where they drank thirstily.

After tending to the horses, he made camp and spread the saddle blankets on the ground and sat down to rest.

He finally got enough energy to build a fire. He dug into his supplies and withdrew a few of the cans. He examined them by the fire, trying to read the labels.

Fortunately, two had pictures. One looked like tomatoes and one looked like a fruit. The third had a picture, but he couldn't tell what it was. He read it slowly: 'Po-arkan-been.' He had never seen a 'Po-arkan-been.'

He opened it with his knife and tasted it. It was good, this 'Po arkan been.' He ate the peaches and tomatoes. He thought that it was much better than raw snake. He'd rather have buffalo or even beef, but this was good. When he'd finished, he took out his scalps and examined them. He laid their raw sides up to dry, checked his weapons and slept.

*

Colt and Dixon found Artesian Springs about two hours before sundown. The water was sweet and the grass was almost belly-high to the horses. They let the horses drink, unloaded them and made camp.

They cooked a good meal of hoecake, sow belly, potatoes and canned tomatoes.

Dixon put on a pot of beans to simmer overnight. He told Colt, "Them beans will be real good, come morning.

Well, let's get you some target practice in," Dixon said. "We finally got enough ammo, time, and there is nobody in miles." He patiently went through the procedures and was surprised at how smooth Colt drew his revolvers and fired.

From ten feet away he could draw and fire, without aiming, with very good accuracy.

Dixon said, "Hells bells, son, that's pretty damn good. I can't do a whole lot better. You only hit that little old can seven times but if it had been a man, all ten would have been killing shots. Try it again. This time, load up all six chambers on both those guns."

Colt did and this time he did even better. He got ten out of twelve with two close hits.

They worked on close-in shooting for an hour, replacing the can with various pieces of logs. They then switched to long-distance shooting. Colt did almost as well as short-distance shooting. Before they quit for the day, Colt could smoothly draw and fire either revolver and hit a six-inch target at thirty feet, every time. He still wasn't fast but he was smooth and accurate.

Dixon said, "That's enough for today. Next time we'll work on your off-hand shooting."

Colt said, "My what?"

"Your off-hand. You're right-handed so your off-hand would be your left hand. You'll find that both guns can be reached real easy with either hand. If you carried them with the butts to the rear, they'd be a little faster to pull—but if you ever take a hit in one arm, you aren't gonna get to the one on the other side with your good hand.

Some man-killers prefer both guns butt forward for just that rea-son. It isn't quite as fast but you can damn well get to them with either hand. Hickock and a whole bunch of others won't carry them any other way. You have to make up your own mind about that. I'm just telling you."

Colt practiced the reverse draw with each hand. It was awkward at first but after a hundred times, it became somewhat smooth and comfortable. During his turn at watch, he worked on that draw the entire period.

The next morning, Dixon showed Colt how to carry the sawed-off shotgun. Colt placed the duster over it and soon he could easily swing it into play. Since he carried it on his right shoulder, Dixon taught him to move to his left as he reached for it.

"If you move quickly enough, it does two things: one, just the motion itself causes the right side of your coat to open, making it easier to get your hand on it. It also might throw off somebody shooting at you. It works for your revolvers, too. If you're pulling your right gun, move left. Left gun, move right. It's only a little edge, but it's an edge. Now, give me that duster."

Colt was surprised to see Dixon take out his clasp knife and cut out the pockets on both sides of the duster.

"This way, boy, you can draw your guns with your hands in your pockets. Just another little trick, but it might save your bacon. Now, today, as hot as it is, I want you to wear this duster over that shotgun. Keep it unloaded, because I don't want you shooting me or your horse.

Now, let's load up and get out of here. I don't think that sheriff is gonna show. We'll just have to drink up as best we can and haul the rest. Our horses been tanking themselves up all night, so they'll be okay for another day."

*

Sheriff Grimes and his four volunteers were half way to Artesian Springs when he heard a shot. He turned and saw Mr. Jacobson, the owner of the mercantile store, slump over.

All five men kicked their horses in the flanks and charged forward, hopefully away from the unseen shooter.

Jacobson managed to hang on for a few moments then fell from the saddle.

Five apparitions rose out of the sand ahead of the posse.

Grimes had pulled his revolver at the first shot. Others in his posse pulled their various weapons. They all started shooting at the five Indians who were calmly shooting at them.

One of the Indians dropped and two of the sheriff's posse were shot out of the saddle.

Grimes let the packhorse loose and urged his horse on through the ambush. The horse jerked a few times but stayed on his feet.

Grimes felt something hit him in the jaw, almost knocking him out of the saddle. Something struck him in the left side, again almost knocking him out of the saddle. He fired his revolver and hung on. He looked over his shoulder and saw only one man still in the saddle. It was Oliver. Of all people, it had to be him.

Grimes galloped on another few hundred yards. Finally his horse slowed down, stopped and dropped to its forelegs.

Grimes slid off, pulling his Spencer from its scabbard as the horse went down. It was lung shot and a red froth blew from its nostrils.

Grimes grabbed the two saddle revolvers and shot the horse in the ear.

Oliver came galloping up. "Get on, Sheriff! They got one coming with horses; they'll be on us in a min—"

Oliver's head exploded in mid-sentence, followed by a shot. He fell from his horse.

Grimes ran to Oliver's horse and was climbing into the saddle when something slammed into his head. He fell to the ground and lay still.

*

The five Apache approached the bodies. They stripped and mutilated them but didn't take their scalps. They took everything else, including what money they found.

*

Douglas Patterson sat on a horse nearby, his hands tied to the pommel and his legs tied to the stirrups. He was having a hard time holding back his tears.

He didn't know what was going happen to him, but it couldn't be any worse than seeing his mother raped repeatedly then killed with a rock to her head. Now this. Before a few weeks ago, violence had never been part of his life.

The Apache got down off his horse, holding the lead rope in his hand.

Douglas knew they would kill him, but anything was better than this. He kicked his horse in the flanks and his horse lunged forward, spooking the Apache's horse. Both horses ran off together.

It took the Apaches, all on foot, a moment to realize what was happening. They scrambled for their guns and started firing at Douglas.

The noise bolted the remaining horses that had been ground-tied.

Douglas, unable to guide the horse, just leaned low in the saddle and kept kicking the horse in the flanks.

It took the Indians several minutes to gather up the spooked horses. Four stayed at the ambush site to try to round up the posse's horses. One took off after Douglas.

*

Douglas kept the horse going as fast as he could and let the horse choose the direction. The Apache's horse was galloping alongside. Douglas twisted his little hands under the rawhide binding until his wrists bled. He kept twisting and pulling, not realizing that the blood soaked the rawhide, allowing it to stretch and also making his hands slippery. Soon he had one hand free. It wasn't long until his other was free as well.

He grabbed the horse's mane and pulled back and yelled, "Whoa."

The horse eventually slowed and then stopped.

Douglas untied his legs from the stirrup and dismounted.

He mounted the Apache's horse and was pleased to find a Spencer rifle in the scabbard and a large leather canteen hanging off the pommel. The saddlebags were filled with something but he didn't wait to find out what it was. All he wanted to do was to get away from the Indians.

Douglas headed south, hanging onto the lead rope of his spare horse.

He galloped as fast as the horse could run, not worrying about gopher holes or anything else.

The horses ran for a good half-hour but soon began to tire.

Douglas looked around for a place to hide. There was none. He eventually spotted some trees ahead of him and made for them.

He saw it was only a small creek, but the horses needed rest and water. He glanced over his shoulder and saw a single speck on the horizon. He knew it was an Indian.

Douglas slowed the horses to a walk to let them blow.

He pulled out the Spencer. It was just like Pappy's. He wasn't a good shot but he had tried it a few times and knew how to load it.

By the time the horses reached the small creek, they'd cooled down enough for Douglas to let them drink.

He looked back and the Indian was close enough that Douglas could distinguish between horse and rider.

Douglas felt a sick lump in his throat. His hands were shaking. He got down off the horse and removed the canteen and saddlebag. He hoped there would be some spare ammunition in it.

He ran about twenty yards up the creek and lay down below the small embankment. He grabbed a handful of mud and worked it into his straw-colored hair and over his face.

Maybe the Indian would take the horses and go away. He waited.

SIXTEEN

Delmar Boni knew that he would catch the boy. He didn't want to kill him, for he could sell him in Mexico.

The white boy was only a child and tied to the saddle so Delmar didn't bother taking any precautions.

His horse had almost been run to death but that would be all right. When his horse fell he would trot on foot. The boy's horses were just as tired and he knew that it would be only a matter of time.

*

He saw the trees ahead. If there was water and the boy stopped, he would catch him. If the white boy continued on without watering the horses, the boy would be afoot within another hour.

If the boy wasn't at the creek Delmar could let his horse drink and rest a few minutes, then go after him. He smiled as he thought how he would beat the boy for running away. Secretly, he admired the boy for his courage.

He was almost to the creek when he saw the brown rump of one of the horses in the trees. He smiled. The boy had apparently given up. He walked his horse to the creek, grabbing a branch.

"Hey, white boy," he called. "It's time for your beating."

He was smiling when he stepped down from his horse into the creek. The horses were there but the saddles were empty; so was the scabbard for the rifle. His smile faded. He felt a prickly feeling between his shoulder blades.

That was the last thing he felt. He didn't hear the shot that killed him.

*

Douglas saw the Indian come into sight not twenty feet away. He was so scared he thought he would vomit. He managed to get his shaking hands to point the rifle in the general direction of the Indian. He heard the Indian call out, and then saw him freeze. His shaking fingers pulled the trigger before he was ready. Out of reflex, he also closed his eyes.

The recoil rocked him backward. Douglas was sure that he was going to die. He curled up, hugging the rifle, and cried, expecting to be beaten or killed at any moment.

He lay there for several minutes. When the beating didn't come he opened his eyes. He slowly sat up and looked around. He couldn't believe it! The Indian was face down in the water, a large hole between his shoulder blades. Very little blood was on his back, but the water was red. He worked the lever of the Spencer, racking a fresh round in the chamber. He crept to the Indian and poked him with the gun barrel.

He'd really killed an Indian! He didn't feel at all bad. In fact, he was elated. He wasn't going to die.

Douglas climbed the shallow bank to check if the other four were coming.

He could see no one. He stripped the Indian of his knife and revolver. He also took the bandoleer of bullets. He wasn't sure they would fit his rifle until he rolled the Indian over.

It was the one they called Delmar Boni. Douglas had shot him with his own rifle.

He gathered the parfleche from the Indian's horse and the spare canteen.

Douglas put the best saddle on the best of the three horses. He unsaddled the remaining two and let them graze to their hearts' content. He mounted the horse and headed south.

*

He rode his sorrel at a walk. He kept looking over his shoulder, expecting to see Indians at any moment. He was more confident now with his Spencer. *Next time*, he thought, *I'll keep my eyes open.*

He rode until dark. He hadn't found water but he did find grass next to some trees on a dry creek.

He picketed and unsaddled his horse. He emptied the saddlebags for the first time.

There was a white canvas bag that was very heavy. He opened it and saw it was filled with twenty-dollar gold pieces. He found his mother's handbag, with her money. He found another bag and opened it. It was filled with cornmeal and some kind of dried meat.

He took the now-empty saddlebag and filled it with water and let the horse drink. The horse drank an entire canteen, leaving only one for him.

Douglas had food but no matches, and nothing to cook it in even if he could start a fire.

He peeled bark from a dead tree and poured a fist full of cornmeal in it. He slowly soaked it a few drops at a time with water from his canteen. He ate half of the dried meat while the cornmeal was soaking. When he finished the meat, he ate the mush-like meal. He rolled up in the horse blanket and slept.

*

When Charley awoke, his groin ached and he had to urinate. The sun wasn't up yet, and he was covered with the morning dew. Fog wafted from the ground like smoke.

He slowly got up and limped a safe distance from his camp and tried to relieve himself.

It took a full ten minutes to empty his flaming bladder. He couldn't believe how much his groin hurt.

He limped to the saddle that carried the cans and jars he had stolen.

Charley thought, *Maybe there was some white man's medicine.*

He found a square bottle containing amber liquid. He looked at the label. It said: 'Horse Liniment.' He tried to pronounce the words. "Hoars Lien Eh Meant. For sorree mussels."

He pulled the cork out and smelled it. It was maybe a drink. He tasted it and spat. It wasn't for drink. It was maybe medicine. He unwrapped the strips of blanket around his chest and dropped his loincloth. He poured the liniment into his hand and rubbed it on his sore side. He took another handful and rubbed his crotch with it.

He felt an immediate cooling effect that made him think this was good medicine. Soon the cooling effect changed to an intense burning sensation.

It was as though coals had been thrust between his legs.

Charley ran as fast as he could to the stinking pond and sat.

He grasped mud and packed it over his groin. The cool water and mud helped, but not enough.

Apache warriors were supposed to have a high tolerance for pain; but in that moment he had no thoughts about being an Apache and he screamed as loud as he could.

The pain was so great that he couldn't sit still and he thrashed around in the pond, splashing water on his testicles and screaming.

It took almost a half-hour for the burning sensation to drop to the barely tolerable level.

Finally, he quit splashing. He was gasping for breath. He gently lifted up his pecker and testicles to examine them.

He could see that they were almost twice their normal size, and his pecker was swollen so much it scared him. The skin was an angry red from the white man's devil medicine.

Suddenly, Charley felt that he was being watched. He slowly turned and saw four mounted Apaches staring at him.

He smiled and started splashing back to the shore, talking to them in his Athapascan dialect. He was afraid that with his short hair, they would mistake him for a Mexican. If they did, then he was dead.

They kept their guns on him as he waded to shore. He finally convinced them he was Apache and had left the Bosque Redondo. They relaxed and lowered their weapons.

Later, he showed them the six scalps he'd taken. They were curious as to why he needed scalps. What good were they? In their practical minds, this was an impractical Apache who took things you could not use.

They had a quiet discussion among themselves. This man was no doubt Apache but he acted more like Comanche. Maybe he was bad medicine. They could let him ride along, kill him, or send him on his own way.

They'd lost two of their men and strength lay in numbers. He had his own supplies and was no doubt a good fighter to have so many white scalps. They finally agreed.

They walked back to the crazy Indian and said, "We have decided. You may ride with us or go your own way. But you act like a crazy Apache."

Charley Tree said, "I go south to join Goyathlay. If you go that way, I go too."

They told him they were going to Mexico to find a larger group of Apache to join. Goyathlay would be as good as any.

They waited while Charley saddled his horse and packed his supplies. The pain in his groin had subsided to a dull burn. He rewrapped his ribs which, surprisingly, felt better. They rode south.

*

Colt and Billy had ridden all day. They had managed to find water at a little place called Encinal.

It was only a couple of shacks set up as a stage relay station.

An old Mexican and his wife ran the combination stage station, saloon and restaurant. Colt and Dixon rested, grained their horses and had some of the best Mexican food they had ever had. They had warm beer and they drank three mugs each, quenching the jalapeño peppers.

It was about twenty-five more miles into Laredo, so they decided to spend the night in the stables and ride in the following day. It would be a long day but they could do it.

They finished their meal and went to the barn. They spread their blankets in the hay and were asleep immediately.

*

Ja-mas-pa was already tired of the one who called himself Charley Tree. The entire day that he'd ridden with them, he'd only complained about his testicles hurting or bragged about those scalps.

Three were of women and two were of old men. The last was, according to its size, a young or very small boy. He and his Dog Soldiers had killed many men, toe-to-toe in combat. All this braggart could talk about was how he had cut their throats after they slept. What use did one have for scalps? Maybe he should scalp Charley Tree and let him live. Maybe then he wouldn't talk so much.

He looked back over his shoulder to see how well-hidden his Dog Soldiers were. He couldn't see any of them. He wanted to leave Charley Tree with the horses but the others didn't trust him. At least the crazy Apache wasn't moaning and groaning now. He turned his attention back to the small buildings about a quarter of a mile away.

The sun was just beginning to come up and it felt good on his bare back. The night had been cool and the two hours they lay in the desert had chilled him. It was too early for the gnats and flies to become a nuisance and he was glad of that.

They'd come upon the settlement the night before, quite by accident, and had decided to wait until morning to see if it was worthwhile and possible to take.

He could see two small buildings and what appeared to be a barn. One of the buildings had smoke coming out of the chimney, so there were people there. The shack was so small that he doubted there were many inside. The other building appeared to be a small store or a large storage shed. He saw no smoke, so probably no one was inside.

He counted several horses in the corral. They were milling around so much, going in and out of sight behind the building, that he couldn't be sure of the number. He guessed that there were eight, or possibly ten. The barn was large enough to have stalls, so there might even be more.

He saw several chickens running about the yard, and a pigpen next to the barn.

A cow was grazing behind the house, tied to a rope.

Ja-mas-pa was too far away to smell the smoke in the still morning air, but he could hear the tinkle of the cow's bell. It was this sound that had given them warning last night, for they'd seen no lights.

This was similar to the stage relay station that they'd hit in Killeen. They'd almost gotten into trouble then, for they'd not expected the stage to arrive.

They'd been armed only with their bows and clubs when they sneaked to the cabin. Fortunately, the man they killed had plenty of guns. When they heard the stage arrive, they'd been able to surprise the driver and guard.

With the hostler's guns, they made short work of the crew and passengers. Had it arrived five minutes earlier, they would have had to fight with only their bows and clubs. At such short range, and in the open, they could've been wiped out.

His mind came back to the present when he saw a man leave the barn, walk a few yards and stand as though he was relieving himself. The man walked back into the barn, only to reappear moments later with what appeared to be a rifle. This person was taking long, purposeful steps as though measuring distance.

Ja-mas-pa counted one hundred such steps, and watched the man bend down as though placing something on the ground. The man stood and paced off another one hundred steps and bent down a second time. The man stood and repeated the process.

The man returned to the barn, where he disappeared.

Moments later, he came back into view with a stool.

The man rested his elbow on his knee and sighted the rifle.

Ja-mas-pa saw the rifle recoil and saw the smoke. The sound followed an instant later. Ja-mas-pa couldn't see the target, so he thought it must be very small. If it was that small, the man must think of himself as a good shot.

He watched as the man fired several rounds, then adjusted the rifle's sights and fired several more rounds.

On one of the shots, Ja-mas-pa thought he saw something shiny spin in the air near the middle target.

It must be one of those cans used by white men to store food. *Yes,* he thought, *this man was a very good shot. He could be trouble.*

*

Dixon woke up at the first sound of gunfire. He grabbed his revolvers and ran to the barn door. He was both relieved and agitated to find that it was only Colt sighting in his new, or at least almost new, Winchester. Dixon stood quietly out of sight to watch. Actually, the boy wasn't doing too badly.

He watched Colt "walk" the first can with each shot. It looked like it was at least a hundred yards away. He watched as Colt reloaded and readjusted his sights, then shot a second can. It was almost two hundred yards away. He saw the can flip and walk away with all but one shot, which seemed close, but no hit. The last shot picked up the can and threw it into the air at least twenty feet.

While Colt was reloading, Dixon said, "That ain't bad, boy. I ain't showed you how to shoot a rifle yet, an' it don't look like I need to."

Colt adjusted the sights for a third time and took aim before he replied.

"I ain't never shot a handgun much before, but I done a little shooting with Pappy's old Spencer. We didn't have much money to waste on ammunition, so Pappy only allowed me one bullet to hunt rabbit for dinner."

Colt stopped talking as he fired. The third can spun in the air. He worked the lever and aimed again. "That old Spencer would rightly tear up a rabbit if you hit him anywhere but the head, so I had to learn to put my one bullet where it counted."

Colt fired and again saw the can spin.

"Well, it ain't no Spencer—but out to about three hundred yards, it ain't too bad."

Dixon said, "Hell, I think I'll let you carry that Buffalo gun I bought. My old eyes can't even see that far. Come on, let's see if we can get us some breakfast before we pull out."

They walked around the barn just in time to see the hostler's wife carrying a milk bucket and short three-legged stool around the house toward the cow. As they approached the house the old hostler came out of the house, stretching his suspenders over a red-and-black-checkered shirt.

Dixon and Colt approached him and Dixon asked, "You reckon we could buy some breakfast before we leave?"

"Si, no problemo. Mi espousa... excuse me, señor, for my bad manners. My wife, I mean, would be happy to make breakfast. Only one dollar, OK?"

Dixon said, "Yeah, that would be fine."

"Come with me, my friends. I will start the fire in the cafe. My wife will be along as soon as she gets the milk. You fellows like milk?"

Dixon said, "Nope, never much cared for it."

"I do," Colt said. "I like milk probably best of all. Especially buttermilk."

Dixon feigned a disgusted look. "Here I am trying to make a real man out of you and all you can think about is milk."

Colt said, "Mr. Dixon, that ain't all I think about. There's something else I think about a whole lot more. As a matter of fact, just about all the time."

Dixon laughed and said, "Well, boy, when you get to be my age, the things that you dream about get fewer and fewer."

They all walked to the combination bar and cafe and went inside.

*

Charley lay not far from Ja-mas-pa. He wondered why Ja-mas-pa didn't like him. Hadn't he shown him the scalps and told how he had taken them? Of course, he'd embellished a little, but didn't he have proof?

Maybe he should leave the group. He would've left earlier but they were four against him and he was afraid they'd want to keep his supplies.

His mind wandered from this to the pain in his testicles. He felt like he had to urinate all the time. He was glad to remain perfectly still.

He also saw the man come out of the barn. It was too far away to be sure, but it looked like Man Who Sits on Log. Soon, he saw a second man. This must be the man who killed his cousins. This was good.

He slowly raised his Spencer and sighted. He wasn't going to shoot, for the distance was too great—even for the Spencer. He only wanted the pleasure of having his sights on this white man. Suddenly, a force knocked his barrel in the dirt. He looked up to see the scowling face of Ja-mas-pa.

"Your name is a good name, Charley Tree," he snarled. "You think like a tree."

Charley said, "I wasn't going to shoot. Never touch my gun again or I will have seven scalps on it, not six."

Ja-mas-pa quickly pulled his knife and had the point on Charley's jugular before he could react.

Charley felt the point break the skin. He could see Ja-mas-pa's lips quivering in anger and the look of death in his eyes. Suddenly, the moment passed.

Ja-mas-pa withdrew the knife, but kept it in his hand.

Charley's fear turned to white-hot anger. He had an impulse to shoot Ja-mas-pa, but he had enough of his sanity to know the others would kill him in a blink of an eye. A shot would also warn the white men. In his present condition, he certainly would be no match for Ja-mas-pa without his gun.

He forced his anger to cool. He would have his turn. No one spoke to him that way, especially in front of others.

Charley said in an even tone, "Now is not the time for us to see who has the big mouth. If we fight now, the white men will hear."

Ja-mas-pa nodded. "Later. We fight later, I promise. For now, we fight the white man. We'll wait to see how many. I see three white man. I see one white man's woman. That's all, maybe, I think. We wait."

Charley nodded. He would wait.

*

After breakfast, Dixon and Colt saddled their horses and headed toward Laredo.

As they rode out of the yard, Dixon said, "I figure we got maybe twenty or twenty-five miles to go. If we make it today, it'll be way after dark. We're getting a later start than I wanted." Dixon looked at his silver railroad watch. "Hell, boy, it's damn near nine o'clock. It'll be hotter than hell before long." Dixon snapped the cover back on the watch and placed it in his vest pocket.

"That's a nice watch, Mr. Dixon."

"Yeah, well, I thought so too when I took it off an old boy who didn't want to go back with me. I didn't figure he'd mind."

"It sounds like you had a lot of people who didn't want to go back."

Dixon nodded. "A few."

Colt studied Dixon. "If you kill 'em, how do you collect any bounty? I mean, if you have to plant 'em, how do they know you caught 'em?"

"Boy, I don't think you really want to know."

"Well, Mr. Dixon, if you don't mind, I really would like to know."

"Son, truth is, if it ain't too far, I'll roll 'em up in burlap and string 'em on the back of a horse and ride on in."

"Won't they start stinking after a while?"

Dixon said, "It depends. If it's real cold, they keep a while. Hot like it is now, I don't want to haul 'em more than a couple of days. They get putrid real fast in the heat. Had to bring one back from Louisiana once. Hotter than hell and the humidity was so thick you wouldn't believe it. That carcass turned plumb black and was stinking so bad after the first day, I just couldn't stand it no more."

"What did you do?"

"Hell, I buried that son of a bitch." Dixon gave Colt a sideways glance. "At least, most of 'em."

"What do you mean, most of 'im?"

Dixon stopped his horse. He put both his hands on his pommel and leaned forward, taking the weight off his rump.

"Well, son, I had a big jar of pickles in my saddlebags. It gave me an idea, so I stopped at the first town I came to and bought me a five-gallon water keg and two gallons of alcohol. I just put his head in that barrel, poured some alcohol over it, and took it on in to Austin. That fellow was worth five hundred dollars and I needed the money."

He laughed. "You sure ought to seen the look on my captain's face when I pulled that old boy's head out of that water barrel. Lost his lunch, he did."

Colt stared at Dixon with wide eyes. "You mean you cut his head off?"

Dixon removed his hat and dragged a sleeve across his forehead. "I don't know any other way to get it off. Do you?"

Colt, feeling a little queasy, said, "No, sir, I reckon I don't." He considered this for a moment. He couldn't imagine any man would cut somebody's head off and put it in a water keg. "Mr. Dixon, I think you're pulling my leg."

"Nope, son, I ain't. Matter of fact, I always carry me a little rubbing alcohol or formaldehyde and a water keg just for that reason."

Colt glanced over his shoulder and, sure enough, there was a wooden water keg tied to the packhorse. The way it was bobbing, it seemed empty. It also didn't look wet from seepage like it would if there was water in it.

"Well, Mr. Dixon, I ain't sure I could cut nobody's head off even if they were dead. Not even for five hundred dollars. I sure wouldn't want to be asleep some night all alone in the desert with somebody's head nearby. I can just hear them hooty owls and coyotes now. No, sir! If you're gonna be carrying somebody's head around, I ain't sleeping near you."

Dixon grinned. "You superstitious, boy?"

"I don't know. I just know I wouldn't like it."

For the next two hours they rode in silence. Suddenly, Dixon stopped his horse and cocked his ear. "Boy, did I hear somebody shooting or was that my imagination?"

Colt heard it too. It was a long way off and behind them. Suddenly, they heard the crackle of several guns firing.

Dixon said, "Son of a bitch! Sounds like a war back yonder. Oh Lordy, I bet them folks we left are in a lot of trouble."

"Let's go back and help 'em."

Dixon shook his head sadly. "Son, it took us almost three hours to get here. At a dead run it would take us an hour to get back, even if the horses could make it in this heat. Getting there an hour from now isn't gonna help no one. Any fight going on will be over by that time."

"There has to be something we can do."

"Son, there is some things you can change and some things you can't. There isn't anything we can do to change what's going on back yonder. It might be them heathen Indians they were telling us about. If it is, they're well-armed, and the last I heard there were six of 'em. That's three-to-one odds, boy.

An' I'll tell you something else: I'd take five-to-one odds against white men over three-to-one against an Apache. No matter what you say about them, they are tough when it comes to a fight. They know this desert an' you almost have to step on one before you can see 'em."

"Mr. Dixon, I know you're right, but maybe them back yonder are the ones killed my ma and took Douglas. I have to go back. I can't leave if there's a chance of getting him back. If you'll let me take some of the food and a couple canteens of water, I'll go back. I'll meet you in Laredo later if I can."

"Nope, I said we were partners and no partner worth his salt would let you go back alone. I reckon that you have to do it, so I have no choice but to tag along and do my best to keep your little ass out of trouble."

Colt was relieved but felt like he ought to resist, just a bit. "Mr. Dixon, you've done enough. You go ahead and I'll catch up with you."

"Nope, I can't do that. Two against whoever it is, is twice as many as one. Let's get going, boy."

Colt turned his horse and put his heels to the horse's flanks.

Blue Eye charged about twenty yards before Colt heard Dixon yell, "Goddamnit, boy, hold on! Hold on a minute."

Colt stopped his horse. Dixon came up to him and said, "Like I said, son, at a full gallop we'd probably kill our horses and it ain't gonna help them people a whit no matter what, so just slow down. Do you notice anything?"

Colt was aware that the gunshots had ceased.

Dixon said, "Whatever has happened has already happened. It's all over, one way or another. Let's just walk our horses on back. If it's who we think it is, they are coming our way, for sure. Why don't we swing off to the east a little instead of backing our own tracks?"

SEVENTEEN

Ja-mas-pa saw the two white men ride off. This was good. What he wanted was the horses and the cow. They could drive them and have meat on the hoof. There'd be enough to last them to Mexico, with enough horses to trade. Anything they found in the house would be extra.

He didn't care about the two white men, but crazy Charley was fit to be tied. He wanted to follow them instead of using his head and going for the livestock. Ja-mas-pa knew he would soon kill this crazy Indian.

They would wait for a while to let the two riders get far enough away. He would not be surprised this time. They were five. There was only one old man and one old woman against them.

He would send one Dog Soldier around the station and position himself a mile down the stage road. He would send one a mile north. If a stage came from either direction, the lookout would shoot one of the horses from the stage. The shot would sound a warning, and at the same time it would slow the stage. It would take the stage crew a while to remove the dead horse, especially if they were under fire.

The remaining three would approach on foot to the one building where the man and woman seemed to spend the most time. One would set fire to the barn and release the horses. The fire and commotion should cause both the man and the woman to rush out, where they could be brought under crossfire. If one remained in the building, they would set it afire; when they came out they would be killed. Either way, it was a good plan.

*

The cool breeze woke Douglas up. He had to think a moment before he realized he was not in the hands of the Indians. He quickly grabbed the Spencer. It was dark and he could hear the horse urinate. He also had to urinate. Which made him think about water. He had one canteen left. That old horse drank a whole canteen the night before and still seemed thirsty. He decided that they would split the remaining canteen.

After watering the horse, he ate the rest of the dried meat.

He wasn't sure what it was because the Indians had butchered a pig, a cow and one of the horses that had been killed at the stage relay station. He thought it was horse. He'd never eaten pork or beef that was this stringy. It was good anyway.

He soaked some more cornmeal and ate. He saw that he'd eaten about half of his supply of meal and all of his meat.

Douglas figured he had one more day of food unless he found a town or a farm. If he failed at that, he would have to try to shoot something. He wasn't sure he could hit anything, even if he saw it.

He was also deathly afraid that if he fired the Spencer the Indians might hear it. He didn't ever want to see Indians again, as long as he lived.

His hair and face were still covered with dried mud. His head itched and he wished that he could spare the water to wash it off.

Douglas saddled his horse and, keeping the sun to his left, headed south.

*

Ja-mas-pa was satisfied. His plan had worked almost perfectly. When the barn blazed up the old couple instinctively ran outside, where they were shot to pieces. The old woman surprised them by managing to stumble back into the building.

He had to admire her, for—shot up as she was—she had charged out the door with a shotgun and shot Esquinosquizn, point-blank, right in the stomach. His backbone was blown right out and stuck up like a stick.

Charley pounced on the already dying old woman and hit her in the head with his club.

Ja-mas-pa watched as Charley cut her throat and yanked her scalp off. *Why does he do that? The scalp is worth nothing.*

Charley looked at Ja-mas-pa, waved the scalps and yelled.

Ja-mas-pa spat. Where was the courage to take the hair from dead people? Charley hadn't even killed the old man, and he'd only technically killed the old woman.

With the death of Esquinosquizn, he'd now lost almost half of his group. Even though Charley Tree was crazy, maybe he wouldn't kill him just yet. He may need him before they reached Mexico.

They gathered all the weapons and ammunition from the station. They filled pillowcases and blankets with goods and trinkets and loaded them on the horses.

Ja-mas-pa searched for money. He knew how much the white man valued money and he could exchange it for weapons and food. It was too bad that the yellow-hair boy got away. He would have brought a lot in trade. To make matters worse, the boy had stolen the horse with all the money from the stage.

He had to admire the little maggot. How such a young boy, unarmed and tied to a horse, could have gotten away and killed one of his best Dog Soldiers was amazing. He knew he could never kill the boy even if they caught him. He acted more like Apache than a white man's son.

He found no money, not a dollar. He knew there must be a secret place but he had no more time. They rounded up the horses and the one cow.

They killed all the pigs and took two, leaving the rest. They chased the chickens, trying to kill them with their clubs. For a few minutes they made a great game of it, but the chickens were far more elusive than they'd anticipated. After killing only two, they gave up.

They torched all the buildings and immediately started east to get away from the road. They would travel east for an hour or two before turning south.

*

Dixon said, "Look yonder."

At first Colt couldn't see anything. Then he saw the smoke. It was still several miles away. To be seen at this distance, it had to be a big fire. The smoke was mostly brown, with gray and black streaks.

"If that was just the barn and hay," Dixon said, "that smoke would be brown. Those black streaks mean that other things are burning. They done torched everything. I guess we know who won the war."

He sighed. "Boy, I doubt if them Indians is gonna stay on the road. You can bet they are heading south, so we got us a fifty-fifty chance that they cut east or west a while before turning south. If they cut west, we're gonna clean miss 'em. If they cut east, you can damn well bet they are coming our way. So check your pieces, son, and keep that Winchester unlimbered. I'd strap that shotgun to your shoulder, and load up your pockets with all the spare ammo you can hold. It wouldn't hurt none if you strapped on one of them canteens, too."

"Why? I have my saddlebags full and my canteen's right here on my saddle."

"If we get into a shooting war, there is a good chance your horse could go down. Them few seconds it's gonna take you to get to them saddlebags and canteen could get you killed. Give yourself an edge, son, always give yourself an edge."

Colt did as he was told. He didn't know if he would ever get to thinking like Dixon. He was *always* thinking ahead.

"Boy, I figure that if it was them Indians, they done grabbed those horses at the station. If they did, they got about ten horses that they are driving, plus what they are riding. That ought to kick up more than a little dust. Keep your eyes peeled for even the slightest thing that looks like dust. It might be all the warning we get. If they send out a scout ahead, we won't even get that notice. They'll be on us like stink on dog shit."

They rode on slowly, trying not to make any dust of their own.

After a few minutes, Dixon said, "Look over yonder, just to your left and a little ahead. Is that dust I see?"

Colt studied where Dixon indicated. "Mr. Dixon, I don't see nothing."

Dixon said, "Take a good look, boy. Your young eyes have to be better than mine. Tell me if it don't look a little hazy off yonder just to your left an' a little in front?"

Colt looked again. "No, sir, I don'... Wait a minute. It does look a little hazy over there."

"If it's them," Dixon said, "it looks like they're about a mile ahead an' a half mile off to our left. Why don't we just Indian over and see if we can sneak a peek, without stirring up a hornet's nest?"

They turned their horses west. It was only a few minutes before they were sure. A definite dust cloud was slowly coming their way. Dixon said, "Well, boy, I don't see any ravine or any place we can set up an ambush. If your brother is with 'em, as soon as we start shooting they'll kill him for sure. I have an idea. Why don't you an' I go up real close to where they're gonna cross. We'll dig me a little hidey-hole and you cover me up and clean up the area. Pull them horses out of sight, and then come back up on foot within your shooting range. If they spot me, maybe you can keep 'em off until I can rabbit out of there."

"Why don't both of us dig in an' just ambush 'em?"

Dixon shook his head and sighed. "Boy, that would be real foolish. We don't know how many they are and with both of us buried in a hole, how we gonna run? We have to find out who they are, how many they are, how they are armed and most important, whether your brother is amongst them. Always remember, boy—before you go into any battle you have to get a look-see. You have to learn about who you're fighting and what you're up against. You just go banging in with guns blazing, you're gonna die real soon. Nope, this is just a look-see. We gonna let 'em pass right by.

After we know everything we can find out, we'll decide what's to be done. Now, let's get busy; we don't have a whole lot of time."

After they dug a shallow depression, Dixon wrapped his Henry and two revolvers in a blanket and lay down face-first in the trench.

Colt shoveled about three inches of sand over him.

"Now, dammit boy, don't put too much weight on me. I have to be able to stand up real quick if they spot me.

Son of a bitch! You're putting so much sand down my drawers I ain't never gonna get it out."

"Excuse me, Mr. Dixon, but I'm only doing what you told me."

After Dixon was covered, Colt planted a dead cactus right over Dixon's rump.

Dixon, looking over his shoulder, said, "Now, why in the hell did you do that?"

"Because, this way, if you have to cut and run I figure you will be doing enough yelling with the cactus sticking to your ass, I'll know to commence shooting."

Colt, laughing at his own joke, smoothed the area around Dixon's head—the only part of him that was exposed.

"If you put any more cactus on me, I'll be shootin' something besides Indians."

Colt placed some brush over Dixon's head.

Dixon spit more dust out of his mouth and said, "Move it just a little more to the left."

Colt did as he was told.

"Now, dust everything up and get out of here. For God's sake, don't shoot unless they do. Just let 'em mosey on past. We can follow later. Now, get back out of sight."

Colt was impressed with Dixon and himself. As soon as he stood up after placing the brush over Dixon's head, he couldn't see anything. So this was how the Apache did it. No wonder they could just appear out of the ground and swarm over some poor traveler.

He walked back about two hundred yards—dusting out his tracks as he went with some mesquite brush—then moved the horses back far enough so that they couldn't be seen.

Colt's only worry would be if his horse caught the scent of the Indian horses and whinnied.

He let a little sand drift out of his hand. Good. The breeze was northerly. It ought not to allow either group of horses to smell the other.

He walked back within two hundred yards of where the Indians were expected.

Colt spread a blanket on the ground behind the ridge of a small sand dune. He laid out his Winchester and both of his revolvers. He placed a small clump of mesquite in such a manner that he could see beneath it and watch part of the trail.

He waited. The sun beat down on his back and he could feel the heat even under the fabric. He'd taken his hat off to keep his silhouette down. Sweat ran down his forehead and into his eyes, making little rivulets in the dust covering his face. Gnats swarmed around him, teasing his nostrils and his ears. He could hear the tinkling of the cowbell and the muffled sound of several horses walking.

Colt knew they were close. He gripped his rifle and tried to peer through the mesquite. He could see nothing.

He kept watching, licking his dry and blistered lips and trying to ignore the gnats. He briefly saw only the top of one Indian's head.

He'd really misjudged his position. He'd thought that he was in a perfect spot, but didn't realize how the undulating sand dunes could fool you. What looked like flat land, wasn't.

Except for that one quick glimpse and the cowbell tinkling, that whole bunch could have passed completely unseen.

He would've never believed it. His blood ran cold. If the Indians spotted Dixon, he wouldn't be able to help him. If he tried to change his position, the Indians would see him. How could he have made such a blunder!

Colt decided that if he heard shooting, he would fire a shot blindly to distract the Indians and then charge them.

It would probably get him killed, but maybe it would at least draw them away from Dixon.

He lay for an hour. The cowbell had faded almost a half-hour before. He raised himself to a crouch, placed his revolvers in his holsters, picked up his rifle and, very slowly, made his way to where he thought Dixon was.

Dixon surprised him by sitting up right in front of him. Dixon said, "You're too damn impatient. You should've waited at least another hour. For all we know, they could have decided to roast one of them horses or that cow a hundred feet away."

Dixon was whispering and Colt found himself whispering too.

"Nah, I heard that cowbell disappear a long time ago. They have to be a mile away by now."

Something over Colt's shoulder caught Dixon's eye. "Get down," he hissed.

Colt immediately dropped to the ground. A lone Indian rode toward them, heading in the same direction as the others. Colt and Dixon were only fifty feet away and in plain view.

The Indian turned his head toward them. His body tensed and Colt knew they'd been seen.

He swung his Winchester up but before he could fire, Dixon's Henry cracked.

The Indian fell from the horse like he had been hit with an ax.

Dixon said, "The fat's in the fire now, boy. Run for your horse. There is three ahead of us and I don't know how many are behind us."

Colt asked, "Where did he come from?"

"I told you, boy. You're too damn impatient. They had a drag rider watching their tail. Get to your horse, quick. They sure as hell heard that shot and they are gonna come a-running." Dixon and Colt ran as fast as they could to where their horses were tied.

Colt had run right over the blanket that he'd earlier laid down, willing to abandon it for speed.

Dixon grabbed the blanket as they ran by.

As Colt was about to mount his saddle, Dixon handed it to him and said, "Tie this around your neck. Leave most of it to fly behind you like a cape. Come on, be quick, boy."

Not knowing the purpose, Colt did as he was told. He saw Dixon tie his own blanket around his neck as well.

Colt said, "What's this for?"

"No time to explain, boy; just do it."

They had no more than goosed their horses into a dead run when Colt felt the wind and buzz of a bullet, followed by the sound of a rifle. An instant later, more sounds like bees flew past; followed by more shots and the sounds of hooves and yelling from the Indians in pursuit.

Dixon was ahead of Colt—leaning low in the saddle with his blanket flying behind him like a cape—when Colt felt the wind of another bullet that narrowly missed. He heard a distinct 'splat' and saw Dixon suddenly sit straight up in the saddle, simultaneously with the sound of yet another shot.

Dixon weaved once to his right than back to his left, almost falling from the saddle. He recovered, and was once again hugging his horse's neck.

When Dixon was shot and sat up, his horse slowed for just a moment, allowing Blue Eye to catch up. Colt pulled up alongside and yelled, "Are you all right?"

Dixon's face was pinched in pain. "I'm okay, boy; keep going."

Suddenly, the Indians' rifles were silent.

Colt risked a look over his shoulder as Dixon's horse caught up with him.

Dixon shouted, "They're out of ammo. Now they'll use their arrows."

Colt glanced back and, sure enough, he saw one of the lead riders reach for an arrow as he brought his bow up, holding the reins in his teeth as he did so.

Colt hugged Blue Eye's mane and tried to prod the horse to go faster. The old no-account nag was losing ground at every stride.

Dixon was ahead and to Colt's right. Dixon managed to draw one of his revolvers and fire a wild shot behind him.

Blue Eye was slowing even more. Colt knew the Indians would be on him at any moment.

He felt something hit him in the back but didn't feel any pain. He saw an arrow fly past and, for some reason, he was fascinated to see it stick in the ground fifty feet ahead.

He was aware of Dixon, even further ahead, firing over his left shoulder. It occurred to Colt that maybe he should be firing, too. He drew his pistol from his left holster and fired over his shoulder without looking.

Suddenly, Blue Eye lunged forward.

Amazingly, Colt saw that he was gaining on Dixon. He passed him and was soon a full length ahead and gaining. Colt was exhilarated. The old crow-bait might have some belly after all.

Colt fired another wild round over his left shoulder and saw

Dixon's hat fly off. Dixon had cut in behind him without Colt knowing it.

Dixon ducked and yelled, "God dammit, boy, watch where you're pointing that damn thing!"

Colt saw that Dixon was laughing. The Indians were dropping back, apparently realizing they weren't going to catch their quarry in a horse race.

Dixon and Colt rode on for another ten minutes.

Finally, Dixon, still laughing, yelled, "Hold up, Colt, I think we outrun 'em."

Colt pulled back on Blue Eye's reins but the horse was bound and determined to keep on running. He had to seesaw the reins—first the right rein, then the left—until the horse slowed and finally stopped.

The horse was blowing hard.

Dixon came up and said, "Well, I guess we know what will get that crow-bait of yours attention."

"What do you mean?"

"Get down and see for yourself, boy."

Colt got down and saw an arrow sticking out of the cheek of the horse's rump.

Dixon chuckled. "Another inch to the left and that Indian would've had a bulls-eye." Now Colt knew why old Blue Eye had decided that he could run after all.

Dixon got down and walked over to Blue Eye. Fortunately, due to the distance and the horse's speed, much of the energy of the arrow had been expended and the arrow didn't penetrate past the arrowhead.

He pulled it out and got kicked for his trouble.

Dixon handed Colt the arrow and said, "Here, boy, you can keep this for a present."

"I don't want it or nothing to do with no damn Indian."

Dixon threw the arrow aside and examined Blue Eye's rump. "Nothing hardly to worry about. I have some creosote salve that'll fix that right up—but not right now. We have to get out of here."

Colt removed his cape, and was surprised to see an arrow sticking from it.

Dixon smiled and nodded his head. "That's why I wanted you to wear that blanket, boy. It don't help much against bullets, but they're mighty effective for deflecting arrows."

Colt's stomach ran cold as Dixon said, "It ain't no guarantee, just another edge."

About that time, the packhorse trotted up.

Dixon said, "Hell, I thought we lost her. I guess she could run better than I thought. Come on, boy, let's get out of here."

Colt said, "I swear, I thought you got shot back there."

"I did, and it hurts like hell, but we ain't got time to worry about it."

"Let me take a look, Mr. Dixon." Dixon raised his shirt and Colt saw several bloody cuts in Dixon's back. He saw Dixon's little back-up pistol missing part of its ivory handle. It looked as though a bullet had hit Dixon smack over his right kidney, striking the pistol he always carried in his waistband and sending small pieces of lead and ivory everywhere. Many of these small pieces had embedded into Dixon's back.

"Well, it looks like you're gonna survive, but I ain't sure about your little pistol."

"What do you mean?"

"That Indian damn near shot your pistol out of your pants. I'd say that it was a good shot. Hell, that Indian did it off a running horse, too."

Dixon reached back and grabbed his gun. "Son of a bitch, that dirty, no-account, heathen bastard! That was my favorite weapon. You know how much them ivory handles are worth?"

Colt said, "No, but at least most of that bullet didn't get into your hide."

"Shit, boy, hide grows back for free. That damn pistol was worth money."

They climbed back on their horses and, keeping a wary eye, turned due west.

Dixon was quiet for a moment, then said, "Boy, all I seen was three Indians go by me and then that one I shot. That's a total of four. Either they're a different group than the ones that took your brother, or they lost some on the way down. I didn't see your brother with 'em, so likely it's a different group."

"Either that, or they done killed my brother."

Dixon hadn't wanted to say as much. "Well, you know it's also possible your brother got away from 'em."

Colt said, "Yeah, it's possible but not likely. Not a twelve-year-old."

Dixon secretly agreed, but said, "Well, let's don't bleed before we're cut, boy. Don't ever bury anybody 'til the body is cold and stiff. You just can't ever tell."

Dixon used one hand to feel the wound in his back. "I figure them Indians is just gonna keep on heading south. They got their hands full trying to handle all that stock, and now there are only three of 'em. I doubt if they will risk scattering their stock to get us. Since there is only three and we are two, it's close to even. A little thinking on our part, we can make it better than even. Why don't we just follow them for a while? Maybe we can get a long shot at 'em with that .45-70 I have."

Colt said, "I want one of 'em alive. I have to find out about Douglas."

"Yep, I agree. Maybe I'll shoot one of 'em real low so he doesn't die right off. Maybe if we ask real polite, he'll tell us what we want to know."

*

They rode west until they cut the tracks of the livestock that the Indians were driving. It was getting close to dark, so they rested and watered their horses and opened some canned beans, peaches and tomatoes. The juice from the tomatoes and peaches was a nice change from the warm water from their canteens.

After tying one of Blue Eye's legs, Dixon applied some creosote ointment to the horse's rump. He then took off his shirt so Colt could pick out the lead and ivory fragments from his back.

"Do you have anything I can put on it?"

"Hell, boy, if that ointment is good enough for your horse, it ought to be good enough for me. Just smear some on and let's get out of here. I figure them Indians ought to bed down soon, an' I don't think they are gonna be expecting us. I figure they think they scared us clean out of the state. Just in case, though, we ought to be real careful. By the way, boy, listen for that cowbell. You can hear that sucker a mile off."

They mounted their horses and rode south, following the tracks. They followed the trail until it became too dark to see. They stopped and fed the horses a little grain from their dwindling supply and watered them again.

Dixon said, "Why don't we just wait here for a while? When that old moon comes out, we ought to be able to see better. That much livestock leaves a pretty clear trail. Tell you what, Colt, you stretch out and get an hour of shut-eye while I watch. We'll switch later and I'll get an hour. By then, the moon should be up."

Colt agreed and rolled up in his blanket. He was soon fast asleep.

EIGHTEEN

Ja-mas-pa was beginning to think his medicine was bad. They'd been more than successful in their raids as far as horses and weapons, but he'd lost four of his original five followers. He had only one dog soldier and a crazy Indian left. He no longer thought of Charley Tree as an Apache. He was just a crazy Indian. It was all they could do to handle so many horses and the cow. Maybe they should kill the cow and eat it. Three couldn't eat much off the cow and they didn't have time to smoke it. It would mostly go to waste. Besides, if they didn't eat the chickens and pigs they killed at the station, they would soon be bad.

He wondered where the white men had come from. They fought like Apache. They hit and then ran away. He hoped they were still running. Most white men would.

He was thinking about the white men when Eskiminzin came to him and said, "There's a creek with grass and water a short distance ahead."

Ja-mas-pa decided they would camp there. He and Eskiminzin would take turns standing watch. The crazy Indian was worthless. Since they had chased the two white mans, all he had done was moan and complain.

He watched the crazy Indian slumped in his white man's saddle with his face tight with pain. Maybe crazy Indian fucked woman with rotten legs.

*

When the small band of Indians arrived at the creek with their ramada, they ran the stolen ropes around four trees making a small makeshift corral. It took them only minutes before the herd of horses was secure.

The cow's udder was swollen with milk and it was bawling, so Ja-mas-pa tethered the cow to a tree and called Eskiminzin over. "Do you know how to take milk from the cow?"

Eskiminzin said, "I see white mans make milk. I never make milk."

Ja-mas-pa didn't really want milk and he didn't care about the cow's discomfort. It's bawling could be heard for miles and he wanted it to shut up. Also, that bell should be removed. It was far too noisy. If he couldn't get enough milk out to shut the cow up, he would have to kill it. That would be too bad. If they ever caught up with Victorio or Goyathlay, the cow would feed a lot of hungry Indians. He told Eskiminzin, "Make milk from cow or kill it."

Eskiminzin caught the cow and started pulling on its teats. Surprisingly, milk started squirting if he held his fingers just right, squeezing from the top down.

Ja-mas-pa was delighted. He quickly got a cooking pot and carried it over to Eskiminzin to collect the milk.

Later, they roasted one of the pigs and drank their fill of the milk.

Charley ate sparingly. He was in a lot of pain and all he wanted to do was lie still. He hurt so bad, he had lost all thought of killing Ja-mas-pa or joining up with Goyathlay.

It was almost midnight when Ja-mas-pa went to the cow and cut the rope holding the bell.

He threw it as far as he could. He heard it clinking as it struck the ground.

*

Dixon held up his hand. Colt started to say something but Dixon motioned him to be quiet. He thought he heard the bell but it was only a couple of sounds. Not like it was on the cow's neck, but he was sure it was the bell. He climbed down and motioned Colt to get down also.

With Colt following, they led their horses back the way they came.

They walked without speaking for half an hour before Dixon stopped.

"Hell, boy, we damn near walked right in on 'em. I heard that bell and it weren't more than a hundred yards ahead of us. I smelled wood smoke, too. Let's park our horses here and flank around 'em to the east. Maybe we can get a look-see. Do you have any moccasins, boy?"

Colt whispered, "No, I don't."

Dixon pulled a pair out of his saddlebags. "Well, as soon as you get a chance, you ought to get a pair. They come in real handy at times like this. Them boots of yours are gonna make too much noise. Get a couple pair of them wool socks we bought and put 'em over the ones you're wearing. The stickers shouldn't go through, but the goat-heads might."

Colt knew all about goatheads. They were a nasty little three-pronged thorn about a quarter-inch in diameter and looked like a goathead with its whiskers and two horns. They could go through a thin-soled boot, and even three pairs of socks wouldn't stop them.

Dixon gave Colt a stern look. "No matter what—not even if you're snake bit—do you make a sound. You do, we're gonna have a real fight on our hands."

Colt did as he was told. He took a canteen and filled both pockets full of shells. He hung his shotgun over his left shoulder, grabbed his Winchester and said, "I'm ready."

Dixon said, "I'm gonna leave my Henry and take the Whitworth. We might get a long shot at 'em. It's only a single-shooter, so if they rush us you'll have to do the fast shooting. I'll do the long shooting. Come on, let's go."

They walked a mile to the east then turned south. They'd traveled south less than a half-hour when they found a small creek.

"Now I know why they stopped," Dixon whispered. "Let's Indian over real quiet like and see if we can spot 'em. No talking from here on and stay back away from these trees. There are too many dead branches and twigs. They'll hear us for sure."

They crouched low and crept slowly north.

After a while, Dixon stopped and whispered, "I think I see 'em. I figure about five hundred yards to our left, and south a little. Let's just stay here 'til it's light enough to see an' then maybe we can pop 'em good."

They squatted behind a small rise and waited.

Eventually, Colt could see a hint of dawn in the east. He turned his eyes to the Indians' camp and saw movement.

Dixon whispered, "I think they're getting ready to pull out. They are already saddling up their horses. Shit, it's too dark to get a good shot. It'll be another fifteen or twenty minutes yet. Son of a bitch!"

The blaze of a campfire flared.

Dixon said, "Hell, they ain't leaving. They're gonna cook break-fast. The damn fools didn't even dig a hole for that fire. Man, they sure don't act like any Apache I ever seen. They have to be the same bunch."

Colt watched Dixon check the Whitworth, put two of the paper cartridges between his teeth, and lie flat on top of the sand dune.

They waited.

As soon as it was light enough to see his sights, Dixon raised the rear sight up to the five hundred-yard notch, and aimed the rifle.

One of the Indians started over to the crude corral with what appeared to be a pot.

Dixon put the bead of his front sight right on the Indian's belly-button and gently squeezed the trigger.

The huge bullet hit the Indian exactly where Dixon aimed, knock-ing him down. The sound deafened Colt and the recoil rocked Dixon back. "Fat's in the fire, boy, get ready!"

Dixon rammed a second load down the barrel before he finished the sentence. The two remaining Indians were on their horses even before the one on the ground quit flopping. One rode east and the other south. They were out of sight before Dixon could get off anoth-er shot.

"Well, would you look at that. Scattered like a bunch of quail.

Nope, they aren't regular Apache, by a long shot. Let's get on down there before that Indian bleeds out. Keep an eye out, because those other two might circle back."

Dixon and Colt cautiously crept down to where the Indian lay. "Keep your eye in that corral, boy. I think they were only three but I could have missed one and he might be in amongst them horses. I hope that Indian hasn't bled out yet. I hit 'im low, but I seen even leg shots kill a man in a couple of minutes. Keep an eye on that son of a bitch, too. I seen people damn near dead rise up and get off a shot. Watch his hands, they're what's gonna kill you."

Dixon held his Whitworth out in front, always sighted on the Indian's head, and approached as though he was stalking game.

The Indian was lying on his back in a pool of blood. His right leg was bent so that his knee was sticking up with the foot flat on the ground. The other leg was sticking straight out. The Indian was moaning and trying to sit up.

Dixon and Colt circled around to approach the Indian from behind his head.

"Indian," Dixon called. "If you speak English, don't you move none. If you move your hands an inch, I'll blow your head clean off. You hear me, Indian?"

The Indian gasped. "Shoot, white man! I think you maybe already kill Eskiminzin. Hurt pretty damn bad."

Dixon didn't see a rifle but the Indian had some type of revolver in his waistband.

"Colt, get that fellow's gun away from him. Get that knife, too."

Eskiminzin said, "Don't worry, white man, Eskiminzin's hands already dead."

After Colt disarmed the Indian, they moved around where they could face him. He was young, no more than eighteen or nineteen. It looked as though he was trying to grow a mustache and beard.

Colt said, "I ain't never seen no Indian with whiskers."

"Oh, I seen a few, boy. Most of 'em pull 'em out, but not all."

The Apache had short hair and wore a red cotton headband. He wore a blue denim shirt, a dark blue pinstriped vest and white man's denim pants. He wore a loincloth in spite of his pants and the typical high Apache moccasins with strips of cloth wrapped around both calves to his knees.

The entire front of his shirt and groin area was soaked with blood. Colt could see a huge hole just below his bellybutton. Thick, dark-red blood pulsed out of the hole.

Dixon said, "Looks like I hit an artery. He isn't gonna last long, so if you have any questions you better ask 'em quick."

Colt looked down at the Indian, whose lips were clenched tight in pain. "Did you fellows have my brother with you?"

"Eskiminzin not know brother."

"A little white boy, about this high." Colt demonstrated by holding his hand about four feet from the ground. "Yellow hair."

The Indian tried to smile and said, "Little Indian killer, your brother?"

"I don't know about no Indian killing, but I think you people took him and killed my ma."

The Indian said, "Your brother make good Apache. All tied up on horse. Stole horse. Kill one damn good Apache."

Colt felt a surge of hope. "You mean he ran away?"

The Indian nodded his head through his pain.

"When? Which way did he go?"

The Indian said, "Yesterday, he go south—Mexico maybe, I think."

Dixon asked, "How many with you here?"

The Indian said, "Only crazy Indian and Ja-mas-pa. Eskiminzin no like crazy Indian. Bad Apache. Take scalp. Scalp no good for nothing. Crazy Indian have bad balls. Always complains."

Dixon and Colt exchanged a glance. "What's this crazy Indian's name?"

Eskiminzin said, "Charley Tree. Bad Apache. No good for nothing Indian."

"Where are they headed?" Dixon asked.

"Eskiminzin no say."

Dixon said, "You will say, all right. If you don't say, and say right now, I'm gonna drag your ragged ass over to that fire yonder and stick your face in it. Then I'm gonna cut out your eyes and stick 'em in your mouth."

Eskiminzin studied Dixon, assessing him. "Crazy Indian go to meet Goyathlay. I think Goyathlay kill crazy Indian."

"What about the other one?" Dixon asked.

"You burn Eskiminzin, still no say!"

Dixon said, "I mean it, you son of a bitch."

"No say!"

"All right, I done told you. Now you're in for it." Dixon handed the rifle to Colt. "Here, boy, hold this Whitworth and keep an eye out. This Indian's gonna tell me everything we want to know." He reached down to grab the Indian by his feet. He stopped and looked at the Indian's face. He leaned over and studied the half-open eyes. Dixon said, "Shit, I think the son of a bitch done died on us." He took his finger and tapped the Indian's half-open eye. The Indian didn't flinch. "Yep, he's gone."

Dixon stood up and said, "I'd say we is having a pretty good day. Looks like your little brother not only got away but killed himself an Indian in the process. We got all them horses back and a whole shit-load of supplies. There're still two Indians out there and one is a bad son of a bitch. Even the Apache don't like him. It looks like every-body, including your little brother, is going south. Let's go get our horses and load up whatever is worth taking and head these horses on down to Laredo. I'd bet the stage line would pay up a couple of dol-lars to get 'em back. Pick up that Indian's revolver, boy, and put it on your saddle for a spare. You may need it one day. Get all his bullets and knife, too."

Colt picked up the revolver. It was unlike any gun he'd ever seen. It had no hammer spur and the grip was ivory.

Dixon looked at it. "Son of a bitch. That's one of them Hart IXL's. I seen one of 'em once—it's double action."

Colt asked, "What do you mean, double action?"

"It means you don't have to pull the hammer back. All you have to do is squeeze the trigger. Here, let me show you."

He took the revolver from Colt, checked the loads, aimed at a nearby stump and pulled the trigger. The hammer came back all by itself, then suddenly dropped, and the revolver bucked in Dixon's hand.

Dixon said, "I can't say I much like the long trigger pull, but it's a fine weapon. Was I you, I think I'd keep this one in my belt for a backup. Except for the caliber, it's a mighty fine gun. It's maybe better than the ones you're already carrying. Anyway, let's load up and get."

Colt asked, "What about the Indian? Shouldn't we bury him or something?"

"Nope, he sure wouldn't bury you. Besides, the critters got to eat, too."

They gathered the horses and headed south. Colt pulled up alongside Dixon and said, "Mr. Dixon, you weren't really gonna put that Indian's head in the fire, were you?"

Dixon looked at Colt real hard. "Damn right I was. Don't you never tell a man you're gonna do something you don't have the stomach for. If you ever get in that habit, come a time nobody's gonna believe you. He would've burned you. Out here, son, it's a hard life. I'll give any man a chance to be square. If they aren't, I'll do anything I have to do. If you ain't willing to do that, you sure as hell ain't gonna last long out here."

They rode on in silence, Colt giving a lot of hard thought to what Dixon said. "Mr. Dixon, I reckon I would've burned him, too, to find my brother, but he didn't know where he was."

"Nope, but that crazy Charley, or that other one—Ja-mas-pa, or whatever his name is—might run across your little brother before we do. I sure wouldn't want that. Even if they don't, you can bet your ass they're gonna hurt somebody else if they aren't stopped. Damn right I would have burned that bastard. Apache aren't like a lot of people. They take a whole lot of convincing to get them to cooperate."

"Well, sir, he told us right out where that Tree fellow went."

"You see, boy, that's because he don't respect that crazy son of a bitch. The other one, Ja-mas-pa—he had respect for him. There weren't no way he was gonna tell us about him without some heavy convincing."

Colt thought about this.

After a long while, Dixon spoke up, "Boy, why don't you call me Billy? Every time I hear you say 'mister' to me I feel older and older. I feel old enough without you pushing me along. Besides, all my friends call me Billy."

"Yes, sir, Billy."

"And stop that 'yes, sir' business, too. 'Sir' sounds as old as 'mister!'"

"Whatever you say, Billy. I guess I have a habit of calling older men 'sir.' My pappy and ma said it was proper respect. I sure enough respect you, Mr...uh, Billy."

"Well, boy, showing respect to a man is like loving a woman. It isn't what you say that counts. It's what you do. 'Course, women do like some pretty talk sometimes. I'm trying to get in the habit for that widow woman I told you about. Comes kind of hard for me, though."

Dixon fell silent and cocked his head in concentration. "Whoa up, boy, I think somebody's coming. Whole bunch of 'em too. Let's get the horses into some brush."

NINETEEN

Colt could see a lot of dust about a half-mile ahead. He and Dixon moved the herd about two hundred yards into the mesquite, ran a quick rope corral around them and tied their horses to a scrub.

Dixon took his Henry. "You stay here, boy; I'm gonna cross the road on the other side. Now, I'll be directly across from you, so if you have to shoot, remember where I am. Don't be wasting any ammo on me."

Colt lay down where he could watch the trail. Dixon was out of sight almost immediately.

He heard metal clanking and saddle leather squeaking amongst the sound of shod horses stepping in the sand. The steel shoes on the horses would click occasionally as they struck a small stone. Colt heard voices. He could hear English being spoken and it wasn't long before a column of soldiers came into view.

He heard Dixon yell, "Hello, there, soldier boy! Hang on. I'm a white man, so don't shoot."

The captain held up his right hand and clenched his fist. The column stopped. The captain sat rigid and made no effort to reach for a weapon. The civilian, however, began sneaking his right hand to the butt of the rifle sticking out of the scabbard. Colt lined up his Winchester on the man's head.

He yelled, "I don't want to shoot you, mister, but if you touch that rifle I'll blow your head off."

The man's hand froze. The captain said, "Show yourselves! Men, hold your fire!"

He turned to the man on his left and said, "Horace, keep your hands clear of that damn rifle."

"Okay," Dixon called. "I'm coming out. Ain't no need to get tense. Boy, come on out, it's okay."

Colt stood up and walked toward the soldiers. He and Dixon reached the soldiers at almost the same time.

Dixon stopped near the captain. "Where're you fellows headed?"

"Well, gentlemen," the captain said. "I think you ought to tell me a little about yourselves first."

"I'm a ranger. My name's Billy Dixon and my partner here is Colt Patterson. We're headed south to try and collect a couple warrants. We picked up a herd of horses that I think belongs to the stage line. Thought we'd drive 'em down with us and maybe collect a couple dollars for our trouble."

The captain said, "Gentlemen, you're very fortunate to have gotten this far. There's a band of Indians that jumped the reservation in New Mexico and have been raiding and burning halfway across Texas. We've been dispatched to intercept them."

Dixon said, "With all due respect, Captain, I wouldn't hardly call it no 'band.' More than likely, I'd call it only two. It was nine or ten, but it's only about two now."

The captain pulled himself up straighter in the saddle. "Sir, I don't mean to be rude, but where do you come by that information? I have it on good authority that there are close to a hundred. They hit a stage relay station up at Killeen and killed a lot of people. They raided a town called Cotulla and killed a bunch of people. The sheriff sent out some volunteers and no one has heard from them since. The sheriff went out with another posse and he's disappeared as well. There's no way nine or ten Indians could have done that much. We're heading up to the relay station at Encinal to secure it. We intend to keep this road open."

"I'm sure you know your business, Captain," Dixon said, "but Encinal ain't there no more. It's burned out. They hit the place yesterday. We killed four of the heathens, but two got away. You probably passed at least one, because he was heading south the last we saw of 'im. The other split east, but I'm pretty sure he'll cut south also."

The captain held up his hand to interrupt Dixon. "Sir, I have no idea what Indians you saw, but the band that hit Killeen had to be large."

"No, sir," Dixon said. "There wasn't more than five or six. Now there is only about two. One's a crazy son of a bitch that calls himself Charley Tree. The other one is named Ja-mas-pa. They all jumped from Basque Redondo a couple weeks ago. It ain't no big band, Captain. There was one bunch of three. They tried to burn my partner, but I killed two of 'em. One—this here Tree fellow—got away. He killed a drummer and a couple a women and stole their stock. It was him that killed those folks in Cotulla."

Dixon continued. "Six or seven others hit Killeen. I think a couple got knocked off along the way, maybe in a fight with the sheriff. They had my partner's little brother with 'em, but, according to one of the Indians we shot, the kid got away somehow and killed an Indian himself. The last we heard, he was on a horse heading south, too. This Tree fellow joined up with them others and I'm pretty sure they killed those folks at Encinal. We didn't go back to check, but we heard shooting and saw the smoke. Later, we seen four of 'em driving the stock. We killed two and got the stock back."

The captain said, "I find your story slightly less than credible, sir. How can I be sure that you didn't steal that stock and blame it on the Indians? How do I know that you haven't concocted that story because we caught you with the stock?"

Dixon spit in the dirt at the feet of the captain's horse. "Well, Mr. Soldier Boy, first off, you didn't catch us, we done caught you. You an' your tin soldiers was making enough noise to wake the dead. We been seeing your dust for miles and hearing your racket for an hour. We could have been miles from here if we were hiding. Second place, had we kept quiet, you and your fancy scout here would have ridden right on by. I bet you couldn't even point out where we got the stock. Third place, Mr. Soldier Boy, I count you two and twelve others. Makes a total of fourteen of you just riding along all nice and neat, right down this old road. Your fancy scout riding right along with you instead of ahead, where he belongs. We could have shot half of you down before you knew what was happening. Those we missed would be so scattered, they wouldn't be able to put up no kind of fight."

Dixon scratched his whiskers. "Fourth thing, Mr. Soldier Boy, if you're interested, I have my commission papers in my saddlebags and a badge in my pocket. Fifth thing, if you still don't believe me, you keep on riding the way you're going a couple hours and like as not you will find a dead Indian with a 45-70 in his belly. His name was Eskiminzin. If you still aren't convinced, you keep your little tin soldiers riding north and you'll find another dead Indian. I don't know his name, though, because I didn't get a chance to ask. An' finally, if you're so inclined, you can keep right on to Encinal. When you get there, you're probably gonna have some burying to do."

The captain was trembling with rage but had kept his silence while Dixon was talking. Colt couldn't help but grin.

The captain, barely able to control his anger, said through clenched teeth, "Sir, no one speaks to me in front of my men in such an insolent manner as you've done. You and your friend may consider yourselves under arrest until we sort this out. You, sir, and your friend shall accompany us back to Encinal."

Dixon raised his rifle toward the captain. Horace started to reach for his rifle but Colt had his Winchester at the scout's chest.

Dixon said, "Soldier boy, I ain't got time to go back to Encinal. I have a twelve-year-old boy to find. He's out here somewhere and scared to death. Now, I can't hardly miss from here. You can ride on, or have your men shoot us down. I guarantee you that you and your fancy guide is gonna be gut shot. I am not fooling, Mr. Soldier Boy. Either you start riding right now, or the four of us is gonna die, right here, right now."

Horace looked uneasy. "Captain, maybe he's right. They could have let us ride on by."

The captain's ego was hurt, but he sensed that this man Dixon meant what he said. The captain was no coward, but he was no fool either.

Finally, he took a deep breath and said, "Mr. Dixon, perhaps you are telling the truth, as incredible as it sounds. If you'll show me your commission papers and where you have those horses, I'll send you on your way."

"Okay, Captain, but if you think I'm gonna turn my back on you so you can have your men shoot us, you're wrong. Why don't you and your fancy guide step down off your horses and walk with me and my partner a little ways over yonder?"

The Captain turned in his McClellen saddle and motioned with his forearm. "Lieutenant, hold your positions. Horace and I are going with these gentlemen. If you hear shots—or if we're not back in ten minutes—it will mean these men have shot us or we'll otherwise be compromised. In that case, you know what to do."

He stepped down. "All right, Horace, let's go and examine this man's papers."

"Captain," Dixon said. "Don't you think you ought to disperse your men? They're sitting ducks out here on this road."

"Sir, I would appreciate it very much if you would cease and desist telling the army how to conduct its affairs. Now, please, if you'd be so kind, show me your papers."

Dixon looked at Colt. "Come on, boy, but keep your eye on them soldiers. I have my eye on Mr. Fancy Guide and the good Captain." They walked over to where the horses were tied.

When they reached Dixon's grulla, he motioned with the barrel of his Henry and said, "Captain, my papers are in a leather pouch inside the left saddlebag. Help yourself."

The captain fumbled at the flap of the saddlebag and soon found the pouch. He untied the leather thong and unrolled it. He unfolded the papers and studied them for a moment. He rolled them back up and replaced them in the bag, buckling the flap back down.

He turned to Dixon and said, "Sir, it appears you are who you claim to be. I am sorry for the misunderstanding, but you must appreciate my position. You're free to go on your way."

Dixon said, "That's mighty kind of you, Captain. I guess in all fairness I must release you to be on your way."

The captain, stung by Dixon's remark, said, "Ranger Dixon, I've always been free to go on my way. I did not arrest you only because I wanted to give you every possible opportunity to clear yourself—which, I must say, you've done."

"Captain, I ain't in your goddamned army and you ain't got no jurisdiction over me." Dixon's eyes blazed with anger. "On the contrary, you're in Texas and I'm a Texas Ranger. You've been under arrest for the last fifteen minutes for obstructing a law officer. Now, because I have other things I have to do, I'm letting you go."

"No civilian law enforcement agency can arrest a military officer," the captain said through clenched teeth.

Dixon said, "Captain, whoever has the drop on anybody can do all the arresting they want. Now, like I said, I'm releasing you. My partner and I will run these horses on down to Laredo to the stage office. You can do what you want."

The captain was about to explode with anger when a shot rang out.

Dixon yelled, "Get down!"

The captain started running back to his men.

Horace hit the dirt along with Dixon and Colt.

The captain ran about a hundred feet when an unseen force threw him backward, followed instantly by a shot.

The troopers, thinking that Dixon had fired the shots, started firing into the brush. The buzz of bullets and the plop of the bullets hitting the sand made the three men lie as low as they could. The staccato of gunfire was everywhere.

The troopers had broken ranks and were galloping their horses in all directions in a wild frenzy.

Horace yelled, "Goddamn it, quit shooting, quit shooting! It ain't us! Hell, y'all are gonna kill each other!"

Eventually, the shooting died down.

"Lieutenant, it's Horace—don't shoot. These boys ain't the ones that did the shooting."

A voice called back and said, "Is that you, Horace?"

"Yes, goddammit! Didn't I just say it was me?"

Dixon yelled out, "You boys better get down behind something. Ol' Charley will pick you off like a monkey picking fleas."

Horace asked, "Lieutenant, are you there?"

The same voice answered. "The lieutenant's dead."

Horace said, "So is the captain. Who's the ranking officer?"

The voice said, "I reckon I am."

Horace said, "Well, dammit, who the hell is 'I am?'"

"Sergeant McGuire."

Horace said, "Well, Sergeant McGuire, I'm coming out, so tell your men to hold their fire." He got into a low crouch and ran towards the road mumbling, "What a hell of a mess!"

*

Charley got off two clean shots before the riders scattered. One horse and rider actually ran right over where he'd been hiding in the sand. He'd quickly crawled deeper into the sage, then stood to a low, running crouch.

He ran to his horse and leaped into the saddle.

He'd not been able to get any scalps or steal anything, but there were two less white men soiling Apache ground.

*

Douglas saw the smoke. He was hungry and almost out of water. He had given the horse another little taste but the horse was dehydrated almost to the point of exhaustion. Maybe that was wood smoke from a nearby farm.

"Come on, horse, let's go, boy." He thought he should give the horse a name but hadn't thought of anything grand enough.

This horse had saved his life and was saving it again, every tired step it took.

What kind of name is fitting for a horse like this? he wondered. The brown gelding wasn't ugly, but he wasn't pretty either. But he had bottom and seemed loyal.

The horse could have run off several times but he hadn't. He seemed to like Douglas, or somehow sense that the boy was in trouble. Douglas thought that he would have to think of a grand name.

General Lee had his grand horse. Pappy said the general called him Traveler. "That's it! That's what your name is, horse. It's General! Now, horse, you can't get any better than a general—except maybe president. President somehow doesn't sound as good as general."

Douglas patted the horse's neck and said, "Yep, that's your name, boy. General. How do you like that?"

The smoke was much further than Douglas expected. Instead of chimney smoke up close, it was a bigger cloud of smoke further away.

Douglas said, "General, I sure do hope that it ain't no grass fire. Maybe it's some farmer burning brush or prickly pear. Come on, boy, we'll make it." The tired horse stumbled, regained its footing, and walked on.

*

An hour later, Douglas could see a windmill and the smoking ashes of what was left of three buildings. A windmill meant water.

He thought, *Musta been a farm that caught fire.*

"General," he said, "it don't look right. How come all three of them buildings burned? Two are far apart and the third is even further. How could the fire spread?"

Then he knew. The Apache. They'd burned out some poor family.

He checked his Spencer and rode the tired horse on down. He saw the two bodies in the yard. He could tell by the way they were spread-eagled and gutted that they were dead.

Douglas turned his eyes away and led the horse to the overflowing water tank.

He cupped his hands under the cascading water and drank.

General was licking the water as it ran over the side of the huge wooden tank.

Douglas let the horse drink a little, then pulled him away. He didn't want the horse drinking too much. He walked to a nearby fence and tied him. He dreaded what he knew he must do.

He walked around the bodies and went to the remains of the barn. He found a shovel with a scorched but otherwise serviceable handle.

He knew that he had to bury the bodies and he looked for a good place.

He selected a place about a hundred feet behind the remnants of the house. He got his horse and lariat and went to the two bodies.

Both were bloated, even with their bellies open. Green flies covered them. The stench and sight made him retch.

Douglas looped a rope around the foot of the man. He tightened it and ran back several feet to catch a fresh breath.

He tied the bitter end to the pommel of the saddle and walked the horse to the grave, then stopped when the body was parallel and even with the grave.

He knew he had to touch the body and he dreaded it. He loosened the loop around the foot and rolled the body into the grave. It fell face down.

Douglas gagged. He wondered if burying somebody face down was all right. He didn't know anything about burying folks.

He took the horse back to the other body and repeated the process with the woman. This time the body landed face up.

He thought, *This is better.*

When he was finished with the first grave, he began covering the woman. He looked in horror as the dirt landed in her open mouth. *Maybe face down was better.*

Douglas turned his head away and shoveled as fast as he could, gagging and crying beyond control.

After filling the graves he ran to the water tank, stripped, and tried to wash the awful smell away.

He sat under the water for an hour, just staring out at the desert. He felt very small and alone. Only a few weeks before, he'd had a warm home and a loving family. Now his pappy and ma were dead, his home gone and a brother somewhere.

He'd been captured by the same Indians that he'd watched rape and kill his mother—in the same manner that these folks had been killed. He'd seen a horrible gun battle and white men mutilated. He didn't know where he was or what was going to happen to him.

Douglas finally got out from under the sprinkling water and walked over to General, buried his face against the horse and bawled.

The horse turned his head and started licking his wet shoulder.

Douglas soon calmed down. Somehow, the horse gave him comfort and he felt better.

He jerked his head up as a stab of fear flew through him. *What if the Indians came back? What if they were out there right now, watching?*

Douglas ran back to his clothes and quickly tried to dress. He was hopping on one foot trying to get his feet into his pants when he fell. He got up and made himself calm down. He picked up the rifle, looked around and didn't see anything.

He filled the canteen and let the horse have more water. This time, he let the horse drink its fill. He tied the horse to the windmill to drink while he searched the remains of the building. The coals were still too hot to check anything but the edges of the smoking ashes.

He heard a sound, turned, and saw a chicken pecking at the gravel about ten feet away.

Douglas found a rock and threw it at the chicken, knocking it down.

Before the chicken could recover, he had it.

He wrung its neck until the head came off.

The carcass dropped to the ground and ran in circles, fluttering its wings, with blood spurting out from where the head had been.

Within a few minutes he had the chicken roasting over the coals. While the chicken was cooking, he unsaddled General and led him to a fenced area behind what had been the house. There was plenty of grass and a feed trough with some grain.

He used the saddle blanket to rub General down and then turned him loose.

"You sure earned this rest, General, you sure did." He was afraid the Indians might come back, but the more he thought about it, why would they? *There ain't nothing left to steal.* He realized he was talking to himself.

"Only crazy people talk to themselves!" he said aloud. He clamped his mouth shut. "I have to watch that. I can't go talking to myself."

He used his horse blanket to curl up by the fire. It was warm and gave him much needed comfort. His Spencer gave him even more.

*

The Troopers finally calmed down and organized a search of the area. Dixon and Colt stayed to help. They found where Charley had hidden and followed his tracks back to where the Indian had tied his horse. There was no doubt in Dixon's mind that it was that same crazy Indian Charley.

He thought, *Shit, that's at least eight people that little son of a bitch killed. Most Apache have some reason for killing. This one just likes it.*

Dixon said, "Come on, boy, let's go to Laredo."

Colt nodded and turned to follow Dixon back to the road. He said, "Billy?"

"What?"

"Billy, I'll stop calling you 'Mr. Dixon' and 'sir' if you'll quit calling me 'boy.'"

Dixon grinned. "I was wondering when you were gonna speak up. Okay, Colt, let's get shed of these here idiots before they get us killed, too."

They walked to Horace and Sergeant McGuire. Dixon said, "It's like I told your captain. It's just one Indian and he's plumb gone. If you old boys ain't careful, that little son of a bitch is gonna kill every damn one of you."

Horace said, "We know what we're doing, Mr. Dixon."

Dixon spat and said, "That's what your captain said."

He mounted his horse and said, "Come on, Colt. Let's leave these Injun killers to their business."

They herded the ramada past the white-faced troopers. It was getting late and, again, it would be nightfall before they got into town.

*

Charley had food in the white man's saddlebags, two canteens of water, his pistol and rifle. He had, unfortunately, lost his shotgun when he and Ja-mas-pa fled the creek.

That was twice now that someone shooting from afar had chased him like a rabbit. He suspected it was the same man. He would one day meet this man and would enjoy himself when he did.

He rode due south until after dark. He could see the lights of a town in the distance when he stopped by a small creek.

The water was flowing and didn't stink like the buffalo wallow had. His testicles hurt and it was almost impossible to urinate. He picketed his horse and sat in the creek. The cool water seemed to help.

He eventually got out of the creek, spread his blanket and slept.

*

Colt and Dixon arrived in Laredo well after dark. They found the stockyard and made arrangements to overnight the cow and horses. They gave the watchman an extra dollar to store their supplies in the tack room with their saddles.

"Come on, Colt," Dixon said. "Let's get us some dinner and a beer before it gets too late. I don't want to have to climb out no window later."

They found both in one place. They were wearing their dusters over their shotguns and each carried three pistols. They were well-armed, even without the knives they were carrying.

Colt liked the way Dixon carried his knife on the inside of his left boot and he emulated him.

"You don't want to carry it on the outside of your boot," Dixon had told him, "because it snags on things. If you have it on your hip and get into a wrestling match, the other fellow might get his hands on it. This way I can get to it with either hand and it's harder for the other guy to get his hands on it. I carry a little-bitty hidy gun in the other one. It's a little two-shot .41 caliber. You ought to think about picking up one for your other boot. Balances out your walk that way. Just a little edge, Colt, you always want that edge. Sometime you're gonna need that edge to do some cutting."

They went into a place simply called 'La Cocina.' When they entered the dim interior lit by coal-oil lamps, the smell of kerosene was strong. Colt had a flashback of that terrible day at the ranch. He almost asked Dixon to leave but realized that every other place would be lit the same way. They ordered carnitas with frijoles and beer.

Colt asked if they had milk and the bartender said, "No, señor. No leche."

They ate their food, left, and found a clean room with two single beds. They were soon fast asleep.

TWENTY

Charley awoke and walked a few feet away and tried to urinate. It was a hard time coming, and then only in dribbles.
It burned like hell and the pain in his groin felt like someone kicked him. That damn buffalo woman gave him a white man's sickness. He wished that he could kill her again.

He stood for ten minutes, groaning each time a dribble would come. He finally finished and turned back towards his blankets, planning on lying down for a while. He looked up to see several Apache quietly sitting on their horses. He recognized one. It was Ja-mas-pa.

One, a very solemn-looking warrior, spoke. "Are you the one who is called Charley Tree?"

Charley immediately sensed that he was talking to someone important. It must be Goyathlay. Maybe even Victorio or Cochise.

"I'm Charley Tree. I am Mescalero from Bosque Redondo. I kill eight white man and women and took their scalps. I kill two more white man yesterday. I caught many guns and horses. I caught many white man's things. I fight with you against the white man that take Apache lands and make Apache go to white man's schools."

The stoic warrior said nothing. Charley tried to walk erect without favoring his swollen testicles. He picked up his Spencer and waved it. "See the white man's scalps? See? Charley Tree can fight!"

The warrior said, in his quiet, but resonant voice, "Why you take scalp? What good are scalp? Can you eat scalp? Can you wear scalp? Can you trade scalp? Why you take scalp, Charley Tree?"

Charley couldn't believe what he was hearing. The scalps proved he was a great warrior. Who was this man to question him? Surely it was not Goyathlay or Victorio.

He asked, "How many scalps you have, old man? How many scalps among your old woman warriors? How come Charley Tree see no scalps, old man?"

The warrior looked at Ja-mas-pa. "You're right, he is crazy Indian."

He turned to Charley with a chilling stare. "Ja-mas-pa tell Goyathlay that your name is Tree and that you think like a tree. Goyathlay think Ja-mas-pa maybe right, Charley Tree. I think you stay with white man too long. Take white man's crazy ways. White man almost as bad as Comanche. Goyathlay thinks Charley Tree bring big problem. Now white man think Goyathlay scalp. Send soldiers. Much fight. Many die I think. When the white man soldiers come to kill Goyathlay and Apache, I will think of Charley Tree. Maybe Charley Tree think of Goyathlay's words. Maybe Charley Tree go ask white mans to hang him. Maybe better for Charley Tree."

Charley was aghast. When he learned that it was the great Goyathlay, he almost pissed on himself, in spite of his swollen urinary tract. Not only was Goyathlay not impressed with his exploits, he was threatening to kill him. Kill him in a way to make hanging a thing to look forward to.

His white-hot anger turned to a cold fear. Goyathlay and his warriors disappeared as suddenly and quietly as they came.

Charley stood watching the empty desert. Slowly his ice-cold fear gave way to white-hot anger. He threw the rifle down in a fit of rage and screamed after the warriors. "Maybe Apache run to white man for hanging! Maybe Goyathlay think about Charley Tree! Take your old woman warriors and eat white man's pig! Fuck white man's woman! Fuck Goyathlay! Fuck fucking Apache! Charley Tree maybe fuck you in the ass!"

His rage finally spent, he sat down on his blanket with his elbows on his knees. Now what? The Apache had thrown him away like a dog turd. The whites would hang him. The Mexicans would scalp him.

He would show Goyathlay. He would show all the Apache. He would show the white man. He would teach them all about Charley Tree. Soon the Apache would come begging for Charley Tree to lead them against the white man. Soon Charley Tree would be known like Cochise, Victorio and Goyathlay. If only his testicles would quit hurting. If only he could piss. If only he hadn't fucked the buffalo woman.

Now what? To ride south no longer had a purpose. He now only must survive. He must find a farm or ranch where he could replace his lost supplies.

*

The next morning, Douglas woke to the warmth of the sun on his back.

The coals in the fire were still warm and he found a few with some spark.

He pulled some dry grass and some partially burned lumber from the charred remains of the barn and got a fire going.

Douglas was busy piling more wood on the fire when he heard a voice.

"You think that fire's big enough, son?"

Douglas looked up to see several soldiers on horseback. His fear turned immediately to relief. White men! He wasn't alone anymore. A lump was in his throat and tears worked their way out of his eyes. He wiped the tears away with a grimy forearm and choked back his tears.

"Yes, sir, I reckon."

All the men were in uniform, except the one speaking.

The civilian said, "Son, my name's Horace and this here is Sergeant McGuire. Your name wouldn't be Douglas Patterson, would it?"

"Yes, sir. How'd you know?"

"We met your brother yesterday and he's been looking for you."

"You seen my brother?"

Horace said, "Yep, we seen 'im. He's heading down to Laredo for a day or two then coming right back up this road. We're supposed to stay here and protect this station 'til this here Indian problem's solved."

Horace glanced at the burned-out buildings. "It sort of looks like we're a little late to be protecting much, though." He looked at Douglas. "Were you here when this happened?"

Douglas shook his head, "No, sir, I come on it last night. Everything was already burned and everybody was dead."

Horace softened his voice. "How many dead, son?"

Douglas's voice quavered. "Two. A man and a woman. They were all naked and cut open and everything. They were scalped, too."

Horace tried to speak as gently as possible. "Where are they now, son?"

Douglas pointed to the two mounds of dirt. "I buried 'em over yonder."

Horace was quiet for a moment, then he said, "You did all that by yourself?"

"Yes, sir."

"Well, I'll declare, that was right decent of you, son."

Douglas said, "I didn't plant no markings or nothing. I didn't know who they were. I didn't have anything to make no markers with, anyway. Everything was all burnt."

Horace stepped down from his horse. "You hungry, boy?"

"Yes, sir, a little. I done killed me a chicken last night an' I have a little left."

"Well, chicken is mighty good an' all but I reckon we can find something else."

Horace turned to the soldier beside him. "Sergeant, this here boy already has a fire going, why don't we make sort of a second breakfast real quick?"

The sergeant got down from his horse. "Corporal Hager, take your squad and set up a parimeter. The rest of you men take a thirty-minute smoke and coffee break. We'll use this here fire, so break out the coffeepots.

Corporal Channey, break out the bacon and them biscuits you been carrying—an' I know for a fact you have contraband in your saddlebags. I'll overlook the whiskey if you give up that jar of honey. I want you to feed this boy all the bacon, biscuits and honey he can eat. Tonight you're gonna split that jug of whiskey amongst all the rest of us. It's either that or you go on report. Do you have any problems with that, Corporal?"

Channey yelled out, "Honey coming right up, Sarge."

Horace asked Douglas, "Is that your horse I seen in that field?"

"Yes, sir. Kinda."

Horace said, "What do you mean, kinda?"

"I sort of stole him from an Indian."

Horace, already having heard the story secondhand, said, "What happened to the Indian?"

"Well, I sort of killed him."

"How'd you manage that, son?"

Douglas then told him the entire story—from losing the ranch, to the death of his mother, to his capture and escape. Before the story was over, Douglas had eaten several slices of bacon, the entire bag of biscuits, and the jar of honey that Channey had been hoarding.

"Well, son," Horace said, "that's quite a story. I tell you what, when you get a couple years older, you come and look me up. I could sure use a partner like you. You'll be one hell of a man to ride the river with. Why don't you just stay right here with us? Your brother will be coming along in a couple days and I imagine he will be real glad to see you. How about it?"

"That sounds real good, Mr. Horace."

"Just Horace, son; that's my first name. I ain't used my last name in so long, I plum forgot. It's just plain Horace."

*

After they finished breakfast, Dixon said, "Colt, I'm expecting a telegram. Let's go see if I ain't got one."

Dixon had been to Laredo many times before and knew right where the telegraph office was. Sure enough, one was waiting. It was apparently very lengthy, for it was in a fat envelope and the telegrapher demanded three dollars.

"Three dollars for a damn telegram?"

The telegrapher said, "Hell, it's a damn book. If you don't want it, okay. If you do, it's three dollars."

Dixon paid and took the envelope. He read its lengthy contents in silence, mouthing each word. He finished and put it in his pocket.

"Colt, tell me about them cows of yours. How long did you have them before they got sick?"

"About three weeks."

"Did you get a good look at them sick cows yourself?"

"Well, Pappy and me checked 'em over real good trying to figure out what was wrong with them."

"And did you see anything unusual, son?"

Colt thought a minute, then he said, "Their bellies was all swollen up and there was a lot of foaming at the mouth."

Dixon asked, "Anything else?"

"No, just that they would lie down and they couldn't get back up. They were just foaming and bawling. That, and the swollen-up stomach."

"Think, son. Are you sure you didn't see no pustules or nothing? Especially on the inside of their legs up near where they connect to the body?"

"What's a pustule?"

Dixon said, "It's sort of like a boil or a carbuncle—maybe real red with a black center."

Colt shook his head. "No. Pap and me both checked them cows over real good and didn't see nothing like that."

Dixon nodded. "There is a gland just inside the pit between the leg and the body. Did you see any swelling, or maybe black or blue discoloration?"

"Nothing. Except for the belly, we didn't see no swelling anywhere. Just before they died, there was blood in the foam. It turned all pink."

"According to this," Dixon tapped the telegram in his pocket, "your cows didn't have no anthrax. Anthrax has an incubation of about seven days. The glands swell up and there are big pustules with black centers. No, sir, something is sure wrong. I thought so in the beginning and now I'm sure."

"Hell, something sure was wrong with 'em. A whole bunch died and they died quick."

"Well, it wasn't anthrax, that's for sure."

Colt was quiet for a few minutes, then he said, "You mean, all them cows slaughtered and the burning of the fields was for nothing?"

"I'm afraid so, Colt." Dixon asked, "Them cows that died. Were they all in the same field?"

"Yeah, about twenty of 'em. Every one of them died."

Dixon said, "Now, think real careful. What did you do different with them twenty cows that you didn't do to the rest? Or what didn't you do that you did do to the rest?"

Colt thought, and then said, "Nothing. They got the same grain and the same water from the same well."

"Well, something different sure happened, that's for sure. It wasn't any anthrax. We'll think on it, son. We're missing something. I just don't know what. Come on. We got to check on these warrants."

*

They spent the rest of the morning asking around all the saloons, restaurants, barbershops, the dental office and even the whorehouses. Yes, a red and green medicine wagon had been seen. Yes, two men came through a few days ago that looked like the poster of the Baker boys, along with three other hard cases. It was believed they were all across the Rio Grande, safe in Mexico.

Dixon asked, "Colt, how's your Spanish?"

"Between almost none and none."

"Sounds like you speak it better than me. Come on, son. We're gonna take a little ride into Mexico."

Colt said, "You don't have any authority down there."

"I have the same authority they had when they decided to kill people," Dixon said. "Are you coming with me? If you want to stay here, it's okay."

"I told you, Billy, I'm with you all the way. Nothing worse can happen to me than what you saved me from."

"We'll take what weapons we need an' our riding horses. We'll just pop over yonder, grab those fellows and be back before supper. Let's go."

They rode about five miles out of Laredo before turning south into Mexico. Dixon didn't want to be seen by any Federales guarding the bridge. He knew the word would spread faster than hiccups.

Laredo was a fairly small town, but somewhat prosperous. Nueva Laredo was little more than a few hovels put together with a blacksmith, a church, a livery, one general store, and three combination whorehouses, saloons and cafes.

They crossed the Rio Grande at a spot where the river was only waist-deep for the horses, then circled around to the south of town about a mile.

They then turned north and rode back into town. About a quarter-mile south of town, they saw an adobe hut with a red and green wagon parked alongside.

A fat Mexican woman was hanging laundry on a line beside the house.

Dixon yelled to her, "Hola, Señora."

The woman turned and smiled. "¿Como esta usted?"

Dixon asked in his rough Spanish, "Por favor, where is the man with the wagon?"

The woman said, "Oh, Señor Peoples. Esta no aqui."

Dixon asked, "Tu sabe Inglés?"

The woman made a gesture with her fingers that indicated small. "I dunno for chure, but maybe at Juanito's Cantina."

"Where is Juanito's, ma'am?"

The woman motioned toward town. "Over there. On the main street, jus' before the bridge, señor."

Dixon said, "Thank you ma'am." They rode down the main street. As they passed Juanito's, Dixon kept his eyes focused straight ahead and mumbled out of the corner of his mouth, "Colt, don't even glance at it, just keep on riding." They rode past and stopped at a tie-rail several buildings further down the dusty street.

"Colt, you hang loose right here. You have your shotgun all loaded up under that duster?"

"Yes. And I checked my revolvers earlier. I'm ready when you are." Colt thought his voice sounded more relaxed than his stomach felt.

"Well, I'm just gonna walk on down to Juanito's and have myself a beer," Dixon said. "Sort of scope things out. If you hear shooting, come running. Otherwise, wait here. I'll be right back."

Colt watched Dixon walking casually toward Juanito's with his duster flopping in the wind.

He tried to appear interested in the leather goods displayed in the window of the store. He could see a reflection in the glass as four federal soldiers rode by. They were all looking at him with hard eyes. He watched them ride past Juanito's and disappear down a side street.

Trying to look inconspicuous, Colt tried to engage the proprietor in conversation—but he spoke no English and Colt spoke no Spanish. He was feeling awkward and felt that everyone was looking at him. He sure wished Dixon would hurry with that beer.

After what seemed a lifetime, he saw Dixon come out of the cantina and walk slowly in his direction.

Dixon stopped and rolled a cigarette, struck a match against his boot and lit it. He strolled across the street to where Colt was standing.

Dixon said, "Colt, you stand out like a sore thumb. Always try to look like you have a purpose. Buy something, do something, or walk, but never stand in one place for no reason."

Dixon lowered his voice. "Now, we done got lucky. There are three of the men that we're looking for. There's that Peoples fellow and both Baker boys. Peoples is sitting at one table playing poker one-on-one with a local. The Baker boys are sitting at a table right behind him, drinking an' carrying on with three hard-case white boys. I figure they're friends."

Dixon shifted a little closer to Colt. "Now, there's a door to the front—the one you seen me come out of. There's a bar about ten paces in from the door. The bar goes from the right and extends to your left for about eight feet, and then it makes a right turn and continues about another ten feet toward the rear door. Peoples is at the first table to your left when you walk in the door, and he'll be facing you.

The Bakers will be with the only group of five sitting together. They are only a couple other locals sitting at another table. I ain't interested in them or the bartender unless they interfere.

Now, I want you to go in an' order a beer. Stand to the extreme right of the bar when you walk in. You'll notice a closed door to a room on your right. There's probably a working girl in there, with God knows who. Be careful of anybody coming out of that door. I done eyeballed that door and it opens inside, away from the bar. If you were to want to go in the door, the latch would be on your left.

Now, the bartender speaks English so just go in and order that beer. I'm gonna go around the back and come in from the alley. When you see me walk into sight, you take a couple steps back so you can cover anybody coming in from the street an' anybody coming out of that whorehouse door. You'll also be in a position to cover Peoples and the Bakers. I can cover Peoples and the Baker crew but I won't be able to see the whorehouse door.

As soon as you hear me say anything, you step back and show that sawed-off shotgun. Hopefully, they'll be too smart to draw down on two shotguns. With any luck, that local that's playing cards with Peoples will duck out of the way. If not, an' the shooting starts, he's gonna be on his own."

Dixon gave Colt a serious look. "Remember, boy, if you hesitate—even for a second—either you, me or both of us is gonna be dead. You go on ahead, now, an' I'll go on around the back."

Colt, now really feeling the butterflies, walked alone down to Juanito's. He'd been so intent on listening to Dixon's instructions, he'd forgotten to tell him about the Federales. Well, maybe there wouldn't be any shooting and they'd be out of there without the Federales being any the wiser.

He crossed the dusty street, feeling the weight of the sawed-off shotgun gently rocking against his hip. He made sure the thongs had been removed from the hammers on his pistols.

Dixon had reminded him to load up all three weapons to six each instead of the five. That gave him two buckshot loads, plus eighteen rounds from his three revolvers.

TWENTY ONE

Colt's stomach was really churning now. Just as he stepped onto the boardwalk, he took several deep breaths, trying to calm himself. He could feel the sweat beneath the duster and on his brow. It was hot, but he knew most of his sweat was not from the heat.

He stepped through the door and found that Dixon's description was exact in every detail. He saw the door to his right as he walked to the bar. He avoided looking to his left as he stepped up to the bar.

The bartender, a fat little man of about fifty with a gold tooth, said, "Yes, señor, what will you have?"

"Just give me a beer."

The bartender said, "Twenty-five centavos, señor. Americano."

Colt knew that was twice the going rate, but didn't argue. He tossed two bits on the bar.

The bartender filled a mug and slid it over to him, pocketing the two bits.

Colt blew off the head and only then did he casually turn just enough to survey the room. For some reason, his case of nerves had disappeared and he was calm.

He was fascinated that there, not more than six feet from him, sat a perfectly normal-looking man who had poisoned at least three—or possibly six—people.

Colt looked further and saw five men sitting at a table. He didn't know which two were the Baker boys but any of them could have been his neighbors. Not a one looked like a killer. He stood drinking his beer. From the corner of his eye, he saw Dixon move into his field of vision.

He set down his mug and stepped back against the wall as instructed.

Dixon pulled his sawed-off shotgun from under his duster and said, "Everybody just freeze where you are."

That was Colt's cue. He exposed his shotgun and pulled both hammers back.

Colt yelled, "I have 'em covered over here, Billy!"

"My name's Billy Dixon an' I'm a Texas Ranger. I have warrants here for the following people. Elroy Peoples—also calls himself Sam Pritchett; that's that son of a bitch over yonder. Eldon Baker—that's the scrawny little bastard on the end that thinks he's a killer. I also have one for Tyrell Baker. That's the dumb- looking, ugly bastard by Eldon.

I am gonna take 'em alive or dead. It don't matter to me because the pay is the same. Everybody else can get up and stand behind the bar."

The room was silent for just a heartbeat. Peoples looked at Colt and said, "I'm unarmed. You wouldn't shoot an unarmed man, would you?"

Dixon spoke up. "If he won't, I sure as hell would."

Peoples said out loud for the room to hear: "The great Billy Dixon, the ranger that cuts off people's heads and puts 'em in pickle barrels. I've heard of you. You have no jurisdiction down here. You're breaking Mexican law."

He spoke to the others in the room. "Gentlemen, you're witnessing an attempted kidnapping and I have over four hundred dollars in gold that I'll give to any man or group who can prevent this dastardly act."

Dixon's voice was like ice as he said, "I'll kill any man that moves."

Colt was watching Peoples. Here was a man as close to death as anyone could come and yet he seemed as calm as if he was only discussing buying a cow.

He saw movement out of the corner of his eye and turned just as the bartender was leveling an eight-gauge greener at Dixon.

Colt instinctively fired both barrels. He saw the bartender's head disappear in a red spray as the bartender's gun discharged, hitting one of the locals and blowing him out of his chair.

Two of the three men stood up with Eldon and drew their weapons.

Dixon's shotgun took out the two standing and one of the hard cases still sitting.

Colt felt a recoil in his hand and saw Eldon go down, dropping his revolver.

Colt looked down and saw his Allen and Wheelock in his hand. He'd not remembered firing it, but he could see smoke coming out of the barrel.

Dixon told Peoples and Tyrell: "Pick up that piece of shit, Eldon, and let's go. I'll kill anybody still sitting in about three seconds. One...two..."

Peoples and Tyrell jumped up and grabbed the coughing Eldon, who was dying at that moment.

Dixon came into full view with both hands filled with revolvers.

He backed to Colt and said, "Put your pistols away and reload that scattergun."

Colt did as he was told. He was only now feeling the adrenaline and shaking so badly that he dropped the first two rounds. He finally managed to recharge the shotgun and lock the breach.

Dixon said, "Now you watch 'em while I reload."

As Dixon was reloading, Colt saw the door to his right open. A bearded man poked a long-barreled pistol out. Colt turned instinctively, firing both barrels of his shotgun again. The shot blew out part of the door and half the man's chest.

Dixon was in the process of reloading his shotgun and had both pistols in their holsters.

Colt's two pistols were in their holsters as well, and he'd just emptied both barrels into the man to his right.

Tyrell, who still had his gun, dropped Eldon and drew it.

Colt couldn't believe how fast it happened.

One second Tyrell was holding his brother, the next he was firing at Colt.

Colt was aware of two shots and a distinct third shot as he dropped his shotgun and reached for his right pistol.

He felt a heavy blow to his right shoulder that spun him around.

Tyrell was in a half-crouched stance and fanning his revolver as fast as he could.

Colt felt a fourth shot buzz by his face and yet a fifth shot. It was all happening in a heartbeat, and yet it was as if in slow motion.

Somehow, Colt was aware of Dixon dropping his partially loaded shotgun and pulling his revolvers.

He saw his own left hand extending toward Tyrell.

The pistol came up to his line of sight and Colt distinctly saw his sights line up as a sixth shot was fired.

Colt's revolver fired. He saw a black spot appear under Tyrell's nose.

Tyrell's head jerked backward and a mist of pink and white halo was seen briefly behind his head.

Colt had a vivid image as Tyrell's revolver spun three complete turns in the air and landed on the dirt floor.

Tyrell bounced off the wall and slid into a sitting position, smearing the wall with his blood.

Dixon said, "Shit! Shit! Shit! The dumb bastards!"

He went to Peoples and smacked him in the mouth, hard enough to break his teeth.

"See what you done, you bastard? You done got five, maybe six, people dead. I ought to blow your fucking head off right here."

He turned to Colt and asked. "Are you okay?"

"I think so, I don't know. I think I've been shot. My right arm is numb. I can't move it."

Dixon, coughing in the dense gun smoke, said, "Reload that scattergun. I think we're gonna need it. Somebody's coming."

Sure enough, Colt could hear people in the street. He heard a voice in broken English.

"Señors. This is Jose Fredrico Gomez, a captain of the Army of the Federal Republic of Mexico. I demand you to throw out your weapons and surrender. You will not be harmed. Please to come out now. We have soldiers surrounding you."

"Son of a bitch!" Dixon said. "Where the hell did they come from?"

Colt said, "I should've told you, I seen Federales earlier. I forgot."

Dixon looked at Colt in astonishment. "You forgot? Hell, if I'd known they were in town, we would've waited."

Peoples was smiling, in spite of his bruised lips and broken teeth. "Well, well, Mr. Ranger. It looks as though I may have the last laugh after all."

Dixon said, "Like hell you will; it just looks like more innocent people may get shot. But your ass is going with me, bought and paid for!"

Colt asked, "What are we gonna do?"

*

Charley was getting hungry. He'd eaten the last of his food. Fortunately, he still had plenty of water. He remembered Ja-mas-pa and the others bragging about robbing the stage in Killeen. This gave him an idea.

Wouldn't white men be traveling the road? If he found a place where he could see them coming, maybe he could rob some white men, get food and maybe more scalps.

He'd decided he wouldn't fuck any more white women, but he'd make them pay for his balls.

He turned his horse west and headed toward the road. He would wait this day and one more. If no one came, he would hunt for a farm or ranch to rob.

*

Dixon moved nearer to the closed door and yelled, "Captain Gomez, can you hear me?"

"Si, I hear you, gringo."

"Captain, we got innocent people in here. We're Texas Rangers down here collecting some white dogshit from your town. I'd like to talk."

Dixon waited to see if the Federale would answer.

When there was none, he went on, "Captain, why don't you and me walk out to the middle of that there street? That way, if either side starts shooting, we both get killed. Is that fair?"

Gomez was quiet for a moment, then said, "Si, I think that would be fair. Come out unarmed."

"I can't do that, Captain," Dixon said. "I'll leave my scattergun and wear only my pistols. You wear yours, but don't bring anything else. Okay, in two minutes, you and I start walking."

"Si, gringo. Two minutes."

Dixon laid his shotgun against the wall. He went over to Peoples and pulled his jacket down over his shoulders. He removed Peoples' belt and secured his hands behind him. Then he pulled Peoples' pants down to his ankles. He removed an over-and-under double-barreled Derringer from Peoples' vest pocket and handed it to Colt. "Here's you a Derringer."

Turning back to Peoples, Dixon said, "I thought you told me you were unarmed?"

Peoples shrugged and said, "So I lied."

Dixon said, "If I ever catch you lying to me again, you're gonna find your head in a pickle barrel."

Dixon searched Peoples, withdrew a leather pouch and counted out twenty-two twenty-dollar gold pieces. He put ten of them in his pocket and handed the rest to Colt. He then took a towel from the bar and gagged his prisoner. Dixon looked at Colt's arm and asked, "Are you sure you're okay?"

"My shoulder hurts like hell," Colt said, "and I can't move my arm." They both saw the bright red blood running in rivulets down Colt's hand and puddling on the floor.

"We ain't got much time," Dixon said. "You're going to bleed out if we don't hurry."

Dixon looked at his watch. "It's time. Now, Colt, I'm going out. Don't you shoot unless they shoot. If they do, don't worry about me. Kill Peoples and anybody else that moves. If you give up, them soldiers are gonna shoot you anyway, so you might as well take as many with you as you can."

Dixon stepped out and closed the door.

Colt looked over at the two locals, who were scared but still apparently uninjured. They were both sitting with their backs to the wall. Colt didn't know if they were armed.

"Any of you fellows speak English?" he asked.

One of them nodded. "I speak pretty good."

"Okay, you and your friend have thirty seconds to strip down and kick your clothes over to me." Colt looked around the barroom. "Who else is in this here whore-room?"

The one who spoke English said, "Juanita. But she maybe gone now."

He told his companion about Colt's instructions and they hurriedly undressed.

Colt peeped out the crack and could see Dixon and the Federales speaking in the street

Dixon was saying, "Captain, as you can see we got a little problem. We don't want anybody else to get hurt. All we want is to take our prisoners back across the border. Now, so far, we got eight dead and one live American. The dead ones resisted and drew on a drop. Two of the dead is Mexicans. We killed one. He pulled a shotgun and tried to kill us, but killed the other one. We got two live Mexicans in there that can tell you what happened. You're welcome to come in and talk to them. I'll guarantee your safety. I'd like to work something out with you on this."

Gomez said, "I have great respect for American lawmen, señor, but I know of no crimes committed by the whites you are speaking of. You have committed a crime of attempted kidnapping and maybe murder in Mexico. From what you say, people have died. That is a very serious crime in Mexico."

"Well, Captain," Dixon asked, "if I can convince you that we only shot in self-defense, do you reckon we could walk out of here with a little fine?"

Gomez said, "If even what you say is true, I think that such a fine would be more than a little."

"Captain, I have two hundred American dollars in gold. That's all we got. You reckon that would cover it?"

Dixon waited, but the captain said nothing.

Finally, Dixon said, "If we don't work something out, I figure your soldiers will shoot us—and we damn sure would kill some of them. There are two innocent people inside might get hit, too. Who knows who else."

Gomez said, "Yes, I see your point. Perhaps a fine would be a good compromise under the circumstances. But first I must talk to the three innocent ones you speak of. If they confirm what you're saying, your fine will be two hundred American dollars. You may pay me directly, of course."

Dixon said, "Of course."

Gomez turned and spoke to his men in Spanish and told them to hold their fire. He would be going inside for one moment.

Dixon said yelled, "Colt, hold your fire, we're coming in."

He and Gomez crossed the street and went into the cantina.

Gomez questioned the three Mexicans at length, in Spanish. Finally, he turned to Dixon and said, "I suppose what you told me is the truth. If you will pay me the fine, you may go."

Dixon nodded and said, "That's good. If you don't mind, Captain, I need you to have one of your men go south of town about a quarter of a mile. There's a red and green wagon. It and them horses down there belong to this piece of shit here."

He nodded to Peoples. "If you'd have your man hitch it up and pull it out front here and load up them two stiffs over yonder, we'll leave your fair town. You can keep these other four. We're also gonna take our prisoner."

Gomez shook his head. "I'm sorry, señor. I can't let you do that. This man has committed no crime in Mexico. To let you take him back would be illegal under Mexican law."

Dixon picked up his shotgun and said, "I guess you leave me no choice."

He aimed the shotgun at Peoples' head and was applying pressure on the trigger. Peoples' eyes got wide and he began shaking.

Gomez saw that Dixon was serious and held up his hand. "No, señor. Please. Perhaps we should discuss this."

Dixon lowered the shotgun and said, "OK, I'm listening."

Gomez said, "If you kill him we will have no choice but to arrest you."

Dixon said, "Wrong, Captain. Nobody is gonna be arrested today. If you try, a lot more are gonna die—including you and me."

Gomez lost his look of confidence and said, "Señor, have you no honor? You guaranteed my safety."

Dixon said, "You were in the middle of the street when I made that promise. You went there at your own risk. I guaranteed your safety from there to here and back to there. If we don't work a deal, the second your foot hits the middle of the street, I'm gonna cut you in half."

Dixon motioned to Peoples. "Then I'm going to execute that son of a bitch and kill as many of your soldiers as I can before they kill me." Dixon fixed his flat eyes on Gomez. "I'm running out of patience, Captain. What's it gonna be?"

Gomez believed that this man with the dead eyes was serious. He asked, "What did your prisoner do?"

"He poisoned some women and maybe a few other folks."

Gomez nodded thoughtfully. "You can take them, but take all the garbage with you."

"Good," Dixon said. "Now that leaves only one more detail."

Gomez asked, "What's that?"

"I know you're an honorable man, being a captain an' all, but if you don't mind I'd like to have you ride with us to the bridge. As soon as we're all loaded up, I'll pay the fine. That way, maybe your boys won't make a mistake and shoot one of us."

Gomez looked at Dixon slyly and asked, "How do I know that you won't shoot me and take the money back?"

"Well, sir," Dixon said, "you get to keep your pistol in your hand. I'll keep mine. You and me will ride in the back with the stiffs and my prisoner. You can have your man drive the wagon and my partner will ride up front with him. If anybody starts shooting, there's a good chance we'll all die. I won't die for two hundred dollars and I don't think you would either."

Gomez smiled. "It sounds like you've done this before, señor."

Dixon nodded. "Once or twice."

Gomez walked to the door and called over one of his men. They spoke for a moment and the man left.

Gomez came back and said, "Your wagon will be here shortly.

You won't mind, I'm sure, if I have some of my men follow us to the bridge. At a safe distance, of course."

Dixon said, "All right, but tell them if they get closer than about fifty feet, I'm gonna get real nervous."

"I will instruct my men."

"Any chance of getting my friend some medical attention?" Dixon motioned toward Colt.

"I'm sorry, señor, but our doctor is not available. I will, however, have one of my men find some bandages to at least stop the blood. It will only take a few minutes to cross the bridge into Laredo. I'm sure you'll find a competent doctor there."

"That's fair enough."

*

It took a half-hour for the wagon to arrive. By that time, Dixon had bandaged Colt's arm. They loaded up and headed back to Laredo. They stopped in the middle of the bridge and bid Gomez goodbye. Dixon climbed into the driver's seat and drove the wagon on across the bridge, with their horses tied behind.

Colt was feeling faint and his stomach churned. The pain in his shoulder was like a ball of fire.

He looked at Dixon and grinned. "That was pretty slick. We let old Peoples pay us out of trouble and made a couple hundred dollars on top of it."

"Colt, if you just calm down and think, most times there is a way out of almost anything."

Dixon glanced at Colt's arm and said, "Let's find you a doctor. Then I'm gonna drop these stiffs off and have the sheriff identify who them other three are. I'll get him to hold old Peoples in his lockup until we're ready to leave."

He smiled as he glanced at Colt. "You done real good back there, except for a couple minor mistakes. You have to learn not to blast both barrels of your shotgun at one time. You always save one for an emergency. Second, you can't be forgetting little things like federal soldiers just before what might be a shootout."

Colt nodded. "That one fellow I shot—boy, was he fast with that gun. He drew and got off four shots before I could blink."

"Most shootouts are that way. It's like I told you: speed doesn't always count. He was faster than you were, but you're alive and he's dead. That was because you slowed down and made your shots count."

Colt nodded his head. "I've never seen so much blood."

Dixon nodded and said, "It gets real messy; especially with a scattergun— and we had two."

"Yeah, and the bartender had one."

Dixon said, "Yep, three scatterguns going off in a room full of people makes for a real mess."

That was the last thing Colt heard before he fainted.

*

Colt woke up on a table to the smell of alcohol and smelling salts.

The doctor looked at him and said, "Well, I see you're awake. How do you feel?"

"Not so good; I think I might throw up. At least my arm don't hurt so much."

"I removed a bullet and pumped some morphine into you. It'll wear off in a while and when it does, it's gonna hurt like hell."

The doctor handed a bottle to Colt and said, "Here's some laudanum to take if the pain gets too bad. Take two capfuls, but no more. Wait at least four hours between doses. You have a broken collarbone and some torn muscles but you ought to be okay in a few weeks. You can leave any time you feel like walking—but you ought to let somebody look at your shoulder in a couple of days."

Colt sat up, feeling lightheaded, but he thought he could walk. "How much do I owe you, Doc?"

The doctor said, "Let's see, it took about a half-hour of my time, so how does five dollars sound?"

"I reckon it's cheap at the price," Colt said. "Where did my partner go?"

The doctor said, "I don't know, but he said that if you got out of here, to meet him over at the sheriff's office.

He said that if you didn't show up in a couple hours, he'd be back to check up on you."

*

The signalman and his escort returned to the burned-out relay station. He went to Sergeant McGuire and said, "Sarge, the wire must be down. I couldn't contact Laredo to the south or Cotulla to the north."

McGuire said, "Well, it's unlikely the wind blew 'em both down, north and south. Them damn Indians probably pulled them down."

The sergeant walked over to where Corporal Donaldson was putting up his tent. "Corporal, the telegraph is down. You're gonna have to carry a dispatch back to Laredo. I want you there tonight and I don't care how late. I think that Dixon fellow is wrong. I have a feeling we might be in for trouble. Deliver the dispatch and get back here by tomorrow night, no matter what. Take Private Davis with you. Leave your tent here and take only enough food and water to get you there. Better see the quartermaster and draw a hundred rounds for your Spencer and another sixty rounds for your revolver. I want you on your way within the hour."

Donaldson definitely did not like the order and Davis would probably like it less. Not only was he worn out, he didn't like the idea of being out alone with just one man. He'd never fought Indians before and, frankly, they scared the hell out of him.

Donaldson said, "Yes, Sarge, we'll leave right away. Only one thing, though. That old nag I been riding is slower than a constipated bug. Davis' horse ain't much better. If we have to run for it, it'd sure be nice if we had something faster between our legs."

McGuire said, "Hell, Donaldson, every woman that knows you says you're already too fast between the legs! All right, take the captain's and the lieutenant's horses. They're the best ones in the bunch. Just don't get too attached to 'em because I have my eye on one of 'em for my own self. You best get cracking—and don't go to sleep out there."

A half-hour later, Donaldson and Davis were heading south at a good canter.

TWENTY TWO

Charley had accidentally crossed under the telegraph wire. He'd seen what Ja-mas-pa had done before and decided to hurt the white man even more by pulling down the talking wire. It was simple enough. All he had to do was toss his rope over the wire, gather up the tossed end and lock it to his saddle horn. He didn't even have to get off his horse.

After pulling down the wire Charley backtracked north; he was about midway between Encinal and Laredo before he found what he was looking for.

He halted at a small creek with good grass. The road dipped down an embankment, crossed through the shallow creek and up the other side.

Several logs had fallen into the creek and some previous flood had washed them downstream about a hundred feet.

He walked his horse in the water to hide his tracks and followed the creek about a half-mile. He secured his horse in some willows. He then walked back to the logs and crawled under them to wait. Waiting was better than riding. His testicles really hurt when he rode and the pain was getting worse.

*

Donaldson and Davis kept their eyes peeled. Fortunately, the desert was fairly flat and they could see for miles. They both knew from yesterday's experience that an Indian could creep up awfully close on foot, even in this terrain. Donaldson felt, however, that if they kept moving no one on foot could sneak up on them. They would also see anyone approaching on horseback. They had held their horses in a canter for the past ten miles or so.

Davis spoke up. "Corporal, if we don't slow these horses down we are gonna kill 'em."

"It can't be much further to that crick we crossed yesterday," Donaldson said. "We'll rest up there. We ought to be there in a few minutes."

*

Charley heard the hooves of the laboring horses several minutes before they arrived. He waited. He still couldn't see anyone, for he was lying flat in the ravine and the riders were out of sight over the ridge.

He listened to the drumming hooves, trying to determine how many there were. If there were too many, he would let them pass.

He heard the hooves slow and stop. He could hear the creaking of leather and knew someone was very close.

A voice said, "We'll rest 'em and let them water here. I don't see any tracks—but just to be certain, let's ride a ways up both sides of this creek. I sure don't want no surprises."

Charley could hear the horses' hooves striking the ground as they approached. They were right above him and he could smell the lathered horses. He hoped he was well-hidden, for if they saw him, he would have no chance. The horses rode on by until he could barely hear the hooves. He heard water splashing and knew they were crossing to the other side.

Soon the sound of the horses' hooves became louder. He heard them pass by him a second time. He still could not see them. About ten minutes later, he heard splashing again from further away. They were checking on the other side of the road. Soon they would come back.

*

Donaldson said, "I don't see any tracks. I reckon we can take a half-hour break—but let's don't unsaddle the horses and let's don't even loosen the cinches. We may have to leave in a hurry."

They reached the road again and rode down into the ravine. They stopped their horses in the middle of the creek and let them drink.

Donaldson said, "Let's get down and stretch our legs and fill our canteen. We can picket the horses and let 'em cool off while they graze."

Davis stepped down, as did Corporal Donaldson. While Davis was driving picket pins into the grassy area, Donaldson opened his fly to relieve himself.

*

Charley waited. He had a clear shot at both, but to shoot now might scatter the horses. He would wait until they were safely picketed.

*

Davis completed securing the horses and said, "Corporal, this may be the last chance to eat. Do you want something?"

"Yeah, why not? I have some biscuits and bacon. We ain't got time to cook nothing, but I like it raw just about as well."

He went to his saddlebags and removed a rolled-up oilcloth, walked about twenty feet to a grassy area beneath a tree, and sat.

Davis soon joined him with his own lunch.

He sat down, just as he heard a smack and an explosion.

A spray of red was all over his hands and red and pinkish tissue spread across his chest. For a moment, he thought he'd been shot.

Just then, Donaldson leaned over and lay what was left of his head in Davis' lap.

"Oh, Lord, no!"

Davis shoved Donaldson's body away and scrambled for his Spencer.

He was screaming in panic as something smacked him in the left side, followed by the sound of a second shot.

The impact knocked the wind out of him and he stumbled. He tried to churn his legs to propel him the last few inches to his rifle, but they weren't moving.

Something was terribly wrong. He dug in his elbows and tried to drag himself, but the strength in his arms was gone.

"Oh, no, oh, no, Lord, no."

Charley was grinning as he walked up. "Why white mans no die good, eh? Why white mans always cry like women, eh? I think Charley make you really cry. You like Charley to really make you cry?"

Davis said, "Just shoot me. Please just shoot me. Don't hurt me any more. Please shoot me. I hurt real bad."

"Charley don't think you hurt enough yet." He stripped Davis and dragged him to a pile of dried driftwood and brush.

"Charley fuck dirty white woman. Now Charley can't piss and Charley's balls hurt pretty bad. Maybe Charley make your balls hurt. How you like that, white man?"

With this, Charley grabbed Davis' scrotum and cut them away.

Davis didn't blink. He knew what was going to happen and was still waiting for it when Charley threw them in his face.

"Why you no scream, white man?"

Davis hadn't felt a thing. As a matter of fact, he couldn't feel anything from his waist down. He smelled smoke. Suddenly, he saw flames come up between his legs.

Oh, God no, he's burning me.

Davis was able to flop up enough to see his lower body burning. He could see and smell the sickening odor, but as yet, could feel nothing.

He opened his mouth and screamed. Soon he felt the heat against his upper back and neck.

Charley sat eating the bacon and biscuits left by the soldiers.

He stood up, took his knife in one hand, holding a biscuit in his right hand, and walked to the screaming man.

"How you like burning, white man? Not pretty good, I think."

He took his knife and cut a circular incision around Davis' head. He popped off the scalp.

The thing before him didn't change its screaming. It was obvious to Charley that the man's mind had snapped.

He wondered how roasted white man tasted. Maybe later he

would find out.

Charley walked away, chewing the remains of his biscuit and holding the bloody scalp in his left hand.

He looked at the other soldier. His head had exploded into several fragments. He picked up the largest piece of skull. It would make a fine plate. He carried it over to the creek and tied both scalps to the barrel of his rifle. He now had eight. How many Indians had eight scalps?

Charley thought this place was a pretty good place. Other white man would come. He'd made a mistake in burning the one white man so close to the crossing. He would have to hide the bodies.

He took their rifles and equipment and loaded them on his horses and hid them with the others.

When he returned, the white man roasting on the fire had quit screaming. It was too bad. He'd died much too soon.

*

Colt was directed to the sheriff's office and he walked the few blocks. He took off his hat when he entered the front office.

"Are you the sheriff?" Colt asked the man sitting at the desk.

The man didn't look up. He merely shook his head and pointed over his shoulder with his thumb. Colt looked in that direction, through an open door, and saw Dixon talking to the sheriff.

Dixon looked up and smiled. "Well, look what the skunks drug up. Sheriff, this poorly-looking man here is my partner, Colt Patterson. Colt, this here is Sheriff Bader Burdett. He an' I go back a long ways."

Burdett stood and offered his hand. "Glad to meet you, Colt. If you're hanging around this old fart, maybe I ought to arrest you on general mopery charges."

"What's mopery?"

Burdett said, "Mopery is slinking around with the likes of Billy Dixon."

"How do you feel?" Billy asked.

"A little weak, I guess. I can't move my arm, but it doesn't hurt too badly. I won't be using it for a while."

Dixon said, "When you feel up to it, we'll head out. The sheriff will entertain our prisoner for a few days if we need to stay a while. He done certified our warrants on the two stiffs. Them other three weren't worth anything. Still, we didn't do too bad. We picked up an even thousand dollars, plus a little extra."

Dixon turned to Burdett. "Sheriff, my partner looks like he could use a little beauty rest, so thanks for everything. I expect we'll be here a couple days, letting ol' Colt here mend a little."

Colt and Dixon left and found a rooming house. Even though it was still light outside, they both lay down and slept.

It was daylight when Colt awoke. He looked over at Dixon's bed and found it empty. He felt drugged and his arm was hurting like hell. Dixon walked in. He'd shaved and was wearing a brand new shirt, hat and boots.

"It's about time you woke up. How do you feel?"

"Okay, I guess. I feel like I slept a week—but it's still light out so I musta just dozed."

Dixon stood in front of the small mirror, admiring his new hat. "Nope, it's light again. You slept all night and it's almost noon. I done had breakfast, haircut, bath and a shave. I even went store shopping. How do you like my new hat?"

Colt had to admit it was a lot better than the old floppy hat he had before. "Nice. What was wrong with the old one?"

"Hell, it's got a hole in it. You shot it plumb off when them Indians was chasing us. I didn't even see the hole 'til this morning. My other clothes was so damn bloody I just threw 'em away, boots an' all. Them boots was soaked plumb through to my socks. Looks like you could use a fresh outfit yourself. Everything you have is blood-soaked, except your hat.

If you feel up to it, come on an' I'll buy you a nice, rare steak. It's real good for someone who has lost a lot of blood. If you still feel up to it afterwards, we'll pick you up some new clothes, including boots. I know an old Mexican who makes the best moccasins in the state. Better than Indians make themselves. You ought to pick up some of them, too."

Colt said, "That reminds me, that money from Peoples is in my pants' pocket."

Dixon eyed himself in the mirror, adjusted his hat and said, "Well, you get dressed and count out my part an' we'll go."

They had their meal and Colt felt a lot better. He was stiff and his chest and arm hurt, but at least he wasn't light-headed.

They visited the old Mexican, who had a pair of soft goatskin moccasins that came up to Colt's knees. The moccasins were double-soled with goat hair between the soles, making them very comfortable.

They picked up a pair of stovepipe boots, some pants, a shirt and more socks for Colt.

By the time the shopping was done Colt was feeling a little weak, so they both went back to the rooming house and went to bed.

*

About the time Colt and Dixon were bedding down, Sergeant McGuire was getting worried. Corporal Donaldson and Private Davis were very reliable. It was only a little over twenty miles to Laredo and they should have been back. It was getting dark and he'd heard the troops murmuring amongst themselves about Geronimo and the one they called Crazy Charley.

He walked over to Horace and squatted down.

McGuire told Horace his fears and the fact that the men were scared to death.

Horace said, "Well, I know Geronimo's been working this part of the country, but I don't think we need to worry about him. He goes after cattle, sheep and things he can feed his people with. He's never been known to attack without provocation, and the Lipan haven't caused any trouble in a long time. Victorio is working over near New Mexico and both he and Geronimo are doing their best to avoid government soldiers. No, I'm thinking that Dixon fellow is right. We have one mean, crazy, son of a bitch Indian out here somewhere, and it looks like he might've met up with your boys."

McGuire said, "Well, my orders are to guard this relay station and keep the road open. The station is gone but we still have a road, so I guess we have to keep it open. What do you recommend, Horace?"

Horace thought for a moment. "How many men do you have left, Sergeant?"

"Well, if Donaldson and Davis don't come back, I have eight. You and me makes ten."

"You're the soldier in charge," Horace said, "but if it was me, I'd split the men into two groups. One group resting and the other group riding. I'd have them riding scout and making a circle about five miles around this place and keep rotating until each scout is relieved. If you do that, and if there are any hostiles, you might cut some tracks. Otherwise, we can all hunker down here and wait. If we do that without scouts out on patrol, some night we could be in for a surprise."

McGuire said, "I didn't think Indians fought at night."

"Sergeant, whoever told you that don't know shit from beans. Most Indians, especially Apache, will fight any time they feel they have the advantage, just like you would. I sure don't know where these stories get started. Hell, you must have heard about Beacher's Island. Those damn Indians fought night and day. They wouldn't let us get any sleep at all."

McGuire asked, "Were you there?"

Horace said, "Yep, I was there and you can damn-well be sure Indians will fight at night."

McGuire stood and walked over to his one remaining corporal.

"Saunders, I want these tents moved out to a one-hundred-foot perimeter. At first light, I want you to divide the men into two groups. Each group will take turns making a sweep around this position for a distance of five miles. You'll be looking for any sign of Indian activity. When the first group gets back, the second group will move out."

Corporal Saunders said, "Whatever you say, Sarge."

*

Charley dragged the cooked corpse of Private Davis off into the bushes. He was pulling the body by the forearm when the flesh of the roasted man slid off the bone. He held the charred meat in his hand and looked at it. Out of curiosity, he tasted it. It wasn't too bad. A little like the pig meat that he'd been forced to eat on the reservation.

He chewed and swallowed. He nodded his head in satisfaction and took another bite. This was good. He would eat the white man and turn him into Apache shit. A fitting ending for all white men. In the future, he would eat a little piece of every white man he killed.

*

Colt woke up the next morning to Dixon's snoring. He saw the half-empty bottle of whiskey on the lamp stand between their beds. Apparently, Dixon had gone out drinking the night before and had brought the bottle back. Colt's arm was stiff, but it wasn't throbbing as bad as the day before. He was also hungry as hell, having missed supper last night. He got up and dressed.

He put his backup gun in his waistband and strapped on his other guns. Dixon was still snoring when he left.

Colt had breakfast and then walked down to the doctor's.

The doctor examined him and said, "I don't see any infection. Looks like I did a good job, in spite of myself. Most of my patients die."

Colt looked at him with alarm and the doctor said, "Eventually, son, eventually. We all die eventually. You have to allow me my little joke. Actually, I'm a hell of a good surgeon. Your condition proves it. We'll keep you wrapped tight for a few more days, then come back to see me."

Colt said, "I can't, Doc. I have to go look for my little brother. He's lost himself out in the desert someplace. I'll be leaving today."

"Son, I sure wouldn't recommend that. You're healing real well right now, but if you aren't careful you could wind up a cripple. I'm telling you to lay off of horse riding for at least a couple of weeks— and don't even think about using that arm for a month. You'll find that, even then, you'll have atrophy and you'll have little strength in it. It may take six months of gentle exercise to get it back to normal."

Colt asked, "What's atrophy? Is there any cure for it?"

The doctor laughed. "Atrophy isn't a disease, son. It's what happens if you don't use a limb like an arm or a leg for a while. You lose your muscle tone and it shrinks."

Colt looked hard at the doctor and asked in all seriousness, "Does that mean everything, Doc? I mean, like, if I don't use something reg-ular it's gonna shrink?"

The doctor, realizing what Colt was asking and that he was in fact serious, laughed. "No, Colt, at least not in your case. Maybe in mine, though. I haven't used a certain muscle in more than ten years and, yes, it has shrunk. That usually comes with age, though. You have a while before you have to worry about your pecker shrinking up like mine."

Colt's ears were burning with embarrassment. "How much do I owe you, Doc?"

"Three dollars." He took the money from Colt and said, "Good luck, son."

Colt walked back to the rooming house and met Dixon as he was coming out. "You don't look too good, Billy, are you OK?"

Dixon said, "I'm all right. Just a little too much of the dog, is all."

"Billy, I can't stick around here while my brother is out yonder somewhere. I have to go looking."

Dixon put a hand on Colt's good shoulder. "I understand what you're saying, but where're you gonna start looking? There are thou-sands of square miles of desert out there. Any tracks left will be mighty cold by now. I reckon he'll show up at some ranch some-where. It doesn't sound like your little brother's got any quit in him."

"I've been thinking. I figure if we backtracked that Indian you killed, I might be able to figure out where Douglas split off and fol-low him."

"That's a possibility, son, but not a very good one. I don't think that your brother's stupid. I figure he hid his tracks best he could from those Indians. If an Apache couldn't track him, I don't give us a whole lot of chance."

Colt said, "Well, I have to try anyway. If you reckon we could leave today or first thing in the morning, I'd ride back with you and help guard your prisoner as far as that creek where we found those Indians and horses. Then, if you don't mind, I'll split off. You can have my share of the warrants. You've already done more than enough to deserve it. Use it to buy some cows for that widow woman that you've been talking about."

Dixon glanced around to make sure no one was within earshot. "Well, I thank you, Colt. I haven't said this to many folks but I have a right-sized amount of cash squirreled away in a bank in Austin. I figure that I have enough money. Besides, you earned your share. I'll give you an address where you can write to me when you get settled in one place. Then I'll send you your share. I figure this is gonna be my last trip, anyway.

When I get old Peoples delivered to Austin, I think I'm gonna resign my commission and head on up to see my lady. If she's inclined, I might just get hitched and settle down. I'm not even gonna bother with these other warrants. If you want 'em, go ahead and take 'em if you feel up to it. I reckon we can head out whenever you feel like it."

Colt said, "I'm not supposed to do any riding for a while, but the doc didn't say anything about riding in a wagon. Maybe I could drive it. We could shackle up old Peoples in the back."

"Not with that arm you can't, Colt," Dixon said. "Why don't we both ride the wagon? I'll drive and you watch Peoples. We can tie our horses on the back."

Colt grinned. "I know the day's half gone, Billy, but I want to get started."

"Okay, son. You go get our things and meet me at the sheriff's. I'll get Peoples and the wagon. We'll load up our tack and get out of here as soon as we can."

TWENTY THREE

Dixon left Colt and walked to the stage line office. He went in and said, "My name's Billy Dixon and I brought in a few horses and a cow. I figure they might belong to you folks. I took them away from some Indians that I think burned out your station up at Encinal."

The short, fat, man sitting behind the desk peered over his glasses and said, "So you're the one. I've already seen those horses. They have the company brand on them and I've already claimed possession of them. You don't have them anymore. What's this about Encinal?"

Dixon said, "Well, I didn't personally see it burn—but I saw smoke, and lots of it, from that direction. Then we saw some Indians driving your stock. We killed a couple of them and got the stock back. We drove them down here. Figured you folks might pay a little reward for us getting them back to you."

"Is that a fact?" The man gave Dixon a sneer. "Well, we already have them back. They are legally ours and nobody asked you to help. Why would you think we would pay you anything?"

"Well, sir," Dixon said, "because it's the right thing to do."

The fat little man said, "If doing the right thing was profitable, we'd all be perfect citizens, wouldn't we? Nope, I don't reckon our company would be willing to pay anything after the fact. So if you don't mind, sir, this matter is closed."

Dixon said, "I reckon I can't make you change your mind," and turned to walk out.

The little man stood. "Now, just a minute. Finish what you were saying about Encinal. How long ago? How many Indians were there?"

"Little fat man," Dixon said, looking him directly in the eye, "Any more information is gonna cost you money."

The man ran around his desk. "Hell, man, people might be dead. You can't keep something like that to yourself. It isn't decent."

"Like you said, mister," Dixon said with a smile. "Being decent isn't always profitable. That information is gonna cost you fifty dollars. I was only gonna ask twenty-five for bringing back your stock. Now it's fifty or you can go to hell."

"There was a safe at Encinal. Did you see any sign of it?"

"I saw a lot of things and a lot of things I didn't see," Dixon said. "Like I told you, it's gonna cost you fifty dollars to find out."

"Hell, I doubt if there was fifty dollars in the safe. Forget it. You're an evil man, Dixon. People might've died—probably have—and you're trying to profit from it."

"Think whatever you want." Dixon turned and left the man sputtering.

*

Dixon hitched Peoples' team and threw his and Colt's tack in the wagon. He tied their three horses to the rear and then climbed inside to survey Peoples' belongings.

Although he'd ridden in the wagon on the trip across the border, his attention was on Gomez and the Federales so he hadn't paid any attention to what was in the wagon.

Looking around, Dixon saw box after box of bottles; some containing powder and some filled with liquid. Most of them had strange-sounding forty-dollar words on the labels. At least half were some type of poison and had the skull and crossbones painted on the label.

He rummaged through a bundle of sour-smelling, dirty clothes and found a sawed-off shotgun and an old Volcanic .30 caliber pistol. He shoved that in his pocket. That gun would go into his collection. He could sell the shotgun for five or ten dollars.

Pushing the clothes aside, he found a decaying cardboard box filled with old newspaper clippings. He thumbed through the obituaries of various people who had died of mysterious ailments. One was about the poisoning of a snake oil salesman and his dog. Elroy Peoples had sold the salesman's wagon and merchandise and had fled Palestine Texas. This was the murder that prompted the rangers to become involved. Killing the salesman was bad enough, but there was something about killing the dog that really bothered Billy.

He rummaged further and found additional newspaper stories about the poisonings of three women in Albany New York—all had been married to Peoples. Most of the clippings had yellowed and faded from age, but there was a more recent one. It was from the Laredo Daily News about an anthrax outbreak.

Dixon studied the article. He reread it and then put it in his shirt pocket. He was climbing into the driver's seat when the hostler came over.

"Excuse me, sir, but you haven't paid for the boarding of those horses."

Dixon settled onto the wagon seat, then said, "Yes, sir, I'll pay for these. But you're gonna have to talk to that little man in the stage office about the others. They're his horses."

The hostler said, "Well, Mr. Jurgen came over and claimed that they were his horses, but I wouldn't let him have them because he said he wasn't gonna pay for the boarding. He said that whoever brought them in was responsible. He refused to pay for anything that he didn't authorize."

Dixon grinned. "Is that right? Well, what would you do with them if nobody pays?"

The hostler said, "I'd damn-well turn them out. I'm not gonna feed any horses I'm not getting paid for."

"Suppose I paid," Dixon said. "How much would you charge to take them about five miles out and scatter 'em?"

The hostler grinned. "Hell, mister, that son of a bitch Jurgen's been asking his due for a long time. You pay those horses up and give me five dollars, I'll scatter those sons-of-bitches so good he won't ever find 'em."

Dixon paid the man his money. He released the brake and slapped the reins to the horses.

*

Dixon met Colt at the sheriff's office, where they loaded up their prisoner and headed out.

Peoples was chained with arm and leg shackles that Dixon borrowed from the sheriff. Another chain was riveted to the one linking his ankle-irons to the U-bolt of the axle. About ten feet of slack was left to allow Peoples to get out of the wagon to relieve himself. His hands were chained behind his back with the steel rings around his wrists locked.

They rode in silence for almost an hour.

Finally, Dixon said, "You know, Colt, if I didn't know better, I'd swear that I smell fried chicken."

"Yes, sir, while I was waiting for you, I had the cafe across from the jail fry us up a couple of hens."

Peoples yelled from the back, "That sounds a hell of a lot better than the mush and beans that I've been eating."

"Shut up, Peoples," Dixon said. "You aren't getting anything but water and a fistful of cornmeal."

"Hell, Billy, we have enough for all of us. We have so much that it may go bad before we get to it."

Dixon shook his head. "It isn't because I'm mean, Colt. When you are transporting a prisoner out here—maybe for several days or even weeks—you can't ever tell what's gonna happen. You give your prisoner just enough to keep them alive. You don't want them overpowering you. You want to keep them pretty weak. If they get loose and run off, it isn't so hard to catch them."

Colt looked at Dixon and smiled sheepishly. "I would've never thought of that."

"It's another edge, Colt. You always have to be thinking about that edge. That prisoner gets one quart of water a day, plus a half fistful of cornmeal and that's it. I don't care if you had a hundred fried chickens and had to throw them away. The prisoner doesn't get any. I'm not trying to be mean. I just know that I always have to have an edge on my prisoner."

Colt sat thinking about that. Dixon and his edges. He had to admit that it did make sense. He looked at Dixon without saying any-thing. No wonder this old man was still alive. He knew more about staying alive than Colt could ever imagine. He was sure lucky to have somebody like Billy Dixon as a friend.

*

Charley was getting hungry. He'd eaten the soldiers' rations the day before. He had plenty of water but no food.

He'd tried to eat more of the cooked soldier, but even partially cooked, the meat stank and tasted putrid. He thought about killing one of the horses. Horse meat was good. Almost as good as mule—which was second only to buffalo. He could not be sure even of that, for he had never actually eaten buffalo and had only heard that it was better from the old people.

Of course, the same old ones complained about the pig meat that the whites made them eat. He always liked pig meat but he would never admit it. The roasted soldier tasted a little like pig meat. His stomach was empty and he was deciding which horse he would kill to eat. He only hesitated because he still fantasized about joining with a large band of Apaches and he knew the captured horses would gain him respect.

Charley smiled as he remembered the chickens that they'd made sport of at the relay station. It was only ten or twelve miles and he could cover that distance easily in three or four hours. If any travel-er came, they would have to pass the relay station. Maybe that would be a good place to wait. He would have chickens to eat in the mean-time. He would also have water. He remembered the big turning wheel the white man called a windmill, pumping water from the ground.

This is good, he thought. I will go to the white man's windmill and eat chickens.

He caught up his horses and rode north.

*

When Colt and Dixon arrived at the creek midway between Laredo and Encinal, it was almost dark. They had made ten or twelve miles and were fairly satisfied with their progress. Considering what Dixon referred to as Colt's 'bent wing,' he offered to unhitch the team and gather wood for the fire. Colt could break out the coffeepot and get fresh water from the kegs.

The fried chicken was more than enough for dinner, so they wouldn't have to cook. Colt spread a ground blanket and set out the coffee and chicken. He walked over to the wagon and unbolted the short chain holding Peoples, allowing him to step down and relieve himself.

After he had re-secured Peoples in the wagon, he walked about fifty feet to some mesquite.

He unbuttoned his fly and froze.

There, just ahead, were two bodies, both gutted and mutilated. One was burnt to a crisp and missing an arm. The other had half of his head missing.

"Billy, you had better get over here!"

Dixon, who was busy digging a hole for a fire, could tell from Colt's voice that it was urgent.

He picked up his Henry and ran to where Colt stood, staring at something.

"What's wrong?"

Colt just motioned to the two corpses.

"Shit! Them heathen bastards."

"Any idea of who they could be?" Colt still hadn't moved.

"Hell, they could be anybody. I tell you what, though, it looks like ol' Crazy Charley's work to me. That burnt one has been scalped."

"Looks like he's missing an arm, too. Reckon you know what happened to it?"

Dixon said, "Damned if I know. Well, let's drag them out of there and get them in the ground. They're stinking pretty bad."

The sound of the green flies filled Colt's ears as he turned away. The laudanum that he'd taken for his pain had his stomach in an uproar already, and now seeing and smelling those putrid bodies made his stomach really churn.

Dixon said, "I'll get one of the horses and we'll drag 'em out of there. I figure we ought to plant 'em away from the creek a ways."

Colt swallowed back the bile that had risen to his throat. "What do you want me to do?"

"Don't worry about it. With your bent wing, there isn't much that you can do. Just keep a sharp lookout while I handle it."

Colt nodded his head, grateful that Dixon was going to take care of the bodies.

Instead of walking back the way he came, he took another route that was closer to the creek. He needed to wash his face badly.

He was almost to the creek bank when he saw the remnants of a fire. Someone had dug a fire-pit. He knelt and placed his hands a few inches above the white ash. Heat was still rising from the pit.

Colt found a pile of debris and he recognized the remnants of a soldier's tunic.

He took a stick and rummaged around until he found a second one with corporal's stripes. Someone had defecated on the discarded clothing. He took his stick and dragged the debris out where he could get a better view. He froze for the second time.

"Billy, I think that you'd better get over here. I've found that fellow's arm. They were soldiers. I found part of their uniforms."

Dixon came over to where Colt stood. "Colt, I sure wish you would quit saying 'Billy, get over here.' I done figured out that you don't have any good news when you say that."

Dixon squatted down and looked closely at what was left of the forearm. There was virtually no meat left on it.

"Hell, there's more shit on those bones than there is meat."

He was quiet a moment, then he said, "I think that crazy Indian has started eating people. I think he ate on that arm."

Colt wrinkled his face in disgust. "How do you know animals didn't do it?"

Dixon said, "Two reasons. One, if animals had done this, why haven't they been at the rest of the corpse? There's no indication that either of those poor boys has been chewed on. Second, animals love the marrow. These bones aren't cracked. No, sir, I'm sure. That Indian ate on that arm. There is something else, too. He stacked up those uniforms and that arm into a pile and shit on them. Yep, I think he was expressing his opinion of the army, and maybe other white folk."

"Billy, that's one crazy fucking Indian."

Dixon stood. "Why don't you go on back and start the coffee. I'll get on with the burying, and then we'll eat."

"I'll make the coffee," Colt said, "but I'm not sure about eating."

Dixon said, "Suit yourself, Colt, but out here you eat, drink and rest when you get a chance, no matter what. Things could change in five minutes and you might not get another chance for any of those things for days. Always do that. It gives you a little extra edge. Eat even if you aren't hungry. If you get a chance to fill your belly with water, you drink all you can hold, even if you aren't thirsty."

Colt watched him go. What Dixon said made sense but he still wasn't sure he could eat. Maybe a little coffee, but food just didn't appeal to him.

After Dixon had buried the bodies, they sat in the shadows away from the fire. Colt drank coffee while Dixon ate almost all of the chicken, with relish.

Peoples was complaining and bumping the wagon, trying to get attention.

Dixon tossed a chicken bone into the fire and said, "Goddamnit, Peoples, if you don't knock it off, I swear I'm gonna put you to sleep the hard way."

Peoples said, "I'm hungry and I'm thirsty. You haven't given me any water or anything to eat all day. This is no way to treat a white man."

"Relax, Peoples," Dixon said. "In the morning, I'm gonna give you some cornmeal and a swig of water. Now, shut up! Those are my last words on the subject."

Dixon picked up his coffee cup and took a swig. "Colt," he said, "I was going through this asshole's wagon and I found something pretty interesting. Our fancy Mr. Peoples here seems to have himself a hobby."

Colt, not even casually interested, said, "Oh, yeah?"

"Yep. It seems like he likes to collect stories about different things. Like those wives of his that he was accused of poisoning. He has clippings of obituaries from different papers about people that have died. Some of them he was suspected of having something to do with helping them on their way. I figure he's kind of proud of his work and sort of keeps those clippings as a scrap book."

Colt said, "I guess a lot of people might do that."

Dixon was quiet for a few moments, making a show of swigging his coffee. "Colt, I've been doing a lot of thinking on your anthrax thing. I know for damn sure it wasn't anthrax."

Colt looked up, startled. "You do? How do you know that?"

"A couple of reasons. First, the incubation period was wrong. Second, you didn't see any pustules. Third is that the only cows that died, died at one time. With anthrax one cow passes it to the other, so at first they go one at a time. It's only after it gets into the ground that they start dying in bunches. Fourth is that none of you folks got sick drinking any milk. And last, according to what you said, all those steers that died, died in one field. Nope, I figure those cows were poisoned."

"Come on, Billy, who would do such a thing?"

"Don't we have us a poisoner locked up in that wagon? Colt, I just happen to know that he went through your part of the country just about the time that your cows got sick."

Colt remembered the day that he'd gone into Cotulla with Mr. Hunt. He hadn't gotten a good look at the driver—but how could he have forgotten a red and green wagon?

He nodded and said, "You're right, Billy. I remember seeing his wagon in town the day after they burned our cows."

Dixon said, "I thought so. There's another thing. When I was going through those clippings, I found this."

He reached into his pocket and withdrew the article about the anthrax outbreak.

Colt read it over twice. He shook his head. "Why would Peoples poison our cows? We haven't done him any harm."

Dixon said, "I don't know, but that clipping was one of his souvenirs. He did it or he wouldn't have had any interest in it."

Colt asked, "But, why?"

Dixon was quiet for a moment, then he said, "Colt, the only reason I can think of is that maybe somebody paid him."

"But, hell, Billy, they had a man down from Austin. I think his name was Stallings. He said it was anthrax and he works for the state. He's some kind of an expert."

"I don't know, Colt. Maybe he was paid off. Even experts can be bought."

Colt shook his head. "I just can't figure who would do something like that. What reason would they have?"

"Maybe somebody who wanted the land, son. Maybe it was the bank. I don't know."

Colt shook his head. "No, the bank sold it only for what was owed. They would've got that anyway. There was just no reason for it, Billy. I don't doubt what you're saying—I just don't see anyone getting any profit out of killing our cows."

Dixon was quiet for a few moments, blowing on his hot coffee and swigging with loud sips. "Colt, you say the bank sold your ranch for what was owed?"

"Yes, they sold ours and the Miller's for just what was owed on it. Like I said, they'd have no reason, Billy."

"Who bought those ranches?"

"Mr. Hunt bought both of them. He was our neighbor. Miller's neighbor, too. His ranch was between the Miller's and ours. Mr. Hunt is a real nice fellow. Hell, he gave Ma five hundred dollars to help us on our way."

Dixon rubbed his chin. "Colt, if your daddy hadn't lost those cows, how much you think your property would be worth?"

"I don't know. The cows were only worth two or three thousand dollars but the property might have been worth ten or fifteen thousand. Now that the ground is tainted, it isn't worth anything."

Dixon didn't say anything for a few moments; he just sipped his coffee. Finally, he asked, "How much do you figure the Miller's place was worth?"

"Oh, a whole lot more. He had over two thousand acres and it was all fenced. It was probably worth at least twice ours."

"In other words, Hunt now has somewhere between thirty and forty thousand dollars worth of property that he got just by settling a bank loan. Do you know how much Miller's loan was?"

"Yeah, Pap told me Mr. Miller borrowed five thousand."

Dixon drummed his fingers on the side of his cup. "In other words, this forty to fifty thousand dollars worth of property only cost your daddy's friend about seventy-five hundred."

As the truth sank in, Colt's stomach knotted.

"Yes, Billy, I guess it did."

Dixon stood and stretched. "Why don't we bring our friend Peoples out here? Maybe offer him some coffee and see if he won't tell us what happened."

Colt asked, "Why would he tell us anything?"

"I think he might be very cooperative. I have some pretty persuasive ways of asking."

Dixon walked over to the tailgate of the wagon and said, "Peoples, you've been begging for something to eat. Maybe I'll let you have something."

Peoples scooted over. His hands were still shackled behind him. His legs were still in irons and the twenty-foot chain was still attached, giving him just enough length to hobble over to the fire.

Dixon motioned to a nearby log and told Peoples to sit. He said, "Let me get you a cup of coffee an' some chicken, Mr. Peoples."

The prisoner eyed Dixon with suspicion. "What's the catch? Why're you suddenly being so nice to me?"

Dixon got the chicken and laid it on the log so Peoples could smell it. He poured a steaming cup of coffee and sat opposite Peoples.

Peoples asked, "How do you expect me to eat with my hands shackled?"

Dixon said, "Hell, I'll hold it for you."

"Well, what are you waiting for? I'm hungry and I'm thirsty."

"Mr. Peoples, we have to discuss that a little. You see, if you want that chicken and coffee, you have to answer a couple of questions that's bothering my partner an' me."

Peoples smiled. "I knew it. I knew there was a catch."

Dixon said, "I went through your wagon and I know you poisoned a bunch of cows up north. I want you to tell me about that."

Peoples laughed and said, "That's preposterous. Go to hell!"

"Peoples, you know as well as you're sitting there that you're gonna hang if I get you back to Austin. Now, I think you know that I'm going to do that if I don't kill you first. Now, I have an execution warrant signed by the governor. Mr. Peoples, do you know what an execution warrant is?"

Peoples shook his head, not liking what he was hearing.

Dixon continued. "An execution warrant means that the court has ordered your death, Peoples. Anybody with this warrant can kill you legally."

Peoples said, "They can't do that. They never caught me. I never stood trial."

"Oh, Mr. Peoples." Dixon stopped to chuckle. "You did stand trial, all right. The only thing is, you weren't there. The State of New York has already tried you in absentee for three murders there and found you guilty." Even if you beat the charges against you in Texas, US Marshalls are gonna haul your ass back to New York and hang you there.

Peoples shook his head. "I don't believe that. They can't do that."

Dixon said, "Oh, yes, they can—and they did."

Peoples, obviously worried, shook his head again. "I still don't believe you. I've never heard of such a thing."

"Believe what you want. But you know that you're gonna hang."

"I don't know that," Peoples said. "Anything can happen."

"Oh, you're gonna hang, all right," Dixon said. "Unless I kill you out here. Do you believe I'll do that?"

"Yeah, I guess you would."

Dixon said, "Well, now that we understand each other, why don't you tell us about those cows. You aren't gonna be in any more trouble than you're already in."

Peoples glared at Dixon. "Why should I? Why should I help you? What's in it for me?"

"Mr. Peoples, stand up."

"Why?"

"Because I said to." Dixon grabbed Peoples by his arm shackles and jerked him to his feet. He threw him towards the fire-pit; just as Peoples was flung forward Dixon stuck out his left foot, causing him to stumble and fall forward, landing across the fire. The coals were only inches below his stomach.

Dixon put his boot in Peoples' back, holding him down. "Mr. Peoples, you tell *me* why you should help us." Dixon was hissing now as he leaned over the terrified man.

"My God, let me up! Let me up!" Peoples screamed. "I'll tell you! Goddamnit, let me up!"

Dixon pulled Peoples to his feet and sat him back on the log.

Colt could see smoke coming from the front of Peoples' shirt.

Peoples was gasping. "You're a maniac. You know that, Dixon? You're worse than I am!"

"You're damned right, I'm worse than you. Now, you have two choices. You can have that chicken and a cup of coffee, or I'm gonna pull down your pants and put you back on that fire. You have about three seconds to decide."

Peoples nodded. "Okay, I'll tell you. Do I still get the coffee and chicken?"

Dixon said, "Yep, you'll get it."

Peoples said, "You burnt my chest; can you put something on it?"

Dixon shook his head. "Nope. Tonight while you're thinking about this little scorching, I want you to tell yourself that next time Billy Dixon asks you something, he expects some consideration. But you can have the coffee and the chicken."

Peoples told the whole story. A man named Thurston Schneider had contacted him. Schneider was only a middleman.

Dixon wanted to know who Schneider worked for.

Peoples said he had followed Schneider and he'd met another man who he'd called Mr. Hunt. Hunt had asked Schneider if Stallings was taken care of.

He didn't know or care who Stallings was. He only cared about his five hundred dollars. All he did was to pour a whole pint of strychnine into a water tank on Patterson's ranch. He also dumped a like amount on some feed bought by the Millers.

Peoples seemed to take pride in his explanation of strychnine. "It's just an alkaloid that can be obtained from plants such as nux vomica."

Dixon stopped him. "I don't give a shit where you got it, Mr.

Peoples. Now, if I ask you, will you sign a statement about your part in this?"

Peoples saw the look in Dixon's eye. "Yeah, I'll sign whatever you want. Schneider and Hunt don't mean anything to me."

Colt couldn't believe what he'd heard. Mr. Hunt had been his father's friend. Their families had helped each other and had even gone on church picnics together.

Colt said, "I'm sorry, Billy. I still don't believe it. There aren't any finer folks then the Hunts. This asshole is lying."

Peoples looked at Colt. "Why would I lie? I don't know any of you people and I've nothing to lose or gain. You wanted to know, and I told you. Believe it or don't."

Peoples turned to Dixon and said, "That coffee's getting cold. Reckon I could have some?"

"Sure, Mr. Peoples, and you can have the chicken, too. Just let me get those cuffs off your wrists so you can eat normal. Right after you sign your statement."

TWENTY FOUR

Horace climbed into his saddle and joined the four troopers. The patrols had been his idea but he was beginning to believe that it wasn't a good one after all.

The men were as tired as the horses and he figured that when they got relieved, he would suggest to Sergeant McGuire that they sit it out at the station. Oh, well, another six hours in the saddle wouldn't kill him.

He spurred his horse and caught up with Private Jorgenson.

*

Charley studied the tracks. At first it appeared that several horsemen, maybe as many as twelve, had crossed the trail.

He noticed a slight difference in the hoofprints. Some had a sharp ridge around the edges. Others looked fairly fresh but lacked the crisp edges.

Charley dismounted and examined the tracks closely. He noted that two sets of tracks had an identical ridge caused by an imperfection in the iron shoe the horse was wearing.

He walked, leading his horse. For some reason, the tracks had made at least two trips going in the same direction. There were no return tracks. This was very confusing.

Charley saw another double set of tracks where the right rear hoof of the horse indicated a small fan of disturbed sand just before the mark. Again, both were going in the same direction. The horses were shod. That meant that they were white men's horses. Maybe it was the soldiers he'd fought. He decided to backtrack the horses.

He mounted his horse and rode due west for an hour before a thought struck him.

Of course! It was a patrol. The stupid white men were following their own tracks. He stopped his horse and jumped down. What appeared to be tracks of at least twelve, maybe fifteen, horses were actually only a few horses going in circles. Yes, not only was there one set that appeared recent, he could also see tracks upon tracks. They had passed at least three times.

He tried to guess the age of the oldest track. One set of tracks appeared less than two days old. Another set, maybe one day, and a third set looked only hours old. That meant every six to ten hours they passed this way. One set of tracks looked almost as fresh as the ones his horses were making. If that was true, they'd crossed in front of him by no more than an hour. That meant they would come back within five to eight hours.

It looked like four, or no more than five, men. They must be soldiers. If he planned it right he might be able to get one, or maybe two, soldiers. If he shot the soldiers and could shoot their horses, too, he would at least get their day's rations.

If they were the same—or of the same caliber as the ones he fought before—they would panic at the first shot. Maybe he could get all five.

Charley found a ravine, hid the horses and walked to where he could watch the trail.

He burrowed under the brush and waited. He could get at least one, and possibly two, before they could react. The remaining soldiers would either run like rabbits, charge his position, or dismount to fight in place.

There were no rocks or brush on the trail that could offer cover for the soldiers. Unless they shot their horses and used them for cover, they'd be exposed. He doubted if they would do that. If they did, he could shoot as many as possible then simply leave. If they ran, he would have the supplies of one, and possibly two, troopers. If they charged, they would be in plain view for several seconds.

If they were that foolish, he would kill them all. If they panicked and ran there was the chance the survivors might split up and try to flank him. He decided that he would shoot and then move to another position. That way, if they did try to flank him, he could pick off one or two more while they thought they were sneaking up on him.

Charley smiled. Yes, it is good. The white man is not smart fighter. If there weren't so many, the Apache would finish them off soon. Maybe Charley would eat more white man meat and turn it into Apache shit.

*

The sun was getting low on the horizon, and Horace was grateful that it was cooling off.

They were almost a third of the way into their patrol and his ass hurt. They'd seen neither hide nor hair of any hostiles. They'd seen nothing. That Ranger Dixon was right. There were only one or two renegades and they were probably in Mexico by now.

He was half-dozing in the saddle, with the four troopers strung out behind in single file. He was staying on the tracks of the previous patrols. This was his third time around and he was beginning to learn the trail by heart.

He casually looked ahead and saw something. It looked like a line in the sand leading out from the previously laid tracks.

Horace slowed his horse as he approached and saw that the line was actually a series of horses' tracks.

As he came upon them, he noted that the angle that the tracks took gave him the impression that whoever belonged to those horses may be trying to avoid being seen.

Now why would that be? It could be white no-accounts or Indians who'd stolen white men's horses.

He turned back to tell the troopers to be on the alert when something smacked his right knee.

The blow was followed by the crack of a rifle. Horace was reaching for his Spencer when his horse went down even before the shot faded.

Horace tried to kick his leg free of the stirrup as his horse fell, but for some reason, his right leg didn't work.

The horse landed on him, pinning his leg and rifle under its body. Horace heard a man yell "Go! Go! Go!"

Several hooves passed over him as the troopers charged forward. Horace heard a smack and a second shot. He couldn't use his right arm and was fumbling with his left hand, trying to reach his revolver. He'd never liked the cavalry's way of carrying their revolvers butt forward, but now he wished that he had adopted their method. He was still fumbling for his revolver when something struck him on top of the head, causing a brilliant white flash that lasted for only a heart-beat. He didn't hear the sound of the shot that followed almost simul-taneously.

*

The three remaining troopers ran their horses for almost a mile before they slowed and then stopped.

They'd all seen Horace go down but it was only then that they realized they were also short Jesse Kline.

Private First Class Ernest Jorgenson outranked the other survivors and he'd wet his pants.

One of the troopers said, "What the shit! I think they got ol' Horace and Kline. What are we gonna do, Ernie?"

Ernie was shaking. He didn't know what to do. He wanted to keep going and just get the hell out of this fucking desert as fast as he could. The same trooper asked, "Were they Indians or what?"

Ernie said, "Hell, I don't know. Probably. Who else would be shooting at us?"

The trooper asked, "How many do you reckon there were?"

"How the hell should I know? I don't know everything. Maybe only a couple." Ernie thought a moment. "If there were more, we'd all be down."

"We can't just leave ol' Horace and Kline back there. We have to do something," the trooper said. "If they're only one or two, maybe we can circle around and sneak up on 'em. Heck, there's three of us and we're trained soldiers. We could take them."

Ernest said, "We have to warn Sergeant McGuire. I reckon one of us ought to hightail it to the station and report. Harrison, why don't you go? Me and Anthony will go back and see what we can do."

*

As soon as Charley shot the two men out of their saddles, he immediately ran back to his second position to wait. Whatever these white mans did, they'd do it soon.

He waited.

*

Sergeant McGuire was pouring himself a cup of coffee when he heard the sound of a distant shot.

He froze. He heard a second shot. The patrol was apparently engaged with someone out there.

"Stand to, men. We may have trouble."

There was a scramble as McGuires's remaining four men kicked out of their blankets and grabbed their weapons.

He heard a third shot. McGuire jumped into the trench with his rifle and asked the nearest trooper, "Marty, what kind of rifle is doing that shooting?"

"Sounds like our sound, Sarge. Sounds like a Spencer."

McGuire said, "I sure hope you're right."

*

Dixon and Colt were in the wagon when they heard the shots.

Dixon looked startled and asked, "Uh-oh. Did you hear that?"

"Yeah, I heard it. Sounds like it's ahead of us and a long way off."

They heard a second shot, followed by a third a few moments later. "It's that goddamn Crazy Charley. I bet my bottom dollar."

Dixon halted the team. "Colt, do you reckon you can handle this team with your sore arm?"

"Yeah, I reckon."

"Why don't we saddle up our horses an' I'll ride on ahead. That way, we won't both be in the same place in case that son of a bitch shoots at us."

Dixon saddled up both their horses. He left Blue Eye tied to the back of the wagon, took his Henry and mounted his grulla.

"Colt, drag Peoples' ass up here and chain him to the seat next to you. If anybody shoots, they might shoot him first, giving you a chance to duck."

"Always that edge, huh, Billy?"

Dixon nodded. "Take an edge every time you can, son. With old Peoples up here, you have a fifty-percent better chance of not getting shot. Now, the sand is too deep off to the side, so you have no choice but to stay on the road. I'm gonna ride about a hundred yards ahead. Mayhaps we can get some warning that way."

Dixon dug his heels into the flanks of his grulla and was soon out of sight.

Colt chained Peoples to the right of the seat. He figured with Dixon on the left and Peoples on his right, he might increase his edge even a little more. He soon had the wagon rolling again.

*

Charley didn't have to wait long. He saw two soldiers riding in from the south. They stopped their horses and tied them to a mesquite. He watched as they came creeping up on his earlier position. He knew there was a third one somewhere. Either that one had ridden for help or he was circling from another direction. He'd have to watch for that possibility.

He lay watching the two soldiers. They would creep up to one bush and then run to the next. One would stay behind to cover while the other ran to the next position.

He waited.

Finally, as Charley knew he would, one of the soldiers found the tracks that Charley had made when he changed positions.

The soldier froze and yelled, "Shit, Tony, he's behind us. Look out!"

The trooper turned and looked right at Charley. He was bringing his gun up when Charley fired. The 56-50 slug hit him in the mouth.

Charley calmly levered another round in before the first trooper's body hit the ground. He heard a splat then a shot. Dirt kicked up in front of his head and flew into his face.

He pulled slightly to his left and fired into the small bush that the second trooper had fired from behind. Charley heard a cuss and a groan.

The trooper fired a second time. Charley felt the buzz of the bullet as it passed an inch or so over his head.

Charley fired again at the smoke. He heard a sound like someone falling and heard the brush rattle. He saw what appeared to be a boot with the toe turned up.

He sighted on the toe, then moved his sights to what he estimated to be about five feet to his right.

Charley fired a third time. He saw the foot jerk. He was sure he'd made a hit.

He knew of a way to be sure if the man was dead or unconscious.

He moved his sights back to the foot. He fired.

Half of the foot disappeared. The rest of the foot didn't move after the impact.

If the man were still alive or conscious, he'd be shaking that foot like a dog shaking a rabbit.

Charley moved his position again. He had to know about that last missing man. He circled completely around the entire battle zone. He found a set of tracks heading east.

The last man had gone for help. He was probably heading for the station where they had killed the old man and woman. If that was where he was heading, the rider could be there by now.

He would have to hurry. The other soldiers could be back in minutes.

He scalped each trooper, took their weapons and gathered their horses.

Charley was mounting his own horse when he got a wonderful idea. He would make Apache shit out of them all.

He dismounted and ran to each body. He cut an arm from each, bundled them up and tied the limbs onto the spare horses.

Charley tied a rope to some brush so that it would drag behind the trailing horse and rode away.

TWENTY FIVE

Dixon, riding out in front, heard more shots. He counted a total of six. They sounded much closer.

Peoples asked, "What's going on?"

Colt said, "Somebody's shooting. Didn't you hear them shots earlier?"

Peoples shook his head. "I don't hear too good. What do you think it is? I mean, who do you think it is?"

"I don't know for sure," Colt said, "but there's a crazy Indian running around shooting an' eating people. You know those two corpses that we buried back yonder? Well, it looks like somebody had been eating on them. Maybe the army has him cornered. I sure hope so."

*

McGuire told Douglas to get into the trench. "Boy, can you shoot that rifle of yours?"

Douglas said, "I shot that Indian, didn't I?"

"Well, that's what I have been told. You just hunker right down in that trench by the windmill. I'm putting you in charge of getting the water if we need it."

Douglas was proud to be told that a real soldier needed him. If the Indians came he would shoot them all. He promised himself that he wouldn't close his eyes this time. That was going to be the hard part. Every time Pappy let him shoot his gun, he'd always closed his eyes.

Somebody yelled, "Rider coming in!" McGuire looked up to see a rider about a half-mile away coming at a dead run. Even at that distance McGuire could see that the rider was using his reins to whip the horse.

That's when he heard more shots. He thought he counted six. Two of them were right together. He had a bad feeling that it wasn't his men doing all of the shooting. That rider coming in confirmed it.

They all watched as the rider galloped his horse right into camp, leaping over the trench and nearly braining one of the troopers.

Trooper Harrison dismounted at a run and stumbled to McGuire.

"Sarge, we were ambushed. Old Horace and Trooper Kline are down. Ernie and Anthony went back to check on them. Ernie sent me here to tell you."

"How many? Were they Indians?"

Harrison said, "I don't know, Sarge. We never did see 'em. Ernie figured it was only one or two. He said that if there were more, they would've killed us all. I figure he was right."

"Well, catch up that horse of yours before he runs off," McGuire said. "Give him an yourself some water then come back here."

McGuire threw his forage cap on the ground in frustration and said to no one in particular, "Shit, we've lost all of our officers and half of our troops. I just don't believe that one Indian or one nobody could do all that. It had to be more. Shit!"

He made a decision. Every time he sent somebody out, they didn't usually come back. They would just stay right goddamn here until they were relieved. If Ernie and Anthony got their Indian that would be well and good. If they hadn't, well, it was too late to worry about them. *Yes, sir,* he thought, *we're going to stay right goddamn here.*

*

Dixon rode at a slow walk. He kept his eyes peeled and his Henry ready. He rode out of a shallow depression and saw the tracks. At first, it looked like ten to fifteen riders had crossed from west to east. He could see what appeared to be three tracks heading in the opposite direction. He recognized all three sets going west. Two were from the horses that had made the tracks heading south on the road. *No doubt ridden by them two dead soldier boys.* The other track he knew for damn sure. *It's that crazy, flesh-eating Indian.*

He rode back to the wagon.

"Colt! I found tracks. It's Indian Charley. He's backtracking somebody. I'm not sure, but it may be a patrol out riding and Charley's laid for 'em. I'll bet you we have some dead soldier boys to the west of us. I feel it in my guts."

Colt didn't speak.

"Well, that wagon ain't gonna make it off that road and it's only about another half-hour or so to Encinal. Let's head over there and see if there're any soldier boys left. If there is, I'll leave you there to rest up and I'll go do some Indian hunting for my own self."

"You aren't going after that little bastard without me, Billy."

"Colt, I hate to say it, but your arm isn't gonna take any hard riding and that's all there is to it."

Colt shook his head. "If you go, I'm going. I said I'd back you all the way an' I mean it. My arm will take it."

"No, Colt, it won't. If you aren't careful you're gonna get it bleeding again. If that happens, you aren't going to be any help to me."

"I'm going, Billy."

Dixon laughed. "You're one hard-headed son of a bitch. Well, we'll talk about it when we get to Encinal."

*

It was dark when they approached the remains of the relay station. Dixon and Colt could see a ring of at least eight fires surrounding the grounds.

"What the hell do they think they're doing with all those fires?"

They started to ride in when they were challenged. "Halt! Who goes there?"

"It's Ranger Billy Dixon and Colt Patterson. We have a prisoner."

"Advance and be recognized."

Dixon said, "Hell, I'm done recognized, I told you who we are." They pulled toward the nervous sentry.

"Where's Horace or that Sergeant McGuire or whatever his name is?"

"Horace is missing and feared dead, sir. Sergeant McGuire is over yonder by the windmill."

Dixon looked over in the direction the trooper indicated. "Where? I don't see anybody."

"Down in the trench, sir. We dug in."

"Come on, Colt, park that wagon by the windmill and let's see what all these fires are about."

Dixon dismounted and tied the grulla to the wagon.

Colt climbed from the wagon, leaving Peoples sitting on the bench seat.

Dixon yelled out, "McGuire, are you here?"

McGuire stuck his head out of the trench. "Over here."

Dixon and Colt walked up just as Douglas's yellow hair popped up out of the trench.

Douglas and Colt froze. They both just looked at each other, neither believing what they saw.

Douglas scrambled out of the trench and yelled, "That's my brother! That's my brother!"

Colt ran over and embraced him.

Douglas burst into tears and pressed his head against Colt's chest.

"I didn't ever think I was going to see you again. They killed Ma, Colt. They did terrible things to her and tied me up and made me go with them. I didn't want to go, Colt. They kept me tied up and beat on me, but I got away."

Colt swallowed the lump in his throat and just hugged his brother.

"It's okay, Douglas. We're together now, and I'm not gonna leave you. Not ever again."

Dixon said, "So that's your little brother. Didn't I tell you that he'd make it?"

Douglas wiped his tears and smiled. "I got one of 'em, Colt. I killed one of those son-a-bitches."

"Douglas, don't talk like that. Ma wouldn't like it."

"I don't care what you say. They're son-a-bitches. I hate 'em. If

I could, I'd kill 'em all."

Colt said, "Well, maybe you earned the right to call them son-a-bitches. I'll call 'em son-a-bitches, too. Okay?"

Douglas smiled. "Yeah, you can call them son-a-bitches, too."

Dixon asked, "Sergeant, what are you doing with all these fires? They can be seen for miles. If old Charley's in the area, he could pick us off like flies."

"Mr. Dixon, the men are kind of spooked. They built them up to see better."

"Sarge, I am not trying to mind your business but, not only are those fires lighting up this whole goddamn place, but no one here is gonna have any night vision. Hell, Sergeant, those fires are about the worst thing you could do next to surrendering to ol' Charley."

McGuire said, "Yeah, I guess you're right." He said, "Men, put out them fires. Right now!"

"Sarge, if you want a cook-fire, dig a hole or put it in that trench. It can't be seen so far that way."

"Mr. Dixon," McGuire said. "Would you mind having a cup of coffee with me? I'd like to talk to you."

"I'd really like a cup of coffee."

"Your partner's invited too."

Peoples asked, "What about me? I could use a cup of coffee. Are you gonna leave me here all night?"

Dixon said, "Peoples, shut your mouth. I'll tell you when you can talk. You just sit there for a while."

Over coffee, McGuire lowered his voice.

"Mr. Dixon, I've been in the army almost four years. All I've ever done is march, parade around or sit on my ass out in the middle of New Mexico. They sent us looking for Victorio and Geronimo. Now, I can't afford to have my men lose confidence in me, but I've never been in a fight before."

Dixon took a long sip of coffee, but said nothing.

"I don't know anything about fighting any Indians, either. Hell, I sent out two men day before yesterday to Laredo with a dispatch. They haven't come back. I sent out a five-man patrol and so far only one's come back. At least two are shot and probably dead. The other two haven't come back, so I figure they're dead, too. We started out with twelve men. Now there are only six of us left. I just don't know what to do."

Dixon sighed. "Sarge, those two that you sent to Laredo didn't make it. We found their bodies about ten miles south. I'm pretty sure ol' Charley got them. Probably got your other ones, too."

McGuire said, "Old Charley. How old is he?"

"Oh, I don't mean old. Hell, he can't be more than about seventeen or eighteen."

"You're funnin' me! Are you telling me a seventeen-year-old kid did all this?"

Dixon said, "Yep. This and a whole bunch more. I hate to give you more bad news, but that crazy son of a bitch ate part of one of your soldiers."

"What?" McGuire, realizing too late that he had shouted, lowered his voice. "You mean he cannibaled one of my men?"

Dixon nodded. "I'm afraid so, Sarge. Charley ate his arm and left the bones on top of their uniforms. Then he took a shit on it. I figure he was sending us a message. He also scalped and tortured one. Burnt 'im up. First Apache I ever saw do that. This one's a real bad one, I swear."

"Mr. Dixon, I can't keep sending men out and not have them come back. On the other hand, I can't leave those other men out there. I have to get them back somehow."

"Well, Sarge, come morning, why don't I take my wagon an' a couple of your men and see if we can't fetch those boys back. There're some deep sand pockets out there so we'll have to hitch a couple more horses to my team. That's one hell of a heavy wagon."

McGuire said, "Mr. Dixon, if you'd do that I'd be much obliged."

Dixon looked at Colt. "Partner, you don't mind if I go out tomorrow with a couple troopers? You can stay here with Douglas and watch old Peoples. We shouldn't be gone more than four or five hours."

"Billy, like I said, if you're going after Charley, I'm going too."

"I promise I'm not going after Charley. I'm just gonna go and get those soldier boys back. I promise."

Colt said, "okay, then I'll stay."

Just then, Peoples yelled, "Goddamn it, I have to piss."

Dixon said, "Hold your water, you piece of shit. I'll be there in a minute." Dixon muttered to no one in particular, "Well, I reckon I better go let him piss. If I have to drive that wagon tomorrow, I don't want to be smelling any piss!"

*

The night passed uneventfully. The next morning, Dixon and two troopers left to recover the casualties from the previous day's fighting.

Colt and Douglas didn't get in too much time visiting since each took their turn at guard duty.

Dixon had chained Peoples to the windmill and that was where Colt pitched his blanket, just out of reach of Peoples' lead chain.

Colt ended his watch at daybreak and immediately fell asleep.

*

Colt awoke to the heat of the sun. He removed the hat that he had placed over his face and squinted in the sunlight.

He heard someone yell, "The wagon's coming back!"

Colt stood and brushed the dust from his clothes. He could see the red and green wagon rocking back and forth as it slowly made its way across the sand. He saw the two troopers riding on the sides. Colt walked over to the perimeter to await the news.

Soon McGuire and the others joined him.

As the wagon approached, he could tell by the grim set of Dixon's jaw that the news wasn't good. Of course, no one expected it to be.

The wagon came to a stop in the clearing. Dixon just sat there a moment looking at McGuire. The troopers dismounted without saying a word.

McGuire asked, "Well?"

Dixon just quietly shook his head. "All dead, Sarge. Worse than that, everyone was scalped and had an arm cut off."

McGuire asked, "Why would Indians cut off their arms?"

Dixon said, "Just one arm, Sarge. And it wasn't Indians. It was just one Indian. It was that same crazy bastard I told you about."

McGuire asked, "But, why? I can understand the scalps and even mutilation, but why just one arm?"

Dixon said, "Considering what we saw of your other trooper, I figure ol' Charley is somewhere right now having himself a feast. He's gonna eat those arms an' shit on the bones. I figure that he's telling us something."

McGuire asked, "Jesus Christ! What kind of animal is he?"

He looked at Dixon with a helpless look and said, "Well, let's get 'em buried."

*

It was mid-afternoon before all the bodies were underground. They made crude crosses out of the charred scrap lumber from the building.

Someone broke out a bugle and blew taps. McGuire said a few words and the ceremony was over.

Just as they turned away, the sentry yelled, "Soldiers coming in!"

Brigadier General Amos Forsyth leading a column of eighty officers and men rode into the station.

Forsyth stopped near McGuire, who saluted. "General, am I glad to see you!"

Forsyth sat on his horse a moment and looked about as he casually saluted back. "What's going on here, Sergeant? Where's your commanding officer?"

"Dead, sir. There're only six of us left."

"What happened, Sergeant?"

McGuire looked ill at ease and said, "Sir, begging your pardon, but didn't Mr. Dixon tell you? He rode into Laredo after the first attack."

Forsyth said, "I never spoke to any Mr. Dixon. We left Laredo right after you did. Someone reported sighting Geronimo on our side of the border. Now, Sergeant, I'm not going to ask again. What happened?"

McGuire told him the story. Forsyth turned to his captain. "Have the men dismount and water the horses."

He turned back to McGuire. "You say one Indian damn-near wiped out your company? One Indian took out eight out of fourteen men? I find that hard to believe. Why aren't you out chasing him? From where I'm standing, I see five men. Why do I see them standing here, Sergeant? Why don't I see your Indian in shackles or dead?"

"Begging the General's pardon, but I thought our orders were to secure this station, sir. We did send out patrols every day except for today. Every time we sent anybody out, they got killed."

"Are you afraid of getting killed, Sergeant?"

"It isn't that, sir. We all took our turns going out. The last patrol got ambushed yesterday. I thought it prudent to hold our position until we could be relieved."

"Private McGuire, consider yourself relieved." Forsyth turned to his captain. "Captain Lilly, I want a detail of ten men and an officer after that woolly Indian. I want to see you and that Indian before me by this time tomorrow. Do you understand?"

The captain said, "Yes, sir!"

Ex-Sergeant McGuire said, "General, sir, if I may recommend it, sir, you might want to speak to Mr. Dixon. He seems to know more about this Indian than anyone."

Forsyth said, "Then go get him, Private. When you come back, I don't want to see those stripes on your arms."

McGuire saluted. "Very good, sir." He did his best about-face and went to fetch Dixon.

McGuire removed his tunic and was tearing off his stripes as he walked. He was greatly relieved. He knew the demotion was intended as punishment, but he couldn't be happier. He was no leader and he knew it. Let somebody else make decisions that got people killed. It was a whole lot easier to just follow orders and worry about himself.

Dixon followed McGuire to where Forsyth was talking to Captain Lilly. When they arrived, Forsyth asked, "Are you Mr. Dixon?"

"Yes, General, that's been my name for as long as I remember."

"Don't smart-mouth me, mister. Just tell me what you know about this so-called one-man war party."

"General, why don't you just go to hell." Dixon stared Forsyth straight in the eye. "If you want any information from me, you're gonna have to ask polite."

"One more impertinent remark from you, sir, and I'll have you in irons."

Dixon watched Forsyth coldly. "Mr. General, I guess you could do that. But I reckon when the governor found out that you delayed a Texas Ranger delivering a prisoner and interfered with the legal discharge of his duties, he might not be too happy. You'd likely get busted down so low you'd be saluting the asshole of every snake that slithers by. Now, you, Mr. General, can change your attitude or you can go to hell."

Forsyth was fuming. He'd never been spoken to in such a crude manner. He didn't know what to do. If this man *was* a Texas Ranger and he detained him, the situation could be embarrassing.

He said, "I was not aware that you are a law enforcement officer, Mr. Dixon. You should've said so. I apologize, sir. Would you please be so kind as to tell me what you can of this situation?"

TWENTY SIX

Dixon told the general what he could about Charley Tree. He and Colt then loaded the wagon and pulled out with their prisoner. It was late, but Dixon wanted to get away from the pompous general before he had to shoot him.

Dixon rode his horse while Douglas drove the buggy, with Colt riding on the seat next to him.

They rode until midnight and dry-camped in the middle of the road.

They were only about five miles from Cotulla but they were tired and the wagon was jostling Colt's sore arm.

Colt and Douglas stood watch until four in the morning, while Dixon slept.

They woke Dixon at the agreed time and switched.

Dixon let them sleep until eight in the morning.

Colt and Douglas woke up to the smell of bacon, coffee and wood smoke. Colt got up and stretched. He walked over to where Dixon was frying bacon in one pan and a dozen eggs in another.

"Where did you find those eggs?"

Dixon said, "Back at the relay station. I found a couple of hens and their nest. Some of those eggs may be three or four days old, but they look alright."

Colt squatted next to Dixon and poured a cup of coffee. "You reckon that general would've got in trouble if he'd arrested you?"

"I doubt it. I was pure bluffing." Dixon grinned. "Sometimes when you only got deuces in your hand, you can make them think you have aces."

"You mean like you did with Peoples?"

Dixon said, "What do you mean?"

"That business about him being already tried and found guilty. That death warrant an' all."

"Yeah, like I did with ol' Peoples. That dumb asshole believed it, too."

"It seems like the general did, too

Dixon laughed. " He will hang though and that's for sure. If he don't hang here, he will be extradited to New York where they got him dead bang on three murders."

Colt finished his coffee and went over to let Peoples have his morning piss and to give him his water and cornmeal.

Peoples was getting weak and after he had relieved himself, Colt and Billy had to help him back into the wagon.

Dixon said, "In a couple more days, even if Peoples got out of those chains, he'll be too weak to go anywhere."

"You're a mean man, Mr. Dixon," Peoples said. "A vile and wicked man."

Colt sat studying his breakfast in silence, seemingly caught up in his thoughts.

Dixon looked up and noticed. "Better eat them eggs, son, they're hard to come by out here."

Colt looked up and studied Billy for a moment and asked, "Billy, after that Charley fellow was gonna burn me, you said something that sorta bothers me."

"What was that?"

"You said that maybe you couldn't really blame those Indians for wanting to burn me. I didn't do anything to anybody. I never wanted to hurt anybody in my whole life."

Dixon set his plate aside and said, "Colt, them eggs that you're eating—notice anything special about 'em?"

Colt looked at the eggs for a moment. "No, sir. What's wrong with 'em?"

Dixon said, "Nothing is wrong with 'em. Son, a few years ago, four hungry Santee Sioux broke into a farmer's chicken coop and snuck a few eggs. They could have taken the chickens, or for that matter, broke into the farmer's house and taken everything, but all they took were just them eggs. They were caught and arrested. Their Chief, Little Crow, went to their defense and tried to explain to the authorities that the only reason them boys stole those eggs was because they were hungry. The reason they were hungry was because the supplies promised to them under the treaty had been diverted by corrupt Indian agents, military personnel, and black marketers—who sold the supplies to local merchants—who resold them to the Indians at exorbitant prices. Want to know what the authorities said?"

Colt nodded his head and asked, "What?"

"They said, 'If they're hungry, let them eat grass!' That's right, son. We had them penned up like cattle, starved 'em to death, and then told them they could eat grass. Things got a little out of hand and the farmer's family was killed and then things really went bad. Soon there were whites killing Indians and Indians killing whites. Little Crow was wounded and his second-in-command, Chief Mankato, was killed. Over 400 Santee were rounded up and condemned to death. All of that over a few eggs—no more than you have on that plate."

Colt was stunned. "Well, that don't give them no cause to want to burn me, kill my mother and scalp good Christian white folk."

Billy said, "Colt, you may not believe this but it was white folk that started this scalping business to begin with. The governor of Sonora, Mexico put out a bounty on Indian scalps. Wasn't long 'til every white and Mexican piece of trash was out looking for anybody with long black hair. Hell, they'd take a Mexican or white scalp right along with an Indian scalp. Pretty soon, the Indians really got plumb pissed off and began taking white scalps. 'Til now, I never heard of an Apache taking scalps at all."

Dixon stared at his coffee in silence. He nodded his head toward the horizon and said, "Now, that boy out there, Charley—I figure he come down from Bosque Redondo. If he did, it's no damn wonder he's pissed off. The American army rounded up every tribe they could find and shoved them in there like pigs in a pen. They rounded up the Navajo who ain't never hurt nobody, burned their peach orchards and their saddles, shot their animals and marched them all the way from Canyon de Chelley in Arizona damn-near to Texas. They starved them all the way so they'd be too weak to fight or run. If any fell—and lots of them did—the soldiers killed them on the spot. That included pregnant women. Like I said, son, I can't really blame that boy for being pissed. If I was him, I'd be pissed, too."

Colt was silent as they loaded up. He finally said, "I ain't never heard of no white man wanting to burn anybody alive."

Billy asked, "Is that right? I didn't hear you complaining when I shoved that asshole Peoples in the fire—and you said yourself that you would have burned that Indian to find out where your brother was. It's a hard life out here, son. When you shove somebody in a corner, take their land, starve and kill their family, they sometimes get a little crazy. There ain't nothing right about any of it. It's just about surviving."

*

It was already mid-morning when they pulled out and Colt figured that they would be in Cotulla in an hour or so. He would need that time to think about what Billy had said.

*

Charley was having a breakfast of his own. He roasted all four arms and ate a little from each. He stripped the cooked flesh from the bone and wrapped it up to save the rest for later. He'd seen the lights from the white man's town the night before and knew that he was close.

He smiled as he got an idea. It would be a good joke to play on the white man.

He gathered the bones from the arms and the sleeves of the soldiers' uniforms.

He bundled them up and jogged to the road, where he left his 'joke,' and then he retreated into the desert about two hundred yards; from there he could watch what happened when a white man or woman found his joke.

*

Less than a half-hour later, Charley heard the rattle of a wagon and the sound of horses. He saw the rider out front and two people on the red and green wagon.

It was Man Who Sits on Log. The man on horseback must be the man who shot his cousins and made him run like a rabbit. He would not miss this time. He would shoot the rider first, for he was the most dangerous.

*

Dixon saw something in the road ahead. He moved his horse to the right side of the road so the wagon could come abreast. When Colt was even, he said, "Hold on, Colt. I see something in the middle of the road."

*

Charley lost sight of the horse and rider as the wagon pulled between them.

No matter, he would shoot Man Who Sits on Log. If the rider came for him, he would hold his ground and shoot him as soon as he showed himself.

*

Douglas said, "Whoa," and pulled back on the reins. Just before the wagon came to a full stop, the left wheel hit a small rock and the wagon bumped as it rolled over it. The sudden lurch of the wagon jolted Douglas and Colt, causing their heads to move backward just an inch.

Colt heard a buzz and felt the wind in front of his nose a fraction of a second before he heard the report from the rifle.

Dixon shouted, "Get down. It's Charley!"

Colt and Douglas ducked down just as a second shot was fired.

Dixon kicked his horse into motion as he pulled his Henry from its scabbard. He'd seen the smoke from the second shot. The big grulla charged forward as Dixon levered a round and fired at the clump of brush where he had seen the smoke. He fired a second and a third shot from the galloping horse.

*

Charley saw the man coming; the horse was at a dead run. He saw the man draw his rifle and fire. He felt the bullet as it clipped the brush and whizzed by his head. The man fired a second shot before Charley could stand up.

He fired at the running horse just as the rider fired a third round.

Charley fired again and the big horse's knees buckled. It went down, throwing its rider.

The man's rifle spun through the air as he tumbled off the horse. The man jumped to his feet, drew two revolvers and ran towards Charley, firing both pistols.

*

Dixon knew the range was too great for his revolvers for anything but a lucky shot. He was just trying to keep the Indian's head down until he could close to killing distance.

He emptied both his revolvers and threw them away. He drew his backup revolver from his waistband and continued firing as he charged.

*

Charley waited. He knew that he was going to kill this white man. He knew the man's pistols were no good at this range.

He aimed the Spencer at the man's chest.

Suddenly, something took the gun from his hand with such force his hands stung. The force was followed an instant later by the sound of a shot. The man was closer now, not more than fifty feet away.

Charley picked up his rifle and found it useless. He threw it aside and drew his bow. He nocked an arrow and let it fly.

He saw the arrow strike the man in the thigh. The crazy man charging him didn't seem to notice.

Charley turned and ran as more bullets flew by. He ran about twenty strides while readying a second arrow. He turned and dropped to one knee, releasing the arrow. The second arrow struck the man just above the waist.

The man fired his pistol again and never broke his stride.

Charley ran a few more feet, turned, and let a third arrow fly.

This arrow struck the man in the stomach just above and to the left of the last one.

The man didn't so much as stumble as he fired again.

Charley felt a blow to his right shoulder that knocked him backward.

He stumbled and dropped the bow.

The wild man was still charging him. He could see the wet streaks of sweat cutting through the dust on his face. Charley saw the crazy man's eyes. They were flat. They looked like death and, for the first time, he felt fear.

He reached for his knife just as the man hit him head-on.

They both went down and the man tumbled away from him.

He recovered just as the crazy white man bounced to his feet, holding the biggest knife Charley had ever seen.

Charley charged, thrusting his knife at the white man's belly. Suddenly, the white man's stomach wasn't there anymore.

The man had spun sideways and struck Charley's outstretched arm with one hand, while slashing the huge knife with his other.

Charley tripped over the man's leg. Stumbling, he almost lost his balance.

As he turned to face the white man, he felt nauseous.

He looked down to see his intestines rolling out of a large slash in his stomach.

Charley stared in disbelief. When had he been cut?

He fought to stand, weaving back and forth. Finally, his legs could hold him no longer and he went to his knees.

He dropped his knife and tried to hold in his intestines with his good arm.

*

Dixon stood panting as the Indian collapsed to his knees. He kicked the Indian in the face, knocking him over onto his back.

He was shaking and out of breath. The adrenaline was wearing off and his stomach was burning like fire. He had to get back to the wagon.

The earth was spinning as he took about three faltering steps and fell. He got up, took one more step, and then fell again. This time he felt someone's hands on him, catching his fall.

*

As soon as Colt saw Dixon charge his horse forward, he told Douglas, "Stay here."

He jumped from the wagon, ignoring the pain in his shoulder, and ran after Dixon. Without the use of his right arm he couldn't use his rifle, so he drew one of his pistols. He saw and heard the exchange between Dixon and Charley. He saw Dixon's horse go down.

Dixon did a complete somersault as he hit the ground and came to his feet, firing his pistols as he ran.

Colt was a good hundred feet behind Dixon. He couldn't fire even if he had been in range because Dixon was between him and the target.

He kept running as fast as he could. He saw Dixon charge the Indian, bowling him over.

When Dixon got up, Colt could see the arrows sticking out of him. He saw the Indian go down again. He was still twenty feet away when Dixon turned toward him, took a few faltering steps and fell.

He staggered to his feet and then fell again, just as Colt caught him.

Colt eased his friend to the ground.

Dixon's face was gray and his tight lips were almost white.

"Colt, that little son of a bitch got me good."

"Just lay back, Billy. We'll get you to a doctor. It's only a couple of miles to town."

Dixon grimaced and shook his head. "No, Colt, it ain't no use. That son of a bitch poisoned those arrows. He probably shit on them, too. It's in my insides and it hurts like hell. I don't think I'm gonna make it, son."

"You *will* make it, Billy. Peoples' got some things in the wagon that'll kill your pain. Just hang on." Colt stood and, cupping his hands alongside his mouth, yelled.

"Douglas, get that wagon over here—and hurry!"

Dixon gritted his teeth and gave a little laugh. "I really gutted that little bastard, didn't I?"

Colt walked over to the Indian.

Dixon was right. Charley's belly was wide open and his entrails were spread at least ten feet. Colt never knew a man's insides could stink so much.

He was surprised to hear the Indian gasp. "Man Who Sits on Log, maybe you help Charley. Maybe you shoot Charley."

Colt knelt down near Charley and looked him in the eye.

"Charley, I'm not gonna shoot you. I hope you live long enough to feel the coyotes eating your guts. I hope you're awake when you hear those buzzards flapping their wings and when they pluck out your eyes. No, Charley, I'm not gonna shoot you. I only wish I had the time to watch. Yep, I sure would enjoy that, except that I have to get Billy to some help. There is one thing I am gonna do for you, Charley. I'm gonna relieve you of your hair. I think you ought to know what you've done before you die."

Colt reached down to cut Charley's scalp when he saw the gold watch around Charley's neck. He pulled it off.

"Well, I'll be damned. Pap's gold watch."

He popped the cover open and saw the inscription engraved on the inside. He thought of his father and mother. He thought of the good life he'd left behind and what he'd become in just a few weeks.

He looked at Charley and said, "Fuck you, Charley. I'll never be like you."

Charley laughed in spite of his pain and said, "Fuck you, white man. Fuck all white man."

*

They got Billy loaded into the wagon and laid him on some blankets.

Billy said in a whisper, "Colt, see if you can't find me some writing material. I want to write a letter to that widow woman. I hope that you'll see that she gets it. Also, see that she gets my share of the warrants. I have some money stashed in a bank in Austin. See that she gets that, too, will you?"

"Sure, Billy—but you're gonna give it to her yourself."

"No, I'm not, an' we both know it. That little son of a bitch put snake poison on those arrows. I got snake bit when I was a little boy and it felt the same way. I don't have a lot of time, son, so get me something to write on."

Colt found some blank leaves at the front and back of several chemistry books that Peoples had in a trunk. He found a quill pen and a bottle of India ink. He sat Dixon up so he could write.

Dixon said, "Peoples, I want you to mix me up something that will ease me through this. It's damn near more than I can handle."

Peoples grinned and said, "Why would I help you?"

Colt said, "Peoples, I'll give you ten good reasons why."

Peoples said, "Boy, I don't think you could name one."

"No, I can name ten right off," Colt said. "If those ten aren't enough I can find a few more. I guarantee you, Peoples, if I hear Billy yell out one time, I'm gonna cut off one of your toes. I'm gonna cut another one off every time I hear him yell out or even groan. Now, I'm gonna leave your fingers, because you might have to use them to mix something up. I know that you don't think I'll do it so I reckon I'll take one off now to start, just to get your attention."

Colt reached over and pulled off Peoples' boot.

Peoples yelled, "That won't be necessary! I believe you. Just hold on, now."

"I'm glad that you're willing to help," Colt said. "What do you have that'll kill the pain?"

Dixon spoke up and said, "Colt, you're gonna have to do more than kill the pain."

Peoples said, "He's right. Those two arrows are in his guts. Even if they aren't poisoned, peritonitis will kill him. The poisons from his own insides will do it. If that *is* Indian shit on those arrows, he hasn't a chance. He'll already have blood poison going right up his gullet, and there's nothing to amputate. The snake poison probably won't kill him by itself. I doubt if there was that much on the arrow."

Dixon said, "Oh, they can get plenty on it if they squish up some liver or something to hold it. I think that's what he did, too. Almost guarantee you that he shit on it."

Colt shook his head. "I don't care. We have to try. We'll get into town in a few minutes. We'll let the doc look at him."

Peoples said, "Get that small blue bottle just over your head. That's concentrated tincture of opium. They make laudanum from it. It ought to cut the pain. Don't give him more than a capful or he'll go to sleep forever."

Dixon said, "Give me that bottle, Colt."

"Nope. When you're through writing and want to go to sleep I'll give you some."

Dixon finished writing the letters and Colt gave him the opium. Dixon was asleep in moments.

*

It was less than an hour when they drove the wagon into town and found a doctor.

They carried Dixon inside and laid him on a table. The doctor took out his stethoscope and listened to Dixon's heart for a moment. He moved the stethoscope around Dixon's chest to another location and listened again.

He looked at Colt. "I'm sorry. Your friend's dead."

The doctor turned to his assistant and said, "Buford, better get the sheriff over here. Sonny, you can wait outside in the waiting room. When the sheriff comes over I'll prepare the body for burial."

Colt swallowed. "Doc, he had a lady up north that has a farm or a ranch. I'd like to take him up there for burial. It's going to take a few days. Is there anything you can do to...um..."

The doctor said, "You mean, help him keep?"

Colt nodded and said, "Yeah, help him keep."

"Let's see, I could wrap and plaster him all up. That would keep the air off him. We could sew him up in an oilcloth and seal him in a coffin. He'd keep a long time that way."

Colt said, "Well, I have some money, so do it."

The doctor nodded. "Just as soon as the sheriff says it's okay. Now, go out and get some fresh air."

TWENTY SEVEN

It took Colt and Douglas five days to get to Austin. They found the ranger barracks and turned Peoples over to Captain Willard Corbett, who was in command. Colt gave him Billy's badge and papers. He also gave a letter to the captain that Billy had addressed to him.

Corbett signed the affidavit on all three warrants and said, "The State Bank will honor those. That's also where Billy kept his account. The letter you have authorizing you to withdraw from his account won't do you any good, though. Since he's dead, his estate will have to go to probate."

"How long will that take?"

"Hell, it could take months. If I were you, I wouldn't put Billy's share in the account. Just cash in the affidavit and take the cash up to Widow Tucker and her boy. It might last them until everything gets cleared up."

Corbett said, "According to this letter, Billy wanted you to have his badge. I can't really do that, as much as I'd like to. You have to be commissioned by the governor to wear that badge. Of course, if you were to ask for a commission, I could give it to you temporary."

"I don't know about that," Colt said. "I do need a job, but I'm not sure that I want to do this kind of work."

Corbett tossed the badge to Colt. "You forgot to give me this. Just don't let anybody see it. If you ever decide you want to wear it, come back and see me. Now," Corbett said, "Billy wrote about Peoples admitting poisoning your cows. Do you have that written statement with you?"

Colt pulled out the confession and showed it to Corbett.

Corbett read it and said, "You wait right here. I'm going in the back to talk to our Mr. Peoples."

Corbett was gone about fifteen minutes. He came back in and told an elderly woman in the outer office, "Mildred, come on with me. You have to witness a statement."

A half-hour later, Corbett came back folding a piece of paper. He told Colt, "Let's go see Stallings. He's in the state building right down the street."

When Colt and Corbett walked in, Stallings looked up from his desk and said, "Hello, Willard. What brings you up here?"

Corbett said, "It's about some dead cows, Mr. Stallings. This man here is Colt Patterson."

Stallings suddenly remembered Colt. His face turned to ash.

He stammered, "What about dead cows?"

Corbett said, "I have a fellow named Peoples over in the lockup and he's signed a sworn statement that he poisoned them cows. Secondly, one of my best rangers did some research and concluded them cows didn't die from anthrax. Third, Peoples swears he overheard a fellow by the name of Hunt talking to another fellow about paying you five hundred dollars to claim it was anthrax. I've known you a long time, Stallings. I always liked you, but goddammit, Stallings, this boy's daddy hung himself over that. Now, you tell me clean it ain't true."

Stallings looked at Colt and seemed to slump in his chair. Tears flowed down his cheeks. He cleared his throat and said, "Willard, I've wished many nights that it wasn't true. When I heard about this man's father, I couldn't believe what I had gotten involved in. I'm glad it's out in the open."

"Mr. Stallings, I think you and I ought to go over to my office now, don't you?"

Stallings just nodded. "Let me get my coat."

After getting Stalling's statement and locking him up, Corbett came and said, "Colt, I knew Sheriff Grimes, but he's dead. I don't know the new sheriff. Do you?"

"No, sir, I don't."

"I could send a wire to lock up that Hunt fellow on suspicion of fraud and grand theft, except I wouldn't want word to get to him. He just might go rabbit on us. Maybe I ought to ride down there my own self. Kind of surprise him. What do you think?"

Colt nodded. "I have to take Billy up to Widow Tucker's and give her some money and Billy's things. It might take me a couple days. I really would like to be there when you arrest Hunt."

"I have a better idea, Colt," Corbett said. "Why don't you go ahead and take Billy up to the Tuckers'. I'll talk to the governor and try to get you commissioned on an emergency basis. You come back through here, and I'll pin Billy's badge on your shirt myself. Then you and me, we'll just ride on down there and you can arrest this Hunt fellow yourself. You can always resign your commission later if you want."

Colt thought a moment and said, "Captain Corbett, I think I'd like that very much."

Corbett said that he would have to hold Peoples' wagon for evidence but that he would loan him his personal wagon.

*

The sky looked blood red from the setting sun as they turned the wagon up the path to the Tuckers' farm. Colt had no idea what he was going to say.

As they pulled up to the house a person came running out the door, banging the screen. "Billy! Is that you, Billy?"

Calvin ran up to the wagon with a huge, expectant grin. When he saw that it wasn't Billy, his grin faded. "You ain't Billy! Billy's my friend, but you aren't Billy. Who are you? You want my ma? Billy's gonna marry my ma. She's in the house. Hey, Ma! It's somebody—but it isn't Billy, Ma!"

An attractive woman who appeared to be about fifty years old came into view in the doorway, opening the screen door as she did so. Her hair was dark and straight with just a few gray wisps beginning to show. Her right hand was hidden behind her full skirt as she stepped out on the porch.

Colt figured the hidden right hand probably held a pistol. "Are you Mrs. Tucker?"

"Yes."

"Ma'am, I'm Colt Patterson, and this is my little brother, Douglas. We're friends of Billy Dixon's. I, us, well, we got a letter for you from Billy. We, uh, well, he's dead, ma'am. I'm sorry."

The woman stood for a moment and then brought her left hand to her face. Her shoulders began to shake and Colt could hear her almost-silent sobbing. The boy's face screwed up and he began to cry. The boy stepped back away from Colt as though Colt had the plague. He turned one full circle, wringing his hands, then ran to the porch and stood behind his mother.

Colt felt like crying himself. It was history repeating itself. He didn't even know this woman, but he felt almost as bad as he had when he told his ma and Douglas about Pap. Colt glanced at Douglas, who appeared to be holding back tears.

Colt climbed down from the wagon. "I'm sure sorry, ma'am." He took off his hat and walked to the porch. He stood in silence, allowing Mrs. Tucker time to absorb what he'd told her.

The woman, choking back her sobs, said, "Excuse me, please." She turned and went into the house.

Colt stood on the porch, not knowing what to do.

Calvin, wiping tears from his eyes, said, "Billy was gonna be my pa. He was gonna move here and show me how to do things. He was gonna show me how to shoot and ride a horse an' things like that. That's all me an' Mama talked about. All we talked about was when was Billy gonna come home. Billy was my best friend; I ain't never had no friend like Billy. He was gonna be my pa."

Colt said, "Billy was my friend, too. He was always talking about you and your ma. All he talked about was how he wanted to quit rangering and come home to you."

Mrs. Tucker, her voice bravely trying to sound calm, said, "Calvin, ask the gentlemen in."

Colt said, "Come on, Douglas."

"No, I'll stay here. You go ahead, Colt."

Colt went inside. Even though the sun wasn't quite down, the cabin was dark.

Mrs. Tucker lit an oil lamp and sat with her face in the shadow.

Colt said, "Ma'am, I was with Billy when he died. I know he wasn't hurting any at the time." Colt omitted the pain Billy felt before he gave him the opium.

He continued, "He wrote this letter just before he died. He asked me to bring it and him to you." Colt handed the letter to Mrs. Tucker.

She said, "Mr. Patterson, my eyes are about gone. I haven't been able to read for almost a year. Would you please read it to me? Please sit down, Mr. Patterson. I've forgotten my manners."

Colt sat at the table and held the letter close to the lamp. He cleared his throat and read:

Dear Ethel,

I'm sorry that I can't tell you in person how I truly feel about you and Calvin. When I would sit with you on your porch swing with my mouth full of pie, I felt like a fourteen-year-old with his first sweetheart. I always wanted to kiss you and I thought you wanted me to, but somehow I was too scared. I've known a lot of women, but none that I'd want you to meet. I kissed most of them. I kissed them and more. I want you to know, Ethel, that since that first night on your porch swing when you and I sat talking until the sun went down, I've never touched any other woman. I saved all my money ever since and I have a few dollars in cash that I'm sending by my friend, Colt. I have a whole bunch more in the bank in Austin. I want you to have it all. If you don't mind, I'd really appreciate it if you would lay my body where I can see your front porch. Sometime if you feel like just sitting there in your swing, thinking about me, well, I'll be there, too. I swore that this was to be my last trip before I came home to you. I guess I was right at that. I could never bring myself to say it to your face, but I sure do love you.

Billy

Mrs. Tucker started shaking and then, as though a dam burst, she was crying with racking sobs. Colt was able to hold the lump back in his throat, but could do nothing about the tears in his eyes. He sat there not knowing what to say while Mrs. Tucker rocked back and forth in her chair, crying.

She finally stopped, choking back her sobs. "Thank you for bringing Billy home. Tomorrow, Calvin and I will bury him under that hackberry tree in front of the house. That way, in the evenings, I can sit on my swing and see him and maybe he will be able to see me."

Colt said, "Ma'am, if you'd let us, Douglas and I would like to stay for the burial. We could sleep in the barn."

"Mr. Patterson, Calvin and I would be proud if you would. Now, could you take me to Billy?"

"Yes, ma'am. He's in the back of the buggy."

Mrs. Tucker and Calvin followed Colt outside. She walked over to the coffin, where she gently laid her hand on the coffin.

She whispered, "I loved you too, Billy—and you're right, I wanted you to kiss and hold me those nights on the swing and I was mad at you for not doing it. Now you never will." Her voice cracked as though out of breath.

She turned and walked away a few steps, her back facing them. Colt could see her shoulders shaking.

Mrs. Tucker cleared her throat. She turned back and said, "Well, I guess you men are hungry. If you'll unhitch your team, I'll make some supper."

Colt said, "Ma'am, that won't be necessary. Ranger Corbett's wife didn't think you'd feel like cooking, so she filled up this box here with a lot of fried chicken, bread, pies and just about everything. If you like, I'll take it in for you, then we'll take care of the horses."

*

The next morning, Douglas and Calvin took turns digging the grave as Colt stood by. By noon, several buggies drove up and people started getting out. It seemed that word had spread and Billy had a lot more friends than he thought. They even brought a preacher and a lawyer.

Colt recognized Ranger Corbett, all decked out in a black suit and hat. He walked over to where Corbett was talking to Mrs. Tucker.

When he approached them he heard Corbett say, "Mrs. Tucker, now there's nothing illegal about it. Mr. Levine here says that there is nothing in the law that says a man has to be alive to get married. Now, if you're the widow, there'll be no probate. Billy always said that he wanted to marry you and we have it in writing, so it would all be perfectly legal."

Mrs. Tucker said, "Somehow it doesn't seem right, just for the money an' all. I've dreamed of marrying Billy ever since I first met him, but not like this."

Corbett said, "Now, it isn't much, but Billy has a little pension coming from the state. If you were his widow you'd be entitled to it. Now, I don't know how to say this, but your boy—well, he's an invalid and if something happened to you he'd continue to get it. If you don't want it for yourself, do it for your boy."

They had a wedding right before the funeral. Billy was finally laid to rest just before sundown. After everyone left, they filled the grave, and on it, placed a simple marker.

As Colt turned to walk back to the house, the sky was red in the west. A gentle breeze picked up and Colt could see the empty swing on the porch rocking back and forth.

TWENTY EIGHT

olt and Douglas drove the buggy back to Austin. They collected their horses and met Corbett. They left Austin for Cotulla the same day.

The ride down was faster and they made it in four days.

They rode out to the Hunt ranch the following day with acting sheriff Ira Poole.

Just before they got to the Hunts' ranch, Colt pulled up. "Captain, if you and the sheriff don't mind, I'd like to go in first. I'd like to talk to Mr. Hunt alone."

Sheriff Poole said, "Boy, I don't think so. You have too good a reason to shoot that son of a bitch."

Corbett said, "Colt, the sheriff is right. I wouldn't want to have to arrest you for shooting him, even though he does deserve it."

"I promise that I'm not gonna hurt anyone. I'll even leave my guns with you. Just give me an hour and then come on in. I promise he'll be on his feet when you get there."

"Well," Corbett said, "leave your guns and that knife that you carry in your boot."

Colt handed over his weapons and rode on to the ranch alone. He approached the ranch just as Orville Hunt was coming out of the barn. Hunt stopped for a moment in recognition.

A big smile crossed his face. "My Lord! It's Colt Patterson. How you doing, boy? I'm glad to see you. Come on up to the porch out of this sun."

"Nice to see you, Mr. Hunt. I don't mind if I do."

Hunt asked, "Boy, how are you getting on? I heard about your poor ma and all. Did they ever find your little brother?"

"Yes, we found him okay."

"That's music to my ears, Colt."

They stepped up on the porch and Hunt said, "Here, grab a chair. Want some water or something?"

Colt said, "No, sir, I brought myself something to drink." He pulled out a bottle of whiskey. "Mr. Hunt, would you join me?"

Mr. Hunt laughed. "I'm not much for drinking; just on special occasions."

"Me either, but I'm celebrating and I was in the area. I thought I'd ask if you wanted to celebrate with me."

"What are you celebrating?"

"Mr. Hunt, I just got hired by the Texas Rangers. No more cleaning out horse stalls for a place to sleep. I'd sure be proud if you'd have a little drink with me."

"Hell, yes. I'll drink to that. Let me go in the house and get a couple of cups." Hunt returned moments later with two cups.

Colt filled each one half full with the amber liquid. "Here's to the Texas Rangers." Colt stood and drank the fiery liquid.

Mr. Hunt swallowed all of his as well. "Whew, that's strong! I didn't know you were a drinking man, Colt."

"I'm not really. Like you, I just drink on special occasions. Like getting this job with the rangers." They both sat down in their chairs and Hunt pulled out his pipe and started filling it. Colt stretched his legs out and put his left hand behind his head with his elbow sticking out.

"Yes, Mr. Hunt, if it wasn't for you, I wouldn't have this job. I really owe you a lot."

Hunt lit his pipe and leaned back. "Why, thank you, Colt, but I didn't have anything to do with it. You got that job all on your own."

"No, Mr. Hunt—if it hadn't been for you, right now I'd be sitting on Pap's front porch talking about fixing the windmill while Ma was making supper."

Hunt sat up. "How's that? What do you mean?"

"Mr. Hunt, if you hadn't had all our cows poisoned by that Mr. Peoples fellow, we wouldn't have lost our ranch and I wouldn't have been looking for a job. See, I wouldn't be a ranger now."

Hunt jumped out of his chair, knocking it over. "How can you say that to me? Your daddy was my friend. I helped you and your ma out after your cows died. I didn't have anything to do with y'all losing your ranch. Maybe you'd better leave."

Colt reached into his pocket and pulled out two small blue bottles. He slowly removed the cap from one and drank it. He put the other back in his pocket.

"Mr. Hunt, we already have statements from Peoples and Mr. Stallings. I think we can prove what you did, no matter what you say. I even think that eventually the Millers and I'll get our ranches back. It'd save a lot of time, though, if you'd sign a statement as to what you did. It would also help if you'd sign over my ranch to me and Miller's back to him. I also think that it'd only be fair if you signed over this ranch to the Millers and me jointly for damages. You'll go to jail, of course, but that'd be the fair thing to do. By the way, are you getting a little sleepy?"

"Maybe, why?"

"Mr. Hunt, if you want me to leave, I will. Charges have already been filed against you, but you won't ever stand trial, because you're gonna be dead about an hour after I leave."

Hunt asked, "What do you mean, I'll be dead? What are you gonna do, shoot me?"

"Mr. Hunt, that whiskey was poisoned. I poisoned you and no matter what you do, you can't change that."

"Bullshit! You drank it, too. I saw you."

Colt pulled out the empty blue vial and tossed it to Hunt. "That, Mr. Hunt, is an antidote. I'm not gonna die, but you are."

Colt pulled out Pap's gold watch. "You haven't much time, Mr. Hunt. You have a lot of writing to do, so if you are gonna do it you had best get started. Your stomach ought to start feeling a little numb right about now. I can see by your eyes that you're already feeling the effects."

Hunt looked scared. "What did you give me, damn you? I'll get my scattergun and we'll see who dies. I saw that other bottle."

A small, double-barreled Derringer suddenly appeared in Colt's left hand. "Sit down, Mr. Hunt. You've already been poisoned. I can fix that, but I can't fix two bullets in your chest. Well, Mr. Hunt, how's it gonna be? I have some friends that I have to go see."

Colt stepped down off the porch and walked to his horse.

"Wait a minute, damn you! Okay! I'll sign what you want, just give me that antidote."

"Well, Mr. Hunt, I figured you would, so to save some time I took the liberty to have an attorney by the name of Levine draw up the papers. I even brought a pen for you."

Colt retrieved the items from his saddlebags and stepped back up on the porch. He handed the papers and a pen to Hunt.

Hunt scribbled his name to the documents. He handed them back to Colt. "Okay, give me the antidote."

"I'll give it to you, but first I want you to call your wife out here to witness it."

"Myrtle," Hunt called. "Get yourself out here—and hurry!"

Colt could hear Myrtle as she approached the door.

She saw Colt and smiled. "Why, Colt, I didn't know you were here. How are you?"

"I'm fine, Mrs. Hunt."

Orville Hunt said, "Never mind the small talk, Myrtle. Just sign these here papers."

She went to her husband, wiping flour from her hands onto her apron. "What's the papers for, Orville?"

"Never mind. Damn it, woman! Just sign right by my signature where it says 'witness.' I'll explain later."

Myrtle looked worried as she signed the papers.

"Now go in the house, Myrtle—right now!"

When she was gone, Hunt handed the papers to Colt and said, "Well, goddammit, I did what you wanted. Now give me the antidote."

Colt took the papers.

"I said give me that antidote!"

"Oh, you mean this?" Colt casually tossed Hunt the other small blue bottle.

Hunt twisted off the cap and drank it down. "It tastes like water."

"Well, it ought to. That's what it is. I poisoned both of us, Mr. Hunt, and there is no antidote. The only thing is, that poison was just a little bit of laudanum mixed with the whiskey. It ought to wear off in an hour or so."

Colt climbed on his horse. "Oh, Mr. Hunt. I have the sheriff and another ranger waiting up the road. I'm gonna go get 'em and it might take a few minutes. That'll give you a few minutes to explain to Mrs. Hunt what you did to her."

He turned Blue Eye around and rode away.

✳ ✳ ✳ ✳ ✳

TWO HEARTS

TWO HEARTS

Elroy was beginning to feel a little more at ease. He was sure that he'd left no sign of his turning east.

He was pleased to see that the trail he was on had actually improved. He had crossed the peak of the mountain chain earlier that morning and was more than halfway down the east face. He could see the flat plain of the desert stretching out before him.

He continued on his downward path, and by sundown he was out of the mountains. He'd been following a second creek down the east side that ended just before he hit the desert.

Just before dark, he reached the flat. He made camp and unhitched and hobbled the team. By the time he'd gathered firewood and built a fire, night was upon him.

Elroy could hear coyotes barking somewhere in the distance. He'd finished his cigar and was leaning forward to pick up the coffeepot when he heard his horses snorting. He glanced up and saw them standing at attention with their ears pricked forward.

He froze as a voice behind him said, "Peoples, just freeze right where you are. I have a double-barreled scattergun pointed right at your back."

Elroy's insides turned to ice and he sat back, keeping his hands where they could be seen.

He tried a bluff. "Who are you, mister? A road agent? Take whatever you want, just don't get tense with that scattergun."

The voice said, "Elroy Peoples, you're under arrest. I'm Colt Patterson, U.S. Marshal. I want you to keep facing that fire and slowly stand up. If you turn around, I'll kill you."

Elroy carefully stood up.

"Now, I want you to keep your right hand up. Using your left hand only, I want you to strip right down to your birthday suit. I mean everything, including your boots and socks."

When Elroy was standing naked, Colt said, "Now walk to your left five paces and keep your back to me."

Elroy did as he was commanded.

"Now lay face down on the ground and put both hands behind your back. I still have this scattergun pointed right at your head and if you so much as move, I'll blow your head off."

Colt stepped over and put his right boot in the middle of Elroy's back. Holding the sawed-off shotgun in his right hand, he snapped on the shackles with his left. He then stepped back and searched through Elroy's clothes.

He checked the pockets of both Elroy's black wool coat and his pants. Upon searching Elroy's boots, he found a .41 caliber Derringer. He pocketed the small pistol and tossed the pants to Elroy.

"Put 'em on."

"How the hell can I, with my hands cuffed behind me this way?"

Colt said, "If you can't figure it out, you're gonna be butt-naked all the way back to New York."

Elroy found it very difficult, but by squatting down he was able to grab his pants by the rear of the waistline and pull them up to his waist.

After Elroy had his pants on, Colt said, "Now lay back down on your stomach."

Elroy complied and Colt soon had leg shackles on him. He told Elroy, "OK, now get up and walk over to the wagon."

Colt attached a ten-foot length of chain to his leg shackles and locked the other end to the rear axle of the buggy.

"Now face the wagon."

Colt released the cuff on one of Elroy's wrists and handed him his shirt.

"Put this on."

"What about my jacket? These nights in the desert get mighty chilly."

Colt retrieved the black wool jacket, rechecked the pockets and handed it to Elroy.

He reconnected the cuffs and dug a shallow hole a few feet from the fire. When it was deep enough, he started a second fire and drowned out Peoples' fire.

Elroy asked, "Why'd you do that? That was a hell of a nice fire."

"It was at that. I imagine that every heathen Indian within twenty miles could see it, too. The one in the hole can't be seen more than a few hundred feet."

Colt took a burning brand and inspected the creek. The creek was somewhat stagnant, with a muddy area extending a hundred feet beyond the small pond where the water actually started. He remembered what his friend Billy Dixon had said about critters in the water. He took his shovel, walked about a hundred feet from the water's edge, and started digging. When he hit moisture, he stopped.

He told Elroy, "If you want to drink from that stagnant creek, go ahead. Frankly, I don't fancy getting any critters in my belly. This hole I dug ought to have plenty of water in it by morning, and it won't have any critters in it.

We'll use it to fill our canteens."

*

Colt cooked himself a good meal; when he was through eating he spread a blanket near the wagon.

Elroy hobbled over to the blanket and complained, "Why can't I sleep in my own wagon? I hate sleeping on the ground."

"There're too many things in that wagon that could get me in trouble. Tomorrow I'll go through it and dump all your potions and poisons. We'll see what happens after that. Tonight you sleep here."

Elroy asked, "What about my boots?"

"Forget your boots. They're going in the fire."

"Why burn my boots? Hells bells, man, that sand's gonna be mighty hot tomorrow."

"As long as you're going to be in the wagon, you won't need boots. If you get away, you're going to be barefoot in this here desert."

"Don't I get anything to eat?"

"You get a fistful of cornmeal plus two pints of water a day, and that's it."

"Goddamnit! That's evil mean. No man can get along on that!"

"Elroy, whether you live or die doesn't make me any never mind. If you get away from me, I don't want you having a whole bunch of energy. Now that's the way it is, so shut up."

"Okay, Marshal, but if I ever do get out of these chains, you're going to be begging me to shoot you."

*

After the fire died down and Colt appeared to be asleep, Elroy rolled to his side and twisted his body so that the right side of his open coat twisted back towards his cuffed hands. He ripped the threads in the lining enough to work a small vial out and into his hand. He buried it under his groundcloth and went to sleep.

*

The next morning Elroy was awakened by the sound of Colt stirring and yelled, "Marshal, I gotta piss and I'm thirsty. Reckon you could unhook my hands long enough for me to do that?"

Colt came over to Elroy, uncuffed his hands and removed the second chain from his leg irons.

Elroy walked a few feet away and pissed against a bush and when he was through, he asked, "Can I have some water?"

"Go ahead." Colt tossed the canteens to Elroy. "Fill these canteens while you're at it."

Dragging his chain, Elroy took the canteens to the waterhole.

"I'll be watching you, Peoples. You get four swallows and that's it. If I see your Adams apple move a fifth time, you won't get any more water for the rest of the day. Maybe not tomorrow either."

Elroy knelt down by the edge of the hole and took exactly four deep swallows. He palmed the glass vial in his right hand, picked up one of the empty canteens and, using both hands, submerged it into the waterhole, emptying the vial as he did so. He dropped the vial into the water and filled the other canteens.

"Do you want the water kegs filled, too?"

"No, they're both full."

Colt took the empty coffeepot to the waterhole and dipped some water into it.

Elroy had a cynical smile as he watched Colt take the coffeepot back to the fire and place it on the coals.

Colt fried up the last of his ham and some hoecake, and washed it down with a couple of cups of hot black coffee.

*

When he was through eating, he poured the remains of the coffee onto the fire and covered up the smoking ashes with dirt. He gathered up his skillet and other utensils and walked to the waterhole to wash them.

He had taken only a few steps when he broke out into a cold sweat. Everything began to tilt and swim before his eyes and he had a distinct feeling that he was going to be sick. His knees buckled and he fell face forward into the dirt.

*

Colt slowly became aware of his surroundings. The sun was hot on his body and he was agonizingly thirsty. His head pounded and it took a few moments for him to remember where he was.

He tried to move, but found himself in leg irons with his hands shackled in front of him. He was totally naked and his boots had been removed. He noted a long chain extending from his wrist shackles to the left side of the wagon. He rolled over onto his side and saw Elroy lying fully clothed on his groundcloth. He was smoking a cigar and smiling at him.

Elroy said, "As they say, every dog has his day. I suppose this dog, specifically me, is finally having his. How does it feel to be in chains, Mr. Marshal? I hope you hate it as much as I did."

Colt tried to speak. His mouth was so dry that he had to clear his throat twice before he finally was able to rasp, "How did you do it?"

"Elementary, my dear Marshal. The next time you search someone, you should be more careful. Of course, for you, there will be no next time."

"What did I miss?"

"Well, don't feel bad. A small glass vial sewn into the lining of a coat is difficult to find. I suppose most people would've missed it. A little tincture of opium in that waterhole worked just fine. I doubt if I could have succeeded had you not dug it. The little pond over there has so much water in it, the opium would've been so diluted you wouldn't have noticed it."

Colt knew that he was completely at the mercy of this smiling madman. He'd made a serious mistake that he'd not survive. He asked, "Why haven't you killed me?"

"Don't be in such a hurry, Mr. Marshal. You'll be killed, but I want to hear you beg me to kill you. I want you to know what it's like to have to slave to a master's demands. I want you to know what it's like to say, 'Yes, boss.' Now stand up and I want to hear a 'Yes, boss' from you."

"Go to hell, you miserable son of a bitch. Go ahead and shoot me. You won't get a 'Yes, boss' from me!"

Elroy smiled and stood. He casually folded up the groundcloth and loaded it into the rear of the wagon.

Colt could see that Elroy had already hitched the team, and Colt's two borrowed horses were tied to the rear of the wagon. He could tell by the sun that it was almost noon and his burning skin indicated that he'd lain in the scorching sun for many hours.

Colt was still lying on the ground when Elroy climbed into the wagon.

Elroy looked over his shoulder at Colt and smiled.

"When I hear 'Yes, boss,' maybe, just maybe, I'll give you a swallow of water. Maybe even a fistful of cornmeal." He slapped the reins against the horses and they bolted forward.

Suddenly, Colt was being dragged through the desert, with sagebrush, dirt, and gravel raking his body.

He twisted and turned until he was able to get to his feet. Stones and thorns ripped his bare feet as he ran alongside the wagon.

Elroy looked at Colt and laughed as he slapped the reins again, whipping the horses into an even faster gait.

At the beginning, Colt's feet only hurt. Soon the pain became agonizing. He half ran and was half pulled for what seemed like miles.

His lungs were bursting and his heart was pounding as he tried to keep up. He stumbled, regained his footing and then fell.

The buggy didn't stop and Colt felt himself being dragged

again. He tried to yell 'Yes, boss,' but nothing except a dry rattle came from his throat.

Diabolical laughter resounded through the desert as Elroy gleefully watched the marshal's body bouncing behind the wagon.